DEFYING HER DESERT DUTY

ANNIE WEST

With profound thanks to
Vanessa, Sharon, Karen and Kandy
for all your support.

Annie West spent her childhood with her nose between the covers of a book—a habit she retains. After years preparing government reports and official correspondence she decided to write something she *really* enjoys. And there's nothing she loves more than a great romance. Despite her office-bound past she has managed a few interesting moments—including a marriage offer with the promise of a herd of camels to sweeten the contract. She is happily married to her ever-patient husband (who has never owned a dromedary). They live with their two children amongst the tall eucalypts at beautiful Lake Macquarie, on Australia's east coast. You can e-mail Annie at www.annie-west.com, or write to her at PO Box 1041, Warners Bay, NSW 2282, Australia.

CHAPTER ONE

HE WAS watching her.

Still.

Soraya's nape prickled. A ripple of hot sensation skated down her arms. She fought the need to look up, knowing what she'd see.

The man in the shadows.

Big. Dark. Broad-shouldered in his leather jacket, the hard lines of his face a study in masculine strength. His upper face was in shadow yet every time she looked across the dimly lit bar there was no doubt his gaze was fixed on her. She felt the intensity of that look in her sizzling blood. And in the curious breathless catch in her throat.

His interest unsettled Soraya. She leaned closer to her group: Raoul and Jean Paul debating politics while Michelle and Marie talked fashion. Raoul roped a negligent arm around her shoulders. Instantly she stiffened, then forced herself to relax, reminding herself it was just a friendly gesture.

Soraya loved Paris's casual lifestyle, but still hadn't overcome her reserve. You could take the girl out of Bakhara but Bakhara still lingered in the girl. Her lips twisted. She'd no need of the chaperone her father had wanted to send.

Movement caught her eye and despite her intentions she turned.

He hadn't moved; he still leaned back just beyond the flickering light of the candle on his table. But now he looked up at a leggy blonde in a red satin mini-dress. The woman leaned in, her low-cut neckline a blatant invitation.

Soraya snapped her head back to her friends, ignoring the way Raoul tightened his hold.

Zahir sank back in his chair and cradled his drink, its cool condensation a respite from the heat. A heat that owed nothing to the close atmosphere of the nightclub and everything to the woman on the other side of the room.

What the devil had he walked into?

Simple, Hussein had said. Straightforward.

Zahir shook his head. Every sense screamed 'alert'. Every instinct warned of trouble.

Still he remained. He had no choice. Now he'd found her, he couldn't leave.

He tipped his head back so the ice slid into his mouth. He crunched it hard, as if the shock of cold might restore his equanimity.

It would take more than ice to counteract his tension.

In other circumstances he might have taken up the invitation of the voluptuous Swedish girl in the short dress. He enjoyed life's pleasures—in his down time.

Never at the expense of his duty.

Tonight was duty, responsibility, obligation.

Yet it was something more too. Something…unfamiliar, evoked by sloe-dark eyes and a full Cupid's bow mouth. By the woman hanging on the words of a scrawny intellectual pontificating as if he had any idea how to run a country!

Zahir snorted and put down his glass.

Whatever it was he felt, he didn't like it. It was a complication he didn't need. Zahir had spent a lifetime learning how to cut through complications.

Over the years he'd learned to curb his impatience. Now he mostly used a statesman's skills: negotiation and discretion. But he'd trained as a warrior from birth. He was still technically head of the Emir's bodyguard, a position that gave opportunities for the satisfaction of hard, physical combat. The clash of one man against another.

He surveyed the *poseur* who was boasting of his intellect and pulling the woman in the dark dress close. The Frenchman's hand hovered near her bare arm. Zahir's fist tightened.

He'd like to get his hands on that buffoon and give him a short, sharp lesson in the real meaning of power.

The intensity of his bloodlust brought him up short.

Premonition skittered like icy fingers down his spine.

This mission was a mistake. He felt it in his bones.

Soraya moved back as far as Raoul's encircling arms allowed.

It was ridiculously late and she'd rather be home in bed. Except her flatmate Lisle had finally made peace with her boyfriend and Soraya knew they needed privacy, even if it meant staying out till dawn. Lisle had been a good friend and friendship was something precious to her.

But she'd made a mistake, finally agreeing to dance with Raoul. She frowned and shifted his straying hand.

Usually Soraya didn't make such mistakes. Keeping her distance from men came naturally. She'd acted out of character, spooked by the need to escape the stranger's unnerving stare. It had made her feel…heated. Aware.

Yet even now she felt his gaze like a brand on her back, her bare arms, her cheeks.

What did he *want*? She wasn't eye-catching. Her dress was modest—positively maidenly, Lisle would say.

Soraya wanted to march across the room and demand he stop it. But this was Paris. Men stared at women all the time. It was a national pastime.

Raoul's marauding hand cut her line of thought and she stiffened. Enough was enough. 'Stop it! Move your hand or—'

'The lady is ready for a change, I believe.' The voice, a deep burr, curled around her like a caress, but there was no mistaking its steely undertone.

Raoul stumbled to a halt then stepped back abruptly as a

large hand removed his arm from Soraya's waist. His eyes flared as he drew himself up. Yet, tall as he was, the stranger topped him easily.

Raoul spluttered as he was shouldered aside. Soraya felt the tensile strength in the intruder's big body as he clasped her in a waltz hold and swung her away.

Torn between relief at being rid of Raoul's octopus hands and stomach-dipping shock at the newcomer's actions, protest froze in Soraya's throat.

It was *him*, the man who'd watched her all evening.

Suddenly he was so near, his breath feathered her forehead, the heat of his body warmed hers and his big hands grasped her so easily it was obvious he was used to being close to a woman.

Soraya shivered as an unfamiliar sensation swirled deep. Not trepidation. Not indignation. But something that tied her thoughts in knots and prompted her to fall in step unthinkingly as he moved to the slow tune.

'Now just you wait—' Over the stranger's shoulder she saw Raoul's face, red with indignation, his fist raised. Soraya's eyes widened. Could he be violent?

'Raoul! No! That's enough.'

'Excuse me a moment.' The stranger released her, swung round to confront Raoul and said something under his breath that made the graduate student pale and falter back a pace.

Then, before she had time to question, he turned back, gathered her to him and swung her across the dance floor.

It was an impressive example of a male staking his territory. But Soraya didn't appreciate being swept away without so much as a by-your-leave.

Even if he had rescued her from Raoul's pawing.

'There's no need for this.' She'd rather just get off the dance floor. But he gave no indication he'd heard.

It chagrined her that her feet automatically followed his lead. She'd never followed *any* man, except her beloved father!

She could wrench herself from his arms and off the dance

floor, but she shied from making more of a scene unless absolutely necessary.

Besides, she was curious.

'What makes you think I want to dance with you?' She jutted her chin defiantly to counteract the strange, breathy quality of her voice.

The movement was a mistake. With her face tilted, her gaze collided with sizzling dark-emerald fire. Shock jolted her and only quick reflexes kept her from stumbling.

His eyes were heavy-lidded, almost lazy. Yet there was nothing lazy about his rapier-sharp scrutiny. She sucked in a breath as it roved her face.

His features were compelling. Strong, with an earthy stamp of male sexuality that melded with sharp cheekbones, a determined jaw and a long blade of a nose to create a breathtaking whole. His skin was dark gold, eyes rayed with the tiny lines that spoke of hours spent outdoors. She couldn't believe they were smile lines. Not on this man who surveyed her so grimly.

Soraya blinked and tore her gaze away, disturbed to find her pulse skittering faster.

'You weren't *enjoying* your dance with him?' He shrugged and she knew in that moment that, despite his perfect French, he wasn't local. There was none of the Gallic insouciance in that movement. Instead she read the fluid yet deliberate action of a man who had more on his mind than a little light flirtation.

He moved with a lithe grace yet every action, from the way he held her hand to the light clasp of his other palm at her waist, was carefully controlled.

For all his agility he was a big man, all hard-packed muscle, iron-hard sinew and bone. Formidable.

Suddenly she felt…trapped, at risk. Ridiculous, since she was in full public view with her friends close by.

Desperately she sucked in a deep breath and sought out her companions. They watched, rapt, elbows on the table and mouths moving as if they'd never seen anything more fascinating than Soraya dancing, and with a stranger. As her eyes met Raoul's, he flushed and moved closer to Marie.

'That's not the point.'

'So you don't disagree. He was annoying you.' His voice was low yet she had an inkling he worked to keep his tone easy.

'I don't need a protector!' Soraya prided herself on her independence.

'Then why didn't you stop him grabbing at you?' There was no mistaking the thread of anger in that deep voice, or the quiver of repressed power that rippled through him in a rolling tide.

It was her turn to shrug.

What was there to say? That despite the freedom of studying abroad she wasn't used to dealing with groping hands? She usually kept a discreet distance from male colleagues. Soraya had perfected the art of blending into a crowd and avoiding individual male attention. Tonight was the first time she'd ever danced with a man.

No way was she confessing that! It was the norm for a well-brought-up girl in Bakhara. Here it would make her seem like a freak.

As would the fact she preferred it that way. She had no interest in a love affair.

'Nothing to say?'

'What I do is none of your business.'

At her words his lips firmed, deep lines bracketing a mobile mouth that revealed tension despite his air of command. One sleek black eyebrow climbed towards close-cropped dark hair.

That superior look would goad any woman's patience.

The music finished and they slowed to a stop.

'Thank you for the dance.' Formal politeness barely masked her annoyance. How dared he suggest she should be thankful to him?

She turned and took a step away, only to find his hold tightening at her waist. Long fingers and a broad palm seared through the soft fabric of her dress, warming her in a way that suddenly seemed too intimate.

The music resumed and with a swift movement he tugged her close so she stumbled against a hard wall of hot muscle.

'What the—?'

'What if I choose to make it my business?' His breath was warm on her face. Those straight eyebrows arrowed down in a scowl that accentuated the intensity of his blazing green stare.

It was as if he memorised everything, from her too-short nose and plain brown eyes to the wisps of hair escaping her once-neat chignon.

The intensity of that look dazed her. 'Sorry?'

'You heard me, princess. Don't play games.'

'Play games?' She shook her head, her jaw clenching in indignation. She planted her hands against his upper arms, trying to prise herself free, and felt only unyielding steel. 'I've done nothing! It's you playing games. Sitting there all night, just watching me.'

Her eyes met his again and her chest tightened at the simmering heat she saw there. Her skin tingled all over.

'You wanted me to do more than watch?' His words were a whispered thread of frayed velvet. 'Is that why you cosied up to your friend over there—to trigger a response?'

'No!' Soraya rocked back on her heels, but his arm at her waist, like a rope of steel, lashed her to him.

For an instant she read something in his gaze, something half-hidden that both disturbed and fascinated.

Then she came to her senses. With a swift, well-executed movement she ground her stiletto heel onto his instep with all her weight.

A moment later she was free. His hand fell away and with it the warmth at her waist she'd almost grown used to.

She strode from the dance floor, head up and shoulders back. A woman in control.

But at the back of her mind lingered the image of his face when she'd fought to break free. There'd been no flicker of pain in his eyes, no hint of a wince on his face, despite what must have been piercing agony.

What sort of man trained himself not to react to pain?

The question unnerved her.

So did the realisation she was only free because he'd *chosen* to release her.

Holding her in his arms had been a mistake.

Zahir grimaced and ruthlessly shoved aside any analysis of *why* it was a mistake.

No need to go there. All that mattered was that she was trouble with a capital T.

He'd known it when he'd arrived at her apartment and found, not the respectable accommodation he'd expected, but a love nest for an almost-naked couple. Clearly they'd tumbled out of bed only because his insistent ringing of the bell had threatened to attract the neighbours.

His assessment had been reinforced when he'd finally tracked her to this seedy club. True, she didn't flaunt herself half-naked like some women. But that dress, the colour of ripe plums, clung lovingly to curves designed to snare a man's attention. Its skirt flirted and flounced around shapely legs when she moved. It slithered enticingly under a man's palm, making him itch to explore further.

Zahir swallowed a curse as his palms tingled.

This wasn't about what she made him feel.

He wasn't in the business of feeling *anything* for her.

Except disgust that she'd played Hussein for a fool. Look at the way she'd snuggled up to that turkey with the ridiculously sculpted excuse for a beard!

He stifled a low growl of anger.

No, she was *not* what he'd been led to believe. And he didn't just mean the fact that the old photo he'd been given showed the round, almost chubby face of an innocent. The woman tonight had the cheekbones, sexy curves and full, pouting lips of a born seductress. And those shoes—spangled four-inch stilettos that screamed *'take me...now!'*.

Heat pooled low. Disgust, he assured himself.

The one time she'd impressed was when she'd stood up to him. Few people dared do that.

The look in her eye when she'd used that damned spike heel had, for a moment, arrested him. And the way she'd strode back across the dance floor, with the grace and hauteur of an empress, had made him want to applaud.

At least she had guts. She was no push-over.

The determined click of feminine heels snared his attention and he straightened from the wall.

Instantly the rhythm of those footsteps slowed and a disturbing fire sparked in his blood. He'd felt it each time her eyes collided with his.

Hell! Now he felt it from her mere glance.

A volatile mixture of fury, guilt and some other darker emotion surged to the surface.

This was *not* the way it should be. Zahir refused to countenance it.

He swung round to face her across the foyer of the nightclub. At this hour even the bouncer had deserted his post. They were alone.

'You! What are you doing here?' Her hand crept to her throat, then, as if recognising that for a sign of weakness, she dropped it to her side and lifted her chin. Subtly she widened her stance. What, did she mean to kick him in the groin if he tried to approach her?

It would do her no good, of course. Overpowering her would be a moment's work.

But that wasn't an option. Despite her flaws, she would be treated with respect. That was why he'd waited till they had privacy to approach her.

He ignored that ill-advised, inexplicable impulse to approach her on the dance floor.

'We need to talk.'

But already she was shaking her head. Flyaway strands of dark chocolate tresses swirled around her slender throat.

Zahir forced his focus to her eyes. Dark as ebony, they held his unflinchingly. He gave her full marks for bravado.

'We have nothing to discuss.' Her gaze skated across his shoulders, his chest and back up again. 'If you don't leave me alone I'll—'

'What? Call out for lover-boy to rescue you?' He crossed his arms over his chest and saw her gaze follow the movement. The low simmer of heat in his veins became a sizzle, igniting a temper he'd almost forgotten he had.

What was it about this woman that got under his skin? It was unheard of.

'No.' She took a mobile phone from her purse and flipped it open. 'I'll call the police.'

'Not a wise move, princess.'

'*Don't* call me that!' She quivered with outrage, her mouth a pout of wrathful indignation.

Too late, Zahir realised why he'd baited her.

Not because she deserved it.

Not because he was naturally crass.

But because he wanted her to look at him, respond to him, as she had on the dance floor. There, despite her defiant words, her body had melted against his just for a moment in an unspoken invitation as old as time.

Hell and damnation!

What was he playing at?

'Forgive me, Ms Karim.' Carefully he blanked his expression, speaking in the modulated tones he used when brokering a particularly difficult negotiation.

'You know my name!' She stumbled back a half-step, alarm in her eyes.

Registering her fear, Zahir tasted self-disgust on his tongue. Nothing he'd done tonight had gone as intended. Where was his professionalism, his years of experience handling the most difficult and delicate missions?

'You have nothing to fear.' He spread his palms in an open gesture.

But she backed up another step, groping behind her for the door into the bar. 'I don't hold conversations with strange men in places like this.' Her gesture encompassed the empty foyer.

Zahir drew a deep breath. 'Not even a man who comes direct from your bridegroom?'

CHAPTER TWO

SORAYA froze, muscles cramping in shock as that one word reverberated through her stunned brain.

Bridegroom...

No, no! Not yet. Not now. She wasn't ready.

Her heart rose in her throat, clogging her airways, lurching out of kilter. Her senses swam. It couldn't be. She had months yet here in Paris—hadn't she?

Soraya staggered back till the hand behind her met a solid surface. Fingers splayed, she pressed into the wall, needing its support.

Through hazy vision she registered abrupt movement: the stranger striding across the small space, arm raised as if to reach for her.

She stiffened and he slammed to a halt, his hand dropping. This close she should be able to read his expression but in the dim light his features looked like they'd been carved from harsh stone, betraying nothing. His eyes blazed, but with what she couldn't discern.

At least he didn't touch her again.

She didn't want his hand on her. She didn't like the curious heat that stirred when he did.

She dragged in a deep breath, then another, trying to calm her racing pulse. With him so close, watching like an eagle sighting its prey, it was impossible. She had nowhere to retreat to. And even if she did she knew he'd follow.

He had the grim, resolute aura of a man who finished what he started.

Her heart give a little jagged thump and she forced herself to stand tall. Even in her new shoes she still had to tilt her head to meet his gaze. He was big—broad across the shoulder and tall. Yet his physical size was only part of the impact. There was something in his eyes…

Soraya jerked her gaze away.

'You've come from Bakhara?' Her voice was husky.

'I have.'

She opened her mouth to ask if he'd come direct from *him*, but the words disintegrated in her dry mouth. It was stupid, but for as long as she didn't say the words she could almost pretend it wasn't true.

Yet even in denial Soraya couldn't pretend this was a mistake. The man before her wasn't the sort to make mistakes. That poised, lethal stillness spoke a language all its own. There'd be no errors with this man. She shivered, cold to the bones.

'And you are?' Soraya forced herself to speak.

One slashing black eyebrow rose, as if he recognised her question for the delay tactic it was.

'My name is Zahir Adnan El Hashem.' He sketched an elegant bow that confirmed his story more definitively than any words. It proclaimed him totally at home with the formal etiquette of the royal court.

In jeans, boots and black leather, the movement should have looked out of place, but somehow the casual western clothes only reinforced his hard strength and unyielding posture. And made her think of formidable desert fighters.

Soraya swallowed hard, her flesh chilling.

She'd heard of Zahir El Hashem. Who in Bakhara hadn't? He was the Emir's right-hand man. A force to be reckoned with: a renowned warrior and, according to her father, a man fast developing a reputation in the region as a canny but well-regarded diplomat.

Her fingers threaded into a taut knot.

She'd thought he'd be older, given his reputation. But what made her tense was the fact that the Emir had sent *him*, his most trusted royal advisor. A man rumoured to be as close to the Emir as family. A man known not for kindness but for his uncompromising strength. A man who'd have no compunction about hauling home an unwilling bride.

Her heart sank.

It was true, then. Absolutely, irrefutably true.

Her future had caught up with her.

The future she'd hoped might never eventuate.

'And you are Soraya Karim.'

It wasn't a question. He knew exactly who she was.

And hated her for it, she realised with a flash of disturbing insight as something flickered in the sea-green depths of those remarkable eyes.

No, not hatred. Something else.

Finally she found her voice, no matter that it was raspy with shock. 'Why seek me out here? It's hardly a suitable time to meet.'

His other eyebrow rose and heat flooded her cheeks. He knew she was prevaricating. Did he realise she'd do almost anything not to hear the news he brought?

'What I have to say is important.'

'I have no doubt.' She dragged her hand from the supporting wall and made a show of flicking shut her phone and putting it away. 'But surely we could discuss it tomorrow at a civilised time?' She was putting off the inevitable and probably sounding like a spoiled brat in the bargain. But she couldn't help it. Her blood chilled at the thought of what he'd come all this way to tell her.

'It's already tomorrow.'

And he wasn't going anywhere. His stance said it all.

'You have no interest in my message?' He paused, his eyes boring into her as if looking for something he couldn't find. 'You're not concerned with the possibility that I bring bad news?' His face remained unreadable but there was no mistaking the sharp edge to his voice.

The phone clattered to the floor from Soraya's nerveless fingers.

'My father?' Her hand shot to her mouth, pressing against trembling lips.

'No!' Colour deepened the razor-sharp line of his cheekbones. He shook his head emphatically. 'No. Your father is well. I'm sorry. I shouldn't have—'

'If not my father, then—?'

An abrupt gesture stopped her words. 'My apologies, Ms Karim. I should not have mentioned the possibility. It was thoughtless of me. Let me assure you, everyone close to you is well.'

Close to her. That included the man who'd sent him.

Suddenly, looking into the stormy depths of Zahir El Hashem's eyes, Soraya realised why he'd pushed her. How unnatural of any woman not to be concerned that sudden news might bring bad tidings about the man she was supposed to spend the rest of her life with.

Guilt hit her. How unnatural *was* she? Surely she cared about him? He deserved no less. Yet these last months she'd almost fooled herself into believing that future might never come to pass.

No wonder his emissary looked at her so searchingly. Had her response, or lack of it, given her away?

'I'm glad to hear it,' she murmured, ducking her head to cover the confusion she felt. At her feet lay her phone. She bent to retrieve it only to find her hand meeting his as he scooped the phone up.

His hand was hard, callused, broad of palm and long-fingered. The hand of a man who, despite his familiarity with the royal court, did far more with his days than consider protocol.

The touch of his flesh, warm and so different from her own, made her retreat instinctively, her breath sucking in on a gasp.

Or was it the memory of that same hand holding her tight against him on the dance floor? Fire snaked through her veins, making her aware of him as *male.*

'Your phone.'

'Thank you.' She kept her eyes averted, not wanting to face his searching stare again.

'Again, I apologise for my clumsiness. For letting you fear—'

'It's all right. No harm done.' Soraya shook her head, wishing it was the case, when all she could think of was that her reaction betrayed her as thoughtless, ungrateful, not deserving the good fortune she'd so enjoyed.

Worse, it was proof positive the doubts she'd begun to harbour had matured into far more than vague dissatisfaction and pie-in-the-sky wishing.

'Come,' he said, his voice brusque. 'We can't discuss this here.'

Reluctantly Soraya raised her head, taking in the deserted foyer, the muffled music from the club and the mingled scents of cigarette smoke, perfume and sweat.

He was right. She needed to hear the details.

She nodded, exhaustion engulfing her. It was the exhaustion a cornered animal must feel, facing its predator at the end of a long hunt from which there was no escape.

She felt spent. Vulnerable.

Soraya straightened her shoulders. 'Of course.'

He ushered her out and she felt the warmth of his hand at her back, close but not touching. Something in the quiver of tension between them told her he wouldn't touch her again. She was grateful for it.

Fingers of pale grey spread across the dawn sky, vying with the streetlights in the deserted alley. She looked around for a long, dark, official-looking vehicle. The place was deserted but for a big motorbike in the shadows.

Where to? She couldn't take him home; not with Lisle

and her boyfriend there. The place was roomy but the walls were thin.

'This way.' He ushered her towards the main road then down another side street with a sureness that told her he knew exactly where he was going.

She supposed she should have asked for proof of identity before following him. But she dismissed the thought as another delaying tactic. There was no doubt in her mind that he was who he said.

Besides, she felt like she'd gone three rounds in a boxing ring already. And this had only just started! How would she cope?

A shudder rippled down her spine.

A moment later weighted warmth encompassed her. She faltered to a stop. Around her shoulders swung a man's heavy leather jacket, lined with soft fabric that held the heat of his body and the clean fragrance of male skin.

Soraya's nostrils flared as her senses dipped and whirled, dizzy with the invasion of her space and the onslaught of unfamiliar reactions.

'You were cold.' His words were clipped. In the gloom his face was unreadable, but his stance proclaimed his distance, mental as well as physical.

He stood tall, the dark fabric of his T-shirt skimming a torso taut with leashed energy. His hands curled and the muscles in his arms bunched, revealing the blatant power his jacket had concealed. Resolutely she stopped her eyes skimming lower to those long denim-clad legs.

He looked potent. *Dangerous.*

'Thank you.' Soraya forced her gaze away, down the street that had begun to stir with carriers hefting boxes. A street market was beginning to take shape.

Relief welled. Surrounded by other people, surely the unfamiliar sensations she felt alone with him would dissipate? She'd been like a cat on burning sand for hours, all because of him.

She dragged his jacket in around her shoulders, telling herself the shock of news from Bakhara unnerved her. Her sense of unreality had nothing to do with the man so stonily silent beside her.

Zahir shortened his pace to match hers. She had long legs but those heels weren't made for cobblestones. They slowed her walk to a provocative hip-tilting sway far slower than his usual stride.

Resolutely he kept his eyes fixed ahead, not on her undulating walk.

Heat seared his throat and tightened his belly. How could he have been so stupid? So thoughtless? The look on her face when she'd thought he brought bad news about her father had punched a fist of guilt right through his belly.

Damn him for a blundering fool!

All because he'd judged her and found her wanting. Because she wasn't eager to hear the news from Hussein. Because she didn't care what tidings he brought if they interfered with her night out.

Because she wasn't the woman he'd presumed her to be, a woman worthy of Hussein.

Not when she spent the night snuggling up to another man, dancing with him, bewitching him with those enormous, lustrous eyes. Letting him paw her as if he owned her.

Zahir cupped the back of his neck, massaging it to ease the tension there.

Resolutely he shoved aside the whisper of suspicion that he'd have welcomed the chance to keep her in his own arms, feel her lush body pressed close.

This wasn't about him.

It was about her.

And the man to whom he owed everything.

'Thank you.' Soraya hugged the jacket close as he stood aside, holding open the door to a brightly lit café.

Entering, she felt she'd strayed back in time a century.

Wooden booths lined the walls, topped with mirrors etched in lush *art nouveau* designs. There were brass fittings of an earlier age, burnished and welcoming, and posters from a time when women wore corsets and men sported boaters or top hats.

But the whoosh of the gleaming coffee machine was modern, as was the sultry smile the petite, female *barista* bestowed on Zahir.

Something tweaked tight in Soraya's stomach. A thread of annoyance.

No wonder he was so sure of himself. He must take feminine adulation as his due.

Not this female.

Her heels clacked across the black-and-white tiled floor, giving the pretence of a confidence she didn't feel. Her legs shook and each step was an effort.

Sliding into a cushioned seat she focused on the café rather than the man who sat down opposite her.

If she'd had to guess she'd have said he'd favour a place that was sleek, dark and anonymous. Somewhere edgy, like him. Not a café that was traditional and comforting with its beautiful fittings and aura of quiet bustle.

A waitress had followed them to their table, her eyes on Zahir as they ordered.

He was worth looking at, Soraya grudgingly admitted, averting her gaze from his hard, sculpted jaw with its intriguing hint of morning shadow.

'You've come all the way from Bakhara,' she said flatly when they were alone. 'Why?'

She needed to hear it spelled out, even though there was only one reason he could be here.

'I come with a message from the Emir.'

Soraya nodded, swallowing a lump in her dry throat. Tension drilled down her spine. 'And?'

'The Emir sends greetings and enquires after your wellbeing.'

She speared him with a look. An enquiry after her health?

That could have been done through her father, who updated the Emir on her progress. Suddenly she was impatient to hear the worst. The delay notched her tension higher.

'I'm well.' She kept her tone even, despite the fact she couldn't seem to catch her breath. 'And the Emir? I hope he is in good health.'

'The Emir is in excellent health.' It was the expected response in the polite give-and-take of formal courtesy.

The sort of courtesy that had been so completely lacking in her dealings with this man.

Soraya's heart pulsed quicker as she recalled those overpowering emotions—the fury and indignation, the compulsion to know more, the feel of his gaze on her. The blast of untrammelled awareness when he'd held her.

She blinked and looked away.

Silence thickened, broken only by the eager waitress returning with their coffees: espresso for him, *café crème* for her. Automatically her hands wrapped round the oversized cup and she tilted her head, inhaling the steamy scent of hot cream and fragrant coffee.

'The Emir also sent me with news.'

Soraya nodded and lifted the cup to her lips, needing its heat. Even draped in his jacket she was cold. Cold with a chill that had nothing to do with the room temperature and everything to do with the creeping frost that crackled through her senses. The chill of foreboding.

'He asks that you accompany me to Bakhara. It's time for your wedding.'

Her slim fingers cupped the bowl of milky coffee so tightly Zahir saw them whiten. She didn't look up, but kept her eyes fixed on her drink. Following her gaze, he saw the creamy liquid ripple dangerously as her hands shook.

Instinct bade him reach out before she spilled the hot coffee and burned her hands.

Sense made him keep his hands to himself.

Bad enough that he knew the feel of her in his arms. Worse that he'd wanted…

No! He thrust the insidious thought aside.

Tiredness was to blame. The freedom of travelling the open road on his bike was what he'd needed after weeks locked in diplomatic negotiation on Hussein's behalf. But it had been a long journey.

As for the hum of awareness deep in his belly—it was a while since he'd shared his bed. That was all.

'I see.' Still she didn't look up. Nor did she drink. Instead she slowly lowered the coffee to the table, her hands still clamped round it as if for warmth.

Zahir frowned.

'Are you all right?' The words were tugged from his lips before he realised it.

Her mouth quirked up in a lopsided smile that somehow lacked humour. 'Perfectly, thank you.'

She lifted her head slowly, as if it was an effort.

Yet when her eyes met his he read nothing in them but a slight shimmer, as if the coffee's steam had made her eyes water. They were remarkable eyes. In the gloom of the club he'd thought them ebony. Here in the light he realised they were a dark, velvety brown, rich with a smattering of lighter specks, like gold dust.

Zahir sat back abruptly and lifted his espresso. Pungent and rich, the liquid seared his mouth and cleared his head.

'The Emir has set a date for the wedding?' Her voice was cool and crisp, yet he sensed strain there. Just as he saw strain in the rigid set of her neck and shoulders.

He shrugged. 'No date was mentioned to me.' As if Hussein would consult him on the minor details of his nuptials! That was what wedding planners were for. No doubt there were hordes of them, eager to have a hand in what would be the wedding of the decade.

'But…' She frowned and caught her bottom lip between her teeth. Resolutely he shifted his gaze from her lush mouth and turned to survey the café. It was doing a roaring trade in early-morning coffees for the market workers eager for a take-away caffeine fix. Yet here at the rear Zahir and his companion were totally alone.

'The Emir wants me to return?'

Hadn't he just said so? Zahir turned and found himself drowning in dark eyes that, if he didn't know better, he'd say held fear.

Nonsense. What was there to fear? Any woman would be ecstatic with the news he'd come to take her back to marry the Emir of Bakhara. If Hussein's character weren't enough to attract any woman, his personal wealth, not to mention his position of supreme authority, were bonuses few women could resist.

Soraya Karim had nothing to fear and everything to gain.

'He does.'

Zahir watched her shift in her seat. Her shoulders straightened, banishing the hint of a slump. Her chin lifted and her posture morphed into one of cool composure. Like the woman who'd stalked away from him in the club.

His heart gave a kick of appreciation and the dormant fire in his veins smouldered anew.

Hell! Since when had any woman had such an effect on him? Not even his last lover, naked and eager in his bed, would have garnered such an instantaneous response.

He rubbed his hand across his jaw, noting the stubble he hadn't bothered to remove. Lack of sleep was the problem. He'd been awake for thirty-six hours—eager to get here and get this over quickly so he could return to the new challenge that awaited him.

His reactions were haywire.

'The Emir has asked me to escort you home.' He curved his mouth in a reassuring smile and reined in his impatience—as if he had nothing better to do with his time than act as her minder on the trip from Paris to Bakhara.

Yet he couldn't begrudge Hussein this favour. Soraya Karim

would soon be his bride—of course he wanted her kept safe on the journey.

A pity no-one had thought to keep an eye on her while she partied in Paris!

'I thank the Emir for his kindness in providing an escort.' Her smile didn't reach her eyes. 'However, it would have been helpful if you'd contacted me before you arrived. That would have given me time to prepare.'

Zahir frowned at the hint of disapproval in her carefully polite tone.

What was there to prepare? Surely, as an eager bride, she'd jump at the chance to return to Bakhara and the opulent bridal gifts Hussein would shower upon her.

After years of delay Hussein was finally ready to proceed with the wedding. His chosen bride should be grinning with delight.

Instead she surveyed Zahir coolly.

'I'm here to assist. You can leave the details to me.' Winding up the lease on her apartment and organising a team of removalists would be the work of a few phone calls.

She nodded. 'I'm obliged to you. However, I prefer to make my own arrangements.' She paused. 'When is the Emir expecting me?'

'I've organised a flight tomorrow night. The royal jet will fly us back.' A day to complete his nursemaid duties and deliver her safely to Hussein. Then Zahir could make his way to his new post. He'd been itching to get to it for weeks.

'The Emir expects me *tomorrow*?' Her face leached of colour, leaving her looking unexpectedly fragile.

Zahir opened his mouth then shut it again.

This wasn't going to plan. He'd envisaged her eager to return to Bakhara and embrace her new life as wife of the country's ruler. He'd expected excitement, gratitude, even.

Instead she looked horrified.

A thread of curiosity curled within him till he blanked it out. He wasn't interested in understanding Soraya Karim, especially as he had a fair idea he wouldn't like what he found on closer inspection. He prized loyalty above all things and Hussein deserved better than a fiancée who couldn't be trusted to keep away from other men.

'There's a problem with tomorrow?' He didn't bother to hide his disapproval.

His nostrils flared with distaste as he wondered if she needed extra time to say goodbye to that lanky fool from the nightclub. Surely she wouldn't delay her departure for *him*? Or had he been a ploy? Perhaps she'd been trying to make the handsome blond guy at their table jealous.

He'd observed the covetous glances she'd attracted in that bar. Anger stirred at the notion she'd played fast and loose with Hussein's trust.

'No, tomorrow's not convenient.' Just that. No explanations, no apologies, just a shimmer of defiance in those fine eyes and a hint of mulish wilfulness in her down-turned mouth.

Despite himself, Zahir felt a spark of appreciation for the way she stonewalled him. The negotiators this last week could have done with some of her spunk. They might have come out of the joint-venture deal with a better share of the profits.

But that didn't negate the fact that she disrupted his plans. True, Hussein hadn't specified a date for his bride's return, but Zahir wanted to conclude this task and move on to his new role. He hadn't been so eager for anything in years.

'And when will it be *convenient*?'

Colour rose in her cheeks and her lips parted as if to protest his curt tone. Zahir's pulse missed a beat and heat combusted deep in his belly as he watched her mouth turn from sulky to an enticing O. With his jacket pulled around her shoulders and her hair coming down in soft curling tresses, she looked inviting, available, *tempting*.

Not like the fiancée of his mentor and best friend.

Her eyes widened as if she read his response despite the savage control he exerted to keep it hidden.

The tension between them notched higher. It trembled in the

air, a pressure that had more do with his reaction to her than with the subject under discussion.

This couldn't be!

It *wouldn't* be.

By hook or by crook he'd have her back in Bakhara, safe with her fiancé and out of his life, before her feet could touch the ground.

CHAPTER THREE

SORAYA knew disapproval when she saw it.

Despite his almost expressionless face, that flat, accusing stare said everything his words didn't.

If it hadn't been imprinted on her so early perhaps she'd never have recognised it. But nothing, not time or distance, could erase the memory of her father's relatives whispering and tutting over the sordid details of her mother's misdemeanours—or their certainty that, if unchecked, Soraya would go the same way to ruin. Even the servants gossiped in delighted condemnation.

Stifling the urge to lash out, Soraya withdrew into herself. What did she care if the Emir's lackey didn't approve of her? Even if, far from being a lackey he was one of the most powerful men in the country?

She had more on her mind than winning his approval. His news changed her life.

'Give me tomorrow,' she said, her voice husky with tension that threatened to choke her. 'Then I'll have a better idea.'

How long to pack her gear, say her goodbyes and, above all, get her research in some sort of order? She feared however long it took wouldn't be enough.

Anxiety welled and she beat it back. Time enough to give in to fear when she was alone. She refused to let this man see her weak.

Abruptly she stood. He rose too, dwarfing the booth and

crowding her space. Instantly she was transported to the club where his touch had sapped common sense. Where just for a moment she'd wanted to lean close to his powerful frame rather than escape his hold. Fear closed around her.

'I want to go home.' Even to her own ears her voice held a betraying wobble. Paris had become her home, a haven where she'd been able to spread her wings and enjoy a measure of freedom for the first time. The idea of returning to Bakhara, to marriage…

'I'll see you back.' Already he was ushering her through the café, one hand hovering near her elbow as if to ensure she didn't do a runner. He dropped payment on the counter where the waitress beamed her approval.

What was wrong with the girl? Couldn't she see he was the sort of bad-tempered, take-charge brute who'd make any woman's life a misery?

Clearly not. The waitress's gaze followed him longingly, needling Soraya's temper.

'Thank you but I can make my own way.'

To her chagrin he was already hailing a taxi—a miracle at this time of the morning. It was daylight but the city was just stirring. Before she could reiterate her point he was opening the door for her then climbing in the other side.

'I said—'

Her words disintegrated as he gave her address to the driver. Her heart thudded and she sank back in her corner.

Of course he knew her address. How else would he have located her? But the thought of Zahir El Hashem shouldering his way into her cosy flat sent disquiet scudding through her. Instinct warned her to keep her distance.

She didn't want him near her.

The fact that he sat as far from her as the wide back seat allowed should have pleased her. Instead it struck her as insulting. He didn't have to make such a conspicuous issue of keeping his distance, so grimly silent.

What she'd done to annoy him, she had no idea. *He* was the

one whose behaviour was questionable, following her every move in the nightclub. What was that about?

Fifteen minutes later they stood on the pavement before her building. He'd overridden her assurance that he needn't see her to the entrance, just as he'd paid the taxi fare as she fumbled for cash. Polite gestures no doubt but he insidiously invaded her space, encroaching on her claim to be an independent woman.

Never before had that claim seemed so precious.

Her heart plunged as she thought of what lay ahead.

A promise to keep.

A duty to perform.

A *lifetime* of it.

So much for the tantalising sense of freedom she'd only just found. The dreams she'd dared to harbour. She'd been mad to let herself imagine a future of her own making.

'Here. Thank you.' She tugged his jacket off her shoulders. Instantly she missed its heavy, comforting warmth and, she realised with horror, its subtle spicy scent. The scent of *him.*

She looked into his shadowed face, unable to read his expression. But there was no mistaking the care he took not to touch her as he took the jacket from her hands. As if she might contaminate him!

Why had she, even for a moment, worried what he thought of her? She'd long ago learned to rise above what others thought, what they expected. Only by being true to herself and those she cared for had she found strength.

'Goodbye. Thank you for seeing me home.' What did it matter if her voice was stilted with indignation? She inclined her head stiffly and turned, unlocking the door.

'It's no trouble.' His deep voice rumbled, low and soft as a zephyr of hot desert wind, across her nape. Too late she realised she *felt* his warm breath, a caress on her bare skin as she stepped into the foyer and he followed.

Soraya slammed to a halt and felt the heat of his big frame behind her. Static electricity sparked and rippled across her flesh. It dismayed her. She'd never known anything like it.

But, she rationalised, till tonight she'd never been so close to a man other than her father.

Would she feel this strange surge of power in the air and across her skin when she went to the Emir?

Despite the heat of Zahir's body Soraya shivered.

'I'll see you to your apartment.'

Flattening her lips at his assumption she couldn't look after herself in her own building, she strode across the foyer. No point arguing. She had as much chance of budging him as of moving the Eiffel Tower.

But she refused to share the miniscule lift. The thought of being cocooned with him in that cramped space sent a spasm of horror through her. She'd rather take the five flights of stairs, even if her new shoes *were* pinching.

Soraya was ridiculously breathless when she reached her floor. She shoved her key in the door and turned to face him.

He wasn't even breathing quickly after their rapid ascent. Nor did he feel that strange under-the-skin restlessness that so unnerved her. That was clear from his impassive face. He looked solid and immoveable. Nothing pierced his control.

'Here.' He held out a thick cream card. On one side was a mobile-phone number. No name, nothing else. On the other he'd scrawled in bold, slashing strokes the name of a hotel she knew by reputation only. 'Call me if you need anything. I'll make all the necessary arrangements.'

No point in assuring him again she'd do her own organizing; it would be a waste of breath. He had the look of a man who heard what he chose to hear. She'd sort out the details later when she wasn't so weary.

'Thank you,' she murmured, resolutely hauling her gaze from his clear-eyed stare. 'Good night.'

Behind her she pushed open the door to the apartment.

'Is that you, Soraya?' From inside, Lisle's husky voice shattered the stilted silence. 'We're in the bedroom. Come in and join us.'

A stifled noise made her look up. Zahir El Hashem looked

for once shaken out of his complacency. His eyes were wide and his mouth slack. He blinked and opened his mouth as if to speak but Soraya had had enough.

She stepped through the door and swung it closed. For the length of five heartbeats she stood, her back pressed against the door, waiting for his imperious summons, for there was no doubt he'd been about to speak.

Instead there was silence. Even through the door she sensed his presence, like a disapproving thundercloud. Her skin prickled as if she'd touched a live wire and her pulse pattered out of sync.

'Soraya? Julie's here too. Come on in.'

'Coming,' she croaked, knowing she had no hope of escaping Lisle or her sister. Julie must have stopped by to see how things were with her twin as soon as Lisle's boyfriend had left.

Girly gossip wasn't what Soraya needed but at least it would take her mind off the news she'd just received: that her wonderful adventure in Paris was over and she was returning home to fulfil the duty she'd been bound to from the age of fourteen. The duty she'd become accustomed to thinking was in some far-off future that became less real with every passing year.

Yet as she snicked the bolt shut and scooped up Lisle's carelessly discarded camisole, Soraya was surprised to realise it was Zahir El Hashem's strong features that filled her mind. Not those of her betrothed.

Zahir stared at the door, one hand still raised as if to stop it shutting. Or force it open.

Shock held him rigid. It wasn't a familiar feeling. He was a man of some experience. Little surprised him. To be at a loss because she'd been invited to make up a threesome with the lovers he'd seen last night should be impossible.

Yet he rocked back on his feet, his gut clenching as if he'd caught a hammer blow to the belly. Searing bile snaked through his system.

Despite what he'd seen earlier, he'd almost convinced himself he'd been mistaken about Soraya. That the woman who carried herself with such poise and grace, yet with that intriguing shadow of anxiety in her eyes, was special. When he'd relaxed his guard he'd liked her, despite his doubts.

Stupid wishful thinking!

Had she deliberately sidetracked him?

Valiantly he'd tried to keep his eyes off the syncopated sway of her pert backside as she climbed the stairs in precarious heels. Even when he'd managed not to look he'd imagined the slip of soft fabric across warm, rounded flesh. His palms had tingled with remembered heat.

Anger welled. His hands fisted and his jaw ached as he clenched his teeth against the need to bellow out her name.

She'd played him for a fool. Tried to con him.

He felt…gutted.

He slumped against the door, hand splayed against it for support, recalling that discarded scrap of lingerie casually discarded just inside the door.

He'd spoiled her fun at the club and, he realised now, with the news she had to return to Bakhara where her every move would be scrutinised. Was she even now hauling that slinky dress over her head to join her friends in a little early-morning debauchery?

Nausea writhed.

Breathing heavily, Zahir sought calm.

Could he have misread what he'd seen and heard? He had so little evidence. Was he wrong to assume the worst? It was tempting to hope so.

Till he realised how much he *wanted* to be wrong. Fear feathered his backbone as he registered the sense almost of longing within him.

From the first his instinct had screamed a warning about Soraya Karim: she was dangerous. She tested his control to the limit and messed with his judgement.

He couldn't let her undermine his duty too.

Zahir sighed and scrubbed his hand over gritty eyes, suddenly more tired than he could remember. How could he break it to Hussein that the woman he planned to marry might not be fit for the honour?

'I'm sorry, madam. I'm afraid the guest you enquired about isn't available.'

'Not in or not available?' Soraya tamped down the steaming anger that had been simmering for hours. 'It's important I see him as soon as possible.'

'Excuse me a moment while I check.' The receptionist turned to confer with a colleague, leaving Soraya free to focus on her surroundings.

The foyer was luxurious in the bred-in-the-bone way you'd expect of one of Paris's grandest hotels. From the crimson carpet leading in from the cobblestoned pavement to the discreetly helpful staff, exquisite antiques and massive Venetian glass chandeliers, the placed screamed money, but in the most hushed and refined tones. The guests, whether wearing couture, business suits or staggeringly mismatched casuals, took the opulence in their stride, as only the super-wealthy could.

Soraya in her workaday jeans, T-shirt and loose jacket had never felt so out of place. Her family, one of the oldest in Bakhara, was comfortably off but had never aspired to this sort of rarefied luxury.

Even her shoes, her one pretension to elegance, had been snaffled in a miraculous end-of-sale bargain.

She stood taller. None of that mattered. All that mattered was seeing *him.* A tremor of repressed fury skated down her spine. Hadn't he promised her a day to get her bearings and then contact him? He'd had no right…

'I'm sorry for the delay, madam.' The receptionist was back. 'I'm able to tell you the guest you asked for has left strict instructions not to be disturbed.'

Soraya's lips compressed. That was why he hadn't answered his phone for the past two hours and she'd finally had to leave her work and come here in person. As if she didn't have more important things to concern her!

Why give her his phone number if he was going to be incommunicado for hours?

An image flashed into her brain of the waitress at the café melting at the sight of his blatant masculinity.

Was that why he couldn't be disturbed? Some assignation with an adoring woman?

'Thank you.' Her voice was crisp. 'In that case I'll wait till he *is* available.'

With a humph of disgust, Soraya stepped away from the desk.

Zahir El Hashem would soon discover she was no pushover.

In the early hours of this morning she'd been numb with the shock of his news, so dizzy with it she'd let him take charge. Now she'd had time to absorb the fact that she had no choice but to face her future head-on. That didn't stop the regrets, the anxiety, the downright fear. But she had to be strong if she was to survive the ordeal ahead. At the moment that meant teaching Zahir she wasn't some lackey to be ordered about at his convenience.

She was, like it or not, his Emir's future queen and a woman in her own right.

Soraya stalked across the room, oblivious now to its refined opulence, and plonked herself down on a plump sofa. She unzipped her laptop case and switched on the computer.

She'd rather be angry than fearful. And better than either was to immerse herself in something she really cared about. Two minutes later she was focused on her report, seeking an elusive error in the heat-transfer calculations.

Soraya didn't know what finally tugged her attention from the latest projections, but something made her look up, a sixth sense that sliced through her absorption.

A cluster of men in dark suits stood on the far side of the lobby. She recognised one as a senior French politician, his face familiar from news reports. But it was the tallest of the group who drew her frowning attention. His skin was burnished a dark honey gold, his features arresting.

Abruptly he looked up, his eyes locking instantly with hers. Shock danced down her spine at the impact.

Just like before.

The world had fallen away when he'd looked at her last night too.

Her hands jerked on the laptop keys. From the corner of her vision she saw a stream of extra rows appear in the carefully constructed table of technical analysis. Yet she couldn't drag her eyes from his.

In leather and denim he'd been a virile bad boy with an undeniable aura of danger.

Today, in exquisite tailoring and with an air of urbane assurance, he looked like he'd stepped from the ranks of the world's power brokers.

Who *was* Zahir El Hashem? Politician or heavy? Sophisticate or rogue?

Why did locking eyes with him make Soraya's heart thud to a discordant beat that stirred unfamiliar sensations?

She jerked her gaze away, blindly hit 'save' on her document and fumbled to shut down the laptop.

She'd had no sleep and she was stressed; no wonder she imagined things. There'd been no instantaneous pulse of connection between them. She'd simply imagined its heavy weight constricting her lungs and drawing her belly tight.

Shoving her laptop into its case she looked up to see him striding towards her.

Trepidation struck her. An awareness that, despite his elegant apparel and their rarefied surroundings, there was an elemental toughness about him she'd do well to remember. Only last night she'd recognised the desert warrior in him. Now as he approached Soraya knew she hadn't imagined the subtle scent of danger clinging to him.

'What's wrong? Why are you here?' His low voice drew the

fine hairs on her nape to prickling attention even as dark heat pooled low inside. It only fuelled her anger.

She refused to feel fear…or anything else for him.

'To see you, of course,' she hissed, jerking to her feet and wishing she was taller so he couldn't loom quite so effectively over her.

His narrowed eyes surveyed the room quickly and comprehensively. It was the sort of look she'd seen bodyguards use, searching for threat.

She'd give him threat!

'We had an agreement.' This time she kept her voice low and even. 'You broke it.'

His dark eyebrows climbed high but he gave no other reaction. 'Come.' He gestured for her to precede him.

Instantly Soraya shifted her weight, widening her stance a fraction as if to plant herself more firmly. She had no intention of meekly following him anywhere.

'I think not. We can talk here.'

Something flickered in those deeply hooded eyes. Something that might have been surprise or annoyance. Frankly, she didn't care. Instinct told her not to be alone with him. She knew next to nothing about him and looking at that granite-carved jaw, she wouldn't put it past him to try coercion.

'This is not the place for our conversation. This is a delicate matter and the person I represent—'

'Would perfectly understand my preference for meeting you here, rather than in a private room.'

He said nothing, just surveyed her with a look that was impossible to interpret. A look that seemed to take in everything from her too-fast breathing to the laptop she clutched like a shield to her chest.

Finally he nodded. 'Of course. If that is what you wish.' He turned and indicated a couple of chairs grouped at the rear of the room. 'Though perhaps we could go some place where we're less likely to be overheard.'

He had a point. Soraya nodded stiffly and let him usher her across the room.

Zahir frowned as he followed her. That instant surge of adrenalin in his blood, the momentary fear that something was wrong, had undermined his calm. All because she'd come looking for him when it was the last thing he'd expected.

It was absurd. Clearly she was in no danger. Panic was a weakness he didn't indulge in. Yet his pulse thundered in his ears as he watched her thread her way across the room.

He didn't like her, didn't approve of her, so why the instant, gut-deep need to protect that had made him hurry to her? He wanted to put it down to duty honed by years of training, but it wasn't that. From the first she'd stirred instincts and feelings that discomfited him. However much he fought it he felt… connected to her. Ever since that first, blinding moment of recognition.

She settled on a gilded sofa and made a production of crossing those long legs. As he seated himself opposite her, Zahir forced his gaze from the way the soft denim clung to each dip and curve.

'You wanted to see me?'

'Not really, but I had little choice.' Her neat white teeth snapped off each word. 'You weren't answering your phone.'

Ah. That was why she was in a temper. When she'd wrecked his plans to return to Bakhara today he'd used the extra time to fit in some meetings. Clearly she expected him to be at her beck and call like some underling.

'As you saw, I had business to conduct.' He refused to apologise for not being available at her whim. 'How can I assist you?'

Her eyes flashed ebony fire. 'By keeping your word.'

Zahir stiffened. 'That is not in question.' Did she have any concept of the insult she offered him?

'Isn't it?' She leaned forward and her scent insinuated itself into his nostrils. Light and delicate, like a field of mountain flowers awakening to the day's first sun. It had haunted him all day, a sense memory he'd tried to forget. 'We agreed you'd give me today to get organised yet my flatmate rang me at five this afternoon because a team of removalists had turned up wanting to pack my belongings.'

Zahir settled back in his seat and inclined his head. 'We agreed that you'd have today. We also agreed that I'd take care of the arrangements. I've done so. You've had your day to organise yourself.'

Colour mounted her cheeks and her eyes glittered with temper. Women could be so predictable when they didn't get what they wanted. He waited for a blast of ungoverned rage.

It didn't come.

Instead she sat back against the silk brocade of her seat.

'You don't approve of me, do you?' Her voice was coolly measured. 'Is that what this is about? Is that why you're being so high-handed?'

Momentarily he was thrown by her directness. He encountered it so rarely since he'd moved into the diplomatic sphere. It was the sort of tactic he used himself to great effect when others preferred to circle the truth. Cutting through the niceties to the heart of the matter was sometimes the most effective way forward.

He hadn't expected it from her.

Unwilling admiration stirred.

'My opinion of you is not in question, Ms Karim. My role is simply to facilitate your safe arrival to Bakhara.'

'Don't give me that! You're more than a courier.' She nodded to where he'd stood saying farewell to his guests. 'That's clear from the leaders who came here to meet you. You're trying to railroad me for your own reasons.'

She was clever too. Obviously she'd recognised the man tipped to become the next French foreign minister.

But what disturbed him was her accusation he was pushing her to hurry because it suited him.

He should have contacted Hussein this morning and voiced his concerns about Soraya Karim. But he'd baulked at the notion. That sort of conversation had to take place man-to-man, not long distance. It had the added advantage that Zahir could then walk away from her and concentrate on the work he'd been preparing for all his life.

'What is it about Paris that keeps you delaying? What's more important than your promise to marry?'

The colour faded from her cheeks and for a second he saw something flicker in the rich depths of her pansy-dark eyes. Something that looked like genuine pain. It surprised him for it seemed at odds with his image of a selfish pleasure-seeking woman.

'I have things to wrap up before I go.'

Things or relationships? His jaw tightened.

'Surely it won't take more than a day to say goodbye to your special *friends*.' He nodded curtly to her laptop. 'And no doubt you'll stay in contact.' Was she the sort who suffered withdrawal if disconnected from social media?

Her smooth forehead puckered then she shrugged. 'I have some work to finish too.'

Soraya almost laughed aloud as a flash of disbelief widened his eyes. Clearly he thought her some dilettante who used university as an excuse for a holiday in Paris.

He recovered quickly. 'It's summer. University break.'

'Have you heard of summer school? Between semesters?'

'I applaud your diligence.' But his tone belied his words. 'Are you saying you have to be here to complete your work? Surely alternative arrangements can be made?'

Circumstances being the fact that she was expected to return home meekly and marry a man, a virtual stranger, more than thirty years her senior.

Cold wrapped itself around Soraya's chest and seeped into bones that seemed suddenly brittle and aged. She drew a deep breath, willing away the panic that threatened whenever she thought too far ahead.

That was the problem; she'd forgotten to think ahead. For too long she'd assumed the future was nebulous and unreal. From the moment at fourteen, when her father had explained the honour bestowed on their family by the Emir's interest in her, through every year when Emir Hussein had remained a distant yet benign figure.

At fourteen the betrothal had been exciting, like something from an age-old tale. Later it had grown less and less real, especially when her fiancé had shown little interest beyond polite responses to her father's updates on her wellbeing and educational progress.

Now it was suddenly all too real.

'It's not just the work,' she blurted out. 'I'd planned to be here longer and I want to make the most of my time in France.'

'I'm sure you're doing just that.' His lips twisted.

She ignored his disapproval. 'I can finish up some of my work elsewhere, but not all of it.' She gestured to the laptop. 'Besides, I don't want a direct flight to Bakhara.'

His only response was to lift his eyebrows, stoking her impatience.

'I intend to travel overland. In all these months I haven't been out of Paris and I want to see more of the country before I return.'

And store up some precious memories—of her last days of freedom. It wasn't too much to ask. Once she returned she'd be the woman the Emir and his people expected. She'd marry a man renowned for his devotion to duty and her life would be circumscribed by that.

She needed this time, just a little time, to adjust to the fact that her life as an individual was ending. The alternative, to return immediately, stifled the breath in her lungs and sent panic shuddering through her.

'That's not possible. The Emir is expecting you.'

She nodded, glad now that she'd found the courage to do what she'd never done before and call the Bakhari Palace, giving her name and asking for the Emir. It had been surprisingly easy.

'Yes, he is.' For the first time she smiled. 'I spoke to him today. He thinks it's a wonderful idea that I take my time and soak up some of the sights along the way. He agrees it will be educational for me to get a better understanding of other places and people, not just Paris.'

It had felt odd talking to the man who for so long had been a distant figure and who soon would be her husband.

Zahir's stunned expression would have pleased her if she'd wanted to score points off this man who always seemed so sure of himself. But she had more important concerns.

'I've got till the end of the month.' That would give her the breathing space she so desperately needed. There was only one problem, but right now it should be the least of her worries. She squared her shoulders and met his eyes. 'The Emir's only stipulation was that you accompany me.'

CHAPTER FOUR

'I KNOW it's not what you planned, Zahir, but I see huge benefits in this trip. Soraya was very convincing.'

Zahir gritted his teeth. He just bet she had been. He heard the smile in Hussein's tone even over the phone. No doubt she'd employed her soft, sultry voice to best advantage in her long-distance call to Bakhara.

'But a week is more than enough, isn't it? The sooner she returns the better, surely?'

'It will be a big change for her,' Hussein answered slowly. 'Living as my wife in the palace. Meeting VIPs, playing a role in diplomatic functions. Plus there's the work that will be expected of her with our own people. She'll be an advocate for many who, for whatever reason, are daunted by approaching their ruler directly. Giving her a chance to mix with as wide a range of people as possible can only be an advantage.'

He paused. 'That's one of the reasons I supported her studying in Paris. She needs to broaden her horizons, ready for her future role.'

Zahir stared unseeingly at the lights of Paris. His heart sank. Not just because Hussein supported Soraya's plan to delay her return. Far worse was the burden of suspicion she wasn't fit to be his mentor's bride.

He thrust a hand through his hair. How could he disabuse Hussein?

How could he not?

He'd do anything to save Hussein pain. The older man was more than a father to him. Friend, mentor, hero, he'd shown Zahir care, regard and even love when no one else had. He'd brought him up more like a son than a charity case. A not-quite-orphan shouldn't have warranted the Emir's personal attention.

Zahir owed him everything: his place in the world, his education, his self-respect, even his life.

He was caught between shattering Hussein's illusions about his bride and letting her dupe him.

His belly churned. 'Hussein, I—'

'I know you're disappointed, Zahir. You're eager to take up the post of provincial governor.'

A sliver of guilt carved its way through Zahir's gut. 'You know me too well.'

Hussein's chuckle was like the man himself, warm and compelling. 'How could I not? You're the son I never had.'

Something rose in Zahir's chest, a welling sensation that tightened his lungs and choked his vocal chords. Despite their closeness, the regard between him and Hussein was rarely spoken. Bakhari males left emotion to their womenfolk, focusing instead on masculine concerns such as pride, duty and honour.

'You make it sound like your time has past. You're in your late fifties, not your dotage. You've got plenty of time to father a son. A whole family.'

And, with a young, sexy bride, nothing was more likely.

Out of nowhere Zahir glimpsed an image of Hussein holding Soraya close, pulling her to him and letting his hands slip over the curve of her hip, the soft fabric of her dress enhancing the femininity of her shapely figure.

He swallowed hard as a jagged spike of pain skewered him. His breath shallowed and he turned to stride down the length of the suite, fighting sudden nausea.

He was tired of being cooped up. He longed for the clean air of the desert, the wide sky studded with diamond-bright stars. *The total absence of Soraya Karim.*

'Well, time will tell,' was all Hussein said. 'But as for the governorship...'

'That doesn't matter.' Zahir splayed a hand against one wall and stared out at the glittering spectacle of the Eiffel Tower sparkling with a million electric lights. He'd trade it in a second for the light of the moon over the desert, highlighting dunes and silhouetting proud, ancient citadels.

'Of course it matters. You'll be the best governor the place has had.'

Silence engulfed them. No doubt Hussein, like himself, was remembering the long period when Bakhara's largest province had been ruled by a ruthless, decadent and utterly unscrupulous tribal leader. A man who'd tried many years before to increase his prestige by backing a coup to unseat Hussein.

Zahir's father.

His biological father, never his *real* father.

It sickened Zahir that he shared the blood of a traitor, a man who'd clung to his position only because of Hussein's forgiveness and the fact that removing him would have caused more unrest at a dangerous, volatile time.

'Your faith in me means everything.' Zahir bowed his head. It was the closest he'd ever come to expressing aloud his devotion to the man who'd rescued him, ragged, neglected and virtually feral at the age of four from his father's palace.

Rather than speak it, Zahir had spent a lifetime demonstrating his loyalty, his regard, his love.

'As does yours, Zahir.' Hussein's tone held a husky warmth that spoke far more than words. 'As for the governorship—it will be there waiting for you. I think my bride isn't the only one who'll benefit from a break. You've pushed yourself hard lately. Take your time and relax. Who knows?' He chortled. 'You might even enjoy the novelty of a vacation.'

Zahir opened his mouth to say he didn't need a vacation. He thrived on responsibility, challenge, pressure. The prospect of managing the vast province held an allure he couldn't put in words. To have total responsibility, rather than be another's aide: it had captured his interest from the moment Hussein had broached it.

'It's not simply the time away.' Zahir paused, wondering how to continue. He wasn't used to being at a loss for words.

'Go on.'

He drew a difficult breath and wished his concerns were about something as simple as the next bilateral trade agreement or progress on a major public-works programme.

'Your fiancée. She's not what I expected.'

Silence. Zahir knew Hussein valued his opinion on so many difficult issues. He'd even trusted him with his life. But this was different.

'I see.'

Zahir shook his head. Hussein *didn't* see. That was the problem. He'd left Soraya to her own devices in Paris, believing she was worthy of his trust.

'I'm not sure she's…quite the woman you expect.'

'Taken you by surprise, has she?' Hussein's chuckle was rich.

Zahir's hand clenched in a taut fist. 'You could say that.' No, he mustn't hide the truth any longer. 'I'm afraid she may not be the right woman for you.'

Hell! He'd give anything not to have to break this news. Hussein deserved better, so much better than a party girl who shared her sexual favours freely.

'Your concern does you credit, Zahir. But I know more of Soraya than you think. I know she's exactly the woman I need.' When he spoke again his words silenced Zahir's protests. 'We will talk on your return. In the meantime, know that I believe in her as I believe in you, Zahir. I trust you both.'

'What are you doing here?' The words shot out of Soraya's mouth before she could stop them. She wasn't used to opening her door to find six-foot-something of male leaning indolently against the doorjamb.

Her heart leapt up against her throat and she felt light-headed at the impact of him.

He was so close she recognised the clean, spicy scent of his skin. It reminded her of the strange sensations she'd experienced when he'd held her in his arms and she'd felt…

'Good morning, Soraya. It's good to see you looking well.' He straightened but only so he could loom imposingly.

'How did you get into the building?' She sounded absurdly breathless given the fact she'd expected to meet him downstairs in ten minutes. But, she was learning that meeting this man head-on was marginally easier if one was prepared.

His gaze raked her face. Heat combusted and spread under her skin.

Who was she kidding? There was nothing easy about this. She only wished she understood what it was about him that screwed her tension up to such dangerous levels.

He shrugged and she couldn't help but follow the movement of his broad shoulders beneath the pale, exquisitely laundered shirt. Casual, expensive elegance; that was the theme of the day. Scrupulously shaved jaw and a heavy yet discreet watch she was sure she recognised from one of Lisle's fashion magazines.

'One of the tenants let me in when she saw me waiting outside.' His glimmer of a smile drew the tightness in her belly even harder.

Soraya breathed deep. Of course it had been a woman. Had she taken one look at Zahir's compelling face and melted deep inside the way Soraya had in the nightclub?

She stiffened her spine.

'I'd expected to meet you at the car.'

'And I thought you might appreciate help with your luggage.' The hint of a smile had vanished and his eyes held that hard glitter she knew masked disapproval.

She forced down the churlish impulse to refuse. The way he took control so smoothly exacerbated her deepest fears about giving up her independence, reminding her that, once married, she would be bound to honour and, above all, obey. She repressed a quiver of apprehension and looked away.

'Thank you. That's very kind.' She stepped aside and invited him in.

'No farewell party?' He looked past her to the neat sitting room and the small, empty corridor.

'No.' She'd said her goodbyes earlier. Parting with Lisle in particular had been difficult. She'd had no intention of doing that under Zahir's assessing gaze.

Despite their different backgrounds, Soraya and Lisle had forged far more than a casual friendship. For the first time Soraya had glimpsed what it might be like to have a sister. Outgoing where Soraya was reserved, flamboyant rather than contained, funny, warm and impulsive—Lisle had been a revelation to a woman who'd spent her life in cloistered, sedate, correct social circles. Lisle was a whirlwind, ripping into Soraya's quiet life and setting it on a new path. One that had opened her eyes to all the world could offer a woman with her life ahead of her.

Except that now those possibilities crumbled to nothing. Soraya's future was set, had been since she was fourteen. It was too late to change it now.

'Soraya?'

She blinked and looked up to find him closer. For a split second she'd have said she read concern in his hooded eyes. She blinked again and the mirage was gone.

'Here.' She gestured to the case behind her in the hallway.

'That's all?' He looked past her as if to locate a secret stash of luggage.

'That's all. Your removalists were very efficient. My books and other bits and pieces are already on their way to Bakhara.' Her voice dropped to a husky note. She really had to pull herself together.

Despite the claustrophobic sense of the future smothering her, she knew the man she'd agreed to marry had reputedly been a devoted husband to his now-dead first wife. He was decent, generous and honourable.

That was more than many women could say.

It would have to be enough. It wasn't as if she was eager to seek out love. She knew what a devastating emotion that was.

As for her tentative dreams—instead she'd have to put her energies into the goals that had enticed her when she had been a starry-eyed teen: being a queen who made a real difference to her people. Being a good wife. At least with her qualifications she could be the former.

'I'll just get my shoulder bag.'

Thirty seconds later she was in her room, hugging close the oversized bag she'd haggled for in the markets two weeks ago. Only it wasn't her room any more. Stripped of her possessions, it was an empty shell. Not the place she'd been so happy.

Stupid to be sentimental about it.

There was no point dwelling on what was past. She'd learned that as a child, bereft and confused.

She turned and found Zahir in the doorway, his gaze, as ever, fixed on her. A subterranean tremor quaked through her, threatening to destabilise the control she fought so valiantly to maintain.

Turning quickly, she scooped up her laptop.

'I'm ready.'

The Loire River snaked below them like a bright pewter ribbon. Studded along its banks and beyond were neat towns, a patchwork of farms and a scattering of chateaux.

But Zahir's attention wasn't on the view, even when the chopper swooped low over quaint towns or stately homes.

It was the woman next to him who riveted Zahir's thoughts and his gaze. Uptight from the moment he turned up at her door, she'd grown coolly distant when he'd informed her they wouldn't travel by car as she'd planned.

She seemed to think he'd countermanded the idea out of a need to take control!

He huffed silently to himself. He had no need to prove his authority.

What he had was a burning need *not* to be cooped up alone with Soraya for the time it would take to drive to their destination.

Zahir couldn't pinpoint what it was about her that made him edgy—it was more than his qualms about her unsuitability as Hussein's bride.

Yet as they headed south-west from Paris he hadn't been able to drag his attention from her. He'd read her initial nerves, watched as she gradually relaxed and began to talk with the pilot. Initially dour, the pilot now chatted easily, flattered no doubt by her questions on everything from pilot training to wind speed and the local topography.

She was a woman who could charm a man with ease.

'You're enjoying the trip?' Zahir found himself asking. He suppressed the suspicion that he'd spoken only to break the camaraderie building between the other two.

'Absolutely.' There was a breathy quality to her voice that told him she was smiling even though she faced away, peering at the view. 'I love seeing everything laid out like this. It's fantastic.'

'I'm glad you like it.'

'Thank you for organising it.' She swung round and the pleasure on her face arrested him. It lit her from within, making her eyes glow and her face come alive.

Something inside Zahir shuddered into being: a recognition, a sense almost of rightness, he couldn't explain.

He'd seen her angry, defiant, exhausted. He'd seen her furious and frigidly cool but, he realised, he'd never seen her happy.

Maybe it would have been better to travel by car after all. *Safer.*

'You've never been in a helicopter before?' It was easier to talk than dwell on the impact of that knockout grin.

She shook her head and a tendril of dark hair slipped free of the knot at the back of her head and coiled down past her breast.

Involuntarily his fingers twitched, as if needing to feel its softness.

The preternatural feeling of recognition grew to something like déjà vu: as if Zahir had been with her before, had watched her joyous smile and felt that deep-down explosion of blistering heat. He could envisage her pulling her hair free of its pins so it swung in a seductive silk curtain, inviting his touch.

'No, I've never flown in a helicopter before. Isn't it terrific? I love the feeling when we swoop low then rise up high again.'

On cue the pilot angled the chopper down to circle a bluff crowned by a half-ruined tower then lifted them back up.

A throaty gurgle escaped her lips. 'Like that. Thanks, Marc.'

The pilot nodded silently and Zahir knew a moment's searing discomfort. As if the easy friendliness between the two had the power to annoy him.

The notion was absurd.

'I can't wait to try it again. I've decided I like air travel after all.' She turned away to watch as they passed over a field of sunflowers, head bent as if utterly absorbed.

'You didn't enjoy it before?'

'My only other flight was on the jet from Bakhara to Paris, so I couldn't be sure.'

Zahir sat back in his seat, processing that. 'You'd never been on a flight before then?' He'd imagined her spending holidays at foreign resorts then shopping till she dropped in the expensive boutiques of various capital cities.

She shook her head and he watched, transfixed by the wistful smile that shaped her face as she half-turned. 'I'd never been out of Bakhara before.'

No wonder Hussein had seen benefit in her studying abroad. No wonder he thought exposure to other places and people would do her good.

Bakhara was no longer the feudal state it had been till recently. The wife of the country's ruler would need polish, poise and some exposure to the wider world.

A pity her exposure hadn't been more carefully supervised.

Zahir frowned. Had she been wild for the hedonistic pleasures Paris offered or had she been seduced by them? He remembered the husky voice inviting her to bed the other morning, and the blatant lust in that pseudo-intellectual's face at the club. There'd be no shortage of people eager to introduce Soraya to life's seamier pleasures.

Heat trickled through his belly. What had Hussein been thinking, letting her loose in Paris without a chaperone? Without someone to guide and protect her, had she been easy prey?

Yet, even as he thought it, Zahir *knew* he was wrong. Soraya Karim was no easy victim. Beneath the feminine sway of hips and that delicious pout of a mouth was a will of iron. Look at how she'd managed to get her own way over delaying her return to Bakhara. Whatever she'd done, she'd done with her eyes wide-open.

The heat in his gut twisted in a sickening swirl.

He vowed he at least wouldn't succumb to her blandishments.

Ahead Soraya glimpsed spires amidst a dark swathe of green. As they approached, her breath hitched at the sheer fairy-tale beauty of the chateau below them. Pale grey, almost white in the bright sunlight, it boasted an abundance of towers capped with conical slate roofs. The windows were large and mullioned, reflecting the sun glinting off the moat that surrounded it. An arched bridge led across to vast lawns and ornamental gardens. The whole was enclosed by a forest that isolated it from everything else. Like an enchanted world.

She sighed. It was so beautiful, so different from anything she'd seen either in Paris or at home. No wonder Lisle had told her she couldn't miss the Loire Valley! She'd said it would appeal to the dreamer in her.

Just the place for Prince Charming to appear and spirit her away on his milk-white stallion.

Her smile twisted. She wasn't in the market for a rescuing

prince. She'd never yearned for romance, not after weathering the destructive aftermath of her parents' disastrous love match.

Besides, one prince was enough in any girl's life.

More than enough.

She wrapped her arms around herself as a chill invaded her bones.

Try as she might, nothing could take her mind off the fact that in a few short weeks she'd be at the Emir's court, preparing for her wedding—to give herself to a stranger.

Dread carved a hollow in her chest, leaving a yawning hole where she'd once nurtured fledgling dreams. Not earth-shattering dreams, just the chance to make her own choices. To build a career she loved and live as she chose.

Right now they seemed as likely as flying to the moon.

It was only as the thud of the helicopter's rotors died that she realised they'd landed. Bewildered, she looked out to see they were between the forest and the river. In front of them rose the exquisite chateau she'd admired from the air.

Soraya tried to dredge up her enthusiasm for the fanciful architecture, the elegant embellishments, the beautiful symmetry. But the cold, hard fact of her looming future marred her appreciation.

She fumbled for her seatbelt, annoyed with herself. She should be making the most of every moment, of each new place and experience. Yet here she was doing what she'd vowed not to do—dwelling on what she couldn't change.

'Let me.' Zahir's warm fingers tangled with hers and she stiffened.

There had to be a scientific explanation for the pulse of energy that sparked under her skin whenever he touched her. Once it had been surprising—twice, too much of a coincidence. Now she found it…disturbing.

'Thank you.' She scrambled out of the door before he could come around and help. Her knees felt ridiculously weak but she put that down to the after-effects of her first chopper flight.

She went forward to thank Marc. He'd been friendly and so patient with her questions.

She'd barely thanked him when Zahir loomed beside her.

'This way.' He didn't touch her again but with him so close she found herself cutting short her goodbyes and preceding him to the chateau.

'I think you'll like this,' he said as they crunched up the white gravel path. 'There's swimming, tennis, archery, riding—all the usual—and the restaurant has a couple of Michelin stars, of course.'

Of course.

'The day spa is renowned and you have a reservation there in—' he glanced at his watch '—forty minutes.'

Soraya shifted her stare from the opulent chateau to the man striding at her side.

'We're staying *here*?' She'd thought they'd stopped to get a better look since she'd wanted to visit the region.

'You don't approve?' He slashed a sideways glance at her then away, never slowing his pace. The set of his shoulders and the clench of his solid jaw spoke of impatience. Or was it anger?

From the very first, disapproval had emanated from him in waves. She was tired of it.

Soraya shook her head. 'No, it's not that.' She just wasn't accustomed to such grandeur; it made her uncomfortable. But, she reminded herself, she'd have to get used to it soon. The Emir of Bakhara was one of the wealthiest men in the world. 'I'm sure it will be…lovely.'

Zahir must have picked up her cautious tone for he stopped, blocking her path. 'If you have a problem, tell me.' His eyes iced over, chilling her anew. 'I'd rather know now than have you running to the Emir and bothering him with your complaints when he's busy.'

Soraya's head jerked back as if he'd slapped her.

The Emir hadn't minded her calling. In fact, he'd sounded pleased she'd rung and surprisingly delighted with her plan for a slow route home.

Nor had she any need to explain herself to Zahir El Hashem. Whatever it was that twisted him in knots wasn't her concern.

She met his glacial stare with what she hoped was casual disdain. 'As you pointed out a few days ago, the Emir is my future husband. I will call him if I wish.'

No need to say she had no intention of making further calls. She refused to let the man looming like a thundercloud think he could bully her. She stepped forward, intending to brush by him, but he didn't budge, just stood before her, blocking her way—unless she chose to scramble through the rose bushes edging the path. He seemed all solid muscle and bone—broad enough to blot out the chateau with those shoulders and towering over her even though she wore her heels.

'One thing you should know.' His voice was soft, a low, lethal growl that sent primitive fear scudding down her spine. 'You betray him and you answer to me.'

Soraya's head shot up, her eyes clashing with his.

Gone was the coolness, the icy detachment. He was all heat and fury. She felt it sizzle around her like a force-field, drawing her in, trapping her. The air between them zapped and crackled with the emotion radiating from him.

For the first time Soraya saw *him*—not the polished, unreadable veneer of a man who hid his true thoughts behind impenetrable barriers.

She'd wondered what lay behind that façade. Now she had a glimpse and was stunned by what she discovered.

For all his appearance of detachment, and despite his reputation as a diplomatic trouble shooter, Zahir El Hashem was a man of passion and volcanic temper. He *cared* about the Emir, and not just as the man who paid his salary.

Prickles of heat broke out across her flesh as she met his glare and refused to back away.

'Your sentiment does you proud,' she said when finally she found her voice. 'But your judgement is seriously flawed if you think I intend to betray him.'

That was just it. She wasn't the sort to blithely walk away from a promise, even a promise given so young.

Her past had moulded her into a woman who understood the value of honour. And the destructive force of betrayal. Besides, she couldn't disappoint her father, who saw this as her bright, wonderful future. Nor could she betray the Emir, the man who'd given her back what she'd almost lost. She owed him so much.

No matter which way she looked at it, she was shackled to her destiny.

'Now,' she continued, her voice husky with weariness, 'please step out of my way. I want to go to my room.'

CHAPTER FIVE

IT WASN'T guilt Zahir felt.

He'd been right to warn her. Let her know he was watching her. That he had Hussein's back covered.

Zahir had willingly put himself between Hussein and danger in the past. It was what he'd trained to do. What he was proud to do. Dealing with an unfaithful woman was nothing compared to facing down a would-be assassin.

Yet something niggled at him. Something was *wrong*.

Gut instinct warned he'd missed something. That he didn't have the full picture—till he reminded himself he wasn't the sort to be swayed by a show of bravado and a flicker of pain in eyes like bruised pansies.

Yet he found himself pushing open the door to the hotel's plush day spa. It reeked of perfume, hothouse orchids and flushed female flesh.

'Can I help you, *monsieur*?' A pretty redhead looked up from the reception desk.

'Yes, I'm looking for Mademoiselle Karim.'

'Karim?' The woman frowned and turned to her computer. 'Ah, I thought I recognised the name. That booking was cancelled this morning.'

'Cancelled?' He'd made no such cancellation.

The redhead nodded. 'That's right. Mademoiselle rang from her room. She'd changed her mind and…' She looked up to find the plate-glass door to the spa swinging closed.

Twenty minutes later Zahir was on the road. At least he knew he wasn't chasing a runaway; her luggage was in her suite. Even her beloved laptop.

Only Soraya was missing.

He cursed himself and accelerated too soon out of a sweeping bend in the road.

How had he let her slip away? Why hadn't he confirmed she was set for a day's pampering rather than assuming it, before settling down with his own laptop?

Because he'd been too eager to put distance between them.

Whether pensive or defiant or giving him the cold shoulder, Soraya Karim tugged at something hot and hungry deep inside him.

Something he had no business feeling for the woman who, rightly or wrongly, was to marry Hussein.

That was the hell of it.

Why her?

He had his choice of women now he was *someone*. His mouth twisted in a smile of derision, remembering his youth, when lack of status had lost him the woman he'd fallen for so desperately. He'd thought his heart broken.

Of course he'd survived. As for his heart—he harboured no fantasies now about love. He never let women close to him emotionally. They barely caused a ripple in his life.

Until Soraya Karim.

Tension crawled through him. He'd had to force himself to give her space. Had he provided her with an opportunity to take off and meet a lover?

His only clues were the details of the car the concierge had organised for her and the map he'd provided—a map on which he'd marked the places Soraya had queried: a couple of chateaux, an old house and what turned out to be a nuclear powerplant. That last had to be a mistake. He mentally crossed it off his list and accelerated down a straight stretch of road, his mouth set.

* * *

It was late when he tracked her down.

A familiar, husky voice caught Zahir's ear. He slammed to a halt at the base of the stone stairs in the old house-cum-museum. Swinging his head round, he saw her.

She was safe.

Relief hit him so hard his knees weakened for a moment. An instant later fury descended, swirling through him like a desert storm.

Hussein trusted him to keep her safe yet he'd let her slip away. For the first time ever Zahir had let emotion interfere with his judgement, with his duty.

Inevitably she was talking with a man, her head bent close.

Zahir pushed away from the stairs, outrage pounding through him that he'd let himself worry about her. Then his mind processed what he saw and he stopped again, frowning.

This was no assignation. The man had stooped shoulders and greying hair. Beside him was a trim woman in her late sixties, smiling benignly as Soraya and her male companion discussed…mechanical gears?

Zahir moved to one side and saw what fixed their attention—a display of machinery. His frown deepened as he flashed a glance around the cellar of the old house.

All around were models of half-familiar machines. A whirligig that looked like the precursor to a helicopter. A model of a tilting bridge. A contraption for hauling water uphill by turning a huge screw.

It hit Zahir then that he'd been right: he *didn't* understand Soraya. He'd missed something vital.

He intended to find out what it was.

'Ah, we mustn't keep you any longer. Thank you for your time, my dear. I've enjoyed our chat.' There was a twinkle in the old man's eyes as he looked past her and up.

Soraya's nape prickled and the hairs on her arms rose as if someone had walked over her grave.

Slowly she turned. Her gaze hit a broad chest in a snowy

shirt then climbed past a strong, sun-burnished throat to a familiar, rock-hard jaw, firm, sculpted lips, lean cheeks and eyes of dazzling emerald.

Heat snaked from her chest to her abdomen, circling there as he held her eyes.

'Hello, Soraya. You take some tracking down.'

Behind her she was aware of the older couple moving away and knew regret. She'd so enjoyed their discussion. Now her day of freedom was over. Was it imagination or did the sunlight dim, as if obscured by sudden cloud?

'Then why did you bother? I'm perfectly capable of looking after myself.' Anger bit deep that she'd not been allowed even a day of freedom. Was this what it would be like in Bakhara? No time to herself? Always watched? Silently she railed against the future she couldn't change.

'So I'm discovering.' Instead of the scowl she anticipated she read only curiosity in his gaze. 'Shall we?' He gestured towards the door that led into the garden.

Reluctantly she led the way. There was no point continuing with her plans to see the rest of the estate now he was here. He'd have some reason why she had to return to the chateau-hotel.

Choosing a seat at a shaded courtyard table, Soraya slipped her sunglasses on. She needed all the protection she could get against his piercing scrutiny.

Zahir didn't say anything, simply ordered iced water and coffee then lounged, one arm slung along the back of his chair as if totally relaxed, watching her.

Soraya's blood tingled in response to that look.

It was almost a relief when their order came. Surely now he'd break the brooding suspense to berate her for leaving and not telling him her plans?

She stiffened her spine in readiness and lifted her glass of chilled water.

'Tell me about yourself,' he said at last, and her hand jerked so she almost spilled the drink down her dress. It was the last thing she'd expected him to say.

'Why?' Sourness tinged her response. 'I'm just the package you need to courier to Bakhara, remember?'

Slowly he shook his head, his eyes never leaving hers. He held her pinioned just with the force of that look. Her limbs felt heavy as if invisibly weighted.

How could he *do* that?

A flutter of apprehension stirred. No other man had the power to make her feel anything like it.

'You're far more than that and you know it, Soraya.'

Her brow puckered. There was something in his tone she couldn't fathom. A keen edge that matched the coil of tension swirling its way down to the pit of her stomach.

'I thought you were here to whisk me back to the hotel.' He said nothing. 'Why *are* you here, then?' After his threat back at the chateau, she'd put nothing past him.

'Hussein entrusted me with your safety. You're my responsibility till you return to Bakhara and—'

'I'm perfectly capable. I don't need to be watched over.' Indignation welled.

'Be that as it may, I was concerned when I found you gone. You're in unfamiliar territory, alone, when by your own admission you have limited experience of foreign travel. I needed to make sure you were all right.'

His voice rang with sincerity and abruptly Soraya's bubble of anger punctured. He was doing his job. It wasn't his fault it felt like he was her own personal gaoler. As for his disapproval—she saw no evidence of it now.

'Why did you come *here*?' He reached for his coffee.

'You make it sound as if Amboise is an unusual choice. It's a quaint old town with a chateau, cliff dwellings—'

'Not the town. *Here*.' His gesture encompassed both the old house and the sweep of park-like gardens she'd yet to explore. 'It's pleasant, but it doesn't match the opulence of the royal chateaux.'

'And, of course, I should be interested in opulence, is that it?' What did he think, that she'd somehow snaffled the Emir for his wealth?

Was that why Zahir had installed her in that beautiful, luxurious hotel that, to her overwrought nerves, felt ridiculously like a gilded prison?

'That's just it.' He leaned forward. 'I don't know what interests you.' His gaze dropped from her face. 'Apart from shoes with more sex appeal than substance.'

A flush rose from the vicinity of her ankles where the scarlet straps of her wedge-heeled espadrilles ended in saucy bows. Heat flooded up her thighs, through her body and scorched its way to her cheeks.

Because he thought her shoes sexy.

Her heart gave an odd little flutter.

Why did that observation sound like an admission of some sort? And why did it unsettle her so?

Zahir lifted his espresso but he didn't look away. Soraya gulped down some icy water, hoping to ease the rush of blood under her skin.

'Clos Lucé is where Leonardo da Vinci lived the final years of his life.'

'I thought he was Italian?'

'He was, but the King of France thought him so special he offered him a home.' She nodded to the open window above them. 'He slept in that room.'

'So you're a fan of his art?'

She shrugged. 'I never saw the Mona Lisa in Paris. There were too many other things to do.'

Zahir's eyebrows rose. 'Hussein mentioned you were studying art history in Paris.'

'I was.' Her chin tilted higher, on the defensive now.

Zahir said nothing but his silence told her he was waiting. For long moments she held his gaze, then she shrugged. What was the point in prevaricating?

'It wasn't my idea, it was my father's. He thought an understanding of art would be useful given my…future. A sort of wider cultural education.' What he hadn't said, of course, was that studying art was more genteel, more suitable for a lady. Not that he'd ever say that out loud.

Soraya smiled. Her dad had never quite understood her interest in the unfeminine sciences, but he was her staunchest ally against the traditionalists who'd looked down their noses at her chosen path. They'd seen her lack of interest in the usual female occupations as dangerous—a possible sign she was like her unnatural mother.

Her smile faded.

'Soraya?'

She looked up to find Zahir's eyes narrowing. 'Sorry?'

'You didn't enjoy the course?'

'No, I did. It's not what I would have chosen myself but it was interesting.' She paused, relishing the warmth of the filtered sunlight and the gentle bird calls, the sense, illusory as it was, of freedom.

'I should have made an effort to see his art. He was gifted in so many fields. Did you *see* the models of his inventions?' That had been such fun, especially when she'd met two amateur inventors eager to discuss them.

'I saw them.' His voice told her Leonardo's breakthroughs were mildly interesting to him, no more.

'Where do you think the world would be without people like that, finding new ways to solve problems?'

'What, like that multi-barrelled gun to mow down as many people as possible at a time?'

Soraya found herself smiling ruefully into eyes that had lost their hard edge and crinkled appealingly at the corners. That hint of amusement eased the hard lines of Zahir's face, making him more relaxed, not the stern figure of the last few days.

She'd thought him in his mid-thirties. Now she reassessed. He was younger than she'd assumed.

'It takes the gloss off his "man of the arts" image, doesn't it? But he was working on what people wanted.'

'You could say that about nuclear weapons.'

'True. It's the age-old issue, isn't it? What people do with what scientists invent.'

'That's what interests you? Science?' His eyes widened a fraction.

'Careful, Zahir. You're not in danger of typecasting me because I'm female, are you?' She'd come up against enough raised eyebrows in Bakhara for her supposedly unconventional interests. Inevitably she felt disappointment stir. 'Women aren't all interested in the same things. We're as varied as men.'

'So I'm learning.'

Soraya raised her eyebrows. Her guess was he expected women to focus on luxury and be dependent on men to make the decisions. No wonder they had been at loggerheads.

'If you weren't so interested in art history, why were you concerned to finish your project before you left?'

She sat back in her chair, surveying him carefully. 'You are sharp, aren't you?'

'I could say the same about you.' This time she caught it—a tiny flash of appreciation in his eyes. She felt an answering flicker of pleasure. 'Are you going to tell me what you were doing or is it a secret?'

'No secret. I just took more than one class.'

He said nothing, simply put down his cup and waited, as if he had all the time in the world and nothing more important to do than listen. Yet that stiff, judgemental attitude was missing. What had changed?

'Not really a class, actually. A job.'

'You *worked*?'

She couldn't help it. A gurgle of laughter escaped at his astonished expression. 'Is that so hard to believe?' She held up her hand. 'No, don't answer. I can guess—you thought I pretended to study but secretly majored in shopping.'

A twist of his lips told her she was on the right track. Despite her amusement, annoyance stirred.

'I'm rather fond of shopping, actually. Paris is a real treat for that—everything from haute couture to street markets.'

Soraya looked down at her shoes, but instead of remembering her thrill at getting such a bargain it was a different thrill entirely that rippled through her. Had she imagined the heat in Zahir's stare? He'd made her feel *sexy* with that casual reference to her footwear.

Her skin tingled and her blood throbbed with that weird, unfamiliar blast of heat. Unfamiliar till three days ago, that was. Till Zahir had singled her out in that bar.

She lifted her head.

'That night in the bar. Why did you stare at me like that?'

Zahir read the curiosity in her gaze and knew he'd seriously underestimated her. She had a sharp intellect as well as a strong streak of independence—characteristics he admired.

Yet he hadn't wanted to like her since the moment he'd seen her with another man. Had he let that blind him to other aspects of her character? Had he rushed to judgement?

'I was assessing the situation. You wouldn't have liked me interrupting your night out.'

Her head tilted to one side. Her brow wrinkled and her mouth pouted in a moue of concentration.

Zahir's breathing shallowed as he stared at those lush lips. He dragged his gaze to her dark eyes.

'No, that's not right.' She shook her head. 'You had no compunction about interrupting my night out. Once you decided to make your move, that was it.'

If he'd decided to 'make his move', that night would have ended very differently.

The thought exploded out of nowhere as he imagined doing what he'd been tempted to do on the dance floor—not release her, as she'd demanded, but sling her over his shoulder and carry her somewhere private where he could ravage her sultry mouth and possess her seductive body with the thorough attention they deserved.

A flash of incendiary heat roared through Zahir's veins, tightening his body to instant, painful readiness. His hand clenched so hard on the tiny coffee cup, he feared he'd break the handle. With stiff fingers he released it and slid his hand from the table.

With one casual remark she'd accelerated his pulse from zero to the speed of sound in an instant. It was unprecedented. It was *dangerous.*

'Zahir?' Dark eyes searched his. This time the throb of electricity between them was more than sexual. It struck right at his core, as if she could do the impossible and delve into his psyche. 'Why did you watch me like that?'

She was persistent. And naïve, he realised with shock, if she really had to ask. If she had any sense, she'd leave such questions safely unspoken. Was she more naïve than he'd assumed? The notion disturbed him.

Or was this a double bluff from a woman who knew her sexual power and was trying to toy with him?

Resentment surfaced. He was no woman's pawn.

'I assumed you wouldn't want me approaching the table and discussing your business in front of everyone.'

He saw from her frown she wasn't satisfied with his answer.

'But you sat there for *ages*.'

Silently he held her gaze. He had no intention of pandering to her ego by explaining a response that shouldn't be: his instant, logic-destroying attraction to Hussein's chosen bride.

Damn it. Why couldn't Hussein have sent someone else—a whole team of someone elses—to bring his fiancée home?

His heart plunged. The answer was easy. Because Zahir was the one Hussein trusted above all.

Shame drenched him.

Abruptly he shoved his chair back across the gravel and shot to his feet.

'Did you want to see the grounds?'

'You don't need to stay. I'll meet you back at the hotel.' From the corner of his eye he saw her spring to her feet. Eager for more sightseeing? Or for another chance to escape his vigilance?

For the first time in years Zahir felt unsure. Usually instinct combined with thorough research gave him all the certainty he needed. With Soraya he'd skipped the research, believing this a quick, simple task. As for instinct… He firmed his lips against a bitter laugh. He no longer trusted his instincts where she was concerned.

'I have no other pressing business.' He slipped some cash under his cup and gestured for her to lead the way, ignoring the flash of dismay in her dark eyes. 'I'm curious to see what the place has to offer.' Especially if it meant getting to know the real Soraya Karim.

CHAPTER SIX

SORAYA told herself she was disappointed he didn't give her the choice to explore alone. Yet disappointment didn't explain the curling awareness in the pit of her stomach, nor the tingle of heat between her shoulder blades where his gaze rested as she led the way down the path beside the wide sweep of lawn.

They stopped at a model of a spiral blade for a flying machine, big enough for a person to stand beneath and turn the handle to make it rotate.

'It's more elegant than the modern design.' She tried hard to focus on the model rather than the man beside her. Her nostrils twitched appreciatively at the scent of his warm skin with a hint of desert spice. She'd carried that scent on her own skin after wearing his jacket. It disturbed her how much she relished it.

'Personally I don't care how it looks,' he drawled. 'So long as it keeps me in the air. I'd rather a modern chopper that works than one that looks elegant.'

Soraya huffed with amusement and looked up at the sail turning above her head. She didn't want to relax with Zahir, for there was an undercurrent between them that unsettled her. These tiny hints of dry humour appealed to her too much. It was far easier not to like him.

'That's my line. I'm supposed to be the one focused on functionality.'

She smiled as a big family group arrived with children eager to experiment, then she led the way downhill to where more models of inventions studded the wooded grounds.

'Because you're a scientist?'

'Engineer. I qualified before I left Bakhara.' She flashed a look over her shoulder but no hint of surprise marred those indecently attractive features.

Swiftly she looked away, stopping before a model of a paddle-wheel boat and pretending to survey it closely.

The other group caught up with them again and children of all ages swarmed over the model, while some tiny tots crouched by the stream, playing a complicated game with sticks and leaves.

'That explains why you asked for directions to a power plant.' Zahir's words drew her attention.

'Sorry?'

'The concierge showed me the places you were interested in seeing.'

'Oh.' She'd forgotten to ask how he'd found her. Zahir must have searched for hours, yet instead of being angry he'd shown only curiosity. Every time she thought she had him pegged, he surprised her again.

'I visited a chateau instead. Far more *opulent* and appealing than a utilitarian power station.'

His chuckle surprised her, sneaking across her skin like a caress. A traitorous part of her enjoyed sharing a joke with him, wanted to see him smile at her.

Abruptly she turned and moved away down the path. She couldn't remember ever being so responsive to a man.

Or was it simply that she'd never spent time alone with such an attractive man? Had lack of exposure made her susceptible? She'd had no trouble keeping her head around her colleagues. But from the moment her gaze had locked with Zahir's she'd felt a zap of high-voltage connection. She couldn't shake it and that made her nervous.

'Somehow I suspect that's not why you changed your mind about visiting it.'

'It's not a state-of-the-art facility so I didn't bother.' Especially as nuclear power wasn't her field.

Not that she'd *have* a field once she became wife to the Emir.

'Is what you were doing in Paris? Engineering?'

'Yes. I was lucky enough to land work as assistant in a research project. Mainly I was just calculating data.'

'You must be good to be taken on.'

His simple statement warmed her. In the Women's University in Bakhara there'd been few interested in engineering. Most people viewed her choice as a misguided attempt to prove herself in a male domain. Or proof that she was unfeminine. Many in Bakhara clung to tradition.

'My professor recommended me. She thought even if I was in Paris for the cultural experience it would be a crime not to take advantage of the opportunity.'

'She was right. Opportunities are there to be grabbed. Did you enjoy the work?'

'Loved it! The team was excellent and I learned so much. I—' She looked down at her hands, clenched too tight before her.

'You…?'

She shook her head. What was the point of saying she'd planned to take part in the project's next phase—that the team leader had asked her to take on more responsibility? That she'd begun to see a future for herself that had nothing to do with a royal marriage and everything to do with her own interests and professional skills?

Ruthlessly she cut off the regrets that churned under the surface. No point going there.

'Look at this.' She quickened her pace to circle a large wooden shell. 'An early model for a war tank. Who'd have thought it?'

Zahir watched her duck her head and step up into the structure. A flash of shapely legs drew his eye but he managed not to stare. Her dress was light and summery rather than revealing, but the way she filled it in all the right places would be pure distraction to any red-blooded man.

Soraya was a captivating mix. She made a show of keeping him at arm's length but regularly forgot and relaxed into unguarded moments. She was intelligent and sexy, a woman he enjoyed crossing swords with.

Until he remembered pleasure was an emotion he shouldn't feel around Hussein's fiancée.

Yet that didn't prevent him wondering what she'd been going to say. She didn't hide her emotions as well as she imagined and he had no doubt she'd changed the subject rather than pursue a line of thought that bothered her. Something about the team she worked with in Paris.

'Your friends at the club the other night—are they engineers too?'

'Sorry?' She looked up, her eyes wide as if surprised at the change of subject.

'The guy you danced with. Does he work on the same project?'

Was it imagination or did her lips tighten?

'No. They're from the university but not in my field.'

Zahir waited for her to elaborate but she said nothing.

'So you don't have a passion for engineering in common?'

'Who? Me and Raoul? Hardly.' She stepped down, pretending not to notice the arm he extended to steady her.

'What do you have in common? You seemed *very* close.'

Her head jerked up and her eyes clashed with his. Sparks of sensation flared and burst across his skin like a brush fire igniting from a summer-lightning strike. It disturbed him that he'd never known such a reaction to a woman. Even in the throes of first and only love, it had taken more than a look to set his blood simmering.

'That's none of your business.' Soraya's breathing shallowed. Zahir became tantalisingly aware of her breasts' jagged rise and fall as she struggled to remain calm.

'It is, when I'm taking you home to marry Hussein.' He let

the words crash out, harsh and honest, as if saying them would break the strange spell she wove around him.

Something had to.

Her eyes rounded and her mouth formed an 'O' of shock. Finally she found her voice.

'Is that what you were doing all that time? Spying on me?' Her voice rose in outrage.

Zahir said nothing. He'd had no plan that night other than to track her down and tell her about Hussein's request that she return. It had been the shock of seeing her. The shock of recognition that had rooted him to the spot. As if he *knew* her, not as the subject of his next mission, but as someone intrinsically important to *himself.*

For once he hadn't known how to proceed. Not when his overwhelming impulse had been to ignore his mission and stake a personal claim on her.

Guilt pooled in his belly. No wonder he'd made a hash of everything that night.

'I don't spy,' Zahir said at last. 'But I won't shy from telling Hussein anything I feel he should know.'

'Like the fact that I had the temerity to *dance* with a man in a public place?' She shook her head. 'What century did you crawl out of, Zahir?'

'If it was only dances, I'm sure Hussein won't be concerned.' He paused, telling himself his urgent need to know was pure altruism. A favour to a friend. 'Is that all there was, Soraya?'

Colour seeped across her cheekbones and her eyes snapped a warning. 'My personal life is just that. Personal. If the Emir has questions, he can ask me himself.'

Her chin jutted belligerently as she faced him toe-to-toe. He applauded her backbone. Few men in Bakhara or elsewhere would have stood up to him this way.

'What about your friend's invitation when you got home?' The words slipped out before he could reconsider. 'She asked you to join her and her lover in bed. Does your bridegroom have a right to know if you make a habit of sharing so *intimately* with your flatmate?'

Her head jerked back, her cheeks leaching of colour as she goggled up at him.

He opened his mouth to speak again—to say what, he didn't know—when her laughter erupted. It had a ragged, raw quality that spoke of disbelief, amusement and something else that made him wish he'd kept his mouth shut.

'You heard that?' She shook her head, wiping her eyes. 'Then it's a shame you didn't hear Lisle mention her twin sister was visiting and they were in her room having a catch-up since her boyfriend had left.' Her hand dropped and her eyes sizzled defiantly.

'Don't presume to judge me by the standards of others. Or are they your standards, Zahir?' She raised a hand when he'd have spoken. 'No, don't tell me. Contrary to your lurid imaginings, I didn't lead a life of debauchery in Paris, nor did I develop a taste for threesomes.'

It was the truth. He read it in every outraged bone in her stiffly held body. In the shock shadowing her eyes and the distaste twisting her full lips.

More than that, he felt it deep within, a truth he'd deliberately ignored.

Why? Why draw conclusions on such flimsy evidence when he'd spent a lifetime learning balanced judgement?

Because he'd needed a reason not to like her.

Because from the instant he'd clapped eyes on her he'd felt an attraction so strong he'd sought any excuse to pretend it didn't exist. It had rocked his world, as if the earth's tectonic plates had shifted beneath his feet.

Because distrusting her gave him a reason not to acknowledge that inexplicable attraction. He'd hidden behind it rather than face the truth.

'Do you always leap to conclusions about people?'

'No.' He shook his head. 'Never.'

'Just with me?' Her sceptical look froze as she read his face.

'Yes.' Shame burned him. Soraya was right. He'd taken one look at her and his judgement, his brain, had shut down. 'I'm sorry, Soraya.' He held her gaze, restraining himself against the impulse to step forward and comfort her. As if she'd welcome his touch! 'That was crass of me, as well as wrong. I apologise unreservedly. The accusation was unworthy of you.'

'So now you pretend to know me? That's rich.'

'I don't know you. That's why I'm here now, because I want to understand you.'

'To spy for the Emir.'

'No!' What a mess he'd made of this. No one would ever believe him the same man who brokered multinational deals on a regular basis.

'Then why?' The anger had gone from her eyes, replaced by a searching curiosity as strong as his own.

Zahir drew in a fortifying breath. He owed her the truth, no matter how vulnerable it made him.

'For myself. Because I need to.'

Her eyes widened and his heart crashed faster as he read comprehension in her eyes. Soraya stared so hard she didn't even seem to notice the straggling group of families pass by—adults, a couple of teenagers and younger children.

'No,' she said at last. 'I don't want you here.'

'Soraya, I'm truly sorry. I—'

'It's not because of what you…assumed about me. I'd just rather be alone.' Zahir's stomach knotted as he read awareness in her dark gaze and a flicker of fear.

He should be relieved one of them was behaving wisely.

She turned away. 'I'll see you back at the hotel.'

Zahir knew it was the right thing to do. Some things were better hidden and never acknowledged. Yet not following her took far more will-power than it should.

He stood, watching her go, until a curve in the path brought the family group back in view. He saw two empty prams and one of the toddlers holding the hand of an older child.

Frowning, he surveyed the group, checking his recollection from when their paths had crossed before.

His heart kicked up a pace as adrenalin surged. He wasn't mistaken: the group wasn't complete. It was the sort of detail he'd been trained to notice. He breathed deep, double-checking.

The toddler in the yellow T-shirt was missing.

Even as the thought formed in his head, Zahir loped onto the track, cutting across Soraya's path.

'Zahir, I'd really rather—'

He quickened his pace, away from the families and back in the direction they'd come. The area was lightly forested and open enough to see for some way. Unless the child was down near the tempting little rivulets that meandered through the grounds.

Zahir's neck prickled as he jogged forward.

'Zahir?' She must have followed him.

Then he saw it: a flare of sunshine-yellow in the shadows. *In the glinting water.* His heart seemed to judder to a stop mid-beat even as he broke into a run.

'Here,' he called over his shoulder. 'Ambulance!' He didn't pause to see if she caught the phone he tossed.

'Soraya? Are you okay?'

She looked up, tugged from her thoughts by Zahir's rich baritone. Around them the discreet chatter of the hotel restaurant resurfaced, the sense of being with others, even if in a secluded corner of the great gilded dining salon. The sky glowed with the sun's last syrupy, pink light as indigo darkness closed in from the forest, cutting off the chateau from the outside world.

It was peaceful and pleasant. So different from the scene branded on her brain. The toddler's face, that awful waxen colour. The screams of his mother. The dreadful, wrenching terror that had reduced everything to slow motion.

Even now the remembered scent of fear clogged her nostrils, vying with the rich scents of their superb meal.

'I'm fine. Thank you.' She cast Zahir a perfunctory smile and lifted a morsel of fish to her mouth. Yet her limbs still felt ridiculously shaky. As if she'd run for her life that day, not simply called the medics and corralled the toddler's family while Zahir had saved his life.

She hadn't even realised there *was* an emergency. She'd been so absorbed, thinking about Zahir, how he'd insulted her then apologised so gravely she'd had no choice but to believe he regretted it. Especially when his eyes mirrored her own deep confusion. She'd struggled to grasp what had happened even as Zahir hauled the boy from the creek and puffed air into his little lungs.

Her knife and fork clattered onto her plate.

'Thank heaven you were there today. If you hadn't been, if you hadn't noticed he was missing—'

'There's no point dwelling on "what ifs". The child is safe.' Zahir reached across the table as if to take her hand where it clenched in a tense fist on the linen cloth. At the last moment he reached instead for his water.

Soraya knew she should be glad he didn't invade her personal space. Yet that didn't douse her longing for the comfort of his touch. Despite the long soak in her suite's oversized bath, she still felt chilled by the afternoon's events. Zahir's hand would be warm, solid and real.

'I know,' she murmured. 'I can't help it. I keep going over it again and again in my head.' She drew a shuddery breath and reached for her glass.

'It was a shock. That's a natural reaction.' There was understanding in his voice.

'*You* weren't shocked.' She bit her lip. 'I'm sorry. I didn't mean for that to sound like an accusation.'

'I understand.' The ghost of a smile softened his mouth and that invisible thread of connection between them twanged tighter, dragging at her internal muscles. 'Don't worry, I was running on adrenalin too. It's just that I've been in emergency situations before. Too often.'

That glimmer of a smile died, obliterated by a sudden harshness that transformed his features. It reminded her that she knew next to nothing about this man with whom she would spend the next few weeks—more, since he was the Emir's right-hand man. In Bakhara their paths would cross regularly.

'Tell me. Please.' Her words escaped without conscious thought and she met his surprised gaze. 'It's none of my business I know. I just…' Soraya bit her lip, not understanding her compulsion to know him. It had nothing to do with prurient curiosity and everything to do with the awareness that had shimmered so strongly between them this afternoon. From the first it had been there. He'd all but acknowledged it himself today.

She needed to know what it was.

'I don't *understand* you.' The words tumbled from her lips. 'And this afternoon…'

How did she explain something fundamental had shifted today when they'd shared laughter and she'd glimpsed a man who appealed far too much, when he'd apologised so sincerely she'd felt his shame and then when he'd saved that child? He wasn't the cold, arrogant man she'd tried to cast him. He was so much more.

She sensed it was dangerous to like Zahir too much. She'd felt safe in her indignation. Yet she couldn't keep pretending he was her unfeeling enemy. It just didn't ring true.

'If it had been left to his family he'd have drowned. They wouldn't have realised till too late.' The words burst out. 'If I'd been there without you, as I said I wanted, I wouldn't have been able to save him either. Only *you*—'

'Don't beat yourself up, Soraya.' His voice was calm, mellow and reassuring. 'You did wonderfully, keeping everyone in order till the medics came.'

Strong fingers covered hers and instantly heat seeped back along her veins.

She'd been right. There was magic in Zahir's touch. This time she wasn't going to question it or pull away.

A sense of wellbeing grew, a glow that wasn't simply the

physical warmth of flesh touching flesh. She looked from their joined hands then up into eyes that had darkened to the colour of the encircling forest.

'I want to understand.' Though she wasn't sure what exactly she needed to know. It was all tangled together—today's events and the enigma of Zahir's true personality. This…*something* between them. The unsettling realisation she didn't understand herself as well as she'd thought.

Absently he rubbed his thumb over her hand and some of the tightness in her belly unravelled. Her rigid shoulders dropped a fraction.

'There's not much to understand. I've seen violence in my life, too often. I learned to react quickly. Even as a child.'

'So young?' At her query his mouth twisted and he looked down at their joined hands.

'One of my first memories is of blood pooling across a stone floor and wondering why the man with the funny stare didn't move before the red stained his clothes.'

'Oh, Zahir.' Her free hand closed over his as he held her. 'I'm so sorry.'

He shrugged. 'It was no one I knew. Just one of my father's cronies.' He spoke with such matter-of-fact coolness it sent a tiny quiver through her. 'He'd had too much to drink and was unsteady on his feet. When he fell, he cracked his skull.'

'How old were you?'

'Three, perhaps. Maybe four.'

'That's dreadful.' Something deep inside twisted. He'd been so young. So vulnerable. What had his life been like that he'd come across such a scene?

'I remember my father stumbling across the room, cursing about the mess. And making myself scarce. I was good at that.' His mouth was a flat line, no trace of insouciance now.

Soraya felt him stiffen under her touch and wondered what he was remembering. The look on his face as much as his words told her it hadn't been pleasant. What had his mother been doing while her son had watched that horrible scene?

'There were other…incidents too. Enough to learn how swift and unpredictable violence can be.' His gaze fixed on a point beyond her but she wondered if what he saw was far beyond the walls of the hotel. 'It was useful training, in a way. It meant I was always half-prepared.'

Soraya blinked and stared. Zahir painted a picture that, despite the lack of detail, horrified her. A childhood where the most valuable lesson learned was a readiness to confront violence.

'It sounds like your childhood was eventful.'

Swiftly he turned his gaze on her and she caught a flicker of amusement in his eyes. 'Obviously Hussein knows what he's doing, choosing you as his wife. That's a diplomatic response if ever I heard one.'

He looked down and frowned as if registering for the first time their linked hands. Abruptly he drew his away, leaving her oddly bereft.

She laced her fingers together and slipped her hands into her lap. They still held the imprint of his, hard and comforting against hers.

'My early childhood was a disaster, but I survived. Then I joined the royal household. I was safe, well-fed, educated, comfortable. But I trained with the warriors. I saw my share of accidents and wounds. I could diagnose a dislocation, a broken bone or sprain by the age of twelve.'

'That must have been tough.'

'I loved it.' Zahir's sudden grin took her by surprise and she sat back, her pulse thudding an uneven response to the sheer glory of it.

Oh my. Oh. My!

It was the second time she'd glimpsed the man behind the wall of steel. The first, when he'd threatened her with such fervour if she ever injured the Emir. And now a look of such unadulterated joy it was like swallowing sunshine, just seeing it. It took Soraya a moment to find her voice.

'Why did you love it?'

He picked up his cutlery but didn't move to eat. 'I belonged,' he said at last. 'That became my world.'

Soraya frowned, more curious than ever for details. But she had no right to push for what was clearly private and difficult territory. As it was, she sensed Zahir had revealed more than he usually deigned to share.

'Eventually I joined the Emir's bodyguard, even led it. So you see I've had lots of opportunities to deal with crises.' His smile now was more restrained, a polite curve of the lips only, not that blinding flash of pleasure that had thwacked her senses into overdrive.

'But no one would want to harm the Emir.' She, more than most of his subjects, had cause to know what a generous and honourable man he was.

Zahir shook his head. 'There is always the possibility—from someone who seeks fame through a violent act, to someone disturbed or ruthless. There have been times when noticing a small detail, or sensing something amiss, made all the difference.'

Soraya slid her hands up to rub her arms. 'Like noticing that boy wasn't with his family.'

Zahir nodded. 'I was trained to register the smallest details. To take note and act quickly when necessary.'

'No one asked you to monitor them.'

His straight shoulders lifted. 'You don't entirely switch off even when you're no longer on close personal protection duty. I haven't done that for years but the skills stay with you.'

'Just as well.'

He shot her a quick glance but she felt its intensity to the tips of her toes.

'Eat, Soraya. It's over. The child is safe and the family reunited. There's nothing to worry about.'

She picked up her cutlery and made a show of eating her meal, as he did. But her niggle of anxiety grew rather than faded with the knowledge she'd gained.

It had all been easier when she could write Zahir off as bossy, arrogant and interfering. Before he'd revealed a humanity and tenderness that made a mockery of her easy assumptions. He'd thought badly of her, but his apology had been genuine and his contrition real. She'd seen the shame and regret in his eyes. And at least he'd been up-front with her.

She recalled him, his clothes plastered to his tall body, cradling the toddler and crooning to him once he had begun to breathe again. He hadn't turned a hair when the child vomited comprehensively and begun to cry. He'd been patience itself with both the boy and his distraught mother, managing to calm them both and monitoring them till professional help had arrived.

The sight of the small child held so easily and safely against Zahir's powerful frame ignited a blast of emotions Soraya couldn't label, but felt to her core.

Nor had he been eager for acknowledgement. As soon as the child was with medical staff he'd taken Soraya's trembling hand, offered his best wishes to the group and led her away for a restorative coffee. He hadn't turned a hair at the stares he'd received with his muddied trousers and his wet shirt clinging to his powerful torso. He'd been solicitous of *her*, as if she'd been the one injured.

Zahir was quietly competent, caring, strong when she was weak.

And he…appealed to her.

He appealed too much for a woman who wasn't interested in men. Who'd seen the pitfalls of romance and decided early not to go there. That had been one of the reasons she'd agreed to her royal betrothal—the belief that an arranged marriage to an honourable man was safer than a so-called love match.

She'd never been romantically interested in any man. Given her background, maybe she'd even worked a little too hard to avoid such temptation.

Why then did Zahir fascinate her so? Why did she need to understand him?

Because she wasn't as self-sufficient as she'd thought?

Because, perhaps, she was susceptible to the charm of a strong, handsome man? A man who hid surprising gentleness and a mile-wide streak of heroism behind a cool façade?

CHAPTER SEVEN

TWO DAYS later Soraya and Zahir returned to the hotel to find a familiar family group in the car park.

'Mademoiselle Karim!' a teenage girl called out. Soraya remembered her; she'd been pale and distraught, blaming herself for her little brother's accident.

'Lucie, how are you? How is your brother?' Soraya smiled as she neared the group, pleasure filling her as she saw the little boy safe in his mother's arms.

'Recovered fully, as you see.' The older woman smiled tentatively before glancing at her husband, clearly uncomfortable beside her. 'We came to thank you both.' Her gaze rested on Zahir. 'Without you…'

'Without them he would have died,' her husband said, his voice harsh. 'Because you couldn't watch him.'

Soraya stiffened, stunned at the venom in his tone.

'In my experience,' said a firm baritone beside her, 'a man casts blame when he holds himself responsible but hasn't the guts to acknowledge it.' Zahir stood so close she felt the fury emanating from him. 'It's a father's duty to protect his family.'

The bristling man before them seemed to deflate. Enough to reveal the hollowed eyes and pallor of a man still working through shock.

'It's very hot out here,' Soraya said quickly. 'Why don't we go inside for a cool drink?' She smiled at the children. 'Or ice-cream? They have terrific ice-cream here.'

* * *

It was a relief to escape outside again with the children. Despite Soraya's calming presence and his own tight control, Zahir could barely stomach being with a man who refused to accept responsibility for his son's safety and blamed his womenfolk for his shortcomings.

'Well done!' Zahir congratulated one of the girls on her archery skills. 'You hit the target this time. Now, try it again, but don't forget to hold the bow this way.' He leaned in to demonstrate.

He glanced at the window where Soraya sat with their older guests, her smile warm. The mother had relaxed enough to relinquish the toddler into Soraya's arms and she bounced him on her knees. Even the woman's husband had unwound enough to nod at something she said.

Zahir's dislike for the man would have stifled the atmosphere. The child's father had struck his personal sore spot: neglectful fathers topped his list of dislikes.

He shook his head as he helped one of the children aim her bow.

Soraya had marshalled the group before he'd even got a grip on his anger. She'd charmed them all, reassured them and acted as hostess as if born to it. He remembered how she'd organised the crowd at the accident. Without her it would have been mayhem.

Her skills would make her perfect in the role of Hussein's queen. She was gracious, charming and able to put people at ease in difficult circumstances.

Hussein had chosen his bride well. Socially accomplished, quick thinking and feisty enough to hint at a passionate nature. She would make a fine wife: an asset in public and the sort of spouse a man rejoiced to come home to at the end of a long day.

The realisation should have reassured him that his mission to return her to Bakhara was important. But it brought no pleasure.

Just a twist in his gut that felt horribly like envy.

* * *

'You've got an ice-cream addiction, Soraya.'

'*I* have?' She looked at the remains of the double-scoop pistachio-and-coffee ice-cream he held and shook her head. 'I don't hear you complaining.'

Zahir shrugged and she averted her eyes lest they cling too long to the movement of his broad shoulders. She'd discovered a weakness for Zahir's wide, straight shoulders and rare, spectacular smile.

She looked instead around the stone-built town. Its square was hung with flags for Bastille Day and lights in the plane trees had just been turned on. In the background a small but enthusiastic band entertained onlookers.

'I'm just keeping you company.' Zahir's deep voice tickled her senses. 'Being a good companion.'

As he had been ever since Amboise. It was as if his accusation and apology, not to mention the crisis there, had cleared the air between them. No word of reproach or disapproval passed his lips. Nor—and she told herself she was relieved by it—did he refer to the shimmering attraction between them.

She'd begun to wonder if, after all, it was one-sided. Who wouldn't be star-struck by a man like Zahir? Even if his attention was for her as bride to his mentor.

'Watch out!' She saw the football before Zahir yet he managed to whip around and stop its wayward trajectory. He kicked it up, bouncing it easily off his knees and feet as he scanned the playing field beside the river.

A grinning boy waved and Zahir kicked the ball straight to him.

'You play football?'

'I used to. When I was young.'

'Me too.'

'Why aren't I surprised?' A slow grin spread across his face and Soraya wondered if she'd ever be able to see it without her pulse stuttering out of control.

'What else did you do when you were young?' They'd been

careful to avoid personal topics. They discussed France and the places they saw, or politics and books.

The one subject they never touched on was Bakhara.

'I rode. I discovered chess. I learned to fight.'

Soraya laughed. 'Of course. You sound like a traditional Bakhari male.'

'I *am* a traditional Bakhari male.'

She shook her head. A traditionalist wouldn't have let her drive his precious car, or listen attentively to a woman explaining the principles of geothermal power.

'What did you do when you were young?'

'Learn to cook, keep house and embroider.' She sighed, remembering hours of dutiful boredom. 'And sneaked out to play football.'

'And dreamed of marrying a handsome prince?'

'No!' The word shot out sharply. 'Never that.'

Zahir watched her intently. 'Marrying Hussein isn't the fulfilment of a lifelong ambition? I thought little girls fixated on a glamorous marriage.'

Soraya lifted her ice-cream, hoping the cherry flavour would counteract the sour tang on her tongue. 'Other little girls maybe. Marriage was never my dream.'

'But things are different now.'

'Oh yes, they're different now.' Bitterness welled, and with it anger at the limitations placed on her life by her engagement. 'Can we not talk about it now? I'd rather concentrate on this.' She waved a hand to encompass the crowd and the holiday atmosphere.

'Besides—' she nodded in the direction of the playing field '—I think you're wanted.'

The football sailed through the air to land near Zahir. The same grinning teenager waved for him to join the impromptu game.

Zahir shook his head. 'I can't leave you.'

'Of course you can. I'm perfectly fine.' She reached to pull his jacket off one shoulder then stopped as a sizzle of fire shot through her fingertips. Beneath her touch his muscles stiffened. His eyes darkened and her breath snagged as heat pulsed between them.

Just one touch did that.

'Go,' she said hoarsely, her hand dropping. 'Please.' She needed time alone to regroup. So much for her innocent belief that things were easier between them. On the surface their relationship was pleasant, friendly, even. But beneath the surface lurked emotions she didn't want to stir.

'If you wish.' He stripped his jacket off and handed it to her. 'Unless you'd prefer to play?'

That made her smile. 'It's you they want. Go.' Studiously she ignored the warmth of his jacket over her arm. She made a production of waving him off then leaned against a tree, watching him lope down to the field.

It didn't surprise her that he sided with the younger players who seemed outclassed by their more experienced rivals. Soraya had seen him with children before. He was a natural, treating them as equals, yet with a patience that made him a good teacher and role model.

She watched him sprint across the field, take the ball almost to the goal and deftly avoid several tackles till a boy of thirteen or so had time to join him. Zahir passed him the ball, then applauded as the boy's shot at goal missed by a whisker.

Pride surfaced. She *liked* Zahir, admired him. She wondered what he'd be like with his own children. She guessed he'd be fiercely loyal and supportive, a true friend. He'd be the same with the woman he loved.

Soraya caught the direction of her thoughts and slammed them shut with a gasp of horror.

Fixing her gaze on the river glinting beyond the playing field, she focused on the last few licks of her ice-cream and the sound of music filling the dusk.

A tentative voice intruded. 'Would you care to dance?' The man's smile was open and the hand he extended marked by hard work. She guessed he was a farmer with his craggy, sun-bronzed face. The music beckoned.

Why not? She'd promised herself she'd make the most of these last precious days of freedom. Placing Zahir's jacket and her bag of purchases on a nearby seat, Soraya took the stranger's hand.

Zahir felt like a kid again, light-hearted and spontaneous. He was even showing off for the girl in the floaty, floral dress standing in the shade at the edge of the square, as if he had nothing more on his mind than making the most of the day.

He couldn't remember the last time he'd felt this way. As if life was simple and full of pleasure, rather than a complicated series of manoeuvres to be plotted carefully, a contest to be won. More and more he felt it, the infectious joy of being with Soraya. As if weighty matters of state weren't the be-all and end-all of his existence. As if, imperceptibly, his priorities had changed.

The sensation was alluring. Like Soraya.

He glanced up, expecting to see her there, watching, but she'd gone. She was fine, he told himself. She'd be in the square, tasting local delicacies or chatting with someone. But a few minutes later he excused himself and jogged over to where he'd left her.

His jacket lay folded on a chair beside her cloth bag that was filled to the brim with her haul of goodies from the market stalls. He turned and surveyed the crowd. Sure enough, there she was, smiling as she danced with a husky young man. Her joy was infectious, even from this distance, and he wished it was him holding her as they danced over the cobblestones.

But discretion was the better part of valour. Holding Soraya would be inviting trouble. Instead he folded his arms and watched as the sky darkened and the woman who filled his thoughts moved from partner to partner.

* * *

'Time to stop?' Zahir's words interrupted her partner's thanks as the music ended. Soraya swung round, breathing heavily after that last mad polka. In the dim light Zahir loomed. Was that disapproval in his voice? His face was set in harsh lines she hadn't seen in days.

Instantly resentment stirred. And disappointment. She'd thought they were past the disapproval.

'Why?' She tucked a strand of hair behind her ear then crossed her arms defensively. 'Because I'm too boisterous? Because it's not the behaviour of a soon-to-be-queen?' His gaze bored into hers and, despite her annoyance, secret heat flared. The heat a woman felt for a man. 'Surely you don't think I'm flirting?'

'Nothing like that. You've been dancing nonstop and I thought you needed a rest.' His eyes skimmed the rapid rise of her breasts before he looked away.

'Sorry.' She ducked her head. 'I thought you were taking me to task.'

'Not surprising, given the way I jumped down your throat initially.'

Surprised, Soraya looked up. One thing about Zahir, he didn't hide from the facts. Even reminders of his mistakes. He wasn't like anyone else she knew. Or maybe it was her feelings for him that were unique.

'Dance with me?' The moment she said it she realised how much she wanted to.

'Surely you've had enough. Let me buy you a cold drink while we wait for the fireworks.'

Soraya shook her head. She wanted Zahir to hold her. She'd spent a lifetime doing the right thing, was facing a future of duty, and for this day wanted something for herself.

'Please, Zahir? Just one dance? It's Bastille Day, after all.' She held out her arms and after a long moment he took her in his arms, holding her gently and not too close. Even so her senses clamoured in delight as the music struck up and they moved together.

'You're not French. Bastille Day means nothing to you.'

'You're wrong.' She fought to keep her voice even when her bloodstream bubbled with pleasure. 'It's about liberty. There's nothing more important than freedom.'

Zahir heard the edge in her voice and tried to read her face in the darkness. She was like fluid quicksilver in his arms. He had to make an effort not to drag her close. Instead he focused on her words.

'Liberty? You speak as if it's threatened.'

She didn't answer for a moment. 'This is *my* time,' she said eventually. 'When I reach Bakhara I won't be able to do as I want or make my own choices. I'll be constrained.'

Because she'd be Hussein's bride.

'You don't sound enthusiastic.'

This time her silence was even longer. 'It's a great honour to be chosen as the Emir's bride.'

Yet he heard no pleasure in her voice. Or was it that he didn't want to hear it? Damn him for his jealousy.

'You're right,' he said at last. 'Your life will be restricted.' Hadn't his own become tightly constrained by duty, loyalty and the demands placed on it? Maybe that explained his dizzying sense of freedom with Soraya. This was a vacation from a life of responsibilities. Yet he couldn't help suspecting the wonder of it would continue if he had Soraya by his side, always. 'But there will be benefits. Hussein is a good man. He'll look after you.'

Though he shied from the thought of them together.

The music ended and they stopped moving in the shadows at the edge of the square. He told himself to let her go but didn't move. Nor did she.

'I know he is,' she said quietly. 'But it's an enormous step, giving up the life I know.'

Zahir breathed deep, dizzy with her sweet, fresh scent, revelling in the feel of her in his arms.

'Would you ever consider not going through with it?'

His hoarse words seemed over-loud in the charged silence.

Appalled, he wished he could retract them. What sort of mad, wishful thinking was that?

'Why would I do that?'

He told himself this was just a hypothetical discussion. 'If you fell for someone else.' Yet he held his breath as he waited for her answer, his pulse drumming in his ears.

'Imagine the fallout.' Her head drooped towards his chest so that he looked down on her vulnerable nape. He gathered her in to him. Just to comfort her, he assured himself. Yet his arms moulded to her as if they belonged.

She sighed. 'The scandal would be enormous, especially after my mother.'

'Your mother?'

'She disgraced herself and the family and my dad bore the brunt of disapproval for not vilifying her. Poor Dad, I couldn't do that to him. His business would be ruined and he'd be an outcast.'

And so would she, Zahir reminded himself. A man who truly cared for her wouldn't do that to her.

'Anyway, I'm pretty sure it's against the law to break a contract with the nation's ruler.' Her laugh was hollow. 'Besides.' She lifted her head and looked him straight in the eye. 'What man would dare steal the Emir's bride? He'd be punished, surely?'

Soraya's upturned face was beautiful, her eyes almost beseeching, and Zahir knew a crazy urge to kiss her till the world faded and all that was left was them.

'He'd lose all claim to honour or loyalty to the crown,' Zahir said slowly, feeling the full weight of such a prospect. He'd made honour and loyalty his life. 'He'd never be able to hold his head up again. He'd be stripped of official titles and positions and the council of elders would banish him from Bakhara.' He drew a deep breath. 'Hussein could never call him friend again.'

'As I thought.' Her hands dropped and she stepped abruptly out of his hold. 'No man would even consider it.'

CHAPTER EIGHT

It wasn't working.

Zahir hefted in a determined breath and thrust off from the end of the pool, forcing his burning lungs and overworked body into another lap.

No matter how hard he pushed himself, he couldn't strip her from his mind. Soraya was there constantly.

He was at the end of his tether. Sleep grew elusive. His attempts to focus on the future and the governorship which would be his greatest challenge to date faded into the background. Soraya took centre stage.

He'd thought to change her mind about taking a slow route back to Bakhara since their time together was fraught with perilous undercurrents.

She'd said she wanted to see the countryside and he'd given it to her. They stayed in a friend's manor house in the Perigord, surrounded by walnut groves, tiny villages and winding narrow roads. No boutiques. No nightclubs.

Soraya loved it.

So much for his plans to convince her to cut short their stay and head for the bright lights! She found everything fascinating; from the stone-building styles to the local accent and the people they met. Even the limestone caves with their prehistoric paintings captured her interest.

Her delight in it all, her vivid joy in each moment, made

every experience fresh and new to him too. He was rediscovering simple pleasures.

Yet there was nothing simple or innocent about his feelings for her.

Zahir hauled himself from the water. It was still early and he was taking the chopper to Paris. Ostensibly it was a meeting that called him. In reality, it was as an excuse to absent himself from Soraya.

He enjoyed being with her too much. He found himself opening up to her. He'd even told her about his childhood, something he never shared. More than that, he felt emotions stirring that he had no business feeling. For years he'd locked emotions behind a wall of steel. Now it seemed there were fissures in the barricade he'd built around himself. He was a different man from the one who'd met her in Paris. He *felt* more, experienced more, cared more.

Zahir was halfway to the house when he saw the garage door open. He frowned. The old estate manager wouldn't be up at dawn working, but with the owners in Paris, who else could it be?

One step into the building and he knew.

The breath sucked from his lungs as he saw her on her back beneath an old four-wheel drive; neat sneakers, white socks and the most mouth-watering legs he'd ever seen.

With those light summer dresses she wore he'd had ample opportunity to recognise Soraya had world-class legs. But her clothes were always modest. Now for the first time his gaze trawled up past her knees to smooth, slim thighs that made him think of cool sheets and a hot woman, of passion and endless hours of erotic pleasure.

Humming off-key, Soraya wasn't sure at first, but she thought she heard swearing, low-voiced and urgent. She paused and wiped her brow with a grimy hand.

A stream of whispered words vied with the early-morning birdsong.

Her skin prickled as she realised she wasn't alone. An instant later she scooted out from beneath the vehicle.

Long legs were braced wide before her. Bare, sinewy feet. Powerfully muscled thighs in sodden board shorts. A towel clutched in one large, white-knuckled hand.

Soraya's throat dried as she yanked her gaze higher, skimming over a washboard abdomen, wide pectoral muscles and straight shoulders. Higher, till she got lost in green eyes turned dark and smoky in the early-morning light.

Her heart jumped and she sat up quickly.

'Zahir.' Her voice was breathless and high. She swallowed and tried again, ignoring the feverish pleasure that surged at the sound of his name on her lips. Ever since the Bastille Day celebrations she'd been ultra-aware of him.

Who was she kidding? She'd been aware of him from the start, only in the beginning she'd been able to hide behind dislike.

'You surprised me.' Great. Now her conversation had dried up with her brain.

Despite the affinity she felt for Zahir and her pleasure in his company, she grew more on edge daily.

It was as if another woman inhabited her body. A woman with desires and needs utterly foreign to her. A woman whose eyes followed this man's every move. Whose breasts were swollen and tender with longing for his touch. Who felt hunger curl hard in her belly just at the sound of his deep voice.

Maybe the critics of her childhood were right. Maybe after all she was doomed to follow in her mother's footsteps—unable to resist the lure of a handsome man. Perhaps her father's protectiveness had been well-founded, and her own innate caution, her wariness of intimacy, had been more valid than she'd realised.

At twenty-four she'd begun to think herself completely immune to the male sex, for none had ever stirred her blood.

Now she knew better.

Whatever it was she felt for Zahir, it wasn't immunity. It was wild and strong, exciting and frightening. Worse, it wasn't just because of his looks. She enjoyed his dry humour, his intelligence, the fact that he was a decent man who took his responsibilities seriously. He was marvellous with kids and patient with a woman spooked by her looming future.

'What are you wearing?' His voice was husky.

She glanced down, then hurriedly folded her legs close, wrapping her arms around them.

'I didn't have any shorts so I cut off some jeans. It's too hot for them here.'

She'd made a mess of the job. Sewing had never been her forte, to the dismay of her female relatives who'd spent so many hours trying to interest her in embroidery and a dozen other housewifely skills. She couldn't even hack the legs off her old jeans in a straight line!

Zahir's dark eyebrows crunched together. 'That doesn't explain why you're down in the dirt.'

Ridiculously his words reminded her of the scolds she'd received from aunts about unladylike behaviour. For a moment the old guilt rose: about the fact she was her mother's daughter. That she was impulsive and strong-willed. That she didn't fit the mould.

Soraya lifted her chin. 'I'm tinkering with the car. Hortense had trouble with it and I thought I'd take a look.'

'Hortense?' Zahir rubbed his chin ruminatively and Soraya almost thought she heard the whisper of early-morning bristles against his hand. His chin was shadowed, accentuating the proud angle of his jaw.

'The housekeeper,' Soraya explained. 'She can take another vehicle.' She waved towards the new models filling the rest of the garage. 'But she's used to this one.'

'You don't have to do that. You're a guest.'

'But I *enjoy* it.' Soraya braced herself for a look of dismay or disapproval.

Instead she was rewarded with a grin that kicked her pulse to top speed.

'Better you than me, Soraya. Horses, people or computers I'll willingly spend hours with. But the underside of a chassis? You can have it and welcome.'

Warmth curled round Soraya's heart and squeezed hard. Zahir's eyes danced and she felt her mouth tilt in an answering smile.

'Yet you drive like a professional.' She loved sitting beside Zahir as he drove them through the countryside. He was competent; not afraid of speed, but she'd never felt in safer hands.

'That's because I *am* a professional. I was trained by the best. Defensive driving, off-road navigation and dune-driving for starters.'

He slung his towel casually over one shoulder, not bothering to wipe away the stray droplets of water that ran from his hair down his collarbone. Soraya followed their progress over his burnished flesh and found herself clasping her hands together far too tightly.

'I can strip down a motor and get it back together in record time,' he continued, oblivious to her stare. 'But that doesn't mean I'd do it for fun.'

'What *do* you do for fun? How do you relax?'

Zahir's easy smile faded.

'You must do something to unwind,' she persevered.

'I find ways.' His voice dropped so low it plucked at her nerve ends and made her tremble.

Green fire blazed beneath his now-hooded lids and Soraya felt an answering conflagration start somewhere in her midriff. As his eyes held hers that ball of heat plunged down to her pelvis. The thud of her heartbeat swelled to a roar that clogged her senses.

Women, she realised. He relaxed with *women*.

The sexual awareness in his stare was so blatant even someone as inexperienced as she couldn't miss it.

But he wasn't thinking about other women now.

Zahir was looking at *her*.

That look was a caress, trailing across her skin and drawing every muscle and nerve ending into singing life.

Soraya revelled in it. Gone in an instant was a lifetime's caution, obliterated by a welling force so elemental it muted any opposition.

Suddenly that tension, the unspoken awareness they'd tried to pretend didn't exist, was back full force. Soraya had tried to convince herself she'd imagined it. Now she saw it in Zahir's intense look. Its impact dragged the air from her lungs.

Did she look at him the same way?

The air between them shimmered as if with heat haze. Honeyed warmth pooled low between her legs and a strange lethargy stole through her.

If Zahir were to close the space between them and reach out his hand she'd welcome his touch.

She *willed* him to do it.

His eyes dropped to her mouth and her lips throbbed as if in response to the brush of his mouth against hers.

What would his kiss be like? Urgent and fiery or slow and sensuous?

Soraya's eyelids drooped as if weighted. Her lips opened, ripe for his. Her hands slipped from where they'd looped around her legs. Her chest rose as a fractured breath became a sigh of expectation.

Zahir stepped close, so close she felt a drop of pool water land on her ankle. She looked up, stretching her neck to hold his gaze.

Did she imagine a tremor pass through his solid frame?

'I…' He speared a hand through his hair. 'I have a meeting in Paris,' he said finally, his voice harsh. 'I won't be back for dinner. Don't wait up for me.'

A moment later he was gone.

A day alone had done nothing to douse the flare of sexual excitement smouldering within her.

Soraya was honest enough not to pretend it was anything

else that made her skin seem too tight for her body and her pulse points ache with longing.

It was an awful irony that now, mere weeks from going to the man she had to marry, she was finally experiencing sexual desire. A desire she'd believed herself immune to.

That didn't mean she had to give in to it. She'd busied herself, thinking if she kept herself occupied every minute of every day until her return to Bakhara she'd conquer this yearning.

It hadn't worked so far—despite tuning the four-wheel drive till it purred, putting in hours on the laptop finishing her report, catching up on emails, driving to a local market and stocking up on so much mouth-watering fresh produce poor Hortense had been cooking all afternoon.

Now, as the day drew to a close and Zahir hadn't returned, Soraya knew she couldn't settle with a book or film.

What better time to face what she'd been putting off ever since they'd arrived?

She took a deep breath and walked down the first step into the outdoor pool. The water was like warm silk on her feet and ankles, yet goose bumps broke out on Soraya's flesh.

Another step and she tried to concentrate on how the underwater lights made the depths look appealing, the blue and gold key-pattern mosaic that ran the sides of the pool.

Her pulse revved as she moved deeper. But her hand was firm on the sun-warmed flagstone at the pool edge. She had nothing to fear, she reminded herself.

Only the fear she'd never been able to conquer.

Her brain filled with the image of that toddler, ghastly pale as Zahir hauled him from the stream. Her stomach twisted and terror was sharp metal on her tongue.

Had she looked like that the day she'd almost drowned?

This time she was determined to conquer her phobia.

Finally she reached a point where she couldn't proceed without submerging. Her heart hammered but she made herself turn and grip the edge with both trembling hands.

Her legs stretched out, weightless behind her. Soraya was

torn between a thrill of exhilaration that she'd ventured so far beyond her comfort zone, and crawling horror at what might happen next.

Experimentally she kicked her legs. It was easier than she'd expected. But how to coordinate arms and legs? Better to concentrate on floating.

It took a while but finally she let go with one arm. If she could just relax enough she was sure she could float. Everyone said it was so easy. Daringly, she let her body stretch out, till she gripped the edge by her fingertips. See? It wasn't so hard. Tomorrow she'd go to the shallow end and try it without holding on. She'd…

'Soraya?' Out of the dusk a figure loomed.

She opened her mouth to reply and swallowed water. Shock swamped her. She scrabbled for the edge, one arm flailing even as she went under.

Panic welled, fed by the taste of treated water in her mouth and nostrils. Shock gave way to fear and she thrashed for the surface.

Till strong arms hauled her up, holding her tight.

She clawed at wide shoulders, desperate for the feel of solid bone and flesh beneath her fingers. Precious oxygen filled her lungs and she gulped it down in great, gasping breaths.

'It's okay, Soraya. You're all right. You're safe. I've got you.' Zahir's voice, like dark treacle, seeped past the panic, finally slowing her frantic heartbeat.

Eyes smarting, she wrapped her arms tight round his neck, burying her face against Zahir's slick skin. He felt warm and solid and so very, very safe.

'But who's got you?' she gasped. 'The water's too deep to stand.' Her lips moved against his skin and she tasted male spice and salt, but she couldn't bring herself to lift her head away.

'I've got us both. Don't worry.'

She registered his big hands splayed warm around her ribs. His legs moved against hers, slowly kicking as he kept them afloat.

'You're sure?' She hated how unsteady she sounded.

'Positive.'

A moment later she felt the tiled steps beneath her feet. His hand uncurled hers from their vice-like grip of his neck and placed it on the warm flagstone at the pool's edge.

'You're safe now. Absolutely.'

Yet it wasn't the stairs beneath her feet that convinced her. It was Zahir's strong, hard form flush against hers.

She'd assumed the next time they met she'd feel awkward, remembering the sizzle of sexual awareness that had charged the atmosphere back in the garage. But embarrassment was obliterated by relief.

'Thank you.' She couldn't seem to let him go, but clung to him with her other arm, her heart galloping. He seemed to understand, for he didn't release her.

'You don't swim?' His eyes held hers.

She shook her head. 'No,' she croaked.

'And you were in the pool because…?'

'I was teaching myself to float.' Her mouth wobbled in a parody of a smile. 'Or trying to.' She clamped her lips shut, not wanting to go further. Yet his constant, silent regard finally dragged the truth from her. 'I'm scared of the water.'

She waited for his look of surprise but it didn't come. He merely nodded his head. 'Sensible of you. I would be too if I couldn't swim.'

A ribbon of heat unfurled within her at Zahir's easy acceptance and matter-of-fact tone. No condescension, no disbelief. He said nothing more, just held her safe as the water lapped around them and Soraya was grateful for his silent support.

'It was the boy,' she finally said, needing to explain. 'Seeing him almost die because he couldn't save himself.' She yanked in a breath. 'I saw him and felt…'

She looked away. What had she felt? Horror, déjà vu, fear. *And more.*

'I felt ashamed I'd never conquered my fear and learned to swim. I don't want to be that helpless.'

Zahir's fingers tightened on her. 'Why are you so scared of the water?'

'I almost drowned as a child. I was playing in the shallows. I thought my mother was watching me but she was…busy.'

Soraya pulled in a searing breath. Her mother had gone to her lover, the man she had eventually ran away with, presumably thinking Soraya wouldn't venture deep.

Somehow through the years the two events had become entangled in her brain—the loss of her mother and her brush with death. As a child she'd almost believed she'd somehow driven her mother to leave with her near-drowning. Of course she knew better now, but the result was a dread of water she'd never been able to overcome.

Zahir's broad palm slid up her back then down again in a gesture of silent comfort that unstrung more of the tension still threading her body.

'What happened in Amboise must have brought it all back for you. No wonder you were white as a sheet.'

Soraya shrugged stiffly. 'It was…horrible. But it made me realise I couldn't go on pretending this fear doesn't matter. I have to do something about it.'

Strong fingers took her chin and lifted it till she was staring into eyes dark as the night closing in around them.

'Promise me you won't do it alone.' Though soft, Zahir's voice had a rough edge that abraded her senses.

'But I—'

'I'll teach you to swim, Soraya. Just promise me you won't try it alone.'

Her heart pounded as his gaze held hers. Soraya's insides melted at the banked heat she saw there.

'I promise.'

'Good.' He nodded and took her hand in his. 'We'll start now.'

'Now?' Her eyes rounded.

'No time like the present. Besides, we don't want tonight's episode to compound your fear, do we?'

It already had, but she bit down on the admission. The thought of going further into the depths horrified her.

Zahir's fingers threaded between hers, his strength and heat melding with hers.

'Trust me, Soraya?'

Her gaze roved his serious, almost grim face. She took in the lines of strength and character carved beside his mouth. There was determination in that solid jaw, arrogance in those aristocratic cheekbones and imperious nose, and a question in his clear gaze.

She thought of all she knew of him. He was capable, dependable and kind. How could she not trust him?

'Yes,' she said finally, and let him draw her into the water.

'Tilt your head back into the water further.'

Soraya did as he bid and Zahir was amazed anew that this was the same woman who a short time ago had been thrashing in panic half a metre from the edge of the pool. Now she floated on her back, his hands beneath her, the safeguard she needed to be confident in the water.

It humbled him that she trusted him so implicitly. Particularly since trust hadn't come easily to her. Initially they'd been like wary, armed combatants in an uneasy truce because of his early misjudgements of her.

Recently that wariness had blossomed into something akin to friendship, or at least understanding.

Except when his libido escaped his constraints and reminded him she was the most seductively attractive woman he'd ever known. Dancing with her in a public square had tested his limits. But this… Even dressed in a tank top and cut-offs rather than a skimpy bikini, she fired his blood.

'Why didn't you wear a swimsuit?' He asked, trying to take his mind off the sensual promise of her body spread before him.

He felt like a sultan offered a feast for the senses. But he had to deny himself and keep his touch brisk and businesslike. He couldn't betray her trust.

'I don't own one.' She darted a look at him then away. 'There's no point when I'd never use it.'

Zahir refrained from pointing out many women wore bikinis that never got wet. They were for display, to show off ripe female curves to best advantage.

The more he knew Soraya the more he understood she was unique. Her shame at not overcoming her fear had surprised him. Her determination to beat it rather than live with what she saw as weakness appealed. She was some woman.

He applauded her pride and perseverance. She had such heart—as much as any warrior he'd known.

Yet her bravery had run close to stupidity tonight. In an instant she'd shattered the hard-won calm he'd spent all day working to achieve. What if he hadn't come down to the pool for a swim? What if she'd drowned here alone? Anger and fear vied for dominance.

'What were you doing in the deep end?' Despite his best efforts his voice had a raw edge.

'I knew if I was in the shallows I wouldn't push myself. I had to face the danger.'

Hot shivers rippled through Zahir's belly. 'Just don't do it again, *ever*, without me.'

She drove him crazy. Pride, fear and desire made for a combustible mix. How much longer could he keep a lid on them all?

'I've already promised I won't.' She looked at him solemnly and his heart kicked against his ribs. 'But I need to learn fast. You won't always be around to help me.'

Of course he wouldn't. He'd be managing Bakhara's largest province and Soraya would be…with Hussein.

Clammy sweat broke out on Zahir's skin and sick dread churned his stomach. He tried so hard to be honourable in thought as well as deed, but lately it was more than he could do.

It was a constant battle to rein in his imagination. As for concentrating on teaching her to relax in the water—it took every ounce of determination to focus.

'Try kicking again but keep your legs straight.'

She did as instructed and together they moved down the pool.

'I'm moving! I'm swimming!'

The delighted look she sent him drove a shaft of pure pleasure through his chest.

It was more reward than he deserved.

Even as he smiled back, his body tensed.

Her long hair, unbound for the first time, spread in a cloud of dark satin. Like mermaid's tresses it caressed his hands, arms and belly as he walked with her. He'd never imagined it was so long. Now he couldn't help but wonder what it would be like rippling down her naked back and breasts as he made love to her.

Unable to take any more, he slipped his hands from beneath her and moved just far enough away to avoid contact. They were in the shallow end and she was in no danger.

Excited at her success, she didn't notice his withdrawal. Her face glowed with effervescent joy.

A man would have to be made of desert stone not to respond to Soraya.

Despite his reputation as a hard warrior, Zahir was made of all-too-human flesh. If only he *were* stone!

How could he hold out against a woman who appealed to him on a level no woman ever had? Not even the girl he'd been head over heels in love with as a youth.

'Zahir? What's wrong?' She was standing, water sluicing down the black top that clung like a second skin.

He shook his head. 'Nothing's wrong.' He turned away. 'That's enough now. We'll continue tomorrow and you can learn to float face-down, ready to swim properly.'

'Really?' She caught his hand and stopped him moving away. 'You think I'm ready?'

Reluctantly he turned and looked down into a face that to his dazzled eyes seemed flawless. Excitement shone in her eyes and her smile wrapped around his heart.

He wasn't aware of reaching out but found his hand cupping

her jaw. Her satiny skin was smooth and sleek to the touch. Her pulse trembled against his fingertips.

Something deep inside, something stronger than logic or caution, roared into life.

Her eyes were wide as she swayed towards him, her lips parting. To warn him off?

It was too late.

His lips met hers and the world collapsed around them.

CHAPTER NINE

SORAYA had imagined his kiss so often. She'd even dreamed of it. The reality obliterated her imaginings as a tidal wave would the ripple of a single stone.

Zahir's broad hands cradled her face, his touch tender yet strong as he held her head just so and angled his own for better access.

His questing tongue slicked her lips, parted them, and she shuddered in great racking waves as sensation exploded within her. Zahir devoured her, invited her, stole her breath with his audacious demands, yet even while plundering rapaciously offered back such sweet, poignant pleasure Soraya was lost.

The fresh taste of his breath was in her mouth. It was the most delicious flavour in the world—spice and salt and the mystery that was maleness. His scent filled her nostrils. His hard body was muscled and intriguing, his heart thundering with hers. His wet skin burned, branding her through her clothes, making her breasts tingle and a curl of indescribable tension twist deep and low.

Instinctively she grabbed his shoulders, swaying as her limbs melted, and the world became a place she didn't recognise.

Nothing had prepared her for the vital life force throbbing through them as if they were one. Or the need spiralling out of control and the sheer wanton delight of being in his arms. Every sense was hyper-alert. Even the softly eddying water was a silken caress drawing her deeper into sensual overload.

She'd never felt more frail, more delicately feminine than now, with his heavy-muscled thighs braced wide around her, his hands trapping her, and his mouth seducing her with sheer, carnal pleasure.

Yet she'd never felt stronger. As if power sizzled and sparked in her blood. As if she could lay mountains low with a single flick of her fingers.

His kiss shattered her and rebuilt her at the same time.

Her hands slid from his shoulders to the back of his neck, up through his damp hair and he growled low in the back of his throat. It was a sound of approval, of male possession, and she revelled in it. Revelled in the power that she, even with her inexperience, had over this man who haunted her thoughts and dreams.

His tongue slid against hers, demanding a response, and she gave it, tentatively at first, then wholeheartedly, lost in the wonder of this heady world of passion.

Her whole body ached, throbbed for Zahir. Only him. She wanted to climb up his tall frame and meld herself against him. She *needed* with a desperation she'd never experienced or thought to know.

Even the rough pressure of his chest expanding against hers incited a thrill.

Soraya pressed closer, needy as never before. She loved the feel of his body, the unfamiliar outline of muscle, bone and sinew. The tickle of his hairy legs against hers. Lifting herself higher into his hold, her hips tilted against him and she registered the solid proof of his arousal.

At the feel of him, hot and heavy just *there* against her, she stilled. A frayed thread of common sense told her to move away, yet some older, sense-deep feminine instinct urged her closer.

Soraya was swaying nearer when firm hands grabbed her upper arms. An instant later she gulped huge drafts of air into oxygen-starved lungs as he put her from him. But nothing made up for the loss of Zahir's mouth on hers, or his body against hers.

Hungrily she eyed his reddened lips. They were drawn flat now, matching the horizontal lines furrowing his brow.

Yet his eyes didn't match his scowl. His eyes were smoky-dark and held a hint of the same shock she felt.

Soraya loved his eyes, she realised. From the first when they'd watched her so intently she'd felt a sizzle of awareness. Even when he'd looked askance at her, Zahir's eyes had fascinated. Now they shared the secret she felt: the secret turmoil of amazing emotions and sensations.

The secret his grim face denied.

'I'm sorry.' His voice was harsh and unrecognisable. 'That shouldn't have happened.'

His gaze left hers to fix on something over her shoulder. As if he couldn't bear to see her. Or as if he couldn't face what he read in her face.

It was the first time he'd ever avoided her gaze.

Soraya felt something crumble inside.

She gulped down a shaky breath and searched for control. Her heart pounded and she had the shakes so badly she wasn't sure she could stand without his support.

'But you can't pretend it didn't happen.' The words emerged breathless and uneven.

She didn't understand what made her say it till he yanked his gaze back to hers and heat exploded inside.

That's why. Because you want to feel it again—what Zahir makes you feel.

Because you want him to admit he feels it too.

But Zahir shook his head, thrusting her further away.

'It was *wrong*.' The last word was dragged from him as if from a tortured soul and she felt his pain as hers. His hands dropped and he stepped back, as if unable to remain within touching distance.

As if she tainted him.

Of course it was wrong. Soraya understood that all too well. To desire her husband-to-be's most trusted advisor was disastrous. Unthinkable!

Yet it felt so right. When it was just she and Zahir, it felt incredible.

'Zahir. Please, I…'

She didn't know what she was going to say. Only knew she couldn't bear the pain she read on his proud features. That she had to ease it somehow.

Yet he didn't give her the chance. Before the words had left her mouth he'd vaulted from the pool, every line of his athlete's body taut with rejection.

He didn't say a word as he strode away.

Sunlight flooded the dining room as Soraya lingered over a very late breakfast. She'd fallen asleep at dawn and couldn't summon the energy to go out, despite the glorious day.

What had she done?

Her flesh prickled whenever she thought of last night's kiss. The way Zahir's body and hers had fused together, driven by a force so potent she'd had no chance of overcoming it.

Or had she?

She shivered and rubbed her hands up her arms.

Her life had been shaped by the mother who'd left when she was six. Her mother had flitted from one affair to another. First to Soraya's father, then to a string of handsome men till her untimely death.

Maybe it was a response to the negativity of those who expected her to turn out like her mum, but Soraya had never sought male attention. She'd happily accepted her beloved father's over-protective ways and steered clear of men.

She'd told herself love was a weakness and desire—

She pushed her untasted breakfast away.

Desire had been a mere word. Safe in the knowledge she'd never experienced it, Soraya had supposed she never would. Until Zahir had caught her in his stormy gaze and nothing had been the same. It was as if he'd branded her as his that night and nothing, not logic or the threat of approaching marriage, could change that.

Her heart dipped.

Was she too destined to make a fool of herself, of honour and duty, for an attractive man?

It didn't matter that duty led her down a path she shrank from. She'd committed to her fate. She couldn't change it. Soraya pressed a hand to her forehead, as if to still her whirling thoughts.

She should be ashamed she'd kissed Zahir and wanted more.

Yes, she felt guilt and horror at what she'd done. Yet that wasn't all. Last night had felt *right*, as if she and Zahir were *meant*. No matter how she castigated herself she couldn't regret that kiss. It was emblazoned in her soul. A single point of perfect happiness.

It did no good to tell herself it was more than sex. That she'd begun to fall for the proud, caring, fascinating man she'd come to know. That just made the situation more impossible.

'Mademoiselle?' Soraya looked up to see the housekeeper in the doorway. 'Monsieur El Hashem sent this for you.'

'Thank you, Hortense.' Puzzled, she took the shopping bag from her hand. Inside Soraya discovered silky material in swirling aquamarine and turquoise.

'*Monsieur* said he'd be waiting for you in the pool.'

'The pool?' Soraya's head shot up, tension crackling through her.

Hortense nodded and tsked as she collected Soraya's still-laden breakfast plate. 'That's right. He said you had a lesson.'

It was foolhardy, Zahir knew. Being alone with her, his hands on her body, would be purest temptation. Yet he'd promised to teach her to swim.

The memory of Soraya flailing in the water, panicking and possibly drowning but for his intervention, froze his veins with a glacial chill. He had to know she'd be safe.

Besides, it would be cowardly to back out. A woman with so much heart and character deserved his respect.

She didn't deserve his tongue in her mouth and his erection

surging between her legs—no matter how much he wanted her. She mightn't be a complete innocent but he'd taken her by surprise with his ardour. He'd felt her shock and tried to pull back. Instead he'd succumbed to pleasure so intense it was like a drug.

Sweat broke out on his brow as Zahir relived the intense pleasure of last night's kiss. The taste of her so deliciously enticing. The feel of her siren's body against his. That mix of sweet tenderness and fiery wanton that had blown him away.

The wanting had been bad enough before he'd touched her. After last night it would be pure torment, knowing paradise was so close yet so far beyond his reach.

A sound made him look up. Soraya walked towards the pool, closely wrapped in a voluminous towelling robe despite the heat. Even seeing her bundled up sent his pulse soaring. Her hair, almost to her waist, trailed over one shoulder like an invitation to touch. Even her bare feet were enticing.

Zahir swallowed a knot of tension.

This would be his penance. Every second would be torture but he deserved it, and worse.

She was Hussein's woman. He'd known it and still hadn't stopped. Now he would face his punishment though it would be the most difficult thing he'd ever done.

She stopped by the pool, eyes wary.

'Are you sure you want to do this?'

'I promised I would teach you to swim. I never go back on a promise.' Yet just watching her played havoc with his breathing. A tremor quivered through his limbs as he met her doubtful gaze.

'I apologise for my behaviour last night.' The words spilled from stiff lips. 'I have no excuse. But, believe me, it won't happen again.'

She met his eyes and for an insane moment he felt a thud of connection between them. It made no difference. It *couldn't* make a difference.

'I'm sorry too,' she murmured, her gaze dipping. 'Last night… It wasn't just you. It was me too.'

Zahir didn't need to be reminded of how she'd undone him with her sweet responsiveness. He shook his head. He knew exactly where the guilt lay.

'I'm responsible for you.'

'For my safety. That's all.' Her eyes sparkled with a militant light but he forbore to argue.

'Thank you for the swimsuit,' she said at last, not quite meeting his gaze. 'You must have been out early.'

He hadn't been to bed, had spent the night alternately berating himself and reliving the guilty pleasure he'd sworn to put behind him.

Zahir remained silent as she fumbled with the tie at her waist and let the robe fall away.

The air sucked from his lungs in a rush as she turned.

She looked like a mermaid, indecently alluring even in the most modest one-piece outfit he could find. He'd been right about her size—too right. The stretch fabric clung like a lover's caress, making his fingers itch as he remembered the feel of her beneath his hands.

She was all enticing curves and supple limbs. The fall of her hair in thick, waving tresses accentuated her femininity, appealing to some primal male part of him that relished each difference between them. Heat roared through him in an out-of-control rush and he fought to retain his composure.

Deliberately he looked at his watch. 'We've just time for another lesson before we leave.'

She faltered at the edge of the pool. 'Leave?'

Zahir nodded and beckoned her down the steps. 'Yes. I've arranged the next leg of our journey. You wanted to see France and you can't do that while we're isolated here.'

He looked away before he could read her reaction. It didn't matter what she said; the decision was made. Immersion in rural quiet had thrown them together. What they needed now was people, cities, action. Anything to keep them occupied and stop him dwelling on Soraya Karim and what she did to him.

Half an hour later Soraya was flushed with excitement and pleasure at what she'd achieved. Even her distress and embarrassment had ebbed to a dull, gnawing ache. For Zahir was utterly businesslike, intent only on her progress.

It was as if last night hadn't happened, except for the jerk of electricity, as if from a live wire, whenever they touched.

Now, breathless, she sank back against the end of the pool, watching as Zahir hauled himself out.

The play of bunching muscles across his back and arms mesmerised her. He really was the most remarkable-looking man. She could watch him for hours. Every movement was graceful despite the raw power he so carefully leashed.

'What's that mark? The one along your side?'

As he turned, his brows jammed together as if he was displeased she'd ended their unspoken agreement to avoid personal topics.

'I've been a warrior all my life. I have scars. It comes with the territory.' He shrugged and reached for his towel.

Soraya noticed then that the dark golden skin of his back was smooth and unblemished. The old scars were on his chest and arms. The marks of a warrior.

Something, a little frisson of feminine excitement, tingled through her, making her frown. It wasn't that she relished the idea of combat, but at a deep, primitive level there was something thrilling about the idea of a strong man prepared to defend what he believed in.

'But that one's different.' She pointed to a white pucker of flesh at his side. It was none of her business but she couldn't stifle the need to know more about him. Surely her question was innocuous?

Sighing, he rubbed the towel over his face. 'A bullet caught me.'

Soraya's breath hitched in a hiss of dismay. Her heart hammered at the thought of Zahir in a gun's sights.

'It's okay, Soraya.' He must have read her horror, for his severe expression eased. 'It was just a flesh wound and a bit of a knick to one rib.'

Just a knick…

'How did it happen?' Prying or not, she couldn't leave it there.

'I used to lead the Emir's personal protection unit, remember? I came between him and someone who intended harm.'

Soraya clung to the side of the pool as weakness invaded her limbs. Zahir had put himself in front of the Emir. Taken a bullet meant for him!

Slowly she shook her head. 'I can't comprehend how you could do that. Put yourself in danger that way.'

'Can't you?' Eyes of vivid emerald caught and held hers. 'Isn't there anyone you'd risk yourself for?'

Before she could answer he went on, 'It was my job. What I'd signed on to do. More than that, Hussein is far more than an employer to me.'

The ripple of emotion across his stern features surprised her. 'Hussein was the one who rescued me from my father's palace when I was just a child. As supreme leader he forced my father's hand into letting me go. Not that my father was bothered about keeping me.' Zahir's austerely sculpted lips curled in a smile that held no humour. It sent a terrible chill prickling down Soraya's spine. What did he mean, his father hadn't been bothered about keeping him?

'Hussein has been father and friend to me. Mentor and role model. I don't just owe him my job, but my life. If I'd stayed in my father's palace I've no doubt I'd have died from neglect.'

The quiet certainty in Zahir's calm tone turned Soraya's blood cold. He'd said his early years were eventful but she'd had no idea.

'What about your mother?'

Absently he swiped his towel over his shoulders. 'I never knew her. She died when I was tiny. So there was no-one to care that I ran feral, barely surviving. No-one to care that my father never legally acknowledged me as his.'

'Zahir!' Having grown up with at least one loving parent, Soraya found the picture he painted appalling. She could barely imagine being so alone.

He shrugged. 'They weren't married. She was one of his mistresses. A dancing girl. Why should he stir himself over a brat who wasn't even legitimately his?' His tone was blank, as if his father's rejection didn't bother him.

How could that be? Soraya knew too well the weight a parent's rejection. She'd carried it ever since she was six. What hidden scars burdened Zahir? It must have been doubly painful for him not to have either parent there for him when he was young.

She'd seen behind Zahir's mask of calm. She knew beyond the formidable control was a man of powerful emotions and blazing passion. A man who felt deeply.

The memory of that man sent heat spiralling in that secret feminine place.

'Hussein gave me a home.' Zahir's voice deepened to that low burr that brushed the back of her neck into tingling heat. 'He cared about me, raised me, made me who I am. I owe him everything, especially loyalty.' Zahir paced the edge of the pool towards her, his words ringing between them, deliberate and measured.

'I could never betray him.'

He was reminding her why there could never be anything between them, despite the shimmering heat that charged the air and the growing sense of a bond between them. Zahir was a man of honour and loyalty. How much more loyal could you get than to offer your life to save another?

No wonder he'd looked sick last night as he'd turned from her. By kissing her, he'd betrayed the man he'd admired all his life.

Against that, the guilt that hounded her paled. To her the Emir was a distant benefactor. How much worse this all was for Zahir, who knew and loved him.

Her heart twisted for Zahir. For the pain he'd borne in the past. For the hurt she'd unwittingly caused him.

And for herself, trapped between duty and desire, with no way out. Her throat closed convulsively. Was that all the future held? Duty?

Once she'd believed it would be enough. She'd thought emotional independence was all she needed.

Then recently she'd begun to imagine a future other than the one mapped out for her—a future of her own making, where she could pursue the half-formed hopes and dreams she'd dared to dream in Paris. Of a career, a future that was about *her* needs and interests, not the nation's.

Now even that seemed unreal, unsatisfactory, a poor facsimile of a *real* future. For the first time in her life Soraya caught a glimpse of what life might be like with more than solely career or duty to fill it. With a man she cared for, a man who made her blood spark and her soul take flight. A man like Zahir…

Like a tidal wave, realisation crashed down on her. She grabbed for the edge of the pool, desperate for support as her world reeled.

'Time to move. We're leaving here, and remember you need to pack.' Zahir turned his back rather than let his gaze run over her again.

The swimming lesson had been as testing as he'd feared. Even the mention of what he owed Hussein only succeeded in racheting up the level of sick guilt in his belly. It did nothing to drive out his fascination with Soraya. It was as if she'd got under his skin, like a desert sandstorm infiltrating every defence.

What *was* it about Soraya? Even in the throes of first love he hadn't felt so…saturated by his feelings. They impinged on every thought after years of him bottling them up. He was aware of her as if she was part of him. Nor was it simple sexual awareness. If only it were that!

He slung the towel round his neck then shot a glance over her shoulder.

She hadn't moved. She stood, hands braced on the flagstones at the edge of the pool, head bent as if winded.

'Soraya?' Concern spiked. He turned back to her. She didn't look up, and he saw her breasts rise and fall quickly as if she'd just swum a sprint. He yanked his gaze higher and realised her face was pale.

He'd thought it impossible to feel more guilt, but he'd been wrong. The way she stood, as if absorbing a body blow, told him she battled pain. Because of him? His chest constricted hard.

Disregarding his resolution not to touch her again, he extended his hand. 'Come on, princess. It's time we left.'

'I told you before—*don't* call me that!'

Zahir's blood frosted as she looked up and he read the haunted depths of her eyes. The slight shadows that spoke of a sleepless night were more pronounced in her milky-white face. Her skin looked drawn too tight. Even her lush mouth seemed pinched.

'Soraya?' His scalp itched with warning. Something was very wrong. 'What is it?'

She shook her head and looked away.

'Sorry,' she mumbled. 'It's nothing. I overreacted.'

Zahir's brow knotted. Even in the face of his blatant disapproval she'd stood defiant and proud. Yet now she looked as if the merest breeze would knock her down.

'Because I called you princess?'

She gave no response, ignoring his hand and clambering stiffly from the pool. Yet even in the sun she shivered, and he draped his towel around her. It said something about her state of mind that she stood meekly while he wrapped it close, rubbing her arms through the towelling.

'Soraya?' She met his gaze but her eyes had a dazed, blind look that worried him. 'What is it?'

'Nothing. I'm fine.' He refused to move away. Finally she spoke again. 'My mother used to call me that, you know.' Her lips stretched in a parody of a smile. 'When I was tiny I even used to believe I was a little princess. At least that I was *her* princess.'

The towel slipped and she clutched it close.

'It just goes to show how gullible children are, doesn't it?' Her voice rang hollow. 'I wasn't special enough to make her stay when her latest lover called. She left me behind then without a second thought.'

A shudder racked her and Zahir had to fight the need to tug her close and wrap himself around her. She looked…fragile.

But a moment later Soraya recovered. She straightened, pushing her shoulders back in that familiar way and turned to survey the pool.

'The last time she called me that was the day I almost drowned. I was wading in a pool and I was sure she was still there, watching me. I didn't find out till later that was the day she'd left us to go to her lover.'

His heart wrenched at the pain he read in her taut features. At the hurt she battled even to think of venturing into water again. He'd believed her strong and determined but he hadn't known the half of it.

'I should have remembered that lesson,' she murmured.

'What lesson?'

'Never to expect too much.' Her expression held infinite sadness as she turned and walked away.

Zahir felt as if someone had taken a knife to his belly and gutted him.

CHAPTER TEN

SORAYA leaned on the railing of the giant motor cruiser and took in the brilliant cluster of lights that was Monte Carlo. Even the water was gold and silver, reflecting the illuminated city climbing the hills.

All around her was luxury. From the multi-million-dollar vessels crammed into the marina to the exclusive party she'd left on the other deck.

Was this what her life would be like as the Emir's wife? A world of untold wealth and privilege?

Fervently she wished she could be thrilled by the prospect. Another woman might have found nothing but pleasure in the comforts of extreme wealth but Soraya had so much on her mind, they left her unmoved. They were comforts Zahir took for granted, fitting easily into this rarefied world of diplomats, royalty and celebrities.

He might have been a bodyguard once, and a lost soul as a child, but he'd moved on. He was strong, confident, a man sure of himself and his purpose, with nothing to prove.

Her heart squeezed haphazardly as she thought of her weeks with Zahir. Despite the caution they exercised, she'd slipped further under his spell.

Riding horses in the Camargue, eating heavenly bouillabaisse in a tiny waterfront restaurant, even visiting lavender fields and a perfume factory; Soraya couldn't have asked for a better companion. He'd been pleasant, amusing and caring.

Yet he scrupulously kept a telling distance between them. He hadn't touched her again. Even during her swimming lessons, and he insisted on those daily. He supervised, instructed and encouraged but kept to the side of the pool.

How she missed his touch! His strong arms around her.

A sigh shuddered through her.

She couldn't ask for more. Briefly she'd been angry at his unswerving loyalty to the Emir, for it meant there was no chance for *them*. But there *was* no 'them'. There were too many obstacles against it. Besides, Zahir's loyalty was part of what made him the man he was.

All she could do was store up memories against a future when he must be a stranger to her. That was what she'd done, gathered memories, as if they could comfort her when she gave herself to another man.

She'd railed at a fate that bound her to a marriage she didn't want. How much worse now when, too late, she'd discovered what it was to care deeply? *For the wrong man.*

Pain tore through her and she gripped the railing harder. She wanted…

No! She couldn't allow herself to go there.

That morning of her second swimming lesson Zahir had thought her upset because he'd called her 'princess'.

It was true the casual endearment had evoked painful memories. But the real anguish had come from the realization that she, who'd thought herself immune from love, had fallen for a man who could never be hers.

She was head over heels in love with Zahir.

The knowledge made her body sing with excitement and her soul shrivel. It was wonderful, delicious and terrible. A blessing that was a curse.

Travelling with him was torture and pleasure combined. Maybe if he felt nothing for her it would be easier, but his punctilious distance told her he felt something for her too. That knowledge kept her on a knife edge of torment, trawling back through conversations, seeking proof of his feelings. Like

Bastille Day, when he'd asked about the possibility of her loving someone other than her betrothed.

If only circumstances had been different.

'Soraya. What are you doing down here when the party's in full swing upstairs?'

Zahir halted several paces away. His eyes ate her up; she was luscious in a long dress of dusky rose. A gown that was innocently demure by the standards of the scantily dressed socialites at the party. Yet it skimmed her body in a way that reminded him too clearly of the hour-glass figure that tempted him during each day's swimming lesson.

Heat clutched deep in his belly.

Her scent, wildflowers rather than hothouse exotics, teased his nostrils. Her hair, held back by jewelled clips, cascaded down her back in a ripple of thick silk.

More than one man had cast covetous eyes on her tonight and Zahir had been busy staking a possessive claim on her to prevent any untoward advances.

Staking a claim on behalf of Hussein, he reminded himself.

She half-turned but didn't meet his eyes. 'I wanted some peace and quiet.'

At her words he stiffened. He'd seen her excited, happy, indignant and angry, but never listless.

There'd been inevitable tension after their kiss. But he'd worked hard not to let her see that taste of her had driven him to the brink of endurance. For her part, Soraya had thrown herself into sightseeing with a fervour that gave no hint she wanted anything else.

At first he'd wondered if she was a little too enthusiastic, then chided himself. It wasn't that he *wanted* her pining for what could never be.

'You're not enjoying yourself?' Tonight he'd sought safety in numbers. This exclusive society party had seemed a perfect alternative to a night alone with Soraya and the terrible gnawing tension within.

Beautiful women with come-hither eyes and smiles that

promised pleasure were here tonight in droves. Yet none had drawn a second glance from him.

Not one could hold a candle to Soraya for beauty or character. She was gentle—despite her bravado in standing up for herself—capable, caring, inquisitive and deeply fascinating. Her fierce independence, her determination and natural exuberance, entranced him. With her he'd felt more than he had in a decade and a half. It was like emerging from a grey half-life into a world of sunshine and colour.

'The party is amazing. Thank you for bringing me.' Yet she didn't sound as enthusiastic as when she discussed her research project. 'So many interesting people. So many celebrities. And I've never seen so much bling in my life.'

'But?'

She shook her head and those long tresses slid and curled around her slim back. Was it ridiculous to resent the fact she wore her hair down tonight? He hated the way men looked at her, imagining that bountiful hair loose around her shoulders as she made love.

He knew they did. Any man would.

He did. God help him!

'But it's only days till our flight from Rome to Bakhara.' Her husky words drew his belly tight. 'It's crept up on me and I needed time to digest it.'

She was going home to marry the finest man he knew.

Zahir ignored the wave of nausea that passed through him at the thought.

'I know Hussein is looking forward to seeing you.' If Hussein had any idea of the lovely woman she'd become, he'd be eager for her arrival.

Soraya bowed her head as if in assent. But her grip on the railing reminded him of a falcon's claws clamped hard and sharp on a leather glove.

'Soraya?' He took a pace towards her then, realising, stopped. '*Are* you all right?'

'Of course.' She tilted her chin up as she stared across the shimmering brightness. 'What could be wrong?'

Something was. He'd come to recognise the way she angled that neat chin as a defence mechanism.

He reminded himself his duty was simply to return her safe to Bakhara, not delve into her thoughts and fears.

Yet telling himself couldn't make it so. Nor could he banish the suspicion he knew *exactly* what was wrong. That, despite her proud front, Soraya felt as he did. That they'd circled an unspoken truth for weeks.

'Tell me!'

Perhaps the harshness in his voice surprised her for she turned her head, eyes wide and it was there again, that jangle along the senses as if lightning had sparked between them.

Damn it. He shouldn't feel this. He shouldn't feel anything except impersonal concern for her wellbeing.

Yet what he felt was personal. Far too personal.

Did she feel it too? Was that why she whipped her head round so fast?

'Soraya. Please.' It was no good telling himself this was merely a job. It had ceased to be 'just a job' the moment he had seen her in that Paris nightclub.

'I don't want to go back,' she said at last. 'I don't want…' Her voice dipped and she swallowed convulsively. That single movement spoke of a vulnerability that tugged at something in his very core. Something he couldn't name.

He found himself behind her, not touching, but mirroring her body with his as if to protect her. He couldn't keep back.

'What don't you want, Soraya?' His breath held.

A deep breath lifted her narrow shoulders. 'I don't want to marry the Emir.'

Like the boom of a bomb blast, her words rocked him back on his heels.

Elation ripped through him, a momentary inward cry of delight, till he smothered it, using every particle of will-power left to him.

It was on the tip of his tongue to ask why she didn't want to marry Hussein. But he wouldn't let the words come. He knew what he wanted her answer to be and he couldn't let either of them go there.

To betray Hussein would make him no better than his traitor father. And it would bring her nothing but shame and public disgrace.

His body snapped taut almost to breaking point. His chest rose and fell hard as he dragged in one sharp breath after another. Silence welled. One wrong word could shatter the world in a way that could never be repaired. The air around them strung close with tension.

'Why marry him then?' He told himself it was time to remind them both that this was what she really wanted. She'd just temporarily lost sight of the fact.

'Because I promised,' she whispered. 'It's arranged.'

'And you can't go back on your word.' It wasn't a question, it was recognition that she, like him, had standards to live by. Zahir had never broken a vow. He knew the value of a promise—particularly a promise given to the man who'd made him who he was today.

If only that reminder could strengthen him now! Temptation was here before him, made flesh in a way that threatened everything he knew of himself.

'That's right. It's my duty to marry him.'

Duty. Another word that ruled Zahir's world.

Wasn't it duty that kept him standing here, his body a mere hand span from hers? That tiny distance represented a yawning chasm, cleaved by his conscience. No matter what he wanted, duty kept her safe from his touch.

Yet it didn't prevent him feeling her heat, scenting her skin and hair, hearing her shaky little inhalations of breath. Almost, he embraced her. He remembered the imprint of her soft body against his and his will-power frayed.

'I promised him and my father. I owe them so much and it's what they both want.'

But not what she wanted.

'Did your father coerce you into it?' The suspicion drove bile to the back of Zahir's throat. Hussein would never do such a thing, but perhaps her father would.

'No.' Her voice rang true. 'My father is a dear man. He would never force me.'

'Then why did you agree?' Zahir hated the plea that broke his voice, but he was past dissembling.

She turned around and suddenly they were just a kiss apart. He ordered himself to move back but his feet wouldn't obey. He shoved his hands deep in his trouser pockets rather than be tempted to touch.

Her beautiful oval face tilted up towards his.

'I was fourteen, Zahir.'

'So young?' He frowned. Despite the old customs of his people, such an early betrothal was no longer the norm.

What had Hussein been thinking? Zahir's heart skipped at the unpalatable suspicion Hussein had been attracted to a girl barely in her teens. But their long engagement countered that idea.

The arrangement was odd. Why hadn't Hussein chosen a woman closer to his own age? Why wait ten years to marry?

Unless the betrothal had been hastily arranged?

The constitution stipulated the Emir of Bakhara had to be married, a family man with the prospect of heirs. Fortunately for Hussein a formal betrothal was as binding as marriage and there'd been no-one eager to hurry him into a second marriage when his beloved first wife had died. Had he chosen an early betrothal to keep the balance of power while he came to terms with his widower status?

'And you wanted to be queen.'

Soraya shook her head. Traditional Bakhari chandelier earrings scintillated at her ear lobes, drawing his eye to her delicate ears and slender throat.

Zahir clenched his hands tight in his pockets rather than reach out and stroke that delicate skin.

'No,' she said slowly. 'Not particularly, though the royal glamour was very exciting. But after a while I saw possibilities. As the Emir's consort I could be useful. Help our people. Devote myself to good works.' Her mouth twisted wryly as if mocking her earlier self.

'There's nothing wrong with that.' It sounded laudable, if distant from a flesh-and-blood marriage.

'Of course there's not.' Abruptly she looked away. 'That's exactly what I tell myself now when I try to imagine the future.'

A future when she would be Hussein's bride. In Hussein's arms.

'So why agree to the marriage?' Zahir's voice was rough. 'For the money? The prestige?'

'Zahir!'

Her shock made him look down, to discover he held her arms in a vice-like grip. Instantly he eased his hold.

'I'm sorry.' Yet he couldn't let her go. The touch of her soft flesh made him war with himself. 'Why, Soraya?'

'Because he saved my father's life.' Her eyes were dark pools of stormy emotion that dragged him down. A self-destructive part of him wanted to dive into those depths and never surface again.

'How?'

It shouldn't surprise him. He had first-hand knowledge of Hussein's generous spirit. Not only had Hussein saved Zahir as a child, he'd never held his father's treachery against him, measuring him against his own deeds rather than the taint of his blood kin.

'My father had a kidney disease,' Soraya responded. 'He needed a transplant, but you know how long the waiting list is for donors.'

Zahir nodded. Organ donation was still new in Bakhara and convincing people to join a donor registry was an uphill battle.

'He would have died while waiting for a transplant.' A tremor passed through her. 'I was too young to donate to him, and he wouldn't give his permission for me to do it.'

Of course she'd wanted to do it. Why wasn't he surprised?

'But the Emir said he owed my father his throne and his life. Apparently years ago there'd been an uprising by several tribal leaders. They'd tried to unseat the Emir and put one of their own in his place.'

Zahir stiffened. 'I know. My father was one of them.' The words scalded his tongue.

'He was?' Her eyes roved his face as if searching for something. 'You're not very like him, are you?'

'What do you mean?' Even now his skin crawled at the knowledge that man's blood ran in his veins. 'You didn't know him.'

'I know *you*, Zahir.' The way she spoke his name was like a caress.

He was so besotted he was hearing things now. He should step back but couldn't shift his feet. As for lifting his hold on her arms—it was impossible!

'I know you're a man of honour. A man who takes his responsibilities seriously.' Her lips curved in a wistful smile. 'I also know you'd never neglect a child of yours.'

'Of course not.' His lips thinned as he thought of the work still to be done to protect the rights of children, and others needing help, in his province.

'Of course not.' She twisted her hands and suddenly it was she holding him, her fingers on his soft yet strong. Ripples of illicit pleasure radiated from her touch.

'I saw you with that toddler. You didn't just save him, you cradled him and comforted him till his mother was calm enough to hold him. Then you made sure all the others were okay too, especially the teenager who blamed herself for not noticing he'd gone. You were gentle and understanding.'

'Anyone would do the same.' His voice was threadbare, stretched tight by the feel of Soraya holding him so tenderly. How he'd longed for her touch.

He should move away.

'Not everyone. Especially when the child was promptly sick

everywhere.' Her smile as she met his eyes was beguiling. He felt its impact deep in his diaphragm. 'You're a natural with kids. You'd be wonderful with your own.'

Suddenly he didn't need to break her hold. She did it, wrapping her arms around herself, as if chilled despite the balmy evening.

He wanted to comfort her, knowing from her stricken expression she felt pain. But he didn't trust himself to hold her then let her go.

'Anyway,' she said briskly, looking at a point near his shoulder. 'When the uprising occurred, my father sided with the Emir. In fact, he was with him when the palace was stormed. He was injured protecting the Emir and apparently it was the sight of blood drawn in the royal council-room that shocked the more sensible leaders into negotiation. The Emir always said my dad saved his life as well as the peace of the nation.'

'I've heard the story. But I hadn't realised that was your father.'

Soraya lifted her shoulders. 'It was a long time ago and I don't think either of them like to talk about it. Later, when my father got sick, the Emir did something truly extraordinary.' Her pale face lifted and he saw a genuine smile there, like a beacon in the shadows. 'He gave a kidney to save my father.'

'I had no idea.' Zahir was stunned. It must have happened the year he'd been sent to study in the USA. 'They kept it very quiet. I've heard nothing about it.'

No wonder. For a nation's ruler to risk his wellbeing like that was almost incomprehensible. Zahir could think of no other who would do it. But Hussein was in a class of his own.

'It's easy to thank someone, but to repay a debt like that…' Soraya shook her head.

'He's a special man.' Zahir had known that since he was four.

'Yes.' Her dark eyes clung to his. 'He is. So when he asked for marriage, my father was thrilled. He knew I'd be marrying the very best of men.'

Zahir nodded, unable to fault her father's logic, even though thinking of her with Hussein made hot pincers tear at his innards.

'So you see,' she added in a low voice that tugged at him, 'I have every reason to marry him and none to refuse.'

'Except you don't love him.'

Her eyes widened but the surprise on her face was nothing to his own. Since when had romantic love featured as even a passing fantasy in his thoughts?

He knew all about dynastic marriages. He'd make one himself one day. He'd tasted love at nineteen and thought his life blighted when his beloved's father had deemed him, the bastard son of a traitor, not a worthy son-in-law. From that day he'd devoted himself to proving himself better and stronger than all his peers.

'No.' Soraya didn't meet his eyes. 'I don't love him.'

Her words hung like a benediction in the air. Zahir's heart felt full.

'But he's a good man. A decent man,' she murmured. 'I owe him my father's life. Without the Emir I would have lost him years ago.'

'So you're repaying the debt.'

She nodded and Zahir had to quell the impatient urge to say the debt had been cancelled with Hussein's actions. It was Hussein who'd owed Soraya's father. But there was no point. He read determination in her fine features. Besides, how could he urge her to go against her conscience?

He could offer her no alternative. Not when he was bound by every tie of loyalty, duty and love to deliver her to Hussein. Not when the alternative would make her a social pariah, an outcast even to her family.

'What of your own dreams? Your aspirations?' The words spilled from him. He'd heard enough about her work to know she needed more from life. The idea of her as no more than a prop to grace Hussein's regal table and be by his side at official functions seemed a travesty. Soraya had so much more to offer.

'My dreams have changed.' Again that small, wistful smile.

'When I was young I had grandiose dreams of helping the nation. Now I…'

She shook her head. 'Now I have the qualifications to do something really useful for our people. I'm hoping the Emir will let me use those skills to support some innovation. We have the resources, and know how in Bakhara to bring power to the outlying regions, for a start.'

'Is that all you want? The good of others?'

Something flared in her eyes, an emotion almost too painful to watch.

'In Paris I'd begun to dream of a different future,' she murmured. 'Where *I* got to choose for myself. I'd follow my career, spread my wings, make my own mistakes.' Her lips twisted. 'I learned how much fun it was to make friends with other women, not because they were from the right families or because we studied together, but because we clicked. I discovered a weakness for philosophical debate and pop music and fantastic shoes.' She lifted her shoulders. 'Nothing earth-shattering or important. Nothing worth pining over.'

Except it was important to her: the right to choose her own path. She'd said as much in his arms on Bastille Day—that there was nothing as important as freedom. He ached at the thought of what she would give up.

'What about you, Zahir? What do you dream of?'

His dreams? Why did they seem less vivid than before?

'Hussein is making me governor of our largest province. It's the province my father misruled as a despot and it will be my job to make it flourish and prosper.'

He waited for the pleasure he usually experienced as he thought of the challenge ahead. The satisfaction of knowing he'd be redressing the depredations of his father.

Nothing came. Not even pride at the fact Hussein valued and trusted him with this important role.

Instead his eyes locked on Soraya's and something swelled between them. An understanding, an emotion he didn't dare name. His body was aflame and the need to touch her again was a compulsion.

Abruptly Zahir stepped back. He kept moving, needing distance before he forgot sense.

He ignored the over-bright shimmer in her eyes and the down-turned curve of her lips as she watched him go. 'I need to talk to our host,' he said.

'Zahir?' He stopped, heart hammering at the sound of his name on her lips.

'Yes?'

'I'm doing the right thing. Aren't I?'

His head whipped round and again that thwack to the solar plexus hit him when her eyes met his.

He breathed deep and searched for the right answer.

He could find none that would satisfy both conscience and desire.

'You're doing the honourable thing.' His voice rang hollow in the silence.

As he forced himself to walk away, he knew for the first time in his life that honour wasn't enough.

CHAPTER ELEVEN

SORAYA paced the luxury hotel-suite, ignoring the view of a quaint Roman square as the sky morphed from peach and bronze to shades of violet and indigo.

Once she'd have watched enthralled, thrilled by the vibrant, fascinating city of Rome. She'd have revelled in today's sightseeing, the historic sites, the curious byways and above all the people, so full of life and energy.

Yet the city had passed in a blur, overshadowed by the fact this was the end.

The end of her freedom.

The end of her time with Zahir.

Her heart shuddered to a halt then picked up again unsteadily.

Rome was their last stop. Tomorrow they'd board a royal jet that would take them to Bakhara.

Desperation was a coiling queasiness in her stomach, a rusty taste on her tongue, as if she'd drawn blood when she bit her lip.

Tomorrow she'd face the man who would become her husband. She was no nearer finding the equanimity she needed for that than when Zahir had broken the news.

Zahir.

She clutched at a velvet curtain for support, reliving the delicious feel of his hair in her hands as they kissed.

That kiss had blasted away the convenient platitudes she'd

hidden behind. It had revealed in shocking, glorious detail how much she wanted him. How much she needed him.

Heat consumed her. Was she so like her mother? So weak in the face of sexual desire? In the face of love?

Yet this didn't feel like weakness. It felt like strength, light and honesty. A heady euphoria edged with terrible fear that it could never be.

She'd tried to convince herself she couldn't be in love with anyone so aloof and bossy. But the frightening man she'd met in Paris wasn't the real Zahir.

Zahir was proud and inclined to take the lead, but he wasn't a bully. He went out of his way to visit places she had her heart set on, patiently waiting as she combed markets, hunting gifts for her dad and Lisle. He took pleasure in the same things she did, chatting to farmers about the harvest, playing with the local kids. He was warm-hearted and caring. A man generous with his time.

He'd continued her lessons daily till she could swim unaided, determined she'd be safe in the water. He'd stuck to his promise despite the strain of those lessons.

Zahir was excellent company, even if he kept a conspicuous distance from her.

How she craved his touch. His affection.

He felt something for her, she knew it. It was there in his carefully blanked expression and in the fierce, possessive light in his eyes when she caught him off guard.

The memory of that look melted her bones.

She loved him. Yet they couldn't be together. The thought scooped a gaping hole inside her chest.

She was destined for the man who'd given her back her father when she'd been about to lose him. Who'd given her years she'd feared she'd never have. Who'd honoured her with his proposal. By all accounts he'd been a faithful and caring husband to his first wife. Soraya knew he'd respect and care for her. *But it wasn't enough.*

She'd been an innocent ever to think devotion to her country or even her career was enough.

Why couldn't she have love too?

The dangerous thought eddied in her brain.

There were a multitude of reasons she couldn't have Zahir's love. She couldn't ask him to run away with her and betray the man he looked on as his father.

Yet she yearned for him with every cell in her body.

Was it too much to ask for a taste of that forbidden dream? For a morsel to comfort her in the long days ahead when she lived not for herself but for her country and the man who, however decent, could never be Zahir?

Soraya's breath escaped in a whoosh. She'd feared she shared her mother's weakness. But her mother had been in love with the idea of falling in love. Instinctively Soraya knew there'd be no other man after Zahir. He was the one. As for the future—that was immutable. She'd be faithful to the man she married.

But couldn't she allow herself a taste of love to sustain her through a future that loomed barren and bare? Just one night?

Zahir was unbuttoning his sleeves as he pushed open the door to his room. He needed a cold shower. Better yet, a couple of hours in the hotel's gym, then a cold shower. Though he knew it wouldn't help. His mind would be full of…

'Soraya!'

He slammed to a stop just inside the room.

Like an answer to forbidden cravings there she was, standing silhouetted by the glow of a bedside lamp. The soft light lingered lovingly on her ripe figure and his throat closed as all his blood drained south. Her hair was down in dark, rich waves that begged for his touch.

'What are you wearing?' His voice was a hoarse rasp.

She fiddled with the tie at her waist but said nothing. She didn't need to. It was obvious that beneath the embroidered silk wrap she was naked. No strap line marred its smooth texture and she'd done it up so firmly the fabric pulled tight across breasts and hips, cinching in at her waist.

His body raced into sexual overdrive, pulse humming, heat escalating, arousal burgeoning. His breath was choppy as he fought to drag in air.

'Soraya!' Somehow he was walking towards her, though he told himself to keep his distance.

Their gazes collided and he almost groaned at the familiar blast of connection between them.

Her nipples pebbled and his palms ached to reach out and cup the proud bounty of her breasts. Yet he managed to stop a pace away. Desire scorched him. More than desire; a yearning that was as much of the mind as the body. It engulfed him with a force that left him shaking.

'You shouldn't be in here.' It emerged as a plea.

'I couldn't stay away.' She swallowed convulsively and the pulse at the base of her neck raced out of control.

His blood beat just as fast. Just as haphazardly.

How many nights had he dreamed of her coming to him? How many mornings had he lashed himself with guilt over the imaginings he hadn't been able to conquer?

It was wrong. But he couldn't overcome it. He felt too much for her. He wanted her as he'd never wanted in his life. That alone told him how dangerous this was.

Soraya trembled as his gaze devoured her. A muscle worked in Zahir's jaw and she felt the tension come off him in great waves. His hands twitched and she wanted them on her. Surely his touch would relieve the ache deep inside?

'I want to make love with you, Zahir.' A weight lifted off her chest with the words and she dragged in her first free breath since she'd come to his room. 'Please.'

He stood stock-still. If she didn't know better, she'd swear he didn't even breathe.

Fear warred with hope. Grabbing the last of her courage she stepped forward, till the heat of his body encompassed her. Still he said nothing, didn't move a muscle. It was as if he'd locked down, rejecting her and what was between them.

Soraya refused to give in so easily. With a daring she didn't know she had, she reached out and grabbed his hand, placing it on her breast.

Instantly his fingers tightened, cupping her, and she swayed against him, captive to sweet, unfamiliar sensations. Fiery threads unravelled from her breast to her belly and lower, to the place where the ache was strongest and she felt hollow with need.

Gently he squeezed and she moaned as pleasure coursed through her. Much as she'd craved his touch, she just hadn't *known*…

She rose on tiptoe and pressed a kiss to his mouth. But at the last moment he moved and her lips landed on the sandpapery skin of his unshaved jaw.

An instant later his hands bit into her upper arms and he put her from him. Cruel fear invaded her bones as she looked into flinty eyes.

'Don't, Soraya.' His voice was harsh.

'Please, Zahir. I love you.' The words came out in a rush, but she couldn't regret them, even as she saw his head rear back in shock. She put her hands on his restraining arms and felt the muscles bunch and tighten. 'I thought—'

'You *didn't* think!' He almost spat the words as he let her go and strode away across the room. 'How could you even consider coming to my room like this?' He braced himself against the far wall, his head hanging down between wide shoulders that rose and fell with each huge breath.

Despair welled. He was rejecting her.

Soraya knew this was her only chance. She had to make him understand.

A moment later she stood beside him, her hands busy with the tie of her robe.

'What are you doing?' His voice was hoarse.

'Showing you I know exactly what I'm doing.' She paused

and hefted in a shuddery breath. 'It's true, Zahir. I love you.' The whispered words sounded loud in the stillness. 'I didn't want to. I didn't plan it. But I…' Welling emotion choked her. 'I can't pretend it hasn't happened. I can't face the future without knowing just once what it's like to be yours.'

Finally her clumsy fingers managed to unknot the belt. She tore it open and shrugged the silk wrap off her shoulders. It slid down sensitised flesh that tingled as if from a lover's caress.

She jutted her chin high; trying not to cower at the realisation she was naked before his gaze. She felt vulnerable and weak, yet at the same time strangely buoyed, freed for now of the oppressive weight of duty and fear of the future.

Zahir's eyes turned hot and hungry and flames licked her deep inside.

'Please.' Her voice was thick. 'I'm only asking for tonight. Just one night.'

He said nothing. Had she made a terrible mistake?

But Zahir's expression told her she hadn't been mistaken. He did care, did want, just as she did.

She lifted one trembling hand and placed it on his chest. Beneath her palm he felt strong and warm. His heart thudded as quickly as hers. They both felt this yearning. She dragged in a deep, relieved breath and with it Zahir's intoxicating scent.

'Don't!' In a blur of movement he grabbed her hand and threw it off.

Shocked, Soraya stared up at a face of fury. The glitter in his green eyes was lethal, the twist of his mouth scornful.

She backed away a pace.

He followed, his face a mask of contempt.

'Don't think you can come to my room like some…some *whore* and tempt me into betraying Hussein.' His coruscating glare lashed her from top to toe and Soraya shrivelled as if under a whip.

'I thought better of you, Soraya.'

Despite the roar of blood in her ears, she thought she heard anguish in his voice. She must have imagined it.

'You go to your husband tomorrow and it won't be with my touch still warm on your body.' He looked away as if the sight of her sickened him. 'Get dressed and go to your room.' He was still speaking as he strode away and yanked the door open.

A moment later the door of the suite slammed behind him.

Blessed silence descended but in Soraya's head his words ran over and over.

A whore. He'd called her a whore!

With a muffled cry of pain Soraya lifted a shaky hand to her mouth, trying to keep back the bile that surged in her throat. Her legs gave way and she found herself huddled on the carpet.

Hours later Zahir stalked across the square towards their hotel. Even the Italians, who seemed to come alive in the evening, had vanished from the streets.

He was alone. Except he bore in his heart the image of Soraya, naked and impossibly tempting, offering herself to him as if he deserved such bounty.

Soraya, flinching under the despicable words he'd thrown at her in a last-ditch effort to shore up his rapidly failing control, when all he'd wanted was to gather her to him and learn the secrets of her beautiful body.

He felt sick with a pain no distance or mindless exercise could numb. How could he have treated her so? In his heart he'd recognised her desperation and need, for didn't he feel them too? To lash out at her had been more than cruel—it had been unforgivable.

Nevertheless, he'd apologise as soon as she woke in the morning. Before they boarded the plane for Bakhara and her bridegroom.

In the hotel doorway he faltered, his hand going out to steady himself as turbulent emotions threatened to unman him. Grief, loss, shame and unrepentant longing.

'Signor?' The concierge moved forward but Zahir waved him away and made for the lifts.

He'd walked the streets for hours and was no nearer finding peace.

It was past time he returned, even if guarding Soraya from harm on this last night seemed like a contradiction in terms. With her pleading eyes, sweetly feminine body and throaty voice telling him she loved him, she was the most dangerous being on the planet.

She made him believe what he felt was meant to be.

Instead his logical brain reminded himself that he'd eschewed love since he was nineteen, preferring to deal with lust. That she was promised to Hussein. That he owed Hussein everything and couldn't betray him.

His heart was heavy as he opened the door of the suite. The lights were on. Hadn't she gone to bed yet?

He'd assumed she'd be locked in her room. Adrenalin surged at the prospect of seeing her again.

For he wanted—more than wanted. He needed her with every breath of his being. How he'd cope after he delivered her to Hussein, he had no idea.

The door to his room was open, the lights on. Surely she wasn't…? No. It was empty. A shuddering breath escaped. Was it relief or regret that made his heart pump faster?

He turned back into the foyer, intending to turn off the lights in the rest of the suite, when he noticed Soraya's door wide-open.

Frowning, he paced closer. The overhead light blazed on an empty room. A familiar splash of champagne silk sprawled across the corner of the bed, trailing onto the floor. He picked it up, inhaling the scent of wildflowers. The fabric was cold to the touch.

The hair on Zahir's nape rose as he knocked on her bathroom door. When there was no response he jerked it open, only to find it empty.

Apprehension skittered down his spine as his senses went on alert. There was no sound in the suite as he strode from room to room, flinging open doors, hauling curtains back from the wall, even checking cupboards.

By the time he'd rung reception to discover Soraya had left no message, and double-checked every hiding place, he was in a cold sweat.

Returning to her bedroom, he rifled through her belongings: suitcase, clothes, purse and laptop. Even her passport and mobile phone were there.

Where was she?

Zahir scowled at the meagre collection of belongings, as if they could tell him what he needed to know.

Twenty minutes later the hotel had been searched from top to bottom, but there was no sign of Soraya.

Dread curled within him, sending tendrils of fear through his frozen limbs.

He'd done this! With his defensive temper and his unforgivable words. He'd never known such guilt, such fear, as sliced through him now, leaving him bereft and trembling.

Soraya was alone in an unfamiliar city at a time when honest people were off the streets. Only the foolhardy or dangerous prowled the city at this time.

Panic swamped him.

He strode to the window and stared at the empty square as if sheer desperation could conjure her. Somewhere out there, distressed and defenceless, was the woman he'd sworn to protect. The woman he cared for.

If anything happened to her…

Soraya put one foot in front of the other and plodded on. She was near the hotel but the fact she couldn't remember its exact location didn't bother her. She'd prefer never to return.

Yet the future had to be faced.

A hollow laugh escaped her. Weeks ago she'd thought life couldn't get worse than an arranged marriage. She'd fretted over it till she had felt sick with anxiety.

Now she knew what real despair was.

To marry one man while loving another.

To have the man she loved despise her for wanting him.

Pain lanced her and she stumbled, putting out her hand to lean against a stone wall. Even now she couldn't stop trembling.

She couldn't remember dressing or leaving the hotel. All she recalled were Zahir's words.

Had she been so wrong? Did he feel nothing for her?

She bent her head till the world stopped spinning. Maybe the grappa had muddled her senses.

She'd been watching water spurt from an old fountain when a motherly looking woman asked if she was all right. According to her, Soraya had been standing there for over an hour.

She'd led Soraya into a tiny courtyard filled with the scent of geraniums and the rumbling purr of a ginger cat. The woman had invited her to sit then pressed a glass of grappa into her unresisting hands. Then she'd taken the other seat and tilted a lamp towards her embroidery.

How long she'd sat there, Soraya didn't know. She'd lost track of time, soothed by the rhythm of the cat's breathing as it stretched across her lap and the chatter of a late-night radio talk show.

Finally she'd noticed the weariness on the other woman's face and, thanking her for her kindness, made her way onto the deserted street. Now she just had to find her way back. A shudder racked her at the idea of facing Zahir's piercing disapproval. But she had no choice.

After all, what more could he do? Her heart had already splintered into raw, jagged pieces.

From somewhere she dredged the strength to walk on. She'd covered just a metre when a figure came in view. A tall man with a purposeful stride.

Instantly she shrank back, her heart battering her ribs. In her dazed state he looked too much like…

'Soraya!'

He sprinted, his feet pounding the pavement, and before she

could gather her wits to retreat he was there, his hands on her shoulders, gripping her tight.

'Are you all right?' He didn't wait for her answer but ran his hands lightly across her shoulders, arms and face, as if needing to feel for himself that she was whole.

'Don't touch me!' She stumbled back a step till she collided with a wall but he followed, hemming her in.

'Tell me you're unhurt.' His voice was as raw as hers. In the dim light she almost didn't recognise him. He seemed to have aged a decade in one evening. 'Please, Soraya!' His fingers shook as he smoothed the hair back from her face. Something sharp twisted inside.

'I'm fine,' she said over a lump of congealing emotion. 'Don't worry; you don't have to soil your hands by touching me.' Though for one precious moment she let herself believe his concern was for her personally, not because he'd committed to bring her back in one piece.

'Soraya. Don't.'

Before her stunned gaze, Zahir dropped to his knees. He gripped her fingers in an unbreakable hold and pressed fervent kisses to the back of one hand then the other.

'Zahir?' Her befuddled brain couldn't grasp the change in him. To have him literally at her feet was unthinkable. His arrogant rejection was too fresh in her mind. Yet there he was, wretchedness written on his once-proud features.

He made her heart turn over despite her anger.

'I'm sorry.' He looked up, his gaze fiercely direct and a wave of emotion rocked her back on her heels. 'What I said to you.' He shook his head. 'It was unforgivable, as well as being untrue.'

His hands tightened and with a sense of wonder she read desperation in his grim visage.

'I lashed out because I felt myself crumbling.' He tore in a ragged breath that pumped his chest hard. 'Every word you spoke pulled me closer to deserting my principles, my duty, my loyalty. You *scared* me.'

He shook his head, though his eyes never wavered from hers. 'I wanted you so badly—*still* want you—it was torture having you offer yourself when I was so weak.'

'You want me?' Her heartbeat stalled.

'How could I not?' His voice was hoarse, his breath hot against her hands. 'I've desired you from the moment I saw you in that club. Every day and every night you fill my waking thoughts as well as my dreams. Soraya. Can you ever forgive me? To call you that…' His breath shuddered out in a rattling rasp. 'You were being honest, when I couldn't even face what I felt.'

He threaded his fingers through hers, turned her hands to plant heated kisses on her palms. Tremors of sensation shot up her arms, to her breasts and down to her womb. Her knees shook so hard she thought they'd give way.

'What do you feel, Zahir?' Soraya was light-headed, overloaded on emotion. She gripped his fingers hard, knowing it was only the current of energy flowing between them that gave her strength to stand.

'This.'

He was on his feet, looking down at her with an expression that melted her bones. His palms were strong and warm on her cheeks, his breath a ripple of heady pleasure as it caressed her lips.

Instinctively her lips parted as, with a groan, he lowered his mouth.

Their lips met and the world exploded. Caution vanished, incinerated by the fierce need devouring them.

Soraya sagged against Zahir, clinging to his broad shoulders as he took her mouth in a kiss that devastated and fulfilled. It pulsed with raw, unvarnished desire and sweetest longing. Soraya couldn't get enough.

His body pressed against hers from thigh to chest, imprinting her with his heat, his hunger. And she was just as eager. Just as unrestrained.

Their lips mashed as she kissed him with more fervour than

expertise. He gathered her close, his hands proprietorial as they stroked down her back till she arched high against him, eager for greater contact.

An instant later he stepped back, despite her moan of protest. Before she could complain, he hoisted her into his embrace and held her close to his pounding heart.

'Not here,' he growled in an unrecognisable voice that set off sparks of excitement deep in her belly.

He turned and strode towards the hotel, a man on a mission. 'We need privacy.'

CHAPTER TWELVE

ZAHIR's hold remained unbreakable as they entered the suite and the door crashed closed behind them.

Soraya carried jumbled impressions of the hotel foyer and the gawping receptionist's stunned expression, though Zahir hadn't slowed his purposeful stride long enough for her to feel anything but excitement at his possessive hold.

The mirrored lift to the penthouse suite reflected Zahir's granite-set visage, his jaw angled in a way that warned he'd brook no interference. No wonder the receptionist had stayed safely behind his desk.

Zahir's expression sent a wave of pleasure coursing through her. A purely feminine pleasure of anticipation.

His pace didn't falter as they crossed the suite's foyer. Lamplight beckoned them into his room where light spilled across the sprawling bed.

Zahir slammed to a stop and in the quiet Soraya heard only their breathing, merging like a single heartbeat, fast and eager.

'Soraya.' It wasn't Zahir's voice; not the easy, calm voice she'd come to know. This sound was dredged from the depths of a tortured soul.

She shivered luxuriously as it wrapped around her, connecting to a deep, visceral part of her.

This was unknown territory yet the world had never felt so right as in his arms. Doubt and uncertainty fled before the force of them together: Zahir the epitome of conquering male, and she all melting, wanting female.

He lowered her to her feet, sliding centimetre by slow centimetre down his taut frame till she was strung so tight with need she could barely stand. She leaned in, latching needy fingers around his strong neck so she could feel his hot flesh.

That simple contact was almost unbearably wonderful.

'If you don't want this, say so,' he groaned, his lips a caress against her hair that set a whole new set of nerve endings into spasms of delight. 'Soraya!' His chest expanded mightily as he dragged in air. 'I can let you go but you have to tell me. Now!'

The way his big hands claimed her hips, pulling her up against him so she felt the rigid length of his erection, it seemed impossible he'd ever release her. Yet she knew his formidable will-power.

'No! Don't let me go.' Part demand, part plea, her words were harsh in the thundering silence.

Don't let me go, ever.

For ever. That was how long she wanted Zahir. She needed him in her life always.

She loved him with a raw, soul-deep passion that cut so deep she knew she'd carry it with her the rest of her life.

Soraya felt a great sigh of relief pass through him and recognised the unsteadiness in his touch—it was the same for her. Zahir needed her so vehemently, so completely he burned up with it. His flesh was hot beneath her fingers and tremors coursed his body.

A lifetime's reserve and caution disintegrated under the onslaught of feelings that welled free at last. Zahir's hot skin against her fingers was a benediction. She watched his brilliant eyes, heavy-lidded and mysterious as he drank in the sight of her.

The way he looked at her…

She slid her hands to his collar and with one quick tug wrenched it open.

His chest, contoured muscle and flesh dusted with dark

hair, beckoned. Her heart galloped as she spread her fingers wide, learning him.

My love.

She leaned in, breathing deep the intoxicating essence of him. Of the man she loved with all her being.

'Soraya.' She felt the breath rise in his chest as his voice trailed across her skin. Still their gazes locked.

The world stopped as they trembled on the brink.

Then, with magnificent disregard for her wardrobe, Zahir copied her action. Yet when he took her dress in his big hands and yanked, the silk ripped. It tore so far it was the work of a moment for him to slide it off her shoulders. The fabric slithered down her body in a furtive caress that made goose bumps prickle her flesh.

She hardly noticed, for the look in Zahir's eyes blotted all else from her mind.

Words poured from his lips, a whispered stream of praise and thanks as his gaze followed her dress down, then rose again to her now-rosy cheeks. That hoarse litany of heartfelt appreciation was enough to make any woman blush.

'No woman is perfect, Zahir.'

Why she demurred, she didn't know, except perhaps that he overwhelmed her. She wished she could be perfect—for him. The heated intensity of his stare, the guttural depth of emotion in his voice made her feel for a moment like the goddess he described.

How could any woman live up to that?

'Yet you are perfect, *habibti*.' He looked into her eyes and she felt that half-familiar shudder rip through her from the impact of an unseen force. 'To me you are.'

The glow in his eyes made her heart swell.

He said more but it was muffled against her throat as he kissed her. She tilted her head back in ecstasy and he lashed an arm around her waist to keep her from falling.

Yet she fell. Into a vortex of tumbling emotion and sensations.

It wasn't just the pleasure of his kiss. It was the way he made her feel: treasured, appreciated, loved.

This time when his hand cupped her breast it wasn't at her clumsy invitation. Zahir's was an expert's touch, moulding, caressing, teasing till wildfire roared through her to rush in a whirlpool of heat between her legs.

Her hands slid to the smooth flesh of his shoulders as he bowed her back, further and further, till she lay draped across his arm. His mouth closed over her breast through the filmy lace of her bra and she whimpered in delight, her fingers clutching at him frantically.

'Zahir.' Did that low, keening throb of sound come from her?

'You have no idea how much I want you.' His lips moved across her breast and throat as he spoke. 'I've tried to resist but I'm only human.'

'I don't want you to resist,' she gasped.

'Just as well.' He licked her nipple and her breath clogged in her throat. 'I couldn't stop now to save myself.'

She felt the mattress beneath her and when his arms came away from behind her they dragged her bra too. Dazed, she watched it arc over Zahir's shoulder as he stripped her panties and shoes away.

She should feel nervous as he ate her up with his eyes. Despite a lifetime's modesty, she couldn't. Not when the pride and pleasure in his expression made her feel like a queen.

He braced his arms wide and a shiver of delicious trepidation shot through her at the sensation of being surrounded by such a virile, dominant male. But, instead of lowering himself to her, he retreated down the bed.

Anticipation hummed through her, knowing that soon, when he'd stripped his trousers off, they'd…

'Zahir?'

'It's all right, little one.' His deep voice reassured but she couldn't relax, not when he settled himself deep between the V of her legs, splayed wide by his gently insistent hands.

'What are you…?' A hiss of indrawn breath clotted the

words in her throat. First his hand and then his mouth stroked her there, where need throbbed strongest.

Soraya's whole body jerked hard, as if from an electric shock. But this was pleasure, pure pleasure so intense it overwhelmed her senses.

One caress, another, and she almost lifted off the bed, held in place only by Zahir's solid weight as a shower of sparks ignited in her blood.

She needed to escape, keep some fragment of control, but delight as well as his imprisoning body kept her there, splayed and open before him.

Her eyelids drooped. Her mouth sagged as she gasped in another raw breath and suddenly, like a roiling tide that grew till it blotted out the world, ecstasy engulfed her. She shook and sobbed with the force of it, abandoned to a delight so intense she could never have imagined it.

A delight of Zahir's giving. Through the maelstrom her hand gripped his where it rested on her thigh. That was her lifeline, her connection to him.

Finally, as she lay spent and gasping, he slid from her grasp. She roused herself to protest, but the press of his mouth to the flesh above her hipbone stifled her words. Just the touch of his lips there evoked a pleasure she should be too spent to feel. His hands skimmed her lightly and she shifted under his touch, like a cat curving into a petting hand.

Except Zahir's hands moved with deliberate, erotic delicacy that soon had fire running in her veins again.

'Come to me?'

At her husky plea, his head lifted. Soraya's heart somersaulted as she saw how the skin dragged taut over those strong features. His eyes held a febrile glitter that spoke of fierce yearning.

'Not yet.'

'Why not?' She grasped his shoulders and tried to haul him close. It was like trying to loosen bedrock. 'Please.'

'I can't.' He shook his head. 'I have no control left. Once I…'

'Don't you understand?' Her voice shook. 'I don't care about subtleties or control. *I need you.* Just you.'

Soraya's heart gave a great leap as she read relief in his face and eagerness. She watched, mesmerized, as he reared up, dragging his clothes off.

She'd seen his body before at the pool, but now, in the golden glow of the lamp, he was hers. Her gaze lingered on the strong, lithe form of the man she loved. Even his scars, reminders of the dangerous life he'd led, seemed precious. Her pulse raced as she read the taut power in his heavy thighs, the wide span of his shoulders and the arrogant jut of his erection. As she stared he smoothed on protection.

She licked her lips, her mouth dry. But as he prowled up the bed, caging her with his body, Soraya felt no hesitancy, just gratitude and fizzing anticipation.

A mew of delight escaped her as he settled over her. To feel his chest against hers, the fuzz of his hair tickling her nipples, the smooth heat of his belly against hers—she hadn't known that alone would be bliss.

Hands tunnelling through his thick hair, she kissed him with all the love and wonder burgeoning within. His response was all she could have hoped for. Tender yet urgent, lavishly satisfying, even as her body stirred anew at the masculine weight pressed high between her legs.

'Soraya.' It was a groan of need as he centred himself above her.

'Yes.' She kissed him feverishly, holding him tight, almost afraid to believe this was real.

Then anticipation shattered, as with one surging movement he thrust sure and strong.

Her eyes sprang open. She was stunned by his overwhelming weight, the fullness that surely was impossible despite being so patently real. She was pinioned in a way that made something like panic rise and spread.

Her breath hitched and she forgot how to breathe as her body locked in shock.

She heard Zahir's heartbeat, loud as her own, fast as her own, and his laboured breathing, harsh in the stillness.

Dazed, Soraya groped for the pleasure that till a second ago had hummed in her needy body. She found only blankness.

'Breathe, *habibti.*' Zahir nuzzled the tender skin below her ear. 'Breathe for me.'

It wasn't his command that broke her stasis but the tiny shimmy of delight raying from the point where he kissed her.

He kissed her again, taking his time to lave her pulse-point and she dragged in a shuddering breath, her chest rising beneath his. Her skin tingled at the friction between their bodies and her next breath was deeper, filled with the male scent of him.

Zahir insinuated his hand between them to touch her breast, plucking delicately at her nipple, and a judder of heat rippled through her. Her frozen limbs eased a fraction and her stunned rigidity eased, replaced by a different, delicious tension.

Slowly, lavishly, Zahir seduced her mouth with his till the hint of panic eased.

'That's my girl. It's all right, see?' He moved, withdrawing from her little by little, till she missed the press of his body above hers and even the strange, too-full sensation of his possession.

Instinctively she slanted her pelvis and he responded with another thrust, this time claiming her body centimetre by slow centimetre. Now the sensations he wrought brought fire to her blood and a different sort of tension.

'Zahir!'

He lifted his head to see her face. To her shock he looked to be in pain, his features pinched. Yet his eyes blazed with a brilliance that stole her breath all over again.

Her hand lifted to his cheek. Tenderness filled her as she read what it cost him not to take as his body dictated, but to harness his impulses.

'Tell me what to do.' She felt so useless.

His lips quirked in a brief smile that looked more like a grimace. 'Lift your legs.' He nodded as she complied. 'Higher. Around my waist.'

Soraya tentatively followed his instructions as Zahir once more slid away, then back with an ease that evoked a stab of pleasure.

Her eyes widened. 'That feels…'

'It does, doesn't it?' His eyelids drooped till she saw only slits of dark green. One more easy thrust and this time she anticipated him, rocking up and back with Zahir, eliciting another sharp pulse of pleasure.

She tightened her hold, wanting to comfort him even as another rush of erotic sensation undermined thought.

They rocked together, finding a rhythm so excruciatingly slow it alternately stoked her arousal to fever pitch and satisfied it with a blinding flash of searing pleasure. The pleasure was the greater for seeing its reflection in Zahir's face.

Each dazzling, joyous pinnacle was shared so intimately it seemed they were one, their bodies moving in tandem, their minds linked as they shared something profound.

Finally, after what seemed a lifetime, pleasure crescendoed. Soraya's eyes fluttered shut and she clung to Zahir as, with a rush, their mutual climax splintered thought in a crash of crystal shards.

The sound of her name on Zahir's lips echoed through the velvet darkness that claimed her.

Zahir paced back from the bathroom into the darkened bedroom.

Was she asleep? He hoped so. He had to think, had to come to grips with what they'd done.

What *he'd* done.

Never, since the day Hussein had rescued him from his father, had Zahir acted on pure instinct without thought or plan.

Never had he acted solely on what he felt.

Until now.

Even at nineteen, when he'd fallen hard for the daughter of

the palace's head groom, he hadn't behaved rashly. He'd thought himself in the throes of love yet he'd never put a foot out of line, courting carefully, respectfully—till her father had put an end to his aspirations, rejecting him as too young, too lacking in prospects, the son of a dishonourable man.

Yet as Zahir neared the bed and saw Soraya, her hair a lush curtain that allowed glimpses of her silvered skin in the moonlight, he felt more than ever in his life.

He wanted her, craved her with all the longing in his battered heart. A heart she'd reawakened.

He wanted to drown out the world in the heady pleasure of her soft embrace.

He wanted that searing sense of rightness, of homecoming, of ecstasy as he became more than just the man he was, stronger for being part of Soraya.

Something tugged hard in his chest as he halted by the bed. He groped for control. Then her eyes opened, dark and fathomless as a desert sky. Her lips curved in a smile so tender it made his heart throb in a new, unfamiliar rhythm.

'Zahir.' The whisper of her sweet voice saying his name was devastating as an earthquake. He trembled at the impact. When she reached out to him that last, almost-sane part of his brain shut down.

He snatched her hand, cupping it so he could press urgent kisses to her palm. Her luxuriant ripple of pleasure was enough to dislodge any foggy shreds of sanity.

'Soraya.' His voice was raw with all he felt and could no longer deny.

Then he was with her, flesh to flesh, his rough body grazing her softness, his aching groin against her tender belly. He tried to hold back, to restrain himself, but she confounded him, her lips at his throat, stalling his breath in his lungs. Then her hand, small and smooth, curled around his erection and his heart stopped.

He surged against her palm, unable to prevent himself, revelling in her gentle, clumsy hold that was more erotic than that of the most practised seductress.

Zahir tugged her close, hands sliding on rippling tresses and satiny skin.

Now she found her rhythm, encircling him in long strokes that drew him tight and rigid as a bow.

It was ecstasy so potent it bordered on agony.

'You have to stop.' He reached for her hand. The rest of his words dried as he held her, holding him. A great shudder passed through him as he groped for something, anything, that would stop him succumbing.

'You don't like it?' Doubt or excitement in her voice? He couldn't tell over the drumming pulse in his ears.

She moved and the caress of her long hair over his shoulders and down his heaving chest drove his desperation to new levels. Her skin, her voice, her hair, her touch; everything about Soraya destroyed him. His limbs lost their strength, his resistance shattered, as she pressed her lips to his collarbone and chest, her nipples grazing his belly in swaying strokes that drove spikes of raw need through him, puncturing resistance and good intentions.

His hands fisted in her hair, holding her tight as she slithered lower.

Her tongue flicked him gently, tasting him, and he bucked, helpless beneath her. Only his grip on her scalp remained strong.

Her lips opened and he was lost.

CHAPTER THIRTEEN

It was late when Soraya woke. She knew without looking that Zahir had gone. She sensed it, just as she always knew when he was near.

Through the night and the early hours they'd lain in each other's arms, always touching. The sound of his breathing had lulled her to sleep after their tumultuous lovemaking.

Her skin glowed, her heart sang, her body throbbed with a pleasurable ache. Her limbs were heavy as if they'd never move again, yet at the same time light, as though she still floated on a plane where nothing existed save herself and the man she loved.

She opened her eyes and saw it was broad daylight. Her heart missed a beat.

She'd tasted bliss but now the real world intruded. She'd known for one short night what it was to be in the arms of the man she loved.

How could she give that up?

She had no choice. Nothing had changed. All the reasons they couldn't be together still held sway. Zahir knew it too. He'd already gone.

Desperate to see him, she flung off the sheet and rose. Her knees wobbled, weak after last night's loving.

A surge of heat tingled from her feet up to her face. Last night there'd been no embarrassment or thought of modesty, yet this morning, without Zahir's embrace, she found she could still blush.

Her clothes were tumbled on the floor. Instead of wearing them, she hurried to the wardrobe and grabbed the robe hanging there. She fumbled as she shrugged it on and cinched it tight. Her fingers as well as her legs shook.

She needed to see Zahir, to cling to the magic just a little longer, before she closed the door on love for ever.

Just one look, one touch.

He was in the living room, fully dressed as he stared at the busy square below. Disappointment stirred as she took in his wide shoulders in the dark jacket, his powerful legs hidden from view in tailored trousers.

He looked so…formal. After last night's potent virility, these clothes made him appear curiously stiff.

She was halfway across the room when he swung round, an espresso cup in his hand. Her pace slowed as he lifted the cup and took a long sip.

He looked different. It wasn't just the clothes. There was an aura around him that reminded her of the fiercely self-contained man he'd been in Paris.

She blinked as shyness assailed her. How could she be daunted by his business clothes? This was Zahir. The man she adored. The man who, she knew in her heart, loved her too. Given his strength of character nothing but that could have prompted him to spend the night loving her as if there was no tomorrow. The knowledge was poignant pleasure and pain intermingled.

'Good morning.' Her voice was husky. The last time she'd used it was when she'd cried out his name in the throes of passion.

'Good morning.' His black eyebrows were a horizontal smudge above severe features and he gave no answering smile. 'How are you feeling today? Are you all right?' His quick concern warmed her. Zahir had been a demanding lover, passionate, but incredibly tender.

'I feel fabulous.' She refused to think of how she'd feel when it was time to say goodbye.

Soraya's steps faltered and her heart lurched as her eyes locked with his. She found blankness there where before there'd been passion, love and even—she could have sworn—wonder. Ice water trickled down her spine.

'What's wrong?' He held himself so rigidly.

His mouth twisted in a brief, brutal smile that spoke of pain not pleasure. 'You can ask that?'

'Has something happened?' she whispered. 'Is there news from Bakhara?'

His fingers clenched so tight on the coffee cup she thought its handle would snap. 'No news from Bakhara.'

Soraya hefted in a sigh of relief, her hand pressed to her chest. For a moment, reading his serious face, she'd wondered if something had happened to her father.

'You look pale, Soraya. You must be worn-out. Why don't you go back to bed and rest?' He took a couple of paces towards her then pulled up short as if yanked back by an invisible rope. The sight of him stopping that telling distance away made every hair on her body rise. His gaze shifted towards the bedroom and colour streaked his sharp cheekbones. 'You must be sore. Last night I should have…'

'Zahir, I'm okay, *really*. I'm just…' What? Feeling needy? She knew their time was almost over and needed Zahir's embrace just one more time to give her strength to do what she must.

She moved towards him then slammed to a stop as he retreated.

It was just a half-step and he covered it quickly, pretending to cast about for somewhere to put his coffee cup, though there was a table right beside him. Yet she couldn't mistake his instinctive movement.

Her heart crashed against her ribs as disbelief swamped her. She grabbed for the back of the sofa to support herself.

'We need to talk,' he said before she could speak.

She nodded. She could barely believe this was the man she

knew. He was so ill at ease and distant. As if last night had never happened.

Or as if he regretted what they'd done.

A knife twisted in her vitals.

Had he been disgusted by her enthusiasm or her untutored clumsiness? She squashed the idea as absurd. Last night had been indescribable pleasure for both of them. The love between them had made each touch, each sigh, magic. It had been so much more than simple physical gratification.

Soraya flushed at the memories, but another look at Zahir's sombre face made the blood drain from her own.

She told herself he only did what he had to—created the distance that must forever more be between them.

Yet her poor heart yearned for one last touch, one embrace, one whispered word of reassurance. How weak she was.

'I'll make the necessary arrangements. You can leave it all to me.'

'Arrangements?' She tilted her head.

'For our wedding.' His gaze meshed with hers, but Soraya saw only flinty determination in eyes that looked curiously flat. 'In the circumstances it will be a small ceremony, and soon.'

'Wedding?' The word emerged as a breathless gasp. She couldn't be hearing this. Yet a flutter of excitement rippled through her, sabotaging her determination to be stoic as she faced the future.

'We're getting married.' She knew that determined look. He was a man set on a course of action and nothing would deter him. The flutter became a tidal wave of excitement.

'But we can't. There's no way…' She spread her arms, encompassing all the reasons they couldn't be together.

'After last night we must.' Strangely he didn't smile at the memory of what they'd shared. 'I've spent the morning working out a way we can be together.'

'It's impossible.'

'I'll make it possible.' A thrill ripped through her. Zahir would move heaven and earth to achieve what he wanted. Was it possible, after all, that there was a way for them to be together? She hardly dared believe it.

'I'll speak to your father as soon as possible and do my utmost to persuade him this will be in your best interests.' Zahir drew in a breath that made his whole chest rise, as if readying himself for some Herculean task.

Her dad. 'I'll talk to him.'

If there was explaining to be done, she'd do it. He'd be horribly disappointed, and worried—not to mention embarrassed that the royal engagement was off—but he loved her. Surely, eventually, she could make him understand, especially if Zahir had a plan that would lessen the fallout? After all, he understood love.

'No.' Zahir shook his head and straightened his shoulders to stand ramrod-straight. Soraya was reminded of a soldier on parade. 'It's my duty. I'll deal with it.'

It. He made news of their feelings sound like a crime. Soraya clasped clammy hands together as the nervous gyrations of her stomach grew worse.

She understood how dreadful this would be. The shock and dismay they'd cause with their relationship. The gossip. The scandal. But despite it all the promise of a future with Zahir at the end of the trauma made exultation bubble through her veins. For it seemed Zahir believed there really could be a future for them. Despite her best intentions excitement swelled.

No matter what sacrifice it took, she was ready. Nothing was more important than the love they felt.

Yet, she realised now, Zahir looked not like a uniformed officer so much as a man facing a firing squad.

'It's not about duty, Zahir. My father will understand better if I explain.' She wanted to take his hand but he'd shoved his fists deep in his trouser pockets.

What was wrong? If he'd found a way for them to be honest about their love…

His grim expression doused her excitement.

He did love her, didn't he?

The way he'd murmured endearments last night, the fact that he'd taken her to bed despite all she knew of his honour-bound code of conduct, had convinced her he shared the same deep emotion she did.

'Zahir?'

'Of course it's about duty.' Zahir's jaw clenched so hard his face looked painfully tight. A laugh jerked from his lips. The sound of it made the hairs on her nape prickle. 'I was going to say it's a matter of honour, but I have no claim to honour now. Not after last night.'

Raw pain stared out from his face as he turned to her and the bright, fierce joy she nursed close to her heart dimmed. Sensation plunged from her chest right down to her abdomen, like a lift plummeting to catastrophe.

'Of course you do.' She hauled in a difficult breath. 'Last night was about honesty and—'

'Don't!' The harsh syllable stopped her as she leaned forward. 'I dishonoured you last night. And I dishonoured Hussein.' Zahir tugged one hand free of his pocket and rubbed it round the back of his neck as if in pain. 'Not to mention your family and myself.'

Soraya's arm slumped to her side. She told herself it was natural he felt guilty. He wasn't the only one. Even now she felt torn.

'You didn't dishonour me. I chose—'

'Not dishonour you?' His bark of laughter was ugly. 'You were a virgin, Soraya. That privilege should have been your husband's.'

Frantically Soraya fought for calm, reminding herself he only spoke as many in Bakhara did.

'It wasn't a privilege, Zahir. It was a gift. *My* gift.'

He swung away as if he couldn't bear to look at her. 'Do you think I'd have taken you as I did if I'd known?'

Soraya froze. Her labouring lungs atrophied as his words sank in.

She opened her mouth and closed it, grasping for words.

Finally she dredged some from deep in her pain. 'You thought I'd already lost my virginity so it was safe to sleep with me?' A great tearing gasp ripped through her, widening with every second he remained silent. 'You're only offering marriage to make good the damage you've done my reputation?'

'No. Of course not.' Yet his face when he swung around wasn't that of a lover. It belonged to a stranger. A stranger who looked at her and felt only horror for the consequences of what they'd done.

He'd wanted her last night, but not enough to withstand the cold, clear light of a new day. There was no joy on his face at the idea of their future together.

No thought of *them*. Just of duty and dishonour.

Dishonour. The word tainted what they'd shared so gloriously.

What she'd thought they'd shared.

Soraya had shared everything. Herself, her hopes, fears and dreams. Her love.

And Zahir? He regretted last night with a fervour that couldn't be faked. Could it be that he'd shared no more than his virile body? She'd blurted her love for him but he hadn't, even in the most intimate of moments, reciprocated.

Finally she realised how significant that was.

She watched him turn to pace the room, his expression brooding. She had to know the truth. Yet still she hesitated, scared of what his answer might be.

'Zahir? Do you…*care* about me?'

His head jerked up. 'Care?' His brow pleated as if she spoke a foreign tongue. 'Of course I care. I want to *marry* you, Soraya. I want to look after you and protect you. Be assured, I will make it all right.'

All right. Hardly the words of a man in love. He made no mention of joy or anticipation.

Wave after wave of shock passed through Soraya. Her knees weakened and she plopped down onto a nearby chair. The leather was cold against her trembling palms.

Would she ever feel warm again?

That's what love gets you. Nothing but trouble!

Soraya shook her head, as if she could banish the voice of doubt in her head.

But she knew it for the truth. Soraya had always feared love with good reason. Wasn't that why an arranged marriage to the Emir had originally seemed such a safe, appealing option?

She looked up at the man with the closed face, pacing with such ferocious concentration. She couldn't focus on his words over the swelling roar of blood in her ears, but she could make out his tone: cool and clipped. No passion. No emotion. None of the love she'd been so sure he felt.

He was in damage-limitation mode. As if she was a diplomatic tangle to be sorted out. An indiscretion to be dealt with.

Her heart gave a single frantic thud that shook her to the core. To have him hold out hope to her of happiness and then dash it was the cruellest torture of all.

She'd do anything, go anywhere with him, if only he'd ask. *If only he loved her.* But she refused to be nothing more than a mistake to be rectified.

She'd thought his actions were proof of deeper feelings. Yet he'd never spoken the words. Never claimed to love her.

Marrying a man who felt compelled to 'do the right thing' by her could only lead to disaster. Zahir would end up resenting her and she—could she cope with loving him and knowing he didn't feel the same?

'Soraya?' She wasn't listening to him. Zahir jolted to a stop, his gaze straying over her: so sweet, so vulnerable in that oversized robe.

His woman.

Despite the untenable situation he'd put them in, he couldn't help but glory in the fact she was his. Incontrovertibly. Totally. His.

Wildfire shimmered in his blood as he remembered how they'd been together. He wanted to thrust the world aside and lose himself in her. But he had to be strong for both of them. He couldn't contemplate a future without her.

That meant dragging himself far enough away, mentally and physically, to be able to confront the implications of their passion. Touching her would addle his brain. It was imperative he think clearly. Besides, he had no right to touch her until he'd made this right for her.

He had to deal carefully with her family, the public and, above all, Hussein if Soraya was to be able to hold her head up in public.

His lungs squeezed tight as he thought of Hussein. Scalding guilt drenched him.

No matter what he felt for Soraya, nothing excused what he'd done. To Soraya. To his friend and mentor.

She might brush it off as 'honesty' but he knew it for selfish weakness. A strong man would have held back, waited till they got to Bakhara, then declared himself publicly.

What sort of man was he?

He'd prided himself on his loyalty, courage and honour. He was weak to the marrow, a hollow sham of the man he'd believed himself. His loyalty to Hussein, his honour, his intentions, had all disintegrated before Soraya.

Had he fooled himself when he'd pretended he wasn't his father's son? That he was stronger, better, honest? Surely his betrayal of Hussein was far worse than his father's disloyalty? *He was his father's son after all.*

The knowledge threatened everything he knew of himself, his life and aspirations. Yet he couldn't afford to dwell on that now. Not when Soraya needed him.

It hadn't been enough to dress, to avoid touching her, to force himself to focus on the ugly public repercussions. All his efforts to strengthen himself ready to face what must be faced crumbled before her potent presence. He wanted to shun the world and take her back to bed. But the world wouldn't go away.

'Soraya?'

Finally she looked up. Yet it was as if she didn't see him. Her gaze was unfocused, fixed on something far away.

She opened her mouth and spoke, but his brain refused to process what she said. He gazed blankly down at her, willing her to break the nightmare horror that suddenly engulfed him.

He crouched before her, hands planted on the leather sofa on either side of her, trapping her close.

'What did you say?' His voice was a hoarse crack of sound.

Her gaze shifted as if she couldn't bear to meet his eyes. His heart pounded. 'I said I won't marry you.'

Zahir stared, vaguely aware that he was still breathing despite the gaping hollow where his heart had been. How could that be?

'No!' Finally he found his voice. 'You must!' She was his. What they shared had transformed him. Made him realise there was more to life than honour, challenge and duty. What in his youth he'd imagined to be love was nothing compared with this all-consuming emotion.

'Must?' She arched a brow imperiously, like the princess Hussein wanted to make her. Her voice was cool, distancing him. 'You have no right to talk to me about *must*. You may be my bodyguard but you're not my keeper.'

Zahir reeled back on his heels, shock slamming into him. Fire exploded in his belly and crackled along his arteries at her attempt to fob him off.

Fury such as he'd never known blasted through him. She couldn't deny him!

'I'm a hell of a lot more than that.' Fear roughened his voice. He leaned in again, close enough to inhale her scent and feel the rapid flutter of her breath on his face. 'You smell of sex, Soraya. Did you know that? Of my skin on yours. My seed.'

Her eyes rounded, her reddened lips parting, and Zahir wanted more than anything to kiss her into capitulation. Seduce away the idea that they couldn't be together.

Instead he reached for the collar of her robe.

'Here.' He yanked it aside to reveal her collarbone. 'I've left my mark on you.'

He'd felt guilty when he'd realised his unshaven jaw had marked the delicate skin of her throat and breasts.

Now all he felt was primitive satisfaction. Despite his anger and shock, his erection surged against the confines of his clothes. He wanted her with every searing breath in his constricted lungs. Not just the sex. He wanted *her*: the woman who'd changed his life and taught him how to feel.

She shoved his shoulders so abruptly he almost lost his balance. As it was she had time to surge to her feet and stride away across the room before he scrambled to stand. He made to follow her and then stopped, reading the pain on her face. An ache filled his chest.

'So we had sex.' Her voice was bitter, unlike anything he'd ever heard from her lips. 'What do you want? Your name tattooed on my skin?'

He'd settle for her smile. Her heart beating next to his. The knowledge she'd be with him, always.

He shook his head. This wasn't Soraya. Not the loving, generous woman he knew. What had gone wrong? He'd worked so hard, spent hours working out how they could be together permanently, and she was throwing it all away.

'You said yourself last night wouldn't have happened if you'd known I was a virgin.' Contempt dripped from her words.

'No!' He paced closer. 'I said I wouldn't have taken you like that. So clumsily.' He waved a slashing hand at the thought of his uncontrolled possession. 'I should have been gentler.' He'd seen the shock of discomfort on her features, read it in every tensed centimetre of her body, and still he hadn't been able to pull away.

The closed expression on her face proclaimed she didn't believe him and he couldn't bear it. He strode across the room, reaching for her.

'No. Don't touch me.' She shrank back.

Instantly he stopped, his belly churning sickeningly.

'Soraya, please. I don't know what's wrong, but we need to talk. To sort this out.'

'Talking won't help.' Her long hair rippled around her shoulders and breasts, reminding him of the sensual delight they'd shared. 'There's nothing to sort out.'

'How can you say that?' Had the world flipped over on its axis? Everything was scrambled. Everything he felt, everything he thought she felt, turned on its head.

'Because there's no future for us, Zahir.'

For long seconds she gazed into his eyes and he read regret there. Regret and pain that tore him apart because he was helpless to stop it. Or did he imagine it? Now her expression was blank and austere.

'Of course there is. If you'll just listen. I've worked out a way—'

'There's no future because I'm going to marry the Emir as planned.'

Zahir swayed on his feet as his world imploded, collapsing around him.

'No! No, it's not possible.' He struggled to draw breath, to banish the wave of blackness that threatened to engulf him. 'You're not serious?'

But her face was set in determined lines. This was *real*. One of the things he loved about Soraya was her honesty. She meant it.

'You *can't* marry Hussein. Not now.' Not when they'd found each other.

'Why not?' Her chin tilted and her dark eyes, once soft as pansies, flashed fire. 'Because you plan to tell him I'm no virgin?'

Zahir shook his head.

'You said you loved me.' The words were torn from him. A desperate appeal in the face of pure torment.

She said nothing. His aching heart longed to hear the words again, to feel the balm of her love surrounding him once more.

Still she remained silent.

Had they been mere words? Lies?

She'd never lied before, screamed his battered soul.

'I'm going through with my betrothal,' she said at last.

He wanted to yank her into his arms and make love to her till she sobbed his name and clung to him, till she recanted and said she wanted him, not Hussein.

But the seed of knowledge he'd nurtured so long had finally burgeoned into full blossom. Once before he'd sought marriage and been rejected because he was the son of a miscreant, with no prospects. He'd vowed then to work harder, be stronger, more successful than any of his peers. To make a name for himself that would be respected.

He'd thought he'd succeeded. And it was true that his reputation, his talents, his position, had been won by sheer hard work and devotion to duty.

A duty he'd failed abysmally last night. Just as he'd failed the tests of loyalty and integrity.

Soraya had said she wanted to make the most of her last days of freedom. Now she'd tasted forbidden fruit. She'd sated her curiosity and her desire for him.

She'd made her choice. Zahir was good enough for a fling, a night's pleasure before a lifetime of fidelity.

But to marry the illegitimate son of a notorious traitor when she could have Bakhara's ruler? Why settle for less than the best?

Why settle for a man who'd proven himself without honour?

Zahir turned on his heel and strode from the room.

CHAPTER FOURTEEN

INSTEAD of escorting Soraya to the palace, Zahir found himself superfluous as her father, ecstatic at her return, met them at the airport and took her to their home.

A courteous man, he invited Zahir to accompany them for refreshment, but Zahir refused.

As for Soraya, she thanked him with formal courtesy. Raw pain skewered him as he watched her treat him like a stranger.

As if last night hadn't happened.

As if they meant nothing to each other.

But she wasn't an accomplished actress. Zahir didn't know whether to be buoyed or furious when he saw, for an instant, the betraying wobble of her lower lip. Her stiff, angular walk, unlike the gentle sway of her natural gait, told him she wasn't as indifferent as she pretended.

Then why…?

'Sir?'

Zahir turned, recognising one of the palace servants.

'Sir, the Emir asks that you attend the council chambers as soon as possible. The negotiations over disputed territories have commenced and you're needed.'

Zahir turned towards the main concourse. Through the glass doors he saw a royal limousine waiting. Yet he had to force himself not to follow Soraya and her father instead.

'Sir. It really is urgent.'

Zahir frowned. 'I'm sure the Emir is well able—'

'That's just it, sir. The Emir is away in his desert palace. He'd expected you earlier and in the meantime left the negotiations to his diplomatic staff.'

Zahir's frown became a scowl. Hussein was in the desert? Odd behaviour from a man expecting his bride-to-be. After a decade-long betrothal, surely he was eager now to claim the bride he'd ordered home?

'The Emir…' Zahir lowered his voice. 'He is well?'

His companion nodded. 'Yes, sir. So I understand. If you'll just come this way…'

It took two full days to turn the talks around into something productive, another day to develop an agreement for consideration by the various nations and a day to ensure the delegates were farewelled with formal courtesy.

Despite the heavy load placed on his shoulders, Zahir performed his official duties as if by rote. He was distracted. Tormented.

By Soraya, who'd said she loved him, only to reject him. Who'd turned from searing passion to icy detachment.

By the puzzle of Hussein's behaviour when he remained uncontactable during these vital discussions. It wasn't the action of the forthright, capable man he knew.

But, above all, by his own turbulent feelings.

Four days neck-deep in sensitive, world-changing negotiations and he'd felt none of his usual pleasure in a difficult job well done.

His priorities had changed.

Because he'd fallen for a woman who meant more to him than the life he'd carefully constructed. What did any of it matter when Soraya was denied him? Worse, when she herself denied what they'd shared?

Pride shredded, desperation welling, he could find no equanimity, could barely maintain a pretence of it.

Now, on the fourth night since his return, he finally had the luxury of solitude. Instinctively, he'd turned to the desert.

Behind him stretched the glittering city, lighting up the night. Before him, the moon-silvered open ground of the wilderness. He urged his horse forward, inhaling the evocative scent of wild herbs, dusty ground and the subtle indefinable scent of exotic spice borne from the east.

As they picked their way into the desert a perfume teased his senses, of some night-blooming flower, rare and fragile.

It reminded him of Soraya and her delicately perfumed skin, sweet as mountain blooms. Of her beauty and grace, how she made a simple smile a thing of rare joy. His heart crashed against his ribs at the thought of never seeing it again. Or seeing her smile at another man: Hussein.

Pain tore at him like great talons ripping his flesh.

It wasn't just her beauty or her smiles he wanted. It was her love. The way she made him feel. When she'd said she loved him, something inside had glowed incandescent: a hope, a dream he'd never known existed until Soraya.

She'd seduced him not with sex but with the wonder of herself. A woman like no other. Proud, determined, prickly, emotional, giving, warm-hearted, loyal. Loyal to the father she loved and the man to whom she'd promised herself.

But not to him.

Hadn't she felt the same joy at his love for her? Hadn't she—?

The horse whinnied and skittered to a halt as Zahir yanked on the reins.

She *must* know how he felt. It had been there in his every desperate caress, in every breath, each murmured endearment. His desire for marriage.

Yet, reeling back time to that night, the morning after, it struck him that he'd never said it aloud. Never declared his feelings.

He shook his head. Of course she knew he cared for her. Why else would he strategise so frantically to find a way they could wed?

But did she know he loved her?

He sat unmoving so long the stars wheeled in the darkness overhead and the moon inched towards the horizon. Finally his patient mount shifted and Zahir let him have his head, cantering down a slope into the network of valleys that marked the border of the great desert.

When finally they stopped, Zahir had reached a decision.

It was beyond him to believe he could win her for himself, though he couldn't completely stifle a sliver of outrageous hope. Yet he had to act. He had to declare what he felt so Soraya knew and Hussein too.

It wasn't in Zahir's nature to hide behind silence.

Suddenly Soraya's words about honour and honesty made sense. What he felt, however problematic, was honest and real.

He'd been honest with Hussein all his life. It was his honesty above all that had built his reputation as a man who could be trusted, especially in matters of state. He couldn't change now. He couldn't face his friend and benefactor hiding what he truly felt.

He couldn't let Soraya turn from him without knowing.

He couldn't live a lie. Not even if it meant banishment and loss of both the prestige he'd built and the dreams he'd held. Loving Hussein's wife doomed him to leaving all he'd once held close, even his best friend.

He would lose everything.

Yet hadn't he already lost the one thing that mattered?

He turned the stallion and headed back to the city, his heart lighter than it had been since Rome.

The royal audience-chamber was vast, richly ornamented and exquisitely decorated with murals and mosaics of semiprecious stones. Designed to reinforce the majesty of the nation's ruler, it could hold hundreds.

Zahir stopped on the threshold, surprised to find it virtually empty with only a few score in attendance.

There was Hussein, looking stately as ever and reassuringly fit, greeting guests. To one side was Soraya, gorgeous in amber silk with a gilt embroidered veil covering the back of her head. She was pale but composed.

His heart jerked with mingled delight and pain.

Would this be the last time he saw her?

After this he'd no doubt be escorted to the border and never allowed to enter the country again, much less approach the royal presence. The trembling in his belly spread to his limbs and for a moment he doubted he had the strength to go on.

Moving his gaze, he saw Soraya's father, hovering close to her. The rest of the guests he recognized: the country's most influential leaders, tribal elders and government ministers. Men he dealt with every day. Men he respected.

Men who'd shun him when this was over.

He watched Hussein, the benevolent, extraordinary man who was as precious to him as a father. Who trusted him implicitly. His stomach dived as he thought of the yawning rift he'd create between them and the hurt he'd cause.

Shifting his gaze back to Soraya, warmth stole through him. Not the heat of lust. This was stronger, fuller and more profound.

Taking a deep breath, he strode towards his fate.

Soraya held herself stiffly, beset by doubt.

She'd never been in the audience chamber and its brilliance daunted her, reinforcing the Emir's power and wealth. Reminding her she was to marry a stranger, as unfamiliar to her as the opulence that surrounded them.

When summoned to the palace this morning, she'd almost welcomed the invitation. For, despite what she'd told Zahir in her pride and hurt, she was less convinced than ever that she could marry the man who held centre stage in this auspicious gathering.

Yes, he was generous and decent, good-looking too, if you had a penchant for much, much older men.

But he wasn't Zahir.

It didn't matter that Zahir didn't love her. She'd given her heart to him and she knew that, like her father's, her love once given could not be rescinded.

She'd hoped for a chance to talk with the Emir in private. He had a right to know his bride loved another.

Instead she and her father had been ushered into a formal reception of VIPs so daunting she'd had difficulty doing more than respond to polite greetings. She very much feared the purpose of the gathering was to introduce her formally as a royal bride and announce a wedding date. Why else was she included amongst all these eminent people?

As soon as this was over she *had* to find a way to speak with the Emir privately. She owed him the truth, though she cringed, thinking of the consequences.

A stir in the crowd caught her attention. Heads turned towards the grand entrance. At the same time a frisson of awareness scudded down her spine, drawing her flesh taut and tingling, as if she'd been dipped in fizzing champagne.

Her breath caught. That sensation was unmistakeable.

It was Zahir. No one else made her feel that way.

Despair flowered deep inside as she realised there was no escape. She'd hoped to put off this first public meeting till she'd gathered her defences more strongly about her, ready to project an aura of disinterest.

Would she ever be able to pretend so well, when just the knowledge he was in the room made her knees weak?

Unable to resist, she turned and there he was, his long legs eating up the marble vastness as he strode towards the throne.

Her pulse rocketed as she took him in. Zahir as she'd never seen him. Zahir in a pure white robe that flowed from broad, straight shoulders, loose trousers tucked into traditional Bakhari horseman's boots. A belt secured a curved scabbard for the customary knife.

There was nothing ostentatious about him. His clothes were simple but of the finest materials. Yet no other man in the room matched him for sheer presence and masculine magnificence. Not even the Emir.

Zahir's face was drawn in harsh lines, as if he'd just come in from the blinding desert sun. Or as if he had momentous matters of state on his mind.

'Zahir! Welcome.' The Emir moved forward to greet him, arms outstretched for an embrace.

'My lord.' Zahir stopped several paces away, bowing deeply.

The Emir halted, his brow pleating as if Zahir's formality surprised him. 'It gladdens my heart to see you, Zahir. You are well?'

'I am, sire. And you are in good health?'

Soraya listened to the exchange of greetings with half an ear, all the while bracing herself for the moment Zahir looked past the Emir and noticed her. Would he come and greet her, or simply nod, as passing acquaintances might? She didn't know which would hurt more.

She must have missed part of their conversation. For suddenly the Emir was ushering him forward and Zahir was shaking his head.

'Before the business of the day begins, I have something I must tell you.' Zahir's eyes, like polished emeralds, flashed straight to her, pinioning her where she stood. As ever, she felt the impact of his gaze from the roots of her hair to the tips of her feet in their embroidered silk slippers.

So he'd known she was there all along.

She shifted, a sense of terrible premonition welling.

'Of course.' The Emir gestured for him to continue. 'You are among friends. Let us hear what is on your mind.'

Zahir turned back to the Emir, his facial muscles so taut she wondered if he was in pain.

'It concerns the lady Soraya.'

Her heart skated to a halt then took up a quick, faltering rhythm. A murmur of interest resonated around the room but she barely registered it. Her whole being focused on Zahir.

What was he going to do—broadcast what he considered her shame to all and sundry? Accuse her of disloyalty? Unworthiness?

She found she'd clasped her hands together, fingers entwined and shaking. Her feet were rooted to the spot.

'Go on.'

'There is something you should know before you marry.' Zahir paused and you could have heard a pin drop in the massive room.

Soraya's father reached out and touched her arm but she couldn't tear her gaze from Zahir.

What was he doing? Why?

Her stasis shattered and she stumbled forward, her long dress sweeping around her unsteady legs.

The Emir half-turned to acknowledge her as she joined them. Yet Zahir didn't shift his gaze. He stared straight ahead at the man he'd called his best friend and mentor.

As if he blocked her out.

Panic swirled up from her stomach, prickling its way through her whole body. Or was it pain? The ache of waiting to be betrayed by the man who'd stolen her heart?

'I know you prize loyalty,' Zahir continued.

'I do.'

'Then you should know that I can no longer remain in Bakhara. Not once you marry this woman.' Zahir's voice was firm and strong, eliciting a ripple of gasps and whispers from the assembled group.

Heat roared through Soraya's cheeks then receded, leaving her cold and strangely empty. Then she felt the clasp of a sustaining hand on hers as her father moved to stand by her. That proof of his love almost shattered her, knowing how unbearably disappointed he would be at the news Zahir would break.

She opened her mouth but no sound emerged.

'Why is that, Zahir?' On her other side the Emir sounded unperturbed, as if he couldn't read the dark sizzle of emotion in Zahir's eyes or the thundering pulse at his temple.

'Because I love her.'

Silence descended, broken only by the rattle of Soraya's breath in her overburdened lungs. Surely she imagined the words? For Zahir to say them now, here, in front of the nation's elite… She tried to take it in but couldn't.

'I love her,' he said, louder this time, making himself heard over the immediate clamour of protest that rose around them. 'Therefore I can't be part of your court. I can't remain here, a loyal subject, when she—' he swallowed hard '—is your queen.'

Zahir's gaze flickered to her and she read haunting anguish in the depths of his eyes.

Her heart gave a great leap, battering up against her throat. She felt light-headed.

'You have never been precipitate before, Zahir.' The Emir spoke over the swelling roar behind them. 'I counsel you not to make rash statements now.

'Soraya?' At the Emir's questioning tone, she dragged her gaze to the weathered, stern face of the older man. 'What are your feelings for this man?'

He spoke with a gravity that confirmed all her fears for Zahir. Had he destroyed in one moment everything he'd worked for? She knew how much his position, his work—and above all this man's regard meant to him. Dismay gnawed.

She sensed the horror of the onlookers and knew he'd just willingly given up all he'd strived for. For *her*.

Yet she couldn't stop the elation singing in her bloodstream. Her lips curved in a smile she hadn't a hope of hiding.

'I love him.' She turned to Zahir. Pulling free of her father's hold, she stepped closer to the man who stood poised as if for battle, alone against the crowd. 'I love him with all my heart.'

She no longer heard the others. No longer noticed the older men. All she knew was the dawning light in Zahir's clear gaze. The pride and love that softened his severe features as his eyes devoured her. The sweet joy that filled her.

She could scarcely believe it. *He loved her.*

Not only that, he had declared it in defiance of protocol, of tradition, of everything that stood between them.

How long they remained there, gazes enmeshed, cocooned

from the uproar, Soraya didn't know. Finally the Emir's voice penetrated. He spoke in deep, carrying tones.

'My kinsman Zahir's announcement has rather pre-empted my own. I've brought you all here today as witnesses.'

Soraya spun around, alarm rising. He couldn't mean to continue with the wedding now? *Surely* he couldn't? She started forward in protest but a hand stopped her.

'Wait, Soraya.' It was Zahir's voice in her ear, quelling the worst of her panic. His fingers engulfed hers and she squeezed back. If they were to be parted now…

Her face flamed as she faced the crowd, read the strain on her father's features and the avid curiosity of so many strangers.

The Emir spoke again. 'I called you here because it's been my intention for some time to abdicate.'

Shocked silence greeted his words. Zahir's fingers spasmed on hers and she heard his swift intake of breath.

'That decision will affect others.' He turned and Soraya found herself meeting kindly hazel eyes. There was no trace of the anger she'd anticipated in his face.

'In the circumstances, it would be unreasonable of me to ask my betrothed to feel committed to me now I've taken a decision which will so substantially alter her future.'

He was letting her off the hook?

A buzz of questions and protests surfaced but Soraya couldn't take them in. All she could process was the solid warmth of Zahir beside her, his strength flowing into her from their linked hands and the knowledge she was free.

The Emir raised a hand as he turned back to the crowd and silence fell. 'I have of course thought carefully about a successor. A man of my own blood. A man who has proven himself capable and trustworthy in so many capacities. A man who just this week saved our peace negotiations when they were in danger of foundering.'

He turned and all eyes followed the direction of his gaze. 'I propose Zahir Adnan El Hashem as my most worthy successor.'

* * *

Soraya paced the antechamber, oblivious to its luxurious furnishings and breathtaking view over the city. What was happening? Her nerves crawled with impatience. She'd felt revolt in the air back there, fuelled by shock and Zahir's uncompromising stance over her.

Her father had ushered her here, away from curious eyes, while the future of the nation was decided. He'd been stunned by the scene in the audience chamber. But, once she'd confirmed she really was in love, he'd proved staunchly supportive, only leaving when she forced him to go and take his part in the deliberations.

The door to the antechamber opened and Soraya swung round, ready to throw herself into Zahir's arms. His eyes met hers, glittering with raw emotion, and her heart juddered in the aftershock of that connection.

He loved her...

But he wasn't alone. The Emir walked beside him.

Soraya clasped her hands together and forced herself to be still, dread rising as she saw Zahir's grim expression and the Emir's weary one.

'How could you do it?'

Soraya opened her mouth then realised the question came from Zahir's lips and that he was standing in front of the Emir, legs planted aggressively wide.

'It was necessary,' the older man said.

'Necessary!' Zahir's deep voice rose to a pitch she'd never heard before. He sounded on the verge of violence. 'You *used* her.'

'I regret that.' The Emir cast her a troubled look.

'Regret?' Zahir's hands fisted at his sides. 'You shackled a young, unsuspecting girl to you with no thought of what that might do to her? How *trapped* she might feel? How distressed?'

Soraya rushed forward and grabbed his arm. It trembled with repressed fury. His other hand covered hers possessively and she leaned into him, still dazed by the fact she could. He wanted her, loved her.

The tension in Zahir's strong frame shocked her. As if it would take just one careless word to unleash violence.

His anger on her behalf was like a comforting blanket, reminding her she wasn't alone any more.

'I'd lost my wife, the love of my life,' the older man said, his voice hollow. 'I think now you both have some idea how that felt.' Soraya felt a quiver of distress pass through Zahir. Or was it through her? The thought of losing him now she'd finally found him made her clutch tighter.

The Emir heaved a deep sigh. 'To rule, I had to be married.' His gaze shifted to Soraya. 'Or betrothed.'

He spread his hands wide. 'You remember how things were then, Zahir, how unready the nation was for another ruler. And there was no logical successor.' His lips quirked. 'Though one young man had caught my eye. I knew with experience one day he'd make a fine emir.'

'The illegitimate son of a brutal tyrant?' Zahir's words bit like bullets.

'The honourable, capable man I'm proud to call kin, however distant the connection.' The Emir paused. 'I've been weary a long time, Zahir. A ruler needs a helpmeet. I'm ready to retire to my country estate and study the stars, read my books and watch your children grow.'

Heat suffused Soraya's cheeks at his direct look. The idea of carrying Zahir's babies made a pulse beat deep in her womb.

'But Zahir isn't married. How could you know…?' Her voice trailed off in the face of the older man's smile.

'I knew Zahir would have no trouble finding a bride. It's time he was settled.'

But Zahir wasn't to be distracted. 'You brought Soraya into an untenable situation.'

The Emir nodded. 'I'd planned today to annul the betrothal on the grounds of my abdication. That would leave Soraya's reputation unblemished. I hadn't anticipated your announcement.'

'But it doesn't go anywhere near making up for the trauma she suffered.'

'Zahir!' She tugged at his arm. 'It's all right now, truly.' And it was. Miraculously, it was. She'd have gone through far more than anxiety over her royal betrothal if it meant having the man she loved.

He turned and looked down at her. His breath on her face was a soft caress. The look in his eyes sheer heaven.

'I owe you my deepest apologies, Soraya.' Dimly she was aware of the Emir bowing, but she couldn't tear her gaze from Zahir's. The way he looked at her was like dawn's fresh promise after an endless night. A moment later the door snicked shut and they were alone. Finally.

'Is it true?'

Zahir lifted her hand and kissed it, turned it over and pressed his lips to the centre of her palm. Lightning jagged through her veins and lit up her senses. His eyes glinted with promise, like cool oasis water in the desert.

'It's true, my love. I adore you. And I'll never let you go.' His voice dropped to a gruff bass rumble that made her insides melt. 'If you'll have me.'

'But in Rome…'

He pressed a finger to her lips.

'In Rome I was a fool. I was so caught up making plans and anticipating problems I forgot the most important thing of all: love.' He smiled and a sunburst exploded in her heart. 'I've wanted you since the night I saw you in Paris.'

'But wanting isn't love.'

'And I've loved you almost as long. The more I learned about you the less I could resist.' His finger on her mouth moved in a slow, seductive stroke along her bottom lip that sent delight shivering through her. 'The question is, do you want me?'

Stunned, her eyes widened. 'Of course I do. How can you doubt it?'

'Because right now the royal council of elders is debating whether I should become Emir of Bakhara. It's by no means a done deal, and there'll be a lot of negotiating, but I need to know what you think. You didn't want a royal life. You wanted more than royal duty and who can blame you?' He paused and gathered her close so her heart beat against his, that single pulse all the stronger for being shared. 'I'll step away from it if that's what you want. I couldn't accept without your agreement.'

'Zahir!' She pulled away as far as his encircling arm allowed. 'You can't do that. You're made for the position.' She couldn't imagine anyone better suited. The knowledge filled her with pride. 'Unless you don't want it?'

Green eyes held hers, unblinking. 'I won't lie. The challenge of it is all I could ever want. Except for you.' His voice deepened and sent threads of gossamer silk trawling over her sensitive skin till she quivered. 'I'd rather have you, Soraya. That's my choice.'

Her heart swelled as she stopped his words with her lips. 'Then it's just as well you don't have to choose.' Something inside broke at the thought he'd give up all he'd worked for if it meant keeping her. She felt humbled. At the same time determination filled her. She'd be the best wife an emir could have. 'I'd rather be yours than anything else in the world, my darling.'

'You'll be mine? Even if it means being wife to the Emir?' His voice was raw with disbelief. His hands shook as he pulled her closer. 'You can pursue your engineering, whatever you want. It won't be all duty. I swear.'

She cupped his beautiful, questioning face in her hands, marvelling that he was hers. 'Well, there will be hardships, I know. Think of all the shopping I'll have to do to look the part if you're made Emir. The shoes, the clothes…' Her breath escaped in a gasp as his marauding hands investigated the sheer silk of her bodice. 'Zahir!'

'The attentions of your virile husband?'

'That will never be a hardship.' Soraya smiled with all the joy in her heart. She couldn't believe the world could hold such happiness.

'Just as well.' His head lowered, blotting out the elegant room, and the world faded away.

EPILOGUE

THE oasis encampment vibrated with the hoof beats of so many horses, all beautifully caparisoned, all bearing horsemen in traditional garb. Their white robes shimmered in the moonlight, their heirloom weapons glinting.

The women had just left in a fleet of luxury four-wheel drives back to the capital.

Soraya's breath caught at the spectacle of Bakhara's strongest and finest wheeling their horses out of the oasis.

The slightest of breezes feathered her dress and she shivered, not with cold, but with delight at the scene that wouldn't have looked out of place in some old romantic tale. An instant later warm hands clasped her arms, pulling her back against a strong, solid body.

A sigh of pleasure escaped her lips. It had been so long, a month in fact, since she'd felt Zahir so close.

Even through her silks and his fine cottons, his heat branded her. She snuggled back against him, revelling in the possessive tightening of his grip, the hitch in his breathing and his burgeoning hardness against her buttocks.

She shimmied back as delicious languor filled her.

'Minx,' Zahir growled as a salute of rifle shots thundered in the night sky. 'Wave for our audience, *habibti*.'

Soraya lifted her arm then moaned softly as he ground his pelvis hard against her. Rills of desire ran through her body, pooling deep inside.

The last of the riders disappeared over the ridge, leaving them sole occupants of the oasis.

'I thought today would never end.' Zahir's lips were hot on her neck. 'Why do Bakhari weddings take so long?'

She turned, wrapping her arms around his neck.

'Not any wedding. The Emir's.'

His hooded eyes glinted in the light of the nearby braziers. 'No regrets, my love?'

'None. Except…' She chewed her lip, feeling delight shimmer within as Zahir's hungry gaze honed in on her mouth. It was a wonder she didn't explode from the heat.

'What?' A frown pleated his brow.

'Except you're wasting valuable time talking.'

With a grin that stole her heart all over again, Zahir scooped her into his arms and strode into the richly decorated tent. Antique lamps spilled multicoloured light over thick, silk rugs, embroidered cushions and the widest bed Soraya had ever seen raised on a dais at the centre of the space.

Tenderly Zahir laid her on the satin cover, then propped himself beside her.

The lamplight cast his strong features in bronze, highlighting their severe strength and above all the shimmering emotion in his eyes.

Soraya's heart welled, reading the reflection there of all she felt.

'Your wish is my command, lady. But be warned.' He nuzzled the base of her neck as his fingers slid over the thin silk of her dress. Delicious tension bowed her taut body. 'I intend to tell you often how much I love you.'

It was a promise he kept through their lifetime together.

* * * * *

ONE NIGHT WITH THE SHEIKH

KRISTI GOLD

To my beautiful daughter, Kendall. One of the best Athletic Trainers in the business, one of my biggest fans, and one of my major sources for chocolate.

Kristi Gold has a fondness for beaches, baseball and bridal reality shows. She firmly believes that love has remarkable, healing powers and feels very fortunate to be able to weave stories of love and commitment. As a bestselling author, a National Readers' Choice Award winner and a Romance Writers of America three-time RITA® Award finalist, Kristi has learned that although accolades are wonderful, the most cherished rewards come from networking with readers. She can be reached through her website at www.kristigold.com or through Facebook.

One

King Rafiq ibn Fayiz Mehdi possessed keen intelligence, vast power and infinite riches. Yet none had aided him in preventing a devastating tragedy—a tragedy for which he had been partially responsible.

As the sun began to set, he stood on the palace's rooftop veranda and peered at the panorama stretched out before him. The diverse terrain he once revered now seemed ominous, inviting disturbing recollections that cut into his composure like a well-honed blade.

A dark, winding road at midnight. Silence and dread. Flashing lights illuminating the bottom of a cliff. The twisted metal wreckage…

"If you believe you'll move mountains by staring at them, I assure you it will not work."

At the sound of the familiar voice, Rafiq glanced back to see his brother standing only a few steps behind him. "Why are you here?"

Zain claimed the space beside Rafiq and leaned back against the stone wall. "Is that how you greet the man who so generously handed you the keys to the kingdom over a year ago?"

The same man who had abdicated the throne for the sake of love, an emotion Rafiq had never quite embraced. "My apologies, brother. I was not expecting you for another month."

"Since I completed my initial preparation for the water conservation project, I felt the timing was right for my return."

Under normal circumstances, he would appreciate Zain's company. Lately he preferred solitude. "Did you travel alone?"

"Of course not," Zain said in an irritable tone. "I do not travel without my family unless absolutely necessary."

Rafiq had never believed he would hear his womanizing brother utter those words. "Then Madison is with you?"

"Yes, and my children. I've been anxious for you to finally meet your niece and nephew."

Rafiq did not share in Zain's enthusiasm. Being in the presence of two infants would only serve to remind him of what he had lost. "Where are they now?"

"Madison and Elena are tending to them."

At least he could temporarily avoid the painful introduction. "I am glad you have finally returned Elena to her rightful place. The household does not run well without her."

"So I have heard," Zain said. "I have also heard you are in danger of causing an uprising among the palace staff if you continue to terrorize them."

Rafiq admittedly had trouble maintaining calm in recent days, but he did not care for the exaggerated accusation. "I have not terrorized the staff. I have only corrected them when necessary."

"It's my understanding you have found it necessary to *correct* them on a daily basis, brother. I've also learned you have not been cooperative with the council."

Rafiq began to question the real reason behind Zain's surprise appearance. "Have you been speaking with our younger brother?"

Zain's gaze faltered. "I have been in touch with Adan on occasion."

His anger began to build. "And you have clearly been discussing me."

"He only mentioned you've been having a difficult time since Rima's death."

Rafiq's suspicions had been confirmed—Zain had arrived early to play nursemaid. "Despite what you and Adan might believe, I do not need a keeper."

Zain leaned forward, his expression suddenly somber. "We both understand how devastating it must be to lose your wife and your unborn child—"

"How could you understand?" No one would ever understand the constant guilt and regret unless they had experienced it. "You have a wife and two healthy children."

"As I was saying," Zain continued, "it's understandable that you are still harboring a good measure of anger, particularly with so many unanswered questions about the accident. However, your attitude is proving disruptive. Perhaps you should consider taking a sabbatical."

Impossible and unnecessary. "And who would run the country in my stead?"

"I would," Zain said. "After all, I prepared many years to assume that responsibility before I gave up the position. Adan is willing to assist me."

Rafiq released a cynical laugh. "First, Adan has no interest in governing Bajul. He's only interested in flying planes and seducing women. As far as you are concerned, our people have not forgotten you abandoned them for a second time."

Barely contained fury called out from Zain's narrowed eyes. "I still have an abiding love for this country, and I am quite capable of seeing that it runs smoothly, as I promised before I returned with Madison to the States. Do not forget, I alone developed the water conservation plan that will secure Bajul's future. And I have earned the council's support."

Rafiq recognized he had been wrong to criticize Zain. "My apologies. I do appreciate your support, but I assure you I do not need a sabbatical."

"A sabbatical would allow you to assess your feelings about the situation."

Rafiq was growing weary of the interference. "My *feelings* are not significant. My duties to Bajul are of the utmost importance."

"Yet your emotional upheaval has understandably begun to affect your leadership. Grieving requires time, Rafiq. You have not allowed yourself enough for that."

He had grieved more than anyone would know. "It has been six months. Life must continue as planned."

Zain whisked a hand through his dark hair. "Plans go awry, brother, and life sometimes comes to a standstill. You have suffered a great loss and if you choose not to acknowledge that, you will only suffer more."

He could no longer suffer through this conversation. "I prefer not to discuss it further, so if you will excuse me—"

The sound of footfalls silenced Rafiq and drew his attention to Zain's blonde American bride walking toward them, a round-faced, dark-haired infant propped on one hip. He immediately noticed the happiness reflected in his sister-in-law's face and the obvious adoration in her blue eyes when she met Zain's gaze. "I have a baby girl who insists on being with her daddy."

Zain presented a warm smile. "And her father is more than happy to accommodate her."

After Madison handed the infant to Zain, she drew Rafiq into an embrace. "It's good to see you, my dear brother-in-law."

"And you, Madison," he said. "You are looking well, as usual. I would never have known you had given birth." Ironically, only a few days after he had buried his wife.

She pushed her somewhat disheveled hair back and blushed. "Thank you. Elena told me to tell you that she'll see you as soon as she has Joseph in bed. She seems to be able to calm our son better than anyone, but then after raising the Mehdi boys, she's had quite a bit of experience."

Zain moved closer to Rafiq and regarded his child. "Cala, this is your uncle Rafiq. And yes, we do favor each other, except for that goatee, but I am much more handsome."

Rafiq experienced sheer sadness at the sound of his mother's name that his brother had given his daughter.

The mother he had barely known yet still revered. "She is a beautiful child, Zain. Congratulations."

"Do you wish to hold your niece?" Zain asked.

If he dared, he risked destroying the emotional fortress he had built for protection. "Perhaps later. At the moment I have some documents to review." He leaned and kissed Madison's cheek. "You have honored my brother by giving him the greatest of gifts. For that, I am grateful."

Needing to escape, Rafiq strode across the veranda, only to be halted by Zain, who handed the child back to Madison and followed him to the door. "Wait, Rafiq."

He reluctantly faced his brother again. "What is it now?"

Zain rested a hand on Rafiq's shoulder. "I understand why it would be difficult to discuss anything involving emotional issues with your siblings. For that reason, I believe you should seek out a friend who understands you better than most."

He could only recall one soul who would currently meet that requirement, and they had not interacted as friends in quite some time. "If you are referring to Shamil Barad, he is away while the resort is being renovated."

"I am referring to his sister, Maysa."

The name sent a spear of regret through Rafiq's heart, and a rush of memories into his mind. He recalled the way her long, dark hair cascaded down her back and fell below her waist. The deep creases in her cheeks that framed her beautiful smile. He remembered the way she had looked that long-ago night when they had made love—their greatest mistake. He also remembered the pain in her brown eyes the day he had told her they could never be together. "I have not spoken with Maysa at length in many years. She severed all ties when—"

"You chose Rima Acar over her?"

He did not care to defend the decision, but he would. "I was not consulted when the agreement between our fathers was made."

Zain rubbed his shaded jaw. "Ah, yes. I believe Sheikh Acar trumped Maysa's father's offer during the bridal bartering. I also recall that you did nothing to plead your case. You never attempted to convince either party that you belonged with Maysa."

And he had regretted that decision more than once. "In accordance with tradition, it was not within my power to do so."

Zain's expression turned to stone. "A tradition that forced me to choose between my royal duty and my wife. An antiquated custom that has done nothing but lead to your misery, and Maysa's, as well. The choice the sultan made for Maysa resulted in divorce and nearly ruined her, and you were anything but happy with your queen."

Anger as hot as a firebrand shot through Rafiq. "You know nothing about my relationship with Rima."

"I know what I witnessed when I saw the two of you together." Zain studied him for a long moment. "Were you happy, Rafiq? Was Rima happy?"

He could not answer truthfully without confirming Zain's conjecture. "I cared a great deal for Rima. We were friends long before we wed. Her death has been difficult for me, whether you choose to believe that or not."

"My apologies for sounding insensitive," Zain said.

"As I told you earlier, it's very apparent you are in great turmoil, which brings me back to my suggestion you talk with Maysa. She will understand."

Perhaps so, but other issues still existed. "Even if she agreed to see me, which I suspect she will not, any liaison with Maysa would not be considered acceptable. She is divorced and I have been widowed for only a brief time."

Zain's frustration came out in a scowl. "First of all, I am only suggesting you speak with her, not wed her. Second, if you are concerned that someone will assume an affair, then steal away in the night to prevent detection. It has always worked to my advantage. Should you need assistance, I will be glad to make the arrangements."

He had no doubt Zain could. His brother had made covert disappearance an art form. "I do not need your assistance, nor do I plan to see Maysa."

"Do not dismiss it completely, Rafiq. She could be the one person to see you through this difficult phase."

At one time, that would have held true. Maysa had known him better than any living soul, understood him better, and she had been a welcome source of support during their formative years. She had also been his greatest weakness, and he had been her greatest disappointment.

For that reason, he should stay away from her. Yet as he left his brother's company and returned to his quarters, alone with his continuing guilt, he began to wonder if perhaps Zain might be right. Reconnecting with Maysa again, if only for a brief time, could very well be worth the risks.

* * *

As the village's primary physician, Maysa Barad answered the midnight summons expecting a messenger requesting she tend to an ailing child or a mother in labor. She did not expect to find Rafiq Mehdi, the recently crowned—and newly widowed—King of Bajul. Her childhood friend. Her first love. Her first lover.

The changes in Rafiq were somewhat apparent, but subtle. He was still tall and lean. Still as incredibly handsome as he'd always been, despite that he now chose to wear a neatly trimmed goatee framing his sensual mouth. His eyes and hair were still as dark, much the same as hers, yet maturity had lent him an even greater aura of power. A power that had crushed her resolve on more than one occasion many years before.

She could not remember the last time he had called on her. She couldn't imagine why he was here now, but she intended to find out. "Good evening, Your Majesty. To what do I owe this pleasure?"

"I need to speak with you."

His serious tone and intense gaze prompted Maysa to press the panic button. "Are you ill?"

"No. I will explain why I am here as soon as we are in a private setting."

Maysa glanced around him to see a black car parked in the portico, and surprisingly not one of the requisite sentries. "Where are your guards?"

"At the palace. Only select members of my staff know I am here."

Being completely alone with him somewhat concerned Maysa. She considered asking him to return in the morning, when she was appropriately dressed, well rested and better prepared. However, he was still the king and his wish would have to be her command, an all too familiar concept. During their youth, she would have done anything he asked of her. One fateful night, she had.

Despite all the concerns racing through her mind, and the threat to her composure, she opened the door wide to allow him entry. "I suppose you may come in for a while."

After Rafiq stepped into the foyer, Maysa closed and locked the door, then faced him to find his dark, pensive gaze leveled on hers. "I sincerely appreciate your willingness to see me at this hour," he said without a hint of familiarity.

She sincerely questioned the wisdom in allowing him in her home. "You are welcome. Follow me."

Maysa led him down the corridor and paused when one of the staff appeared from around the corner. She waved the befuddled woman away and continued past the myriad rooms comprising the expansive house belonging to her father, and on loan to her. The same house where she'd gone from teenager to woman in her childhood bed, courtesy of the man walking behind her.

Once they reached her private living area, she shut the door and gestured toward the settee. "Feel free to be seated."

"I prefer to stand," he said as he began to pace the room like a caged tiger, his hands firmly planted in the pockets of his black slacks.

Maysa dropped down onto the sofa, curled her legs beneath her and adjusted the aqua caftan to where it covered her bare feet. She chose to continue to speak in English, should one of the staff decide to eavesdrop. "What can I do for you, Rafiq?"

He stopped to stare out the window overlooking the mountains. "I could not sleep. I've had difficulty sleeping since…"

"The accident," she said when his words trailed away. The mysterious, single-car accident that had claimed the queen's life six months ago. "Insomnia and restlessness are understandable. Rima's death was tragic and unexpected. If you would like me to prescribe a sleep aid, I would certainly be willing to do that."

He turned toward her, some unnamed emotion in his near-black eyes. "I do not wish a pill, Maysa. I wish to go back to that night and find a way to prevent my wife's death. I want to find some peace."

His feelings for his queen apparently were much deeper than Maysa had realized. "It takes time to recover from losing someone you cared about, Rafiq."

"It has been six months," he said. "And I did not care enough, which directly contributed to her demise."

Evidently she had made an erroneous assumption. It seemed Rafiq's marriage to Rima Acar had been little more than a long-standing agreement between their patriarchs. Yet she didn't understand why he blamed himself for her death. "You weren't driving the car, Rafiq."

He crossed the room and joined her on the opposite end of the small settee. "But I did drive her away that night."

She wasn't certain she wanted to hear the details, but since he'd decided to take her into his confidence for the first time in years, she chose to listen. "Did you argue before she left?"

He lowered his head and streaked his palms over his face, as if to erase the bitter memories. "Yes, immediately after she informed me she was with child."

Rima's pregnancy had been kept from the press, but the revelation came as no surprise to Maysa. Unbeknownst to the king, the queen had come to her for confirmation instead of consulting the palace physician, though she never quite understood why. Rima had always been aware of Maysa's close relationship with Rafiq, at times pitting them as rivals. "Were you not happy to hear the news?"

"I was pleased to know I would have an heir. She was not at all pleased to be having my child."

Maysa had witnessed Rima's distress when she'd delivered the results, but she had attributed that to slight shock. "She told you that?"

He released a rough sigh. "Not in so many words, but I sensed her unhappiness. When I questioned her at length, she did not deny it. She disappeared some time later without my knowledge."

Maysa experienced a measure of satisfaction that he'd chosen to release his burden and a good deal of guilt over what she'd chosen to withhold from him. She suspected she knew where the queen had been before the accident, though she had no solid proof. "Do you know where she might have been going when she left?"

His expression remained somber. "No, and I most likely will never know. I do know if I had been kinder to her, then perhaps she would not have felt the need to leave."

She offered him the only advice she could give him at the moment. Advice she had been forced to follow since the day he'd told her he would be marrying another, shattering her dreams of a future with him. "Rafiq, you can spend a lifetime wondering what might have been, or you can move on with your life."

"I told Zain only hours ago that I intended to proceed with my life," he said. "I did not admit the difficulty in that. To him, or until recently, myself."

"It would be nice if your brother were here during this trying time."

Rafiq kept his gaze trained on the floor. "He arrived in Bajul today with Madison and their children."

She realized having the children around could be the basis for his lack of enthusiasm and distress. "That must be very difficult for you."

He finally looked at her. "Why would you believe I would not welcome my brother's family?"

She laid a hand on his arm. "Of course you would, but being in the presence of two infants might remind you of your recent loss."

"I can handle that, but I cannot abide Zain's advice. He is convinced I need a sabbatical."

"Perhaps he is right. Time away would aid in the healing process."

He frowned. "He is wrong. I only need time to adjust. I can accomplish that and still tend to my duties."

As far as she was concerned, he was overestimating his strength. "Does Zain know you're here?"

"Yes. He insisted I talk with you."

Maysa's hopes had been dashed once more. "I thought perhaps you came on your own."

"I would never have thought to bother you," he said.

"It's no bother, Rafiq. I considered visiting you after the funeral, but I wasn't at all certain I would be welcome."

He looked at her somberly, sincerely. "You will always be welcome in my world, Maysa."

The memory hit her full force then. The memory of a time when he'd spoken those same words to her.

No matter what the future holds, you will always be welcome in my world, habibti....

Yet she had not been welcome at all. After his marriage contract had been finalized, they had been expressly forbidden to see each other, yet they had continued to meet in secret. Those clandestine trysts had only fueled the fire between them until one night, they had made love the first—and the last—time.

Maysa wondered if Rafiq remembered. She wondered if he recalled those remarkable moments, or if he had pushed them out of his thoughts. She wondered why she had been such a fool to believe he would have changed his mind about marrying Rima.

She rose to her feet and crossed the room to pour a glass of water from a pitcher set out on a side table. She kept her back to Rafiq as she took a few sips, and swallowed hard when she heard approaching footsteps.

"Have I said something to upset you, Maysa?"

His presence upset her. Her feelings for him upset her. She set the glass on the table and turned to him. "Why are you really here, Rafiq? Why have you come to me after all these years?"

His expression reflected confusion. "You are the one person I have always turned to for solace."

"Not always," she said. "We've been virtual strangers for well over a decade."

His expression implied building anger. "You were the one who left Bajul for the States, Maysa. I have always been here."

"I had no choice after I divorced Boutros."

"A man you should have never wed."

A heartless, angry sultan who had almost stolen her sense of self-worth and security. Almost. "As it was with you and Rima, my marriage was no more than an edict from my father."

Rafiq inclined his head and studied her. "Why did you risk your name and reputation to divorce him?"

She did not dare tell him the entire truth. "He refused to allow me to pursue my profession. I refused to allow him to tell me how to live my life."

He looked as if he could see right through her. "That is the only reason?"

"Isn't that enough? And what other reason would there be?"

Now he appeared cynical. "Everyone is quite aware of Boutros Kassab's reputation for suspect business arrangements and questionable connections."

She would simply allow him to believe that rather than reveal the harsh reality—Boutros was a sadistic, uncaring lecher. "I was eighteen when we married, Rafiq. I had no involvement in his business dealings. I was only required to play the dutiful wife."

He raised a brow. "In his bed?"

She hesitated slightly. "Do you wish me to lie and say no?"

"He is thirty years your senior. I hoped you would say he had little interest in anything of a carnal nature due to an inability to perform."

Many nights she had wished that had only been the case, but it had not. "Boutros is a man, and men rarely lose interest in sex, no matter what their age."

"Did he satisfy you, Maysa?"

She was momentarily stunned. "That is none of your concern."

He streamed a fingertip down her cheek. "I am only curious if he knew how to please you. If he learned, as I did, how to make you tremble with need."

She circled her arms around her middle as if that might afford her protection from his magnetic pull. From the memories. "Did Rima satisfy you, Rafiq? Or did you simply go to her for the sake of producing an heir?" The moment the words left her mouth, she silently cursed her thoughtlessness.

Rafiq reacted by turning away, crossing the room and moving to the window to stare at the mountains once more. She approached him slowly and rested a palm on his shoulder. "I am so sorry, Rafiq. I did not mean to be so unkind. I know how much you are hurting over the loss of your child. I also know that you did care very much for your wife, and you were a good husband to her. You would never ignore her needs."

"And in doing so, I was forced to disregard what I needed most."

"And that was?"

"You."

Without warning, Rafiq spun around and crushed Maysa against him. He claimed her mouth with a vengeance, with a touch of desperation. And as she always had, she willingly accepted the kiss.

She hated that he could so easily mold her into a willing, wanton woman, but not quite enough to stop him. She despised herself for wanting to give in to the ever-present desire. To do so could lead to undeniable pleasure, and quite possibly disaster. He didn't necessarily want her. He only wanted comfort wherever available, as it had been all those years ago. And that made her furious enough to recapture her common sense.

With all the strength she could muster, Maysa moved back, putting some much-needed distance between them. "How many women were there after me and prior to your marriage to Rima?"

Confusion crossed over his expression. "Why does that matter?"

"Perhaps you could call on one of them to provide the escape you so obviously need."

His handsome features turned to stone. "You truly believe that is all you mean to me?"

She folded her arms beneath her breasts. "Yes, I do. You're only seeking a temporary diversion, and after you receive it, you will be gone again."

"I seek the company of someone I trust. Someone I have always cared about."

"If you truly cared about me, you would not have kissed me."

"Perhaps the kiss was a mistake," he said. "Perhaps I should not have come here."

She released a disparaging laugh. "You're right. It was a mistake. Someone could find out, and that would not go over well with the elders. I am a scorned woman, remember? A divorcée and to some, the equivalent of a harlot. And let us not forget you are the almighty king."

"You have never been a harlot in my eyes," he said adamantly. "And at times I wish to forget I am the king."

The sudden dejection in his tone tugged at Maysa's heartstrings. "It sounds as if you *could* use a sabbatical."

"I have nowhere to go where I would be left alone." He fixed his gaze firmly on hers as his lips curled into the familiar teasing smile. The one that had always crushed her determination. "Unless, of course, you would be willing to open your home to me. I would keep to myself. You would not know I am here."

She would know he was there every moment of the day, whether in his presence or not. "I question the wisdom in that plan."

He took her hands into his. "I only wish for time away from my responsibilities, and to become reacquainted with a friend."

How very easy it would be to agree to his request, but… "You have no wish to become reacquainted in bed?"

"I would never ask anything of you that you are not willing to give."

That alone presented a problem—she could find herself willing to give him everything, receiving nothing in return aside from nights of pleasure and more good memories to temporarily overcome the bad. He could also break her heart once more.

Maysa tugged out of his grasp and strolled around the room, all the while weighing the pros and cons. Then something suddenly occurred to her. She could use his presence to her advantage. She could finally show him that improvements to health care for the poor should be paramount during his reign. She could introduce him to exactly what his people endured in the face of illness. And she would do so while keeping her wits about her.

After all, the guest wing was far removed from her private suites, allowing them physical distance. Aside from that, she was a strong, independent woman. She had superb skills honed at the best medical facilities in the United States. She had survived and divorced a known tyrant. She could handle a king—or so she hoped.

On that thought, she faced Rafiq again, lifted her chin, and centered her gaze on his. "All right. You may stay." When he began to speak, she held up a finger to silence him. "As long as you abide by my rules."

He sent her a suspicious look. "What would these rules entail?"

"I prefer to reserve the details for later." When she actually knew what they were.

"All right," he said. "Is there anything else you require of me tonight?"

One response vaulted into her brain. An inappropriate response that she shoved aside. "Not at this time."

Rafiq regarded his watch before bringing his attention back to her. "I must return to the palace now. We shall continue this discussion when I arrive tomorrow to begin my respite."

Tomorrow? "I thought perhaps you would need more time to make arrangements." Or to change his mind.

"I have complete control over when I stay or when I leave the palace. After all, I am—"

"The king. I know." All too well. "I'll see you out."

They walked side by side to the door where Rafiq paused and regarded her earnestly. "I am forever in your debt, Maysa, and I assure you I will give you no cause to distrust my motives."

That remained to be seen. "I'm pleased to know that. And I reserve the right to add conditions should your motives come into question."

"I will strive to win back your trust. The way you once trusted me before our lives intruded on our relationship."

Maysa wanted to believe him. More important, she wanted not to be so drawn to him. Wanted not to feel so lost when he looked at her as he looked at her now—with a heated gaze that traveled from her forehead to her mouth.

They stood for a few long moments, face-to-face, the tension as thick as the mountain mist. Maysa recognized that it would only take a slight move toward him before they found themselves lips to lips. Body to body.

She finally cleared her throat and stepped back before her resolve shattered. "Have a good night, King Mehdi. I will see you tomorrow."

"I will be here before day's end, Dr. Barad."

The formality surprised Maysa and sounded false to her ears. Yet if that formality kept her grounded, she would avoid calling him by his given name. Avoid touching him altogether. Avoid any circumstance that could lead to risks neither could afford to take. But when he leaned and brushed a soft kiss across her cheek, and presented a soft, sensual smile, she worried danger could lurk around every corner when he returned to her home.

After Rafiq opened the door and strode out of the house toward the awaiting car, Maysa considered the first rule. An important rule that could save her from herself. "Rafiq," she called before he could settle into the seat. "I have one more thing to say before you go."

He turned with a wary look on his face. "You have reconsidered?"

She hadn't, though she probably should. "No. I have thought of one rule that we both must follow."

"And that is?"

"There will be no more kisses."

He sent her a knowing smile before he slid into the car. And as Maysa watched the taillights disappear, she worried that King Rafiq Mehdi could convince her to break all the rules.

Two

No more kisses...

As Rafiq sat alone in his office, attempting to tie up loose ends, kissing Maysa remained foremost on his mind. Making love to her again did, as well. He could no more resist the fantasies than he could pick up the palace with his bare hands and move it down the mountainside.

"Have you mentally vacated the premises, brother?"

Rafiq glanced up from his desk to discover his youngest sibling standing before him, wearing his usual standard beige flight suit and mocking smile. "I am preoccupied by my duty."

"Too preoccupied to speak with me, your most loyal supporter?"

Adan rarely supported anyone aside from himself. "Unless you have something important to say, you may return later."

"I do have something of great importance to tell you," Adan said as he claimed the opposing chair.

Frustrated over the intrusion, Rafiq tossed his pen aside and leaned back in his seat. "You have found yet another aircraft you are determined to add to our fleet."

"No. I came to deliver a message."

"From whom?"

"Maysa Barad." Adan's grin widened, as if privy to a secret. "She requests that you arrive before 6:00 p.m., and that you limit your guards if at all possible."

He could only imagine where his brother's thoughts had turned. "Duly noted. You may leave now."

"Not until you explain why you are visiting Maysa, and why she would ask that you not bring along too many guards. Either she feels she does not pose a threat, or she wishes to make certain she has your undivided attention."

"What business I have with Maysa is not your concern."

"Perhaps, but I am curious."

Rafiq resisted telling his brother what he could do with his curiosity, and his British accent. "If you must know, Maysa has agreed to allow me to take a brief respite in her home."

Adan rubbed his chin. "I see. Will you be spending this respite in her bed?"

He was not at all surprised over the assumption, but he *was* angered by it. "Rest assured, I will not be attempting to bed her." Though preventing that possibility would prove to be a great challenge.

Adan released a cynical laugh. "Ah, that is where we differ. I for one would give up flying before I would not take advantage of being alone with a beautiful woman in close confines. And you should consider doing the same."

He felt the need to explain his resistance, whether Adan deserved an explanation or not. "First, I have only been widowed a short while—"

"To a woman you did not love."

"A woman I had known for quite some time before she became my wife. No matter what you believe, I did care for Rima."

"Yet not as much as you've always cared for Maysa."

His patience was beginning to grow thin, frayed in part by the truth. "Maysa is only a friend who has agreed to accommodate my needs."

"Which needs would those be, brother?" Adan asked.

"My intentions are honorable." Though his thoughts and actions the previous evening had not been at all honorable.

"How honorable will you be while spending time with a friend who at one time fancied herself in love with you?"

He could not argue that point. "What Maysa and I shared in the past had more to do with camaraderie than with love."

"Teenage lust, you mean. And that lust could quite possibly carry over into adulthood."

He had spent most of the night considering it. "I am older and wiser. I have learned to maintain self-control."

Adan presented a skeptic's smile. "You are a Mehdi male, Rafiq, and self-control can and will escape you in the presence of a woman you have always desired. You are not made of steel."

Rafiq folded his hands atop the desk and glared at his brother. "Do not project your lack of restraint on me. I have not made bedding women my favorite pastime."

"I have not had as many women as you might believe," Adan said. "And although you have practiced more discretion, I suspect you were not celibate during the time between your agreement to marry Rima and when you finally did wed her."

That fact was not up for debate. "If you are finished delving into my private life, you may take your leave immediately."

"Actually, I'm not quite finished. Did it disturb you that Rima was not a virgin when you wed her?"

Adan's audacity made Rafiq's blood boil. "Why would you assume this?"

"Are you denying it?"

Unfortunately, he could not. Yet he did question how Adan would know something so personal about Rima. He was tempted to ask, but he in turn feared the answer. "This topic is not up for discussion."

"I only wanted to point out that Rima was not destined for sainthood," Adan said. "Neither are you. In fact, you're human, and a man with needs."

The reason behind his brother's insinuation finally dawned on Rafiq. "If you are worried I will bring scandal upon the Mehdi name by sleeping with Maysa, I assure you that will not happen. And if you are also hoping that I will abandon my duty and pass the crown to you, as Zain did with me, you may set those wishes aside immediately."

Adan's expression turned suddenly serious. "I have never possessed any desire to be king, Rafiq. And as far as your relationship with Maysa is concerned, I am an advocate for letting nature take its course. If you and Maysa find you cannot resist each other, then don't. You certainly have my blessing."

Adan had failed to weigh the most important fact. If Rafiq took Maysa as his lover again, the liaison could only be temporary since he would be expected to choose a suitable queen. The thought of being with another woman aside from Maysa was unthinkable. The thought of wounding her again, unimaginable. Yet he could very well head down that path if he acted on impulse.

For that reason, perhaps he should consider canceling their arrangement. Perhaps it would be best if he found another location for his sabbatical. "I will take your counsel under advisement. Now if you do not mind, I have work to complete."

"So much work, *il mio bel ragazzo,* that you cannot give your former governess a few moments?"

Rafiq turned his attention from Adan to Elena Battelli, who now stood at the doorway, a dark-haired infant balanced on her hip. Her silver hair contrasted with her topaz eyes that at times hinted at mischief, and other times reflected wisdom. She had been the Mehdi sons' surrogate matriarch since their mother's death, and always a welcome presence. She had also been free with her opinions, and he expected no less from her now.

Rafiq came to his feet, rounded the desk and accepted her embrace. "I am glad to see you have returned home, Elena. You are looking quite well."

"You are looking tired, *cara,*" she said as she handed the baby off to an overtly surprised Adan. "Take your niece to her father and allow me some time alone with your brother."

Rising from the chair, Adan gripped the child awkwardly and looked as if he had consumed something unpalatable. "What if she begins to cry on the way?"

Elena frowned. "She would not be the first female you've made cry, so I suggest you hurry."

As soon as Adan left with the squirming infant, Rafiq seated himself behind the desk while Elena claimed the chair opposite his. She studied him for a long moment before she spoke. "What is this I hear about you spending time with Dr. Barad?"

He should not be surprised Elena would join his brothers by presenting her thoughts on the matter. Yet her opinion had always mattered most. He also suspected she would side with Zain. "It is not what you might believe it to be."

"I believe, *cara mia,* it is a good idea."

He had not predicted that reaction. "I am beginning to question the wisdom in the plan."

"Because you fear what others might think?"

Because he feared his possible absence of strength in Maysa's presence. "I do not wish to add undue stress to her life."

Elena waved a hand in dismissal. "Maysa is well equipped to handle stress, Rafiq, and perhaps even better equipped to handle you."

He was taken aback by her assertions. "What are you saying?"

"I am saying she knows you very well." Elena laid a palm on his hand. "She has always been your touchstone, and I believe you need that right now, more than you need the throne. And if you are concerned that you might succumb to inadvisable urges, I trust you to be the honorable man you have always been."

If only he could trust himself. "Then you sincerely believe I should continue with my plans?"

"Yes, I do." She rose with the grace of a gazelle. "Do not forget what I've taught you. *Chi trova un amico trova un tesoro.*"

He who finds a friend, finds a treasure.

As Elena started toward the door, she sent Rafiq a smile over one shoulder. "Maysa is your treasure, *cara.* Do not squander that gift."

Maysa had begun to believe Rafiq had changed his mind. When the doorbell chimed, she hurried down the hall to answer the summons but then slowed her steps so as not to seem too anxious, though she was. Yet when she opened the door, the bearded man on the threshold happened to be her brother, not the king. "What are you doing here, Shamil?"

"I expected a more enthusiastic greeting, considering my recent absence," he said as he breezed past her and entered without an invitation.

"My apologies," she said as she faced him in the foyer. "I'm just surprised to see you."

"Were you expecting someone else?"

She chose to withhold the truth and settled for a change in subject. "Are the resort's renovations complete?"

"No, and that is why I am here now," he said. "I will be returning to Yemen tonight, and I would respectfully request you supervise the workers from time to time in my stead."

The request did not surprise her in the least. Shamil

always seemed to have an ulterior motive when he bothered to call on her. He had protested the loudest over her divorce, and had chastised her at every turn—until he wanted something. "I have a medical practice that requires my attention, Shamil. I do not have time to oversee a project that you took on."

"Need I remind you the resort is partially your responsibility?"

She could not believe his audacity. "Our father handed the keys to the resort to you, not me."

"And he handed this house to you," he said as he made a sweeping gesture over the area. "All because he is a generous and forgiving man. I would be remiss if I did not mention that he initially arranged for the hotel's restoration. I am certain it would please him if he knew you were assisting me. He would not be pleased if he learned you refused to provide that assistance."

Maysa was beyond trying to please her father, and immune to Shamil's veiled threats. "I can only promise that I will stop by once a week, provided I find the time."

"Twice a week, or perhaps three times, would be preferable."

She would agree to most anything if it encouraged her sibling's speedy departure. "I will try. Is that all you wish from me?"

"For the moment. I will notify the staff you will be periodically stopping by."

"All right."

When Maysa moved toward the door and yanked it open, she heard the sound of a car pulling into the portico.

"What is *he* doing here?" Shamil asked, both his tone and expression balanced on the brink of contempt.

She ventured a backward glance to see Rafiq emerging from the sedan with a heavily armed guard standing nearby. "First of all, he is the king, and he is allowed to go anywhere he pleases. Second, he is a friend, and at one time, your best friend."

"He no longer holds that distinction."

Maysa's attempt to question her brother further was thwarted when Rafiq joined them at the doorstep.

Rafiq smiled at Maysa and briefly nodded at Shamil. *"As-salam alaikum."*

"Wa alaikum as-salam," Shamil replied in a voice that heralded indifference along with a touch of disdain. "Have you forgotten the way to the palace, Sayyed?"

"Not at all," Rafiq replied. "I am here by invitation."

Shamil sent Maysa a lethal look before returning his attention to Rafiq. "If you are here to discuss health care issues with my sister, it would be appropriate to do so in a less private setting."

Concerned over her brother's caustic demeanor, Maysa stepped aside to allow Rafiq entry. "The staff will show you to your quarters, Your Highness."

"As you wish," he said without offering Shamil even a passing glance.

She sensed her brother's glare before she actually contacted it. She turned and gave him a glare of her own. "How dare you be so ill-mannered."

"How dare you invite him into our father's house."

"Our father has always had close ties to the Mehdi family," Maysa said. "He would not be opposed to having a member as a houseguest, particularly if that member happens to be the sovereign ruler of Bajul. A king who is in need of a respite, which is why he will be staying here for a time."

"Our father would be opposed to you becoming the king's mistress."

Her fury simmered just below the surface of her feigned calm. "You have no right to speak to me this way, nor do you have any reason to hate Rafiq. Or do you still envy his marriage to Rima?"

He looked as if he might strike the wall, or worse, his sister. "Rima meant nothing to Rafiq," he growled. "He did not deserve her."

Clearly Shamil had not moved beyond the past, or his desire for a woman he could never have. But hadn't she been guilty of the same with Rafiq? No. She had moved on, and would continue to do so. "How would you know what privately transpired between the king and queen, Shamil?"

"She deserved far more care and concern than Rafiq afforded her. She deserved the chance to live, and he stole that chance from her."

"Rafiq had no hand in Rima's death."

"You would not agree if you had seen her that night."

Maysa felt as if they might be hurling toward the truth of what had transpired that evening. What she herself had witnessed. "Perhaps I did see her after all."

That seemed to momentarily douse Shamil's wrath. "Where would you have seen her?"

"I drove to the resort earlier that evening and when I saw you embracing a woman on the veranda, I immediately left. Am I correct to assume that woman was Rima?" When he failed to respond, she added, "Shamil, was it Rima?"

His gaze faltered. "She was there for a brief time."

"And how many times before that?"

"That is not your concern."

Oh, but it was. "Were the two of you having an affair?"

"Enough!"

She'd obviously struck a nerve encased in the truth. "And Rafiq knew nothing about your liaison with his wife."

"Rafiq knew nothing about Rima's life because he chose not to know." He sent her a steely look. "And he will never know. Is that understood?"

One more threat among many. "He has a right to know what happened in the minutes leading up to her death."

"He gave up all rights to that knowledge when he discarded her feelings and deprived her of freedom. And if you utter one word of this conversation to the king, then I will see to it you are removed from this house and I will make certain your reputation is ruined beyond repair."

She clung tightly to the last thread of civility. "You do not have that much power, Shamil. You never have. I can find another place to live, and the villagers respect me not only as their doctor, but as a person. They care not about my past."

He narrowed his eyes and stared at her. "Will they be so accepting if they learn their doctor is also the king's *sharmuta?*"

She pointed a shaky finger at the SUV parked at the end of the drive. "Leave now and do not return unless you arrive with an apology."

He released a bitter laugh. "Oh, I will return, yet I

will not rescind what I have said. If you reveal any details to Rafiq, there will be consequences."

With that, he rushed to the waiting SUV and drove away, leaving Maysa standing on the threshold, worrying over how she would tell Rafiq about his wife's whereabouts that fateful evening. *If* she decided to tell him.

Should she confess, the outcome would still be the same. Rima would still be gone, her secrets following her to the grave. Shamil would be bent on ruining Maysa's life if she told Rafiq the details. She had very limited loyalty to Shamil, but she possessed enough common sense not to risk losing everything she had worked so hard to build. Yet the thought of keeping such a serious secret from Rafiq fueled her guilt.

Fortunately, she would not be forced to choose which course to take in the immediate future. Right now, her focus would be on making Rafiq feel welcome.

She seemed uncomfortable. Rafiq noticed that about Maysa during dinner, and now as they relaxed on rattan sofas in the private courtyard beneath the night sky. Regardless that she seemed on edge, she still looked beautiful as she sat with her legs curled to one side, revealing her bare feet and a delicate silver chain circling one ankle that matched the heavy bangles at her wrists. Her long, dark hair cascaded over her slim shoulders, strands of amber highlighted by the moon, and the sleeveless white gauze dress she wore contrasted with the golden cast of her skin. He remembered touching that skin during a time when they had both been completely captivated by one another. So hungry for each other that it seemed they might never be sated—until the one and only night they crossed the forbidden line and made love.

She captivated him still, fed a fire that he had wrongly assumed would be extinguished by time, mistakes and regrets. He wanted to leave the sofa he had claimed and take the space beside her. He wished to do more than only sit with her. Yet her moratorium on kissing left him with only one option—remain where he sat and simply admire her from afar.

Maysa sighed, her attention focused on the jasmine lining the edge of the stone terrace. "I love summer evenings."

He loved the sound of her voice—soft, lyrical. "You have lost most of your accent."

She smiled, deepening the dimples creasing her cheeks. "The time I spent in the States is responsible for that."

"Do you still know how to speak our native tongue?"

She frowned. "Of course I still know how. I have to communicate with my patients here."

He thought of one question he had wanted to ask. "Why did you return to Bajul to practice medicine knowing how you would be treated following your divorce?"

Her gaze wandered away as she began twisting the bracelets around her right wrist. "Bajul is my home, Rafiq, and since Boutros lives elsewhere, it seemed logical to return. I also missed the quiet pace and the peaceful existence."

"You do not seem at peace tonight," he said. "Is something bothering you?"

She shifted slightly and finally raised her gaze to

his. "Actually, yes. I'm concerned about the lack of care for the poorest in Bajul."

"It is my understanding you are an excellent doctor, therefore they are receiving the finest care."

"But I'm only one person, Rafiq. Other physicians could assist, yet they refuse. They only provide services to those who can pay. It's a travesty."

He understood her frustration, yet he had no solution. "I cannot force other physicians to work for no pay."

"But you could see to it that newer doctors are enticed to come here to fill in the gaps."

He leaned back and set his glass of mango juice on the adjacent table. "How do you propose I do this?"

"By offering government-sponsored grants."

"Our current funds are earmarked for the water conservation efforts. We have no surplus to devote to anything else at this time."

"Then perhaps sell one of the new military planes Adan has recently acquired. It would seem you have more than enough for a country the size of Bajul."

"At times it seems we do not have enough to bolster our defense. But I will take your suggestions into consideration."

He noted a spark of anger in her dark, almond-shaped eyes. "That is all you have to say?"

"Maysa, I am only one voice on the council."

"You are the supreme voice, King Mehdi. You have the last word."

He had less power than she realized. "I must do what the majority dictates to keep the peace."

"At the expense of your people?"

"Again, I will consider your concerns and present

them to the council when it is time to prepare the next budget."

She straightened her legs, planted her feet on the ground, and seared him with a glare. "That is over five months away. People could die before then, both elderly adults and children. Mothers with difficult births."

He did not have the means to accommodate her at this time, yet he could not disappoint her. "I will see what I can do, though I can make no promises."

"I suppose that is enough," she said, her expression somewhat more relaxed. "At least for the time being."

Fatigue began to set in, yet Rafiq could not force himself to leave her. He also could not rid himself of the slight pain resulting from an injury he'd suffered in his youth. He lifted the shoulder slightly, once, twice, before he settled back against the cushions.

"It still bothers you, doesn't it?" Maysa asked.

He was not surprised she had noticed. "What bothers me?"

"Your shoulder. The one you fractured in that ridiculous fight with Aakif Nejem."

"I believe we were fighting over you." He smiled. "And I came away with two black eyes and a lacerated lip. I would have been unscathed had it not been for my falling against the iron gate."

Maysa returned his smile, though she appeared to be attempting to keep it at bay. "The very gate you drove through earlier, designed by my father to ward off unwelcome suitors."

"Yet that gate was not strong enough to keep me from you that night."

A brief span of silence passed between them, as well as an exchanged glance that Rafiq remembered very clearly. The same knowing look they had given each other when he had laid her down in her bed, cloaked only by the cover of darkness, the threat of discovery heightening their desire.

Maysa broke the visual contact first and turned her focus back on the flowers. "That was a long time ago, Rafiq. We were both young and very foolish."

"We were consumed by each other."

She raised a thin brow. "Consumed by lust, you mean."

Had it only been lust, he would have long forgotten that evening. Forgotten her. "Have you never considered what would have happened had your father come upon us?"

"Would he have forced us to marry?" She shook her head. "He would have sent me away from you."

In many ways, that is exactly what had happened. The sultan had sent her into another man's bed. A man who had not deserved her.

When Maysa hid a yawn behind her hand, then stretched her arms above her head, Rafiq suspected she would soon be leaving him again, at least for the evening. "It is time for me to go to bed," she said, confirming his theory. "I have several early visits to make in the village tomorrow."

He struggled for some way to keep her there awhile longer, and returned to the issue that had begun their journey into the past. "Would you examine my shoulder before you retire?"

"What do you believe I'd accomplish by doing that?"

She would be closer to him, at least momentarily. He pressed his palm against the spot that always gave him the most pain. "I would like to see what you think about this ridge. Perhaps you can advise me if it is an issue I need to have evaluated further."

She sighed, rose from the sofa and took the space beside him. "Lean forward." After he complied, she rested her left hand on his left shoulder and examined the offending shoulder with her right hand.

"Well?" he asked.

She pushed against one spot, causing him to wince. "Does that hurt?" she asked.

"Slightly." More than he would allow her to see.

"That's your deltoid muscle," she said as she continued to knead the area. "You have quite a bit of tension there."

The tension behind his fly began to increase with every caress of her fingertips. "Perhaps it is only stress-induced?"

"Perhaps, but I cannot tell for certain without an X-ray. You could probably benefit from physical therapy."

The therapy she was offering him now was quite beneficial in terms of soothing the soreness. He could not say the same for his libido. And when she leaned over and applied more pressure, his palm automatically came to rest on her thigh, immediately above her knee, where he drew small circles with his thumb through the dress's thin material.

Her hand froze midmotion. "What are you doing, Rafiq?"

"Nothing." Not presently.

She released a shuddering breath. "We said no touching."

He inched his palm higher. "You said no kissing."

"Rule two, no touching."

Despite her assertions, he did not bother to lift his hand, and she did not bother to shove it away. “Yet you have been touching me.”

“As a physician.”

“And I have reacted as any man reacts to a woman’s touch.”

“For that reason, I should go now.”

Rafiq predicted she would stand and leave, but she remained positioned next to him, both hands still resting lightly on his shoulders. He straightened, bringing their faces close, their gazes connecting immediately. He saw the indecision in her eyes, as well as a spark of need.

And then Maysa did something Rafiq did not expect—she broke her first rule.

Three

She had taken complete leave of her senses, but at the moment Maysa didn't care. She only concerned herself with the play of Rafiq's mouth against hers and the impressions he made with the gentle glide of his tongue.

At some point—and she had no idea how or when—he had shifted toward her and she had moved fully into his arms. A nagging voice demanded she stop before she could not, but she disregarded the caution. For once she wanted to be softly kissed, without undue force. Willingly kissed. She wanted to remember how it felt to be a desirable woman, not simply an object of brutal lust.

Yet all the reasons why she shouldn't be doing this kept crowding her mind. She could be only a means to an end for Rafiq. A source of comfort. A temporary diversion. She was also keeping a secret from him. A secret that could ultimately destroy him emotionally, and her reputation literally.

Still, when he cupped her breast, she focused on the sensations, not solid rationale. He traced her nipple with a fingertip, causing her to shift restlessly against the building heat. But when he left her mouth to feather kisses down the column of her throat, sliding the dress's strap down her shoulder, a barrage of bitter memories prompted her to automatically tense.

Rafiq reacted to her sudden change in mood by abruptly rising from the sofa, leaving Maysa alone steeped in self-consciousness. He walked away, his hands laced behind his neck, and stopped in the middle of the terrace, keeping his back to her.

"I'm sorry," Maysa muttered as she readjusted her clothing. "I have no idea what has come over me. We shouldn't be doing this." She'd begun to wonder if she could do it, even if she wanted to.

Rafiq dropped his arms to his sides and faced her again. "I am not sorry, yet I am convinced this will keep happening between us."

So was Maysa, unless she revealed the absolute truth behind her reluctance. She wasn't willing to do that. "We'll simply need to avoid situations such as this. Following dinner each evening, I will return to my quarters, and you will return to yours. We will keep our distance during the day, as well."

He shifted his weight slightly. "And I will lie awake all night, imagining how it would be to touch you with my hands and my mouth in ways I never did when we were younger. I will dream about how it would feel to be buried deep inside you. And each time I see you, I will want the reality."

The heat returned, prompting Maysa to cross her legs. “Then perhaps it would be best if you found another place for your respite.”

“I care not to be anywhere else.”

Truthfully, she didn’t want him to leave, either. “Then I suppose you will be forced to rely solely on your imagination.”

“Or we could both choose not to fight our desire. No one would know if we became lovers again.”

How very easy it would be to agree. How very foolish if she did. “I would know, Rafiq. Nothing could ever exist between us beyond temporary physical pleasure. You are the king, and I am a woman who most believe is unfit to keep company with you, let alone be your lover.”

He rubbed a palm over his nape. “Again, we could be discreet. We could enjoy each other during the time we have.”

The fact he didn’t say she wasn’t unsuitable was as effective as a frigid shower. Maysa stood, hands fisted at her sides, nails digging into her palms. “I have already been one man’s whore, Rafiq. I will not be another’s.”

“I am prisoner to tradition and acceptable mores, Maysa, as are you. Yet that does not mean I would view you as my *sharmuta*.”

“Yet that is exactly what I would be to you, a woman not fit to be your queen, yet expected to do your bidding in bed. Answer your every need, yet receive nothing in return, as it was with Boutrous. That would make me your mistress.”

Maysa expected to see anger in Rafiq’s expression,

but he only seemed concerned. "What did Boutros do to you, Maysa?"

"This has nothing to do with him." Only a partial truth. "This has to do with us. I have developed a great deal of self-respect during our time apart. I am not that smitten schoolgirl who would have given everything to you, knowing I could never have a future with you."

He released a rough sigh. "What do you wish me to say, Maysa?"

That he would tell the elders to go to hell. That she was an acceptable partner by virtue of her intelligence and skills, not her past. That he would make an effort to change the archaic laws governing the role of women. "Nothing, Rafiq. I wish for you to say nothing. You have already said it all."

When she turned to retire to her room, Rafiq called her back. "I would rather die a thousand deaths than to wound you again, Maysa."

And she would experience a thousand more regrets if she gave in to the sincerity in his dark eyes. "Then don't, Rafiq. Be my friend."

He approached her slowly. "I am your friend. That has never changed, despite the distance between us."

Before she made another monumental mistake and walked back into his arms, Maysa left the terrace and returned to her quarters. And once she was safely in bed, she let herself imagine what it would be like to make love with him again, too. Yet the fantasies could never replace the reality. But the reality was she'd invited him here for a reason, and tomorrow she would begin to implement her plan. And with that plan came the opportunity to educate a king. The beautiful, sensual king of her heart.

* * *

Shirtless, Rafiq faced the double-paned window overlooking the veranda, allowing Maysa a premiere view from the partially open door. The strong planes of his broad shoulders, broken by a slight scar on his right, demonstrated he was still as physically fit as he'd always been. The indentation of his spine tracked into the waistband of his navy pajamas, surrounded by supple, golden skin. And below that, narrow hips and a toned buttocks looked quite touchable.

But she wouldn't touch him. Not today. She had more pressing matters at hand, provided he cooperated.

Maysa moved quietly into the room, several items of clothing clutched in her arms. "Did you sleep well?"

If he was at all startled by her appearance, he didn't show it. He simply turned and presented a half smile. "I slept as well as can be expected in a strange bed alone, knowing that a desirable woman is such a short distance away."

She disregarded the innuendo, but she could not seem to keep her eyes off the downward stream of masculine hair below his navel, or that he seemed quite pleased to see her from an anatomical standpoint. "Well," she said as she forced her gaze to his dark eyes, "I hope you are sufficiently rested since I have plans for us today."

"Plans?" He rounded the foot of the bed and stood a few feet from her. "What do these plans entail?"

"I am traveling to the Diya region and I want you to come with me."

He frowned. "That is over two hours away."

"Yes, and I make the journey every Wednesday to

treat the sheep farmers and their families. Today is Wednesday."

"Why would you wish me to accompany you?"

"Because I believe it's important you begin to understand the health care issues facing your country, including the lack of resources in remote areas."

He appeared to mull that over before he spoke again. "The people of Diya never supported my father. It has been reported several possible insurgency camps exist there."

"Perhaps they did not embrace being ignored by your father," she said. "You could change that."

He strolled around the room for a moment before turning to her again. "Would we be able to communicate by cell phone with the outside world?"

She rolled her eyes. "There are no cellular towers. The villagers only recently received regular phone service, and many do not have electricity. Some do not have adequate water supplies."

"If I accompany you, I would require a contingent of guards for both our protection should I be recognized."

"Not if you are unrecognizable." She tossed him the army-green shirt and cargo pants. "If you put these on and wear sunglasses, no one will know a king walks among them."

He unfolded the clothes and inspected them. "I doubt a change of attire would serve as an adequate disguise."

"If you wear sunglasses and shave, that should suffice."

He laughed. A deep, low, sensual laugh that sent chills down the length of Maysa's body. "I have no intention of shaving."

"Your goatee will grow back, Rafiq. Most likely in two days' time."

He leveled his gaze on her. "Is it that important I join you?"

"Yes, and it should be important to you. A good ruler knows his people. Especially the poor and less fortunate."

He sighed. "All right. I will do this for you, but I still believe it is necessary to bring along a guard."

"That isn't necessary. I've traveled the terrain many times and I have yet to encounter any trouble. I also travel with a firearm should I need it."

His grin arrived slowly. "Do you know how to use it?"

She returned his smile. "I'm certain I could shoot straight should the situation arise. So rest assured, as long as you are with me, your royal body will be safe."

"You are willing to take my royal body into your own hands?"

Ignoring the suggestive words, she pointed at the clothes. "Dress, Your Majesty. I'll meet you at the back entrance to the house."

His smile disappeared. "And I will drive."

"No, you will not."

With that, she flipped her hair over one shoulder and left the room to prepare for the journey. With a reluctant king in tow, it could prove to be quite an adventure.

Rafiq had always known Maysa to have an adventurous spirit. He had seen her take risks most women would not dare undertake. Yet he had never seen her dressed as she was now. She wore a long-sleeved white blouse covered by a white laboratory coat, as well as khaki pants and a pair of heavy boots. Her official apparel concealed her feminine attributes, yet her absence of makeup did not take away from her natural beauty. He knew exactly what existed beneath the clothing—full breasts, round bottom, soft skin.

While Rafiq's discomfort began to grow, Maysa looked entirely comfortable behind the wheel of the Hummer, navigating the rugged terrain with practiced ease. He, on the other hand, was sweltering due to the August sun and in part due to his inability to take his eyes off Maysa. Since last evening, he had not been able to escape the memory of her kiss. Could not erase the images of what he wanted to do with her. To her. But he also could not forget her reaction to his touch, as if she had been somewhat repulsed.

He streaked a hand over his forehead and took a drink of water from the canteen she had brought along. "How much farther?"

"We're almost there," she said, keeping her eyes trained on the dirt road. "Over the mountain."

As soon as they topped the rise, Maysa continued down the incline past a tribesman herding sheep and several young boys playing barefoot along the path. Once they arrived in the primitive town, she pulled in front of a large canvas tent where several people had gathered around the opening.

After Maysa shut off the ignition and climbed out, Rafiq remained seated to observe the interaction between doctor and villagers. Women, men and children converged upon her, shouting greetings and presenting smiles that she returned.

After a time, she managed to make her way to the passenger door to address him. "Keep your sunglasses on at all times," she said in a low voice. "I will tell everyone you're from the States and you do not speak Arabic. In fact, it's best if you do not speak at all."

That could take effort. "If that is what you wish."

She favored him with a smile. "And by the way, I like you better clean-shaven."

His hand immediately went to his bare chin. "Be that as it may, I will begin growing it back as soon as we are finished with this adventure. Otherwise, someone might mistake me for my brother."

She pulled a stethoscope from the pocket of the lab coat and draped it around her neck. "Do what you will, Rafiq, but take it from a woman. Kissing a man with a beard is not always comfortable." With that, she rounded the SUV while Rafiq remained to ponder her words. Did she intend to let him kiss her again? One could always hope.

Rafiq slid out of the Hummer and joined Maysa at the rear to haul the large supply trunk into the tent while she carried a smaller medical kit. She signaled him to be seated in a rattan chair in the corner of the tent and pressed a fingertip to her lips, reminding him to be silent, as if he were an errant schoolboy. She then went to work, tending to the villagers with both speed and skill. She periodically handed out treats to the children and advice to worried mothers. Several men stood nearby, eyeing Rafiq with suspicion and occasionally watching Maysa with lust. He could not blame them though he did not care for their leers. Yet defending the physician's honor would most likely incur the physician's wrath.

As Rafiq continued to witness Maysa deliver her expert ministrations, he experienced a sense of pride, though he had no right. He had never discouraged her from entering the medical field, but he had not encouraged her, either. He had always believed she would be destined to abandon her dreams for the life of a sultan's wife. But she had bravely defied convention and custom, and had suffered severe consequences for her choices.

Watching her care for these downtrodden people, receiving their adoration and appreciation, Rafiq realized that perhaps she had not suffered as much as one would believe. Perhaps she was living the life she was meant to live. A life without him.

A commotion coming from the tent's entrance drew his attention. A young man elbowed his way through the awaiting crowd, shouting, *"Tâbeeb!"*

When he rushed toward Maysa, Rafiq immediately shot to his feet to intervene. Maysa gave him a quelling look as she took the farmer aside and spoke to him quietly.

He could not hear most of the conversation, but he understood the gravity of the situation from the concerned look in Maysa's eyes. She turned and addressed the woman who'd been assisting her and instructed her to do what she could until she returned. Then she gestured Rafiq to follow her out of the tent. Once they were back in the SUV, Maysa followed a truck out of the village and toward the mountains.

"Where are we going?" Rafiq asked as Maysa made one hairpin turn without braking.

"There is a woman in labor," she said. "She's having difficulty delivering."

"Her first child?"

"Fourth, and that's what concerns me."

The man had not looked old enough to father four offspring. But he did not have time to voice his opinion as Maysa pulled into a drive leading to an earthen hut. She had stopped the vehicle, retrieved the smallest medical kit and had arrived at the front door before he had barely left the passenger seat.

Rafiq made haste and entered the house to see Maysa disappearing through a door to the right of the living area. He discovered three children sitting on the low blue sofas, their eyes wide with fear. The oldest could not have been more than six years old, the second perhaps four and the youngest about two years of age. He surveyed the room to find it absent of any adult and assumed the father had chosen to be at his wife's side.

When he claimed another smaller sofa to wait, the oldest little girl came to her feet and crossed the room to stand before him.

He remembered Maysa's insistence he not speak, yet he could not pretend he was not concerned over the child's well-being. *"Shu esmek?"*

She twirled a lock of dark hair around her tiny finger. "Aini."

The name suited her, he decided. With her dark curls and equally dark eyes, she was as pretty as a spring flower. He remembered Elena once saying that children only wanted to be fed, clothed and to feel safe. Aini was clothed, she did not appear undernourished, yet he imagined she did not feel secure at the moment.

For that reason, Rafiq began to recite a story about a lost sheep in search of its mother, a tale he had learned from his own mother. One by one, the other children gathered around and listened intently. When they looked at him with complete trust, he realized, though he had been born to royalty, he had never felt quite as important as he did now. He also experienced a fierce need to protect them. The protection he had not afforded his unborn child.

The sound of mournful moans began to filter from the adjacent room, thrusting away the regret. Rafiq waved the children onto the sofa beside him and set the youngest in his lap. He raised his voice in an attempt to muffle the scream that made his blood run cold. He could only imagine what these innocents were feeling at the moment—hearing their mother in such abject pain.

Maysa emerged from the chamber holding a bundle in her arms, a cap of dark hair showing from beneath the white blanket. To Rafiq, she looked completely natural holding a baby, and in one fleeting moment, he imagined her holding his child.

She approached the sofa and smiled. "Here is your baby brother," she said to the children in Arabic, followed by, "The baby was breech," in English, directed at Rafiq. "The mother has lost a lot of blood and needs a hospital."

While the two oldest children slid off the sofa to view their new sibling, Rafiq moved the youngest child from his lap and stood. "Is the mother in danger?"

"Yes."

Her somber tone demonstrated to Rafiq the gravity of the situation. "How much time does she have?"

"I fear not long enough to make the three-hour drive, but we have no choice."

Rafiq would give her another choice. "Is there a telephone?"

Maysa looked around the room and pointed at an

ancient handset hanging from the wall. "There, though I cannot guarantee it works."

He would soon find out. Fortunately, the telephone was operable, though it took several attempts to connect with the palace, and another two to convince the staff he was in fact the king. Finally, he managed to reach his brother. "Adan, I need your immediate assistance."

"You have bedded Maysa and you need to know how to proceed?"

He was in no mood to put up with Adan's questionable comments. "I need a medevac helicopter sent to Diya immediately. Make certain to have medics onboard, and that it arrives in less than fifteen minutes."

"What is this about, Rafiq?"

"A woman's life is at stake," he said. "We have only a small window of time to deliver her to the hospital."

"I will do the best that I can on such short notice."

"You will do exactly what I say, and you will be expedient!"

"Calm down, Rafiq. I will have the helicopter there in ten minutes, even if I must fly it myself."

"Good. I am counting on you, Adan."

As soon as he hung up, Rafiq recognized his heart had been racing at breakneck speed. He had done what he could and hoped that it would be enough. He had not been able to save his own wife, but perhaps he could save this one.

Even after she'd treated the last remaining patient in the tent, Maysa could not recall feeling so utterly helpless. A few hours ago, she'd watched the helicopter fly away while she stayed behind since there hadn't been room for her and the woman's husband. "I should have left for the hospital hours ago."

Rafiq came up behind her and rested his palms on her shoulders. "She is in competent hands," he said. "The hospital was prepared to receive them immediately. I am certain all will be well."

If only she could feel so confident. "I hope so," she said as she gathered supplies and put them in the kit. "I cannot imagine how her poor husband would feel if he lost his wife, not to mention having to raise four children on his own."

"It is not something you would wish to imagine," he said. "So do not."

Maysa understood all too well what Rafiq was probably feeling at that moment—his own loss. "I hope we receive some news soon."

"Adan said he would find a way to get word to us when there was news to report."

Maysa was grateful Rafiq had been there to offer support, and thankful that his position had opened doors she would not have been able to open herself. She turned with a smile and handed him the kit. "Please put this in the Hummer and we'll be on our way."

"We cannot leave now."

He couldn't be serious. She was so tired she could barely stand. "Why would we wish to stay any longer? I've finished with my work here for the week."

He smiled. "I have been told the villagers have arranged a feast in honor of the *Tâbeeb* and her *American* friend."

As much as Maysa would like to attend, she was simply too tired for a celebration. "As it stands now, we won't be home until midnight."

"You have not eaten all day."

"I had some goat cheese and *lahvash.*"

He frowned. "Would you insult those who have prepared a fine meal in your honor?"

Before Maysa could respond, "I wouldn't if I were you, Dr. Barad" came from behind her.

She glanced back to see a tall, lanky, sandy-haired man with a full beard approaching. A familiar face she hadn't seen in quite some time.

As soon as he came to her side, Maysa drew him into an embrace. "It is so good to see you, Jerome."

He set her back and surveyed her face. "It's good to see you, too, Maysa. It's been at least a month."

"Longer," she said with a smile. "I assumed you returned to Canada."

"I did for a time, but I didn't stay long. After making a few stops, I'm back in Diya to finish my work."

After Maysa heard Rafiq clear his throat, she faced him again. "Jerome Forte, this is…" She struggled to come up with a proper—and false—introduction. "This is Rafe."

Jerome presented a cynical smile. "No. This is Rafiq Mehdi, ruling king of Bajul."

She should have known she wouldn't be able to put anything over on the photographer. "You're right, but I prefer you keep his identity to yourself."

"You may count on my absolute discretion," he said before he regarded Rafiq once more. "It is a pleasure to meet you, Your Majesty."

Rafiq stared at Jerome's extended hand for a few moments before accepting the gesture. "What brings you to this part of the world, Mr. Forte?"

"Please, it's Jerome." He wrapped an arm around

Maysa's waist, much to her chagrin. "I've been photographing the area for an international magazine. Not only did Maysa suggest the region, she has been instrumental in convincing the villagers here to allow me to take their pictures."

Rafiq looked as though he might throw a punch. "Is that all she's been assisting you with?"

She moved away from Jerome and frowned. "Yes, that is all. Jerome and I have been friends for several years."

"Yes, we have," Jerome said as he smiled down on her. "And I've missed our talks."

"We must decide whether we are staying or going," Rafiq said, a definite edge in his tone. "If you choose to leave, then we must do so now."

He suddenly sounded as if he wanted to leave. "We should stay for a while," she said. "You're right. I wouldn't want to seem ungrateful."

Rafiq moved beside her and possessively took her arm. "If you will excuse us, Mr. Forte, we have a celebration to attend."

"As do I," Jerome said. "The party is being held a block away. We can all walk together."

Considering the disapproving look on Rafiq's face, Maysa was somewhat concerned that accompanying Jerome could lead to trouble. She would certainly hate to have to intervene, though she would. She did not appreciate male posturing in any form or fashion. "Then I suppose we should be going before the sun has completely set."

The trio walked the brick streets of the village, Maysa flanked by the men. While Rafiq remained stoic and silent, Jerome chatted nonstop about his recent travels to Tunisia. Fortunately they arrived at the expansive field without incident.

Several fires blazed throughout the area, providing the means to cook the fare for the feast, including spits with roasting lamb. She'd never cared for that delicacy due to her fondness for baby sheep. But tonight she would sample everything to avoid appearing unappreciative.

As they wove their way through the throngs of people, Maysa answered each greeting with one of her own as Rafiq and Jerome hung back. The village men wore summer-weight *bishts,* their heads covered by *mashadahs,* while the women wore the usual *hijab.* She, Rafiq and Jerome seemed out of place in their civilian clothes, yet no one seemed to notice—except for a group of young women who stood to the side of the banquet table, giggling behind their hands when the men walked up to fill their plates.

Maysa leaned toward Rafiq and whispered, "You are making quite an impression on the female population here. Perhaps you could find a suitable wife among them."

"Perhaps you have discovered a suitable lover in your Canadian friend."

She found the jealousy in his voice somewhat amusing. "As I have told you, Jerome is only a friend. Nothing more."

He kept filling a bowl full of *ogdat* until the stew almost overflowed from the vessel. "He would like more. He would like to have you all to himself."

"Don't be foolish, Rafiq. If you'll look to your left you'll notice he is preoccupied with a young woman as we speak."

Rafiq followed Maysa's gaze to where Jerome was standing near one of the fire pits, charming a pretty young woman who seemed to be hanging on his every word, as well as his arm. "She does not appear to be more than a teenager," he said.

"I predict she is well over the age of consent," she said. "And interested in Jerome. I've seen them together before."

Rafiq frowned. "Her parents approve of this liaison with a foreigner?"

She sighed. "I have no idea, and it is not any of my concern. Now let's eat so we can leave as soon as possible."

Maysa followed Rafiq to the nearest fire and sat beside him on the ground. They ate their meal in silence, then afterward watched several men perform the *dabke* in their honor. As badly as she wanted to leave, she felt it would be impolite to depart during the dance. A dance that seemed to go on and on for an eternity.

By the time the group had finished, and the applause had died down, Maysa worried she could fall asleep and land face-forward in the fire. "We should go now, otherwise I might be forced to let you drive."

Rafiq regarded his watch. "It is late. Perhaps we should find lodging here for the night."

Finding herself in a hotel room with Rafiq did not seem wise. "As far as I know, Diya has no inns."

"Is there a family who would take us in?"

"The two of you can use my tent, Your Excellency."

Once more, Jerome had interrupted the discourse by stealing into the area without Maysa's notice. "Then where would you sleep, Jerome?" she asked, though she knew the answer.

He grinned. "I have made other accommodations."

Of course he had—with the young woman who happened to be standing behind him. "I appreciate the offer, but from what I recall, your tent is not that large." At least not large enough to house two former lovers battling chemistry.

"I disagree," he said. "It's very large, and it has enough room for three people, provided you're willing to sleep side by side on the ground. Actually, there's a sleeping bag covering the ground, and a spare should you need it. It's really quite comfortable."

"I really don't think—"

"I believe it will be suitable for the evening," Rafiq chimed in. "We appreciate your generosity, and we accept."

Maysa momentarily gaped. "I don't accept. I am quite capable of driving."

"You are exhausted," Rafiq said. "As am I. We will rise early in the morning and return refreshed and fully awake."

She doubted she would sleep at all with Rafiq in such close proximity. "I truly don't believe it's necessary."

"His Majesty has a point, Maysa," Jerome added. "There's no need to hurry home when you have a perfectly good tent for the night. It's in the same location, so I'm sure you'll have no problem finding it."

With that, Jerome took his paramour's hand and disappeared into the darkness.

Maysa brought her attention back to Rafiq. "I'm not certain it's wise for us to spend the night together in a tent."

"And I do not think it is wise to drive hours in a state of exhaustion."

She decided to give up on that argument, in part because she was extremely tired. "All right, you may have the shelter and I will sleep in the Hummer."

"No one is sleeping in the Hummer, Maysa. We are both adults and I vow to maintain control, if that is your concern."

That was precisely her concern. "Do you promise to stay on your side of the tent?"

He raised a hand as if taking an oath. "I promise that I will be the gentleman Elena has taught me to be."

Could she trust that he was telling the truth? Could she trust herself around him? Of course she could. She would keep her distance, and demand he keep his. And in the morning, she would return home without any regrets.

"All right. We'll stay in the tent."

And she sincerely hoped it *was* big enough for both of them.

Four

The shelter was much larger than Rafiq had envisioned, and not a tent in the true sense of the word. The structure was comprised of a wooden frame covered by canvas, and tall enough to allow him to stand. Yet it seemed much too small for a man who greatly desired the woman with whom he would share the space.

As he sat on the blanket-covered ground to remove his boots, Maysa stood in the corner, washing her face in a basin set out on a small side table. She had removed her blouse, leaving her clad in a fitted, sleeveless undershirt. While he continued to watch her, she slipped the band securing the braid, unwound it and then shook out her hair that cascaded down her back, the ends touching the top of her waist. He recalled that fall of hair surrounding him, flowing over his bare skin. How many nights had he imagined it happening again? Too numerous to count. And when he had made love to Rima, Maysa had oftentimes been foremost in his mind, fueling his fantasies. A shameful secret he would carry to the grave.

Maysa turned and stretched her hands above her head, drawing the shirt tighter, revealing she wore no bra. She removed a brush from her bag and ran it through her hair. "Thank you for all you did today. And be sure to thank Adan for getting word to us that both mother and child received a clean bill of health."

"Do not forget your part in that good news," he said as he followed the movement of her hand sliding the brush through her long locks, back and forth.

"I was only doing my job."

She was clearly bent on torturing him at the moment.

He stripped away his own shirt for the sake of comfort, and as soon as she turned off the lantern, he intended to remove his pants, also for comfort. If that somehow offended her, then so be it. After all, she had made certain their makeshift beds were almost a meter apart. Still, the distance would not prevent his fantasies, or discourage him if she gave him the least bit of encouragement.

Wise or not, he wanted her still. He would continue to want her even after they parted ways. Yet her reaction the night before when he touched her indicated she did not want him as fiercely as he wanted her, if at all.

After replacing the brush in the duffel, Maysa returned to the pallets, lowered herself onto the blankets and crossed her legs before her. "Are you tired?"

Sleep was the last thing on his mind with Maysa so close. "Surprisingly I am not."

"Neither am I. I thought perhaps we could talk."

He stretched out on his side facing her, and bent his elbow to support his jaw with his hand. "What do you wish to talk about?"

"Your relationship with Rima."

He had not expected that, nor did he care to discuss it. "She was my wife for a brief time and that is all that needs to be said."

"Actually, that's what I wanted to talk about. Why did you wait so long to marry her?"

He had had many reasons, but he chose to omit one—he had hoped Rima would eventually tire of waiting. "I attended university, and when I returned, I had to assist my father since Zain had left for the States. We had no indication when he would return, or even if he would return at that point."

"That seems like a logical justification for a man, but I don't understand why Rima would agree to delay a wedding for the sake of duty when your responsibility would still exist after the wedding."

Rima had never pressured him to set a date. He had done so only because it had been expected. "She decided to travel and then after her father passed, she spent a good deal of time with her mother. We were both in no hurry." And they had both believed they had a lifetime to spend together. A life that would include polite conversation and little passion.

"I would say that's obvious," Maysa said. "You waited almost fifteen years to make it official."

In many ways, fifteen years had not been long enough. "I understand why you would be confused over the decision, considering you married Boutros almost immediately after the betrothal."

Her gaze faltered. "I wasn't given a choice. My father demanded I marry him immediately, per the terms of the agreement. Boutros wasn't getting any younger, and he wanted an heir."

"An heir you did not give him."

"Fortunately, no."

When Maysa began to rub her right wrist, only then did Rafiq notice the ropelike scar circling it. When he had called on her the first night, she had been wearing heavy bangles that concealed the mark. Tonight, the wound was uncovered and he needed to know its origination, though he suspected he already did.

He immediately sat upright and took her hand to study it further. "What is this?"

She wrenched out of his grasp. "It's nothing."

He needed more evidence to substantiate his theory. "Take off your watch."

"No."

"Then I shall do it for you."

He anticipated she would fight him when he unbuckled the strap, yet she sat motionless with a blank stare, as if shielding herself from the truth he sought. And he found that truth when he removed the watch—another circular scar.

Rafiq bit back his anger and tempered his tone. "Did he bind you, Maysa?"

"Rafiq, I—"

"Did that *kalet* tie you?"

"Yes!" she said, her voice heralding her fury. "Yes, the bastard bound me. He grew tired of me fighting him."

Rafiq gritted his teeth and spoke through them. "He forced himself on you against your will?"

"Yes, he did, and he also did this." She twisted around and raised the back of her shirt, revealing a series of slashes across her flesh. "He tried to beat me into submission, and when it did not work, he would go for the rope."

Unable to remain still, Rafiq stood and began pacing the area. He longed for a solid wall to hit, a means to expend his rage. "I will kill him with my own hands."

Maysa's laughter spun him around. "You are too late to ride to my rescue, I fear. It's my understanding his heart is failing, though I'm surprised to learn he has a heart at all. I have no doubt it is as black as midnight."

Rafiq returned to her and claimed the space beside her. "Did you not mention this to your father?"

"Yes, I did. He told me that to be a good wife, I would do what was required. Even Shamil sided with him."

His respect for the sultan and his former friend plummeted. "And your mother?"

"She always left the room, most likely to hide her tears. But I never cried. I was determined not to let any of them see my tears or my weakness, especially Boutros."

"Yet you suffered for your strength."

She raised her chin, defiance reflecting from her eyes. "I called on that well-honed strength the night I left him."

He needed to know all the details, both bad and good. "How did you manage to escape?"

"We were at his home in Oman. He was out with one of his many mistresses. I broke into his desk, stole several thousand riyals and caught a plane to Canada. That's where I first met Jerome, on the plane. He assisted me in finding temporary housing. He was also instrumental in finding me employment. I worked as a waitress in a busy café, and once I'd saved enough money, I traveled to the States and began my studies."

Her resilience amazed him. "Your father never offered financial assistance?"

"Of course not. He was furious. But my mother eventually sent me money whenever she could. She enabled me to hire an attorney for the divorce. And as they say, the rest is history."

He formed his palm to her face. "Though I admire what you have accomplished on your own, you should have come to me for help."

"Why would I do that, Rafiq? You all but bid me a final farewell after we spent that one night together, or have you forgotten?"

The bitterness in her tone caused him to drop his hand. "I have never forgotten that night." Nor had he forgotten the sorrow in her eyes when he had told her they could not be together again.

"You told me we would remain friends," she said. "Yet we never really spoke again."

"We were forbidden to have any contact."

"We were forbidden after you were officially betrothed to Rima, but that didn't stop you from taking my virginity, did it?"

"And I recall you came to me willingly that night. You begged me to make love to you."

She lowered her eyes. "Yes, I did, and I never regretted it. I only regretted…"

He raised her chin with his fingertips, forcing her to look at him. "You regretted what?"

"That we only had that one time. But it was enough

to get me through those horrendous times with Boutros. I would close my eyes and escape back to that night. I reminded myself that what we shared was pure and good, not ugly and brutal. Those memories helped ease the pain and tolerate the reminders I still carry with me."

He suspected her internal scars still ran deep. "I did the same with Rima," he said, surprised at how easily the admission flowed out of his mouth. "She came to me willingly, and I always treated her with care and respect. Yet I sensed her thoughts were somewhere else. Perhaps on someone else, as were mine. I always thought of you."

"And the women before Rima?"

"I always imagined you. And the men after Boutros?"

"There have been no other men."

Perhaps that should not surprise him. "No one?"

"No. When you kissed me the other night, that was the first time since I left him. I thought I was immune to desire, but you proved me wrong." She attempted a smile but it faded quickly. "Although when you touched me, I realized I still have lingering issues."

He had mistakenly believed she had no intention of returning his affection. "I understand why you would feel that way, but I would have hoped the passage of time would have aided in your healing."

Her hand went to her wrist again, as if she needed to remember. "My emergency room rotations served as a constant reminder of what I had endured. I treated women who had suffered the same, and I began to realize that marital violence spans all cultures. Some still turn a blind eye to the problem because they believe that a wife should persevere to save the marriage. Fortunately, I was wise enough to leave."

He took her hand again and kissed her palm. "You were brave, Maysa. You still are. Braver than most men."

He saw the first sign of tears in her eyes, but she quickly blinked them away. "I am also damaged, Rafiq. No man would want me."

I want you. "You are a beautiful, desirable woman, *habibti.* Any man would be fortunate to have you."

"Well, I do not intend to give anyone that option. But I do have a favor to ask of you."

"Whatever you wish."

"Would you hold me tonight?"

She asked so little of him, yet so much. "If that is what you desire."

"But can you only hold me without wanting more?"

He could offer her a lie, or be completely honest, which is what she deserved. "If I said I did not wish to make love with you again, that would be untrue. But I will honor your request and be satisfied having you in my arms as we sleep. Shall I turn off the lantern?"

"I'd prefer to leave it on."

To chase away the demons, Rafiq presumed. "Then we will leave it on."

She stretched out on her back and sent him a sincere smile. "Then, Your Majesty, you are cordially invited to join me for an evening of celibacy."

He returned her smile, despite his disappointment. "I accept your invitation, Dr. Barad, as long as you do not steal the blankets."

"I will try to refrain."

When Maysa shifted to her side, Rafiq covered them

both and slid his arm beneath her. He decided to remain clothed from the waist down, at least until he was assured she slept. Then he would strip off his slacks and hope she did not notice.

Yes, she was inadvertently bent on torturing him with her request. And with the floral scent of her hair teasing his senses, her warm body fitted to his, she had succeeded in her mission.

At some point during the night, Maysa roused from a fitful sleep to the sound of steady breathing. A few moments passed before she became fully awake and turned to find Rafiq lying on his back. The lantern had begun to dim, washing his bare chest in an amber glow, yet allowing her to covertly study him. Human anatomy had been a part of her daily existence for years, but she was not immune to prime physical specimens, and the king definitely fit into that category.

His right arm curled above his head on the pillow and the other rested at his side between them. His dark lashes fanned out beneath his closed eyes, and his lips were pressed together. His clean-shaven jaw had already begun to show the signs of a light spattering of whiskers.

She continued her visual journey down the column of his throat and on to the prominent pectorals that indicated he still worked out with weights. He'd developed that passion in his teen years, while his brothers had stayed in shape picking up women, literally and figuratively, according to Rafiq. He had been a serious student, so bent on earning his father's respect. Bent on being his father in many ways. Yet she had known a different prince, the one who had spoken sweet words in soft whispers. The young man who had touched and kissed her so gently.

Those memories prompted her to reach out and touch him now. She sifted through the triangular shading on his sternum and slid a fingertip lightly down his belly, pausing where the sheet was draped loose and low, covering his hips. Realization that she didn't see a waistband dawned on her. She rose up to view his pants piled in a heap at the end of the pallet. Only his pants?

Morbid female curiosity caused her to lift the sheet to take a peek.

Hello...

As she suspected, he was unequivocally—and beautifully—bare. And for some reason, she could not quit staring.

"Are you enjoying the sight?"

She dropped the sheet and glanced up to see Rafiq's half smile and his open eyes full of amusement. "You're naked."

He propped a bent arm behind his neck. "I am, and you seem quite fascinated by that fact."

His voice hinted at arrogance and pride and Maysa had to admit, he had much to be proud of. "The question is, why did you take off your pants?"

"I always remove them when I am in bed. Otherwise, I have difficulty sleeping. You do not remember this?"

Oh, yes, she did, though they had only slept together one time. "I remember."

"Do you wish me to put them back on?"

Did she? "I wouldn't want you to be uncomfortable on my account, Your Excellency."

"Good. Feel free to carry on, although should you

proceed, you are in danger of waking the sleeping dragon."

She sent a downward glance to the place she'd recently inspected. "I believe the dragon has already been roused."

His grin expanded. "And you are surprised by this?"

Not in the least, but she was surprised by her reaction. She felt winded and flushed and…needy. "I apologize for touching you without your permission."

"Never apologize for something so pleasurable. I am yours to do with what you will."

She so badly wanted to return to the time when she had been secure in her sensuality. When she hadn't been afraid to explore, or be explored. She had the perfect guide next to her, a man she could trust. A man she had desired for as long as she could recall. Perhaps he couldn't promise a future, but he could bring her back to that land known as the living. First, she had to ask.

"I have a request for you," she said.

"Your wish is my command."

Before she reconsidered, Maysa sat up, drew in a deep breath, pulled her undershirt over her head and tossed it aside. "I want you to touch me the way you did when we were young, Rafiq."

Obvious desire, as well as a cast of concern, called out from his coal-colored eyes. "Are you certain?"

She stretched out on her back, closed her eyes and fisted her hands at her sides. "As long as we go slowly. I need—"

"I understand what you need," he said. "And you may rest assured I will treat you with the greatest of care. You only need tell me to stop, and I will."

She knew he would, otherwise she would never allow this to happen.

After Maysa nodded, Rafiq took her arm, unclenched her hand, and kissed her palm. He then leaned over and kissed her forehead, then each cheek before brushing his lips over hers. “Open your eyes for me.” When she complied, he added, “I want you to see me touching you. I want you to know it is me.”

He did understand, she realized, and she loved him for it.

Loved him...

She would take that out and examine it later. At the moment, her attention was drawn to Rafiq as he brushed his knuckles down her throat. He circled a fingertip around one breast, then the other, all the while keeping his gaze trained on hers. He seemed to be gauging her reaction, and she reacted with an increase in her respiration. He placed a kiss between her breasts, then sought her eyes again before he dipped his head and closed his mouth over her nipple. The circular movement of his tongue, the gentle pull, caused her to shift restlessly from the sensations. She was so lost in the heat, the yearning, she hadn’t realized he was caressing her abdomen. She wanted him to keep going, yet when he slipped the button on her fly, illogical fear enveloped her.

“Stop.” Her command came out in a raspy whisper.

But she’d been forceful enough to cause Rafiq to raise his head, taking the welcome warmth of his mouth away from her breast. “Do you wish me to stop completely?”

“Yes… No…” She streaked both hands over her

face. "I'm not certain. A part of me is still fearful, and I despise feeling this way."

"I do not want you to be afraid. I want you to feel only pleasure."

She lowered her eyes. "I know. I'm sorry."

"Do not apologize, Maysa. I promised I would stop when you asked, and I am a man of my word."

She finally looked at him. "You're a good man, Rafiq, and always patient with me."

"I will continue to be patient," he said. "You will determine if you wish to continue. Now we should sleep. We have a long drive ahead of us in the morning."

She didn't want to think about morning. She wasn't certain she could sleep. "I suppose you're right."

"First, may I kiss you?"

How odd that he'd asked, yet she appreciated that he had. "Yes, you may."

"You are not concerned with the no-kissing rule?"

She couldn't help but smile. "I believe it's too late to enforce that now."

"I want to make certain you have not changed your mind."

"I will if you do not hurry up and kiss me."

He rolled her toward him, framed her face with his palms and pressed his lips against hers softly. Yet it didn't last long before Rafiq pulled back and smiled. "Now if you would please put your shirt back on, I might possibly be able to sleep."

Feeling strangely wicked, Maysa leaned over him to retrieve her top, intentionally rubbing her bare breasts against his chest. She rose up and replaced the shirt slower than necessary. "Is that better?"

He swallowed hard. “Somewhat. Should I put on my pants?”

“I’m a doctor, Rafiq. I’ve seen quite a few naked men in the course of my medical career.” In afterthought she added, “But I would prefer you keep the dragon covered.”

Rafiq laughed then. A grainy, sensual laugh that almost had her reconsidering sleep. But she wasn’t ready to move forward in their intimacy. At least not yet.

When she settled back onto the blanket, Rafiq again folded her in his arms, providing the security she needed at the moment.

Concerned over the future, Maysa listened to the cadence of Rafiq’s breathing and determined he wasn’t sleeping. “Are you awake?”

“Yes.”

“After all the years, I still feel a connection between us. Do you?”

“Of course,” he said. “Time does have a way of standing still when it involves friendship.”

Friendship... That said it all. “Where do we go from here?”

He brushed a kiss across her forehead. “Wherever we choose to go. And wherever that might be, I promise we will both find pleasure in the journey.”

Did she dare continue with this dangerous emotional game? Did she risk losing herself to him again? Yes. She was no longer that starstruck young girl with unattainable dreams. She could never play a role in his future, but she could be a part of his present. They needed each other. He needed comfort, and she needed confidence.

Wise or not, she would make love with him again, provided she wasn't too broken.

Five

He was surprised she had allowed him to drive. He was more surprised by her current demeanor.

As Rafiq navigated the barren terrain, he afforded Maysa an occasional glance. At the moment, her face was turned toward the morning sky shining in through the moon roof, her unbound hair blowing back in the breeze from the open window. He could not see her eyes, now covered with sunglasses, but he could definitely see her smile and the twin dimples framing her mouth. She had also left her blouse unbuttoned, providing a view of the undershirt drawn tight over her breasts. That had almost proved enough distraction to cause him to veer onto the shoulder, coming dangerously close to the edge of the cliff.

Freedom...

That word immediately came to Rafiq's mind. Both yearned for it, yet Maysa captured the essence of it. He wished to see more of that absence of inhibition in the near future. He wanted more of what they had shared last night. Most important, he wanted revenge on the man who had stolen her security and left her scarred for life. Death was not good enough for Boutros Kassab.

"We should keep driving past the city," Maysa said, turning her vibrant smile on him. "We should escape and not tell anyone where we're going."

Her enthusiasm was contagious, and familiar. Many times in their shared pasts they had spoken about this very thing. "And where do you suggest we go?"

She lifted her shoulders in a shrug. "I don't know. South to the sea, maybe. Or perhaps we could travel north into Saudi. Dine at the finest restaurants and stay at the best resort."

He only wished they could be that carefree. "You have responsibilities, as do I."

She frowned. "What happened to your sense of adventure?"

"Replaced by the crown." Determined by duty.

"That, Rafiq, is a travesty." She pointed to his left. "Pull over up there."

She'd indicated a thirty-meter expanse of dirt breaking into the pavement and a sheer drop-off beyond. "Why?"

"Please, just do it. And back into the spot."

Far be it for him to question Maysa once she had her mind set on something. He slowed the Hummer, pulled off to the side of the road and then put the vehicle in Reverse. He made certain to leave sufficient room between the SUV and the drop-off, though he was tempted to inch close enough to earn a scolding.

Once they had stopped, Rafiq shut off the ignition

and draped one hand over the wheel. “Do you wish to watch the traffic the go by?”

She unbuckled her seat belt and opened the door. “No. We’re going to sit for a while and look at the mountains.”

When Maysa exited, Rafiq did the same and followed her to the back of the vehicle. She opened the tailgate, boosted herself up onto it, and patted the space beside her.

They sat quietly for a time, staring off into the distance. He had seen the panorama countless times, yet he had often taken the majestic mountains for granted. They served as a fortress surrounding the city, nature’s protection against those who envied Bajul’s peaceful existence and autonomy, as well as its resources.

“You can see the palace from here,” Maysa said, breaking into silence. “And of course, who could miss *Mabrúuk.* We should take a day to explore there before your respite is over.”

He did not care to consider the ending of his time with her, though it was inevitable. “When Zain and Madison visited the mountain, they returned with not one but two souvenirs. Zain knew the possible consequences, and he chose to take that risk regardless.”

“You don’t truly believe that fertility mythology, do you?” she asked.

Perhaps not, but he did not wish to take any undue chances. “I only know the villagers still believe it.”

“Well, I can’t say that I do. It takes more than a mountain to make a baby.”

He sent her a teasing smile. “I was not aware of that.”

She playfully swiped at his arm. "I'm certain you don't need me to explain the procreation process."

He rubbed his chin and pretended to think. "I would not object to hearing it in terms I would understand."

She laid a hand above her breast. "Why, Your Majesty, are you asking me to talk dirty to you?"

Precisely. "It would not be the first time if you did."

A blush colored her cheeks. "I was incredibly young back then."

"And extremely bold." He still recalled that night when she had verbalized what she had wanted him to do to her, causing him to shift against the uncomfortable effects of that memory. "I appreciated your candor, and I would hope you still feel that you may say anything to me."

"I do, and I have." She leaned back and supported herself on straight arms. "Do you remember that night when we spent several hours not far from here, looking at the same view?"

He remembered it well. "The night you stole your father's car and whisked me away from the palace?"

"I borrowed his car," she corrected.

"Without his knowledge or permission."

She looked extremely proud of her subterfuge. "I returned it later, and he was never the wiser."

"True. Do you remember the code we used when you would summon me?"

Her smile gave the rising sun competition. "How's the weather. And you would always answer—"

"Hot." And that would start the scramble to find a way to be together.

The silence returned, this time rife with tension as

they centered their gazes on each other. She finally favored him with a smile. "How is the weather?"

"Hotter than a desert blaze."

She leaned to his ear and whispered, "So am I."

He answered the obvious invitation with a kiss. Maysa responded with the passion Rafiq had learned to appreciate years before, and had greatly missed. He had never received the same reaction from his wife, but then their kisses had been obligatory. Absent of passion or undeniable need.

He experienced all those emotions with Maysa, and the intense desire to have her again overwhelmed him. He slid his hand beneath the back of her blouse to feel her bare skin against his palms. She surprised him by guiding that hand around to her breast. The desperate sound she made when he feathered his thumb across her nipple was almost his undoing.

Momentarily releasing her, he shoved the medical kits aside to make a place for them. No words were spoken as they crawled inside the vehicle and immediately moved back into each other's arms. He kissed her again, harder, deeper, as he divided her legs with his knee until they were completely twined together as tightly as braided rope.

"I want to touch you," he said. "Everywhere."

"I want you to touch me." Her voice was winded, her eyes hazy. "I need you to touch me."

The reality sudden dawned. How easy it would be to grant her wish. And unwise. Should anyone come upon them on the verge of making love, the scandal would rock the country. A scandal neither could afford.

He placed a kiss on her forehead. "Not here. Not now. You deserve better than this." That all-important next step would be best taken in a feather bed, not in the bed of an SUV. "We are less than twenty minutes away from your home."

"I'm not sure I can wait another twenty minutes."

Neither was Rafiq. "Then perhaps we should leave immediately."

"Are you sure you wouldn't rather stay here?"

He kissed her again, this time with more restraint to prevent rousing the dragon again. "I am sure. We will have the entire evening to spend together and a bed at our disposal. Provided you are ready to take that next step."

Her smile expanded, showing her dimples to full advantage. "Then what are we waiting for?"

Fortunately, they had waited long enough not to have their burgeoning affair confirmed by another member of the royal family. Had they arrived ten minutes earlier, Zain and Madison Mehdi might have caught them in a thoroughly compromising position.

Maysa wasn't altogether unhappy to see the couple, though their timing wasn't exactly the best. But when they'd come upon Zain and Madison in the living area, both looking extremely serious, she worried this might not be only a casual visit.

Rafiq crossed the room and targeted his brother with a glare. "Why are you here?"

Zain rose from the sofa, his gaze honed in on Maysa. "We have simply stopped by to see how the two of you are getting along."

"That's not true," Madison said as she stood. "We're here because all hell is breaking loose back at the palace."

Maysa exchanged a wary look with Rafiq before she brought her attention back to Madison. "What exactly do you mean?"

"Although arranging for the helicopter was noble, Rafiq," Zain began, "you might have been a bit more discreet. It seems the media has learned you were in Diya with Maysa. You might have made us privy to your plans so that we would have been prepared for the fallout."

"Rafiq had nothing to do with it," Maysa said. "This was all my idea. Had I known it would create a scandal, I would never have considered it."

With his eyes flashing anger, and his hands fisted at his sides, Rafiq looked as if he might fly into a rage. "I was in Diya observing one of Bajul's finest doctors treating the sick and downtrodden. What scandal is there in that?"

Madison lowered herself onto the sofa and folded her hands together. "Because rumor has it you spent the night with the country's finest doctor."

Searing heat began to work its way from Maysa's throat to her forehead. "We slept together in a tent." Could that have sounded more questionable? "In a large tent, and all we did was sleep." Excluding some minor foreplay and major kissing. Hopefully they wouldn't ask about the ride back from Diya.

"Did anyone see you together on your return from Diya?" Zain asked.

Clearly that had been too much for Maysa to hope for. "No one saw us."

"There was nothing to see," Rafiq interjected, sounding a bit too defensive in Maysa's opinion.

"Everyone, please sit," Madison said. "We need to implement a plan."

Rafiq slid his hands into his pants' pockets and remained frozen on the spot. "I prefer to stand."

Maysa preferred to leave for the closest exit, but she claimed the chair adjacent to the sofa before she answered that urge. "What do you suggest we do about this misunderstanding?"

Zain draped an arm over his wife's shoulder. "Madison held a press conference this morning to—"

"Without my permission?" Rafiq interjected.

Maysa affected the calm Rafiq failed to show. "What did this press conference entail?"

"Attempting to answer the usual questions," Madison said. "What business did the king have in Diya? What is the true relationship between the king and doctor? In other words, are they having a sordid affair? Nothing I haven't faced before in my career."

"I really feel badly you're having to work on your holiday, Madison," Maysa said.

Zain kissed Madison's cheek. "Even after blessing me with two babies, my wife is still the best at what she does."

Madison smiled. "Sweetheart, I can lactate and change a thousand diapers a day and still handle my job. That's part of why you love me."

This time Zain kissed her on the mouth. "And you love me for my overt charm, as well as my royal staff."

While Maysa couldn't hold back her laughter, Rafiq grumbled an Arabic curse. "Could the two of you stop mooning over each other and bring your minds back to the issues at hand?" he said. "Specifically, I demand to know every detail of this press conference."

Maysa could only guess at that, but she was certain karma had arrived, telling her to steer clear of any intimacy with the king. Steer clear of him altogether. "I would assume Madison denied the conjecture, Rafiq."

Madison shrugged. "Of course. I said the king wanted to investigate medical care in the outlying villages, and that's why he accompanied Dr. Barad to Diya. He preferred to do so anonymously to allow him a better advantage. I ignored any questions about the sleeping arrangements."

"Madison successfully dodged those bullets," Zain added. "But there will be plenty more if someone discovers the two of you cohabiting here."

As usual, Rafiq began his restless pacing. "Are you saying I should return to the palace?"

"Not necessarily, Rafiq," Zain said. "Madison also informed the press that following your information-gathering, you would be taking a brief sabbatical."

Maysa could see several problems with that plan. "Are you certain that's a good idea with the media already making assumptions?"

Zain wrapped an arm around his wife's shoulder. "Madison and I both agree Rafiq still needs time away."

"But he can't stay here with you," Madison added. "He's going to have to find another place for his mini-vacation."

Rafiq stopped his pacing and stepped forward. "Would you please address me directly? And do not forget I have the ultimate decision whether I stay or go. If I decide to remain here, then that is what I will do."

Maysa looked directly at Rafiq for the first time since they'd received the news. "Madison's right, Rafiq.

You cannot remain here with me. The gossip will escalate, whether it's true or not."

"And that is the last thing you need right now," Zain said. "We are so close to having the council's full support for the water project. They need to know your complete focus is on your duty and not on a woman who…"

When Zain's words trailed off, Maysa's defenses went on high alert. "Whom they deem not worthy to wipe the king's feet?"

Madison reached over and patted Maysa's arm. "Believe me, I know exactly what you're going through, and I personally think the mores are ridiculous and archaic."

"This is not the time to try to change customs," Rafiq said. "It seems I have no other option than to lock myself in my suite and demand I not be disturbed."

"And that holds no guarantees you will not be disturbed," Zain added. "Should anyone learn you are there, the intrusions would continue. I suggest perhaps you leave the country. You could stay in our home in Los Angeles."

Rafiq released a caustic laugh. "If you recall, California is home to the press and paparazzi. I would be bothered there perhaps more than I would here. And I refuse to be so far away should an emergency arise."

"He's right," Madison said. "It would be best if we find a remote location near Bajul."

"He can stay at the resort." Maysa's abrupt, and somewhat loud, declaration had the effect of a gunshot. All eyes turned to her.

Madison appeared totally unimpressed by the suggestion. "I don't consider staying in a resort full of tourists as the best place to relax and avoid publicity."

"No one is presently staying there," Maysa said. "The main hotel is currently closed for renovations, but the stand-alone villas on the far side of the property are available. They're a perfect hideaway."

"What about the staff?" Zain asked.

"Shamil gave them all a vacation. In fact, he requested I stop by from time to time to oversee the workers."

Rafiq frowned. "With no staff available, then I would be charged with preparing my own meals and laundering my own clothing?"

Heaven help him if he had to lift a royal finger to do menial chores. "Every villa is equipped with a full kitchen and normally a private chef. Since that isn't the case at the moment, I would be willing to see you have the proper meals and I can have my own staff do your laundry."

"This could definitely work." Madison pointed a finger at Maysa. "But you'd have to find a way to remain undetected. Zain's guards ran off a few reporters who were hanging around at the gate when we arrived. I assure you, they'll return as soon as we leave."

"I'll travel at night," she said. "The building crews will be gone by then, so the risk of anyone seeing me would be minimal."

When Rafiq failed to respond, Zain turned his attention to him. "Does this appeal to you at all, brother?"

Rafiq finally dropped into a chair and stretched his long legs before him, as if he'd settled in for the unforeseeable future. "I am thinking."

"Don't think too long," Madison said. "We have to

decide now, otherwise you'll be forced to return to the palace whether you're ready or not."

Rafiq remained silent a few moments before sending a quick glance at Maysa. "I will agree to the plan, as long as Maysa is also in agreement."

She saw no reason not to agree. He would have his time away, and she would have time away from him. If he had stayed under her roof, the temptation would have been too great. As it stood now, they would be better off keeping their distance from each other. She would simply deliver his meals and laundry, then leave. If only she truly believed it would be that simple. "I agree it's the best option."

"Excellent." Zain shot to his feet, held out his hands to his wife and pulled her up from the sofa. "Now if the two of you will excuse us, as soon as we return the guards to the palace, we have plans of our own."

Madison checked her watch. "And we only have a couple of hours before your children demand to be fed."

"That is why they invented bottles," Zain muttered.

Madison patted his cheek. "Patience, sweetie. The lake isn't going anywhere, and neither is the mountain."

"Are you planning to have more children?" Rafiq said, sounding somewhat appalled.

Madison's cheeks flushed. "Well, no, we're not. But then we weren't planning the last two."

Maysa couldn't help but laugh again. "Then I suggest you make certain you are prepared to battle the powers of *Mabrúuk*. I have condoms available should you need them."

Zain winked at his wife. "Thank you for the offer, Maysa, but we have everything under control."

Madison sent him a smile. "We better. As much

as I love our babies, I'm not sure how well we could handle two more."

Maysa experienced a tiny bite of envy over the couple's obvious love for each other. A love that had encouraged a king to give up his throne for the unacceptable woman he adored. If only she could be so fortunate.

Shaking off the melancholy, she gestured toward the corridor. "Since I certainly do not wish to delay you further, I'll see you both to the door."

Rafiq didn't bother to stand. "Before the two of you leave, I would caution you both to take care. But if you wish to provide a diversion by swimming nude in the lake during the light of day, you have my blessing."

"We are married and I am no longer the king," Zain said. "The press is not interested in my life any longer. In fact, I can parade naked in the streets if I so desire without earning a second glance."

"I don't know about that," Madison added. "I've seen you naked and it's pretty impressive."

Zain grinned before continuing the lecture aimed at his brother. "On the other hand, you, Rafiq, *are* the king. You are expected to behave with a measure of decorum, so I suggest you avoid being naked anywhere other than the shower."

The warning was not lost on Maysa. "I will make certain he keeps his clothes on in public." Her tongue seemed determined to get her in trouble. "I'll see you to the door so you may get on with your day."

After a brief exchange of goodwill between the brothers, Maysa escorted Zain and Madison to the door while Rafiq stayed behind. "You can both rest assured that we will be on our best behavior."

"I trust you will," Zain said as he kissed her cheek. "Do not let him have the upper hand and order you around. Stand firm."

"I'll try my best, Zain, but you and I both know your brother. He's nothing if not stubborn and persistent." And persuasive.

Once Zain started toward the awaiting car, Madison took Maysa's hands into hers. "If that whole best intentions thing to avoid Rafiq's charms doesn't work out for you, just make sure you're discreet. And most important, don't go anywhere near that damn mountain."

With that, Madison hurried away to join her husband, leaving Maysa alone to ponder her options. She couldn't exactly avoid the mountain since it shadowed the resort, as it did most of the town. And she definitely couldn't avoid Rafiq's charms as she saw to his comfort. But she could—and she would—stand firm. At least she had work to occupy her time and her mind.

"Are you certain you have to work tomorrow?"

They'd barely made it into the villa's door before Rafiq posed the query that sounded like the prelude to a proposition. Maysa set one of the paper sacks containing supplies on the kitchen's black granite counter and began rifling through it. "I have to be at the clinic tomorrow. I have a full schedule."

Rafiq leaned around her and placed another sack next to hers. "Will you not consider staying with me tonight?"

Oh, she had considered it on the drive to the resort. She was considering it now when he rested his palm on her waist and she could feel the warmth of his hand through the dress's cotton fabric. But she still planned to give him an emphatic no. Eventually. Right then she chose to ignore the question and his touch. Or at least try.

"My chef prepared these pastries for your breakfast," she said as she pulled a metal tin from the bag. "She also provided a nice lunch that I'm sure you will enjoy."

She took said lunch, sidestepped Rafiq and placed it in the refrigerator. After she closed the door and turned around, she found Rafiq leaning back against the opposite counter, arms folded across his chest, his eyes looking as dark and intense as a midnight storm.

"I will make it worth your while if you stay with me tonight." His deep, sensual voice, as well as the promise in his words, went straight to Maysa's head like a glass of fine French champagne.

Stand firm...

Turning her back, she continued to unload the last of the supplies. "It's almost a half-hour drive to the clinic."

"I will have one of the guards drive you."

"I have my own vehicle, remember?"

"Yes, I remember. I also recall what we almost did in that vehicle, and our plans to finish what we had barely begun. Had my brother not arrived, we would still be in your bed, and I would be deep inside you."

Maysa fumbled the coffee canister on her way to placing it in the overhead cabinet. The container hit the countertop with a thump, landed on the bamboo floor and rolled behind her. She closed her eyes and cursed her clumsiness. She opened her eyes the minute she heard Rafiq come up behind her. He brushed against her back as he set the coffee in the cabinet with little effort.

Maysa's effort to avoid him began to wane. She ducked under his arm, strode to the adjacent dining room and began rearranging the artificial flowers in the vase set in the middle of the heavy wood table. "I have to admit Shamil did a good job modernizing the villas. With all the granite and stainless appliances, the place looks almost American. There is a nice private pool in the courtyard and..."

A persistent king pressed against her back, generating enough heat to fuel the six-burner stove. Rafiq rested his right hand on her waist and his left hand higher, where he grazed his thumb back and forth along the side of her breast. Then he swept her hair aside and whisked a series of soft, warm kisses along the side of her neck. She could ignore him. She could pretend to ignore her body's immediate reaction. Or she could simply enjoy the moment.

When she tipped her head back against his shoulder, he kissed the corner of her mouth, and without warning, he turned her around and set her atop the table.

A laugh of surprise slipped out of her gaping mouth. "Are you attempting to disarm me?"

He rested his hands on her thighs. "I am trying to persuade you allow me to resume what we began earlier today."

"We're in the kitchen."

He planted his palms on her knees. "We are in the dining room next to the kitchen."

She narrowed her eyes. "Are you having some sort of sexist fantasy about having your way with a woman in a domestic setting?"

"You are my fantasy, and I would like to have my way with you in any setting."

He punctuated his point by kissing her without mercy. So lost in his gentle yet complete exploration of her mouth, a few moments passed before Maysa realized Rafiq was working her dress up her thighs. When she tensed, he brought his lips to her ear.

"Trust me."

She did trust him, so much so she didn't launch into all the reasons why they shouldn't do this as he reached beneath the dress and clasped the band low at her hips. She didn't issue one protest when he began to lower her panties. In fact, she lifted her hips, allowing him to pull them down her legs to drop onto the floor. She didn't question why she was sitting on a table with her hem almost to her waist. She didn't care that she was exposed to Rafiq's eyes as he nudged her legs apart. She certainly didn't care when he formed his hand between her thighs.

She tipped her head against his and lowered her gaze to watch the patently erotic scene. Not once had she climaxed with her former husband, and she worried she might not be able to now. But this was Rafiq, the one and only man who had ever given her one—several—before the foreplay culminated into full-blown lovemaking. He knew exactly where to touch her, how much pressure to apply until she bordered on begging him to hurry. Yet he continued to take his time, measuring each stroke until her legs began to tremble. A sense of relief blended with the heady sensations when she experienced the impending release. She inadvertently dug her nails into Rafiq's shoulders as the orgasm began to build in intensity. She bit back the scream resulting from sheer pleasure, not pain. He captured her gasp with another kiss, moving his tongue in sync with the finger he had eased inside her.

As the final wave subsided, Maysa kept her head lowered and tried to hold the unexpected tears at bay, to no avail. She quickly swiped away the few that slipped free and hoped Rafiq didn't notice.

"Did I hurt you?"

The distress in his voice drew Maysa's gaze to his. "Not at all. I wasn't certain I could feel that way again."

He kissed her forehead so tenderly she almost sobbed. "I despise what that monster did to you, yet I knew he would never break you."

"No, he did not." But Rafiq could very well break her heart again.

He leaned over, swept her underwear from the floor and handed them to her. "Now get dressed, return home and try to have a good night's sleep."

She was stunned he hadn't made another attempt to convince her to stay. "What about you?"

"I will be fine until you are ready to take the final step."

Was she ready? A few moments ago she would have gladly followed him into the bedroom. But perhaps he was right. Perhaps she needed more time to weigh the consequences. "You heard what Zain and Madison said. We should not be entertaining thoughts of further intimacy under the circumstances."

He visually tracked her movements as she slipped her panties back into place. "No one would need to know, Maysa."

"But I would know, Rafiq. If we made love, and a reporter asked me about our relationship, the truth would be written on my face."

"All the more reason for you to take some time away from your practice."

If only it were that simple. "My entire day is booked tomorrow, morning until late afternoon."

"Say the word and I will have my personal physician treat patients in your stead."

"He doesn't know my patients. They rely on me. They know me."

Rafiq clasped her waist, lifted her up and set her on her feet. "Then see your patients and come to me tomorrow night."

The temptation to say yes lived strong in Maysa. Temptation had gotten her into trouble before. "I'll think about it."

"That is all I ask."

His agreement came much too swift. "Then you'll be fine should I decide to have one of your guards deliver your dinner while I remain home?"

"Of course."

He gave her a brief kiss with only a light graze of his tongue. Yet that was enough for her to reconsider.

Before she did, Maysa grabbed her bag and began backing to the door. "I will let you know if I decide to join you tomorrow night."

A slightly arrogant grin lifted the corners of his beautiful mouth. "And if you decide not to come to me, mark my words, I will eventually come to you."

Six

"You have one remaining patient, Dr. Barad."

Maysa leaned over the counter and frowned at Demetria Christos, the fiftysomething office manager, who normally ran the clinic's office like a ship's captain. Tonight the woman seemed as tightly wound as her salt-and-pepper curls. "You told me fifteen minutes ago the last patient had left, Demetria."

She began rapping the desk with a pen. "He's a walk-in. An American traveling through the region. He says he requires a complete physical, although he looked well to me. Very well indeed."

She could refuse treatment, but then again, he could actually afford to pay for the services. She could always use extra money for supplies and salaries. "Where is Jumanah?"

"She left a few minutes ago with her husband, before the man arrived."

And that meant Maysa would be without a nurse to assist. Not necessarily an issue, but it would delay the process if she had to handle the entire treatment herself. "Fine. But please lock the door and hang the closed sign."

"I have already done both."

"What room is he in?"

Demetria resumed her annoying pen tapping. "Room one."

Maysa pushed off the counter then turned when she came upon an idea. "I have a favor to ask. Would you mind having Paulos prepare his eggplant moussaka to go, please?" One of Rafiq's favorites during the time when they would eat together at the Greek restaurant. Now that she had the dinner situation solved, she had to tackle the other—whether she would personally deliver it or summon one of his guards.

She sent Maysa a suspicious look. "You do not like eggplant, Doctor."

A faux pas of the first order. "It's for a friend. Someone who's in Bajul for a visit."

"A man friend?"

A royally gorgeous man friend. "Yes, but he is nothing more than a casual acquaintance." And that was nothing less than a colossal lie.

Demetria looked crestfallen. "I am disappointed you have yet to find a suitable companion. Perhaps you would reconsider using my matchmaking talents?"

She would rather eat eggplant. "No, thank you, and feel free to go to the restaurant now."

"You want me to leave you alone with a stranger?"

The woman had a point. "Does he look threatening?"

"He is very tall and lean and quite handsome." She topped off the comment with a smitten smile.

Not the answer Maysa needed. "But does he appear to be the criminal sort?"

"My instincts say he is harmless, and my instincts are never wrong."

Except for the time Demetria had coerced her into a date with a local banker who was eight years' Maysa's junior and as interesting as a spreadsheet. "Then clearly there isn't any reason why you shouldn't leave."

"This is true. His chart is on the door."

"Thank you, and I'll be by to pick up my order as soon as I'm finished here." Maysa spun around and headed down the tiled hallway, exhaustion weighting her steps. She grabbed the chart from the holder and scanned the intake form only containing his last name as she entered the room. "What can I do for you, Mr. King?"

"I am open to all suggestions."

She glanced up from the page to see Rafiq casually perched on the edge of the exam table, one leg slightly bent, one foot planted on the floor. He wore a tailored white shirt, black dress slacks and an expression that said he was greatly enjoying his little surprise.

"What are you doing here?" she asked as soon as she found her voice.

"As I told your secretary, I am here for a complete physical."

That came as no real surprise. "You have your own physician."

"He is not presently available."

As if she believed that. "Did Demetria recognize you?"

"She did, but I asked her not to tell you."

That certainly explained the office manager's odd behavior, yet it did not explain Rafiq's lack of wisdom. "Do you realize the risk you took coming here? Anyone could have seen your armored car and—"

"I walked from the palace," he said. "I had the guards deliver me there and then set out on foot. That served as a sufficient decoy."

"Since it's at least a mile from the palace to the clinic, obviously you're not in dire straits as far as your physical health is concerned." She would have to question his mental health for walking the streets in broad daylight.

He leveled his dark gaze directly on hers. "I do have an ache that does not seem to want to go away."

She decided to play along, probably at her own detriment. "Where exactly is this ache?"

"I will show you."

When Rafiq slid off the table and began unbuckling his belt, Maysa pointed at him. "Do not remove one article of clothing, Your Majesty."

He had the gall to grin. "Then how will you treat this ache if you do not see its origin?"

Do not humor him, Maysa. She smiled in spite of herself. "Believe me, I don't have to see it to know how to diagnose it. It could possibly be priapism, although that usually occurs when the erection remains long after sexual intercourse."

"I see." He rubbed his shadowed jaw and studied the ceiling before returning his attention to her. "Then how do I find relief, Doctor?"

She tossed the chart onto the counter housing the sink. "I don't believe the answer to that requires my expertise. However, I do require an answer from you. Once again, why are you here?"

He took two slow steps toward her. "I am here to ask if you will be coming tonight."

If he had his way, she would be—in every respect. "It's been less than twenty-four hours since you asked, and I still have not decided."

He moved as close as he could, pinning Maysa against the counter, his hands braced on either side of her. "Is there something I could do to persuade you?"

The images from the dining table incident filtered into her muddled mind. The feelings of absolute desire were still fresh, and threatening to reappear. "Give me more time, and some space."

He straightened and slid his hands into his pockets. "I will not pressure you to make a decision, yet I will be disappointed if you leave me to while away the hours all alone, with no relief for my condition… What is it called?"

"Priapism, and you don't actually have it. You do have the means to relieve it by taking matters into your own hands."

That earned her another one of his deadly smiles. "And what would be the pleasure in that when you could take matters into your hands?"

Maysa was growing very hot, and very bothered. "I suggest you go back to the villa and await my decision like a good little king."

"How will I know what that decision will be?"

"When you see me at the doorstep. Or not."

"Then I will wait all night if I must." His expression turned suddenly serious. "Before I leave, I need you to know I understand your hesitancy, and the reason behind it. You fear the loss of control."

Rafiq had definitely hit the mark with that assumption. "You're right. Losing control is something I no longer take lightly."

"You might also believe I am being selfish." He released a rough sigh. "Perhaps I am. Yet I have learned that life holds no assurances, and the time we have is relatively short-lived. But at the moment, time together is all we have, no matter how brief."

And brief it would be. Once this affair was over, should it actually begin in earnest, they would go back to leading separate lives, as they had been for well over a decade.

He took her hands, turned them over and placed a tender kiss above the scar on one wrist, then the other. "If you decide to join me tonight, I will promise to give you my complete attention, and I will allow you all the control."

He then strode out the door, while Maysa remained in the room to mull over his vow. Rafiq Mehdi wasn't the kind of man to give up control under any circumstance. He was still the man she'd known long ago—an abiding tenderness existed beneath the steel exterior. He'd demonstrated that only moments ago. Would it be worth the risk to her emotional health if she made love with him again? Could she walk away as if nothing had ever existed between them?

She had traveled down that treacherous road before, and she had survived. She would definitely survive this time.

Maysa Barad would never allow any man—not even the man she had always loved—to break her again.

* * *

Rafiq had constantly been decisive when it came to duty. When it involved lovemaking, he was much the same. He had always taken the lead after making the first move. To relinquish that power would be completely foreign to him, yet he would for Maysa—provided she finally arrived.

She had phoned a half hour ago to inform him she was on her way. He had walked the floor as he'd waited, wondering if perhaps she had changed her mind. In accordance with his plan, he wore only a robe and nothing else. A distinct risk, but he had a point to prove. He also had a tenuous hold on his libido when he heard the lock trip.

Maysa entered the front door carrying a brown paper sack. She stopped short the moment her gaze fell on where he now stood, attempting to affect a calm he did not remotely feel.

She clutched the bag tighter and cleared her throat. "Obviously you've run out of clean clothes."

"I still have a surplus. I decided to wait to shower until after your arrival."

The discomfort in her expression indicated she understood what he was proposing. "I brought dinner from the Greek restaurant."

The low-cut yellow gauze dress she wore almost brought him to his knees. "Would you be dining with me?"

She shook her head. "No. I had a late lunch."

"As did I. You may put it away and I will reheat it later in the microwave."

"You know how to use the microwave?"

"I have two graduate degrees. I believe I can find

which button to press." He had one particular button in mind, but it would not be found in the kitchen.

"Far be it for me to force you to eat," she said. "I'll put this in the refrigerator."

"And I will retire to the shower." Without formality or fair warning, Rafiq removed the robe and set it aside on the sofa. "You are welcome to join me."

He expected Maysa to protest his boldness or perhaps leave out the door. Instead, she took a slow visual voyage down his body. He reacted as any man would, particularly a man in the presence of a woman he wanted with a fierceness unlike any he had known.

Her eyes widened slightly when she arrived at the destination that heralded the obvious results of her perusal. "I see your condition hasn't improved."

"It still requires treatment. After your hectic day, are you up for a further examination?"

"You are clearly up for it." She raised her gaze and smiled, presenting her dimples as one more weapon in her female arsenal. "I might be persuaded to lend a hand in a while. In the meantime, I suggest you retire to the shower."

"And you will join me?" He was quite surprised by the eagerness in his voice, and evidently so was Maysa.

"Perhaps, but first I must return a phone call from a patient."

Her profession seemed destined to intrude on their time. "Will this require you to make a home visit?"

"I won't know until I speak with him."

He inclined his head and narrowed his eyes. "Is this truly a patient, or a secret lover?"

She rolled her eyes. "It's a seventy-year-old farmer with a cold. I highly doubt his wife of fifty years would approve of me taking him as a lover. Besides, one lover at a time is all I can handle."

The promise in her words and her eyes lifted Rafiq's spirits. "Then I shall be in the shower, awaiting your care."

Gathering his strength, Rafiq turned away from Maysa, though he sincerely wanted to take her down on the sofa and dispense with further delay, as well as her clothing. He crossed the expansive master bedroom and entered the bath that was truly fit for a king. The stone shower was equally large, perhaps large enough for five people, and well appointed. He depressed the control on the wall that slid the ceiling open to reveal open air and a host of stars. He then set the temperature and started the water for two of the four showerheads.

After stepping beneath the spray, he braced both hands on the tiled walls and attempted to regain some control. If he failed, Maysa's examination would be over before it had begun. *If* she had not decided to take up with the farmer and leave him behind. He decided to bathe and hope for the best.

When several minutes had passed, and he was thoroughly clean and somewhat composed, he began to believe Maysa had changed her mind. Perhaps she had…

"The doctor has arrived."

The sound of her voice drew his attention to the shower's opening. The sight of her standing there, without any clothing and seemingly relaxed, shattered his calm into a million shards of human glass. He had never seen Maysa completely nude, even in their youth when their covert meetings had been conducted in darkness. The golden cast of the overhead light illuminated each detail, from the fullness of her breasts capped with light brown nipples, the indentation of her waist, the curve of her hips and the shading between her thighs.

When she stepped into the shower, he grew painfully hard and extremely aware that he would have to develop superhuman strength in the next few moments.

Maysa moved beneath the spray opposite him and closed her eyes as the water flowed over her. After Rafiq pushed aside the showerhead above him to gain a better view, his anticipation heightened while he watched her bathe. He followed the movement of her hands as she washed her breasts, then her abdomen and lower still. He wanted to go to her, touch her, kiss the moisture from her body one blessed inch at a time. Yet he had promised to relinquish his control. Therefore he had no choice but to wait until she came to him.

She rinsed the soap from her body, slicked back her long hair and finally approached him. But when he reached for her, she took a step back. “Before we continue, I need to outline some rules.”

He could not conceal his frustration. “More rules?”

“For now,” she said. “First, do not touch me until I give you permission.”

“That is not acceptable—”

She held up a hand to silence him. “Don’t forget that I am in control, as you ordained.”

He had not forgotten, though he had begun to regret it. “Continue.”

“Next, you cannot kiss me, at least for the time being.”

He was quickly taking exception to her rules, yet he knew better than to argue. “All right. Is there anything else I might do to accommodate you?”

"Yes." She closed the space between them and reached up to move the spray over them. "Enjoy being stripped of your control."

Her eyes seemed alight with fire as she placed her hands on his chest, pausing to touch his nipples with deft fingertips. He sucked in a deep breath when she drew a path down his belly. He clenched his jaw tightly when she circled his navel, and tighter still when she raked her nails lightly down his thighs.

She seemed to be purposefully avoiding his erection, or perhaps bent on torturing him until he begged her. She undeniably had torture in mind, he realized, when she lowered herself onto her knees. The minute she took him into her mouth, he began the battle to remain in control of his body, the only control he still retained.

When she used her tongue like a feather, from tip to shaft, Rafiq focused on trivial details in an effort to prolong the experience—his least favorite foods, his agenda for the next council meeting, the extreme heat in August. He even attempted to recall the words to the Petrarca poem Elena had forced him to memorize. Nothing worked as a sufficient distraction, until he ventured a glance at Maysa kneeling before him. Seeing her there, appearing subservient, gave him pause, as well as a temporary respite from the need for gratification.

He broke a rule by lifting her to her feet, immediately earning him a look of displeasure. "Did I do something wrong?" she asked, sounding unsure.

"You were doing everything right, and it took great effort for me to stop you."

"Then why did you?"

"Because you should never be on your knees before any man." Least of all him—a man who could give her nothing more than temporary pleasure.

"But you didn't force me on my knees, Rafiq. There is a difference."

"Still, I wish to see your eyes when you touch me."

Her smile reappeared, soft and sensual. "Let's see how long you can keep them open when I continue."

And continue she did, using her hands as effectively as she had her mouth. She increased the cadence of her strokes, making it difficult for Rafiq to draw a breath, or to keep his eyes open. In a matter of moments, he would lose both the battle and the war. He would lose the opportunity to carry her to the bed and bury himself inside her.

"Stop." The demand echoed in the shower like a gunshot.

"No," she replied, then sent a pointed look at his hand circling her wrist.

He reluctantly released her and prepared to plead his case. "If you continue, I am in grave danger of—"

"I know. That is my intention."

She had turned the tables on him, implementing her own plan that would surely drive him to the brink of pleasurable insanity. Yet she was empowered, and he was powerless. Powerless to stop her determined, thorough touching. Powerless to hold out any longer when she brought her lips to his ear and whispered, "Be grateful you are surrendering your control to a physician."

And without warning, she pressed her free hand between his legs at the same time the climax crashed down on him with the force of an explosion. He tipped his head back against the wall as a harsh, guttural moan slipped out of his mouth. The orgasm continued longer than any he had experienced before, and the impact almost buckled his knees. By the time the sensations began to wane, he realized his heart was beating dangerously fast.

He finally opened his eyes to Maysa, who seemed very proud of her accomplishment. "What did you do to me?" he grated out.

She streamed a fingertip along his jaw. "Aside from giving you the most intense orgasm you've ever experienced?"

"*How* did you do it?"

"I happen to know a certain trigger point that reportedly increases a man's pleasure. I've never tried it before, but I assume it worked."

"Had it worked any better, I would be dead."

She laid her cheek on the left side of his chest before returning her gaze back to his. "Your heart is still beating strongly, so I do believe you will live."

"For a moment I was in doubt." And in less than a moment, he would kiss her, damn the rules.

"I'm certain you have no doubts about one particular aspect of the experience."

"What would that be?"

Her expression turned from amused to sultry. "Isn't handing your control to a woman a complete rush?"

And now the time had come to reclaim that control.

He spun her around against the wall, framed her face in his palms and kissed her without hesitation, using his tongue to simulate the act of lovemaking that he planned to undertake tonight. He would need time to recover, but he knew exactly what to do with that time.

He broke the kiss but kept hold of her face. “You do not have the market cornered on your so-called trigger points. I know where they exist on you, and I intend to explore each and every one, perhaps more than once.”

“But—”

He pressed a finger to her lips. “This is my plan, and these are my rules. I expect you to touch me, and I will be kissing you often. Everywhere. Do you understand?”

She appeared as if she might respond but nodded instead.

“Good. Now before I carry you to bed, I have one last remark.”

“Please do, but hurry.” Her words came out in a raspy whisper.

“If you trust me enough to give up your control to me, I will give you an experience you will not soon forget.”

Seven

Maysa wouldn't soon forget the expectation in Rafiq's dark eyes as he awaited her answer. If she agreed to his request, she would acknowledge that she was finally ready for that next all-important step—letting go and letting him make love to her in every possible way, and the possibilities were endless. She wanted to experience each and every one with him. She needed to forget the horror her life had been with Boutros. Rafiq alone could erase those memories from her mind with only a kiss.

She took both his hands into hers. "I trust you, Rafiq. Do with me what you will, as long as you do it very, very soon."

When he swept her up into his arms, Maysa laughed from surprise and a sheer sense of freedom. She continued to laugh as he strode into the bedroom and deposited her on the edge of the mattress. She stopped laughing when he stood before her, his golden skin and thick dark hair still damp from their water play, arms dangling at his sides, every astounding inch of him exposed to her eyes. One prime, naked, beautiful male. All hers to enjoy with touches and kisses. Definitely kisses, and she craved one now.

She turned her focus on his mouth and made a rather ridiculous observation in light of their current situation. "You shaved again."

He rubbed a hand over his jaw. "Yes, and with good reason. As you've said, women at times find facial hair irritating. I would not want that for you."

"I like you better without the goatee."

"I am pleased you are pleased."

Maysa would be more pleased if he would make some move to touch or kiss her. Anything to put her out of her misery. After the shower escapade, she was so sexually keyed up she could jump out of her skin, or jump all over him.

Yet he continued to survey her as if intentionally prolonging her agony. "Rafiq, are you simply going to stand there all night and assess me?"

"No." He leaned forward and planted his palms on either side of her hips. "I am trying to decide exactly what I wish to do with you."

"I don't care. Just do it."

He barked out a laugh. "Patience has never been one of your virtues, but since I am now in control, you will have to find some."

She sighed. "You're frustrating me so much I want to scream."

He gave her a wry grin. "I assure you, screaming

could very well be involved. Or at the very least, moaning."

His words blanketed her body with another round of heat. His sudden, deep kiss landed that heat right between her thighs. After he had kissed her quite thoroughly, he began a trek down her body with his lips, pausing at her breasts to pay each equal attention with the tip of his tongue and the steady pull of his mouth.

When she tried to take him back onto the bed, he rejected her efforts and straightened. "Patience," he reminded her. "I want you to remain where I have placed you."

He wanted her to continue to sit up? "What if I want to lie back?"

"I will inform you when that is permissible."

He was beginning to take the power play to the extreme, but who was she to question him? She had stripped him of all control in the shower, and seeing him that helpless had been a complete and utter turn-on. "Your wish is my command, Sayyed."

"And my command is that you take pleasure in the experience," he said, tossing her words back at her.

"I'm sure I will, as soon as you give it to me."

"I have every intention of giving it to you." When he raked his gaze down her body and back up again, she literally squirmed. "Do you know what you deserve?" he asked.

A medal for remaining upright. "No, what do I deserve?"

He leaned forward again and kissed her lightly. "A man who is willing—" he lowered himself to the floor "—to fall to his knees before you."

His tender words and actions shot straight to Maysa's heart. "I don't know what to say."

"Say nothing," he said. "Only feel."

When he parted her legs, Maysa trembled from anticipation. She became keenly aware that he was about to undertake what no man had ever dared. She had been with two men—and the one before her had never attempted this. The other had only been concerned with his own sadistic gratification, not hers.

Still, she wasn't a child. She knew all there was to know about human sexuality and female anatomy. But she had no personal barometer with which to measure how this ultimate intimacy would feel. She would soon find out, she realized, as Rafiq slid his hands beneath her bottom and kissed his way up her inner thighs.

The minute he reached the intended target, she acknowledged he had a wonderfully wicked mouth, and he used it on her with the skill of a man experienced in the art of lovemaking. As she witnessed the act, she had trouble catching her breath, but couldn't. With every pass of his tongue, she tried very hard to take in all the sensations, but she was beginning to enter the realm where thought was impossible. Her hips involuntarily tilted toward him, prompting Rafiq to be even more deliberate. And that in turn brought about a climax that jarred her like an unpredictable bolt of lightning.

The impact left her weak and winded and momentarily incoherent from the wonder of it all. But she wasn't so mentally jumbled that she didn't notice the typical male pride in Rafiq's expression as he rested his chin on her shaky knees.

"That was quick," she said when she'd recovered enough to speak. "And totally amazing."

"I agree it was over too quickly for you to enjoy the full effect. It will not be that way the second time."

Surely he didn't mean… Oh, yes, he did. "Rafiq, I can't…"

"Do not underestimate yourself," he said. "Or me."

Multiple orgasms had never been a part of her limited sexual repertoire. She knew they were possible, but could she truly hope they were possible for her? She sought confirmation as Rafiq went back to his ministrations, this time using his hand as well as his mouth. She remained more aware of what he was doing this time, but no less excited to have him do it. No less in need of a release. The climax began to gain momentum, more tempered this time, but still potent. And when Rafiq hit her "trigger spot," the orgasm caused her to curl over his head to anchor herself.

Maysa fell back on the bed, closed her eyes and waited for the endless tremors to subside, willing her pulse to steady. Only a few moments passed before she felt the mattress bend beside her.

"Are you all right?"

She opened her eyes and focused on that remarkable, endearing smile. "I have traveled to that state known as euphoria."

His deep laugh gave her the chills all over again. "I believe I visited there in the shower."

"I never knew," she said, struggling to express what she was feeling.

"Never knew what?"

She rolled toward him and touched his face. "I never knew I could feel so much. I truly did believe Boutros had destroyed all that was good about lovemaking. I have you to thank for helping me to see it can be good. Better than good."

He pushed her damp hair back and kissed her forehead. "You are not required to thank me, and the best is yet to come. If you are ready."

How could she not be? "I am more than ready, and weary of waiting."

"Good. Get dressed."

She had not expected that perplexing order. "Is this some new technique you've learned, making love fully clothed?"

"No. I want to take you somewhere special to make love to you."

He was certainly full of surprises tonight. "Where would that be?"

"Our past."

If only they could actually return to those carefree days. If only they could change the course of their history and the confines of their culture. If only they had found some way to be together permanently.

Maysa dealt daily in reality, not impossibilities. Time could not be rewound, and even if it could, she wasn't certain she would turn back the clock. Every heartbreak, every moment of torture, had driven her to succeed. Every disappointment had made her who she was today—a strong, independent woman. A physician. If she had been chosen to be Rafiq's wife, she would have eventually been relegated to entertain dignitaries and churn out royal heirs. She had always wanted to be a doctor, and she probably would not have been allowed the opportunity had she married Rafiq. Resentment might have destroyed their love.

Nevertheless, the past was dead and buried, and the present was all that mattered right now. She would concentrate on that as they set off on their mystery journey.

Yet the mystery ended the moment Rafiq steered the Hummer off the main highway and Maysa realized exactly where they were going—their secret sanctuary.

Ancient olive trees lined the narrow lane, welcoming them back to the large parcel of Mehdi-owned land that bordered the palace grounds. The private grove where she and Rafiq had come of age in each other's arms. Where they had first declared their love, all the while knowing that love would never be enough to sustain their relationship. Not when culture and customs had intruded.

As pavement turned to gravel, Maysa powered down the window, allowing the warm breeze to reintroduce her to the scents and sounds of nature in its purest form. Rafiq pulled between two acacia trees adjacent to the small clearing that had served as their special meeting place. He shut off the ignition and left on the parking lights that illuminated the tufts of grass and aloe plants in a golden glow.

After taking in the sight, she shifted slightly toward Rafiq. "It looks the same as it did before. I do hope the caretaker still keeps the wolves away."

He draped an arm over the steering wheel and stared out the windshield. "No one has spotted a wolf in a number of years."

That gave her only a small measure of comfort. "I suppose we could have brought along one of your guards, although having an audience would be rather awkward."

"They are positioned on the main road in front of the entrance to the property."

Wonderful. "They're not going to be patrolling the area, are they?"

"They will remain in the car, as I have instructed. We will not be disturbed."

"Good. I'd hate to be caught—"

"Naked?" He accentuated the comment with a sensual grin.

"Exactly."

"I will protect you from prying eyes if necessary."

She smiled at a sudden recollection. "If my memory serves me correctly, you insisted on coming to my bed that first time because you worried someone would catch us here without our clothes. Now you're suggesting we take off all our clothes here and the threat is still real."

He reached across the console and took her hand. "With age and experience comes the need for adventure."

"As long as that adventure does not include ants and other creatures of the night."

He brought her face around and kissed her. "I will protect you from all predators."

Maysa fished two condoms from the side pocket of her casual dress and prepared for Rafiq's reaction. "And I am in charge of protecting us from pregnancy."

As she'd predicted, he scowled. "Although I understand the necessity, I am not pleased with having a barrier between us."

"A thin barrier. You'll barely know it's there."

"I will know, and why only two?"

She slapped playfully at his arm with the back of

her hand. "I have a whole box at the resort if this is not enough."

"That is good to know." He reached behind the seat and brought out two of the hotel's blankets. "Now it is time to put these barriers to good use."

Maysa waited while Rafiq rounded the Hummer and opened her door. After he took her hand to help her out, they walked, arms around waists, toward the far side of the field that contained more sand than foliage.

Rafiq let Maysa go to spread out one of the blankets, then dropped the other on the ground beside the pallet. "In case we need to cover ourselves should we be visited by an intruder."

She truly hoped that wouldn't be necessary. "Well?" she asked when neither made a move to undress.

"Shoes first," he said as he lowered onto the blanket and began removing his boots.

Maysa slipped off her sandals while Rafiq stripped out of his shirt. Although the light was limited to a three-quarter moon, she could still make out his body's finer details—the webwork of masculine veins in his strong arms, the bulk of his biceps and the ridged plane of his belly. She had seen those details earlier, among others, yet she found she would gladly study them for hours. She also discovered a sense of daring that had been missing from her life for several years.

After she stepped onto the edge of the blanket, she pitched the condoms to Rafiq, who made a perfect one-handed catch. She reached behind her, slid the back zipper down and then lowered the straps. She let the dress fall in a pool of gauze at her feet, drawing Rafiq's attention to her bare breasts. When she shimmied out of her panties and kicked them aside, he released an audible groan.

"Have I told you how beautiful you are?" he asked, his voice noticeably strained as he lowered his fly.

She didn't need to hear the compliment—she could see the appreciation in his eyes, and elsewhere when he had dispensed with the rest of his clothes. And she had no qualms about taking a long look elsewhere. "Thank you, Your Highness. I feel the same about you." She felt so much for him that her emotions were heading into a tailspin.

Rafiq patted the space beside him. "If you are ready to proceed, join me."

Deciding to take that daring for another spin, Maysa went to her knees, crawled toward him and reached over to retrieve one discarded packet. After withdrawing the condom, she nudged Rafiq onto his back and took the liberty of rolling it into place, with a few added unnecessary adjustments for good measure.

She then stretched out atop the length of him. "I believe I've proven I am more than ready." She shimmied her hips against him. "So are you."

With one smooth move, he flipped her onto her back. She expected to see amusement in his eyes, but instead, she saw worry. "Again, if you wish me to stop, say so. If you experience any pain, tell me."

She loved him for his concern. She loved him for more reasons than she could count. "I'm positive that will not happen. After all, this is what we've been waiting for, and I trust you'll make it worth the wait."

He lifted her chin and kissed her briefly. "I will do everything in my power to make it right for you."

"And you are a very powerful man, Rafiq Mehdi, oh, king of the female climax."

Finally, his smile reappeared. "I will endeavor to continue to earn that title, beginning now."

And he did, without a moment's hesitation. After a few expert touches and one long, hot kiss, he quickly took her to the brink and she was on the verge of pleading and promising him anything if he would take her all the way. Then he removed his hand, raised slightly, moved over her.

Maysa braced for the inevitable, so certain she could handle the culmination of all their foreplay. Yet when he began to ease inside her, her body tensed even though her mind told her this was not an invasion. This was Rafiq, the man she trusted with her life.

Rafiq stilled and responded by uncurling her fisted hands and kissing her palms. He then began speaking to her in Arabic. Soft words. Sensuous words. Descriptive words that painted a picture of how she felt surrounding him. How he had waited a lifetime to be this close to her again. How his greatest desire was to give her the utmost pleasure.

Before Maysa realized it, they were completely joined; she was entirely free of any resistance and once more caught in the throes of an orgasm the moment he began to move. As the cadence of his thrusts increased, she smoothed her hands over his back, memorized every nuance, reveled in his power and remembered that one night when she had given herself to him the first time. When she had willingly handed over her heart, only to have it shattered by his duty. And it would invariably happen again if she allowed it.

She refused to consider that now. She only wanted

to concentrate on these precious moments when nothing mattered but making love with him. Loving him.

After Rafiq collapsed against her with a low moan, Maysa's unwanted tears again broke through despite her determination not to cry in front of him for the second time in as many days. The emotional fortress she had erected for self-protection had begun to crumble in his presence.

"Once more, I have brought you to tears, and I am sorry for that."

Maysa opened her eyes and tried to smile, a shaky one. "These special moments made me cry, Rafiq. Not you. They're good tears."

"I have never known tears to be good."

Spoken like a man who probably hadn't cried since childhood. "Sometimes they're necessary. An emotional release of sorts. You don't need to worry."

He brushed a damp strand of hair away from her cheek. "Yet I do worry. I worry about what will happen after we part ways again."

So was she. "Let's not ruin this by talking about that. We still have time. Tomorrow is Saturday, which means I have nowhere I need to be."

"I need to be with you," he said. "The entire weekend. I do not want to be away from you for even an hour."

"Then I am yours." For the weekend. Beyond that, who knew?

He brought her against his chest and rubbed her arm in a soothing rhythm. "Perhaps we should begin our time together in a real bed."

Maysa smiled in earnest. "I agree. I think I'm lying on a tree root, or perhaps a tortoise."

He shifted to where they faced each other. "Shall we drive back naked?"

"Oh, no, let's walk back naked. If we're lucky, we'll stumble upon some hapless reporter and provide a story that will span the ages. I can see it now—King Rafiq Mehdi Plays Doctor with Local Doctor."

Their shared laughter echoed over the olive grove, drowning out the night sounds and the inevitable goodbye hanging over them like a guillotine. Maysa wanted more laughter in the time they had left. She would reserve the tears for after he was gone.

Rafiq could not recall a time when he had been consumed by such fierce emotion. As Maysa slept in his arms, he held her as tightly as he dared for fear of rousing her. She needed rest as much as he needed her. He planned to wake her in the morning with kisses and make love to her most of the day. Lose himself in her for as long as possible, until he was forced to leave her behind again. Forced to find a more suitable woman in the eyes of the elders and the country at large. He knew no woman who would be as suitable for him as Maysa. But he would not subject her to the cruelty he inherently knew would exist if he took her as his future queen. He would not risk failing another woman.

Oddly, the guilt over his role in Rima's death had subsided over the past few days, yet it once more reared its ugly head. He had selfishly and willingly drawn Maysa into this doomed affair, and now he would suffer the consequences of his actions by losing her a second time.

Before that happened, he had much he needed to tell her, including all that had transpired the night of

Rima's death. Perhaps then Maysa would understand why he did not deserve her devotion. Perhaps then their parting would be easier. Swift and sure, as it should be. Once he confessed, she would not look upon him the same way. She would not be able to forgive him, as he had not been able to forgive himself.

In the interim, he would cherish this fleeting fantasy they had created, and he would show Maysa the depth of his feelings by giving her his undivided attention. He dared not put those feelings into words, for to declare them out loud would only wound her further.

Yet as he gazed upon her beautiful face and saw the girl she had been, as well as the remarkable woman she had become, he whispered those words without thought. With the reverence of a prayer.

"Ana bahebik."

I love you....

Eight

Maysa had always looked forward to Monday mornings, a day when she could leave the boring weekend behind to face the challenges of her profession. Today, with a remarkable man sleeping soundly at her side, she hated Monday.

In a little over an hour, she would reluctantly leave Rafiq to go work after spending a weekend with him that had been anything but uneventful. On the contrary, she'd experienced the best two days of her life to this point. She'd become someone unrecognizable to herself, a woman transformed into a high-voltage mass of sexual energy. She and Rafiq had made love in many different ways, and in many different places. She had done things with him that she'd never dreamed she would do, and the rewards had been phenomenal. He'd guided her into a paradise built on experimentation and a total loss of inhibition. They'd foregone clothing for easy access whenever the lovemaking mood struck them, and it had quite often.

But during the aftermath, when they'd been temporarily satisfied to only hold each other, they talked about times gone by and the road to her career. They'd discussed world politics and Rafiq's role in Bajul's future. They had covered everything but their impending goodbye.

Maysa had been grateful for that. She preferred to focus on the present and quiet, unforgettable moments such as this. She propped up on one elbow, supported her cheek with her palm and took the opportunity to study Rafiq, now stretched out on his back. He had a perfectly sculpted profile, as did all the Mehdi sons, only one of the reasons their photos had been in high demand and plastered all over the internet. Extraordinarily beautiful men with political power and untold wealth. The pinnacle of masculinity in a package of three.

But right now, with his eyes closed and his features slack, Rafiq looked more teenage boy than adult monarch to Maysa. More innocent than experienced. The motherless child who had strived to be worthy of his father's respect. The king of her damaged heart.

When he began to stir, she smoothed a wayward lock of hair back and kissed his forehead. His eyes opened slowly, followed by a patently sensual smile. The adult Rafiq had returned.

"I am surprised you are awake," he said in a sexy morning voice.

"I have to go into the clinic in a bit."

He turned toward her and outlined her lips with a

fingertip. "Can I persuade you to take another day off to spend with me?"

He could, if she let him, but she wouldn't. "This is my life, Rafiq, taking care of people. I have a responsibility to my patients to show up and..."

Her words trailed off the minute Rafiq's hand landed on her breast. She should move it immediately, before he moved that hand significantly lower. But as he began that predictable downward trek, his cell began to ring, momentarily keeping Maysa from throwing caution and obligation to the desert winds.

Rafiq fell back against the pillow, snatched the offending phone from the nightstand and answered with a gruff, "What do you want, Zain?"

Maysa settled her head on his shoulder, her palm resting on his sternum. She listened to the steady beat of his heart, as well as the one-sided conversation that seemed somewhat tense.

"I will be preoccupied for the next hour," he said. "But you may call after that if any issue arises."

Then out of the blue, Rafiq guided Maysa's hand beneath the sheet to show her exactly what had arisen. She attempted to ignore his personal "issue," not by taking her hand away, but by leaving it still.

Rafiq caught her gaze, smiled and winked at her before he continued. "I trust you can handle it." Maysa stifled a laugh when he added, "No, I was not speaking to you, Zain," followed by a long pause when Maysa could no longer resist the temptation to drive him crazy with a few practiced touches.

"What am I doing at the moment?" Rafiq drew in a broken breath and let it out slowly. "I am considering a long morning ride. I will see you this afternoon."

After he hung up, Rafiq immediately tossed the phone aside, while Maysa threw back the covers. After that, everything happened very quickly—fumbling for a condom, touching with abandon, making love as if tomorrow would not arrive. After the frantic session was over, they remained in each other's arms while their bodies calmed and their breathing returned to normal.

Yes, these were the moments she appreciated the most. She would take them to memory and bring them out when they were all she had left of him.

The shrill of the alarm forced Maysa out of the fantasy world and back into reality. She reluctantly left him and sat up. "I have to get ready for work." When Rafiq didn't respond, she glanced to her right to find him staring at the ceiling. "Is something wrong?"

"A complication with one of the council members," he said without looking at her. "I must return to the palace this afternoon."

"Permanently?" She despised the disappointment in her voice, but she wasn't prepared for their parting.

"I am not certain," he said. "It will depend on the outcome of the meeting."

She rose from the bed, grabbed the robe from the nearby chair and slipped it on. "I hope it goes well."

"As do I."

On the chance this could be the final time they would be together alone, she decided to make an offer he wouldn't refuse. "I'm going to shower now. Would you like to join me?"

He moved up against the wood headboard and raked both hands through his hair. "I will shower in the secondary bath. After you are dressed, meet me in the living area. We have a few things to discuss."

A strong sense of dread shot all the way to her soul. "All right. I will see you in a while."

As she bathed, Maysa tried to tell herself this could only have to do with Rafiq's duty, and not their relationship. She had little luck in convincing herself that was the truth. By the time she was finished dressing and out the bedroom door, she was resigned to hearing goodbye.

When she entered the living room, Maysa discovered Rafiq leaning forward on the edge of the small divan, his head lowered and his hands laced together between his knees. When he looked up, she immediately noticed the weariness in his eyes.

She swallowed around the knot in her throat and took the space beside him. "I am fairly certain I know what you are about to say."

He sighed and leaned back against the magenta cushion. "You have no way of knowing what I am about to say until after I say it. And once the words leave my mouth, you will never view me in the same light again."

She clasped his hand to reassure him that nothing he said would ever change her mind about him. "Rafiq, we've both known our time together would eventually come to an end sooner than later."

"You misunderstand," he said. "This is not about us."

Now she was sincerely confused. "Did something happen at the palace in your absence?"

"No. I need to tell you what transpired the night Rima died. I have been carrying the burden far too long."

Relief washed over her, though she was still concerned. “Go ahead. I’m listening.”

He hesitated a few moments before he continued. “Shortly after dinner that evening, she came into my study and told me of the pregnancy. I was pleased with the news and hopeful that having a child together would restore our civility, if not our friendship. She did not agree.”

“Then she wasn’t even the least bit happy about the baby?” Maysa asked, though she had seen indications of that unhappiness when Rima had come to her for confirmation.

“No, she was not happy. I requested we make a formal announcement, yet she refused. She said she did not want anyone to know until she was more than two weeks along in the pregnancy.”

Warning bells rang out in Maysa’s head. “Are you certain she wasn’t further along?”

“I am certain. Why would you believe otherwise?”

She had no one to blame but herself for walking into this snake pit. Still, she was trapped between upholding patient confidentiality and being up front with Rafiq. She chose the former for the time being. “I apologize. You were her husband and you would most likely know when she conceived.”

“I knew the exact night she became pregnant,” he said. “I had recently returned from a diplomatic mission encompassing several countries. It was the first time she had allowed me in her bed for several months, and that was only after I pursued the matter of producing an heir.”

The tangled web of deceit had now grown, wrapping Maysa in its clutches. If he had been traveling during the time of Rima's actual conception, that left only one probability—Rafiq had not fathered the child she'd been carrying at the time of her demise. "You said something else happened that night. What was it?"

"We debated the announcement for a time," he continued, "and then she informed me she did not care to be pregnant with my child, but she did want out of the marriage. I told her that was impossible and I would not divorce her."

Having heard that from her own husband, Maysa experienced a fleeting moment of sympathy for Rima. "I'm sure that upset her further."

He released a rough sigh. "Yes, but not as much as when I told her if she left the country after the birth, I would seek her out and bring the baby back to the palace. I would see to it she would have no contact with our child. She said she would see me in hell before she allowed that to happen. That is when I ordered her out of the palace. I arranged for the car she was driving that night."

And Maysa knew exactly where she had gone—ironically the resort where they were now having this disturbing discussion. "No one knows about this?"

"Only my assistant, Mr. Deeb, who had the car delivered to the palace." He turned his weary gaze on her. "And now you know everything."

She did, but he did not. She could fill in the blanks, and possibly annihilate everything she had worked so hard to gain, because of one man who had played in integral part in this twisted triangle. Her own flesh and blood.

Rafiq streaked a hand over his jaw and sighed. "I

would not blame you if you choose to leave now and never look back."

She rested a hand on his arm. "If you are expecting harsh judgment from me, you won't find it. You're human and not infallible. Neither am I. We all make mistakes, and we can only move on and learn from those mistakes if they cannot be rectified."

He appeared stunned by the comment. "I deserve no less than your condemnation. What honorable man threatens to tear a mother away from her child, then arranges to send that distraught woman to her death?"

"An angry man," she said. "And you had no way of knowing Rima would have an accident. Her death wasn't your fault any more than your mother's death was your father's fault."

He sighed. "I cannot believe you would forgive me so easily."

"Yet I do, Rafiq. More important, it is past time for you to forgive yourself."

The time had also come to tell him the truth about Rima's relationship with Shamil, and the result of that relationship. But after she consulted the clock on the wall, she decided to wait until she wasn't facing a clinic full of patients in less than twenty minutes. As it stood now, she would probably arrive late.

She came to her feet, leaned over and kissed his cheek. "When I return here tonight, we'll continue this discussion, provided you decide not to end your sabbatical immediately." She held her breath while waiting for his answer.

"I will be here," he said. "I cannot stand the thought of leaving you today."

She couldn't stand the thought of him leaving her

ever. But he might not be so willing to stay once she revealed the truth, as well as how long she had kept it from him. "I have to go now, and I'll see you this evening."

Rafiq rose from the sofa, took her hand and walked her to the door where he kissed her soundly and said goodbye. She hoped it wasn't the final one.

After she was well on her way to the clinic, Maysa mulled over everything Rafiq had told her, particularly the part about Rima lying about the length of her pregnancy. She was without a doubt certain of one thing—Rafiq had not been the father of Rima's child. Her instincts told her she knew the responsible party. And as soon as she had a break at work, she planned to track him down and confront him by phone.

When her cell began to ring, Maysa fished it from her bag to find her brother's name on the screen, as if she had somehow willed him to contact her. "Hello, Shamil," she answered with feigned composure.

"Hello, my dear sister. Are you enjoying your status as the king's whore?"

Evidently the rumors had traveled all the way to Yemen. "It's not like you to listen to idle gossip, Shamil."

"True, but I do tend to believe what I have seen with my own eyes. That was quite a passionate kiss the two of you shared at the door of my finest villa only minutes ago."

Utter panic settled over Maysa. "Where are you now?"

"I am staring at two armored cars, but I am about to pay His Excellency a long overdue visit. I have done some soul-searching during my time away and I have decided the bastard should hear the truth."

Unable to concentrate on driving, Maysa pulled onto the shoulder. "The guards will never let you near him."

"That is where you are wrong. I have already notified the king I will be there soon, and he was more than happy to welcome an old friend."

She highly doubted that. "You call yourself a friend when you have betrayed his trust by sleeping with his wife?"

"You are not one to judge after you have spread your legs for him in *my* resort. I will derive great pleasure from demanding he leave at once."

A sense of dread prompted Maysa to tighten her grasp on the steering wheel. "Shamil, please, think about what you are about to do."

"I have thought about it, and nothing you can say will stop me from exacting the revenge the *king* so deserves."

When the line went dead, Maysa jumped into action. She executed a U-turn in the middle of the road and depressed the accelerator, spewing gravel in her wake. If Shamil made good on this threats, she refused to allow Rafiq to face the truth alone—provided she wasn't already too late.

At one time, Rafiq would have welcomed seeing his onetime closest friend. But after learning from Zain that Shamil was still attempting to thwart the conservation project, he was anything but pleased over his unexpected appearance. "I believe our meeting was scheduled at 4:00 p.m. at the palace."

"And I believe this meeting cannot wait."

When Shamil entered the villa without a proper invitation, both guards immediately moved forward to follow him. Rafiq raised a hand to halt their progress. "Remain here. I will notify you if you are needed."

He returned inside to discover Shamil had made himself at home in a chair across from the divan. "Please, sit down on *my* sofa, Rafiq."

Rafiq complied and assumed a relaxed position, though he was anything but relaxed at the moment. "Your insistence upon calling me by my given name is an act of subordination. I will forgive you this time in light of our shared past."

He stroked his graying beard as if it were a cherished pet. "I am sorry to say I cannot forgive you for seducing my sister. But then I suppose she was an easy target."

The true reason behind the visit had become all too clear. "I refuse to discuss Maysa with you."

Shamil crossed his legs and folded his hands together in his lap. "Perhaps then we should discuss the other woman formerly in your life, until you drove her to an untimely death."

Rafiq clung to the last thread of restraint. "I will not speak to you about Rima, either."

"Then I will speak to you about her. I know everything about your sham of a marriage, Rafiq. Every last detail. Who do you think she told about her misery over being wed to the likes of you?"

He momentarily rejected that notion, until he recalled Rima mentioning having lunch with Shamil a few weeks before her death. "I am aware you and Rima maintained your friendship and that you spoke to her on more than one occasion. We were all friends at one time."

"Friends?" Shamil barked out a caustic laugh. "You were never Rima's friend. You were her captor and she, your prisoner."

Rafiq had begun to suspect Shamil knew much more than he had initially believed. "We were bound by a contract made a long time ago. Rima accepted her role as queen and my wife."

Shamil leaned forward and sneered. "Let me ask you something. Did it disturb you to learn you were not Rima's first lover?"

A repeat of the conversation he had had with Adan a few days before. "What Rima did before our wedding was immaterial to me. I only asked that she remain faithful after we exchanged vows."

"Were you faithful?"

"I was." Though he had been tempted a time or two during the year following their marriage. Yet he had never acted on that temptation.

"Perhaps physically true to her," Shamil said. "But not mentally. You have always lusted after my sister."

"You know not of what you speak." A false denial, but Shamil did not deserve the truth.

"When you were forcing Rima to do your bidding in bed to produce another arrogant Mehdi, were you not imagining driving your *sambool* into Maysa?"

It took all Rafiq's strength not to wrap his hands around Shamil's throat. He settled for a curse. *"Ibn il sharmuta!"*

Shamil appeared only mildly insulted. "Please leave my mother out of this. She was a good woman. Unfortunately, Maysa does not appear to have inherited that goodness. She has brought nothing but shame to our family, first by divorcing her husband, and now by allowing you to bed her."

He refused to acknowledge any intimacy between him and Maysa. He would definitely address Maysa's ruthless ex-husband. "Do you know what Boutros Kassab did to her? Are you aware of the torture he inflicted upon her? Or do you have so little regard for Maysa that you do not care?"

Shamil did not seem the least bit disturbed, leading Rafiq to believe the latter held true. "Maysa has always been prone to exaggeration. I am certain the accusations she leveled against Boutros were overblown."

Having his conjecture confirmed, Rafiq's hatred burned bright for this man whom he once considered a confidant. "At one time I greatly respected you, Shamil. Now I see that you are nothing more than a power-hungry, misguided man without a conscience. It is no wonder you have not found a suitable wife. No woman would dare tie themselves to you."

His smile was cynical. "Your wife did not feel that way, Rafiq. Had she not been bound to your contract, she would have been with me. In fact, she was. Many times when you left her alone to travel. Did you not wonder why she always chose to stay behind?"

He had never questioned her reluctance to travel, nor had he objected to the decision. "She had duties to oversee at the palace."

"She had an aversion to spending time with you. And for your information, I was Rima's first lover, and I was her last."

"You are a liar."

"It is not a lie. She came to me that fateful night

when you ordered her out of the palace. She told me you arranged for her transportation and threatened to take your child away from her."

Rafiq now realized he spoke the truth. "That proves nothing other than she came to you seeking advice."

"She came to me seeking comfort, which I gladly gave to her in my bed. If you require further confirmation, ask my sister."

He had erroneously believed the shocking secrets were over. "What does Maysa have to do with this?"

"She saw Rima and I together in this very place that night."

If Shamil spoke the truth, Rafiq did not understand why Maysa had withheld the information. He intended to find out, but first he must deal with the turncoat before him. "I could have you hanged for this."

Shamil appeared unmoved by the threat. "Yet you will not do that. I hold the power to halt the conservation project, as well as destroy your standing with your people. Once they learn you demanded the queen leave her rightful home, subsequently leading to her death, they will not be quick to forgive you."

Rafiq inherently knew that to be true, but he would not give Shamil the satisfaction of an admission. He would present a defense for his actions. "The people are aware Rima's death was an accident, and I do not need your vote to see the project to fruition since I have the majority of council's support."

"Then consider this. Should word leak out that you have taken a scorned woman as your mistress, then you will take Maysa down with you. Since the day you appointed me health minister, I began to make many contacts in the medical field. I will make certain she is stripped of her hospital privileges and quite possibly her license to practice."

Rafiq glared at him. "You would have to show cause to do that. An unfounded rumor of an affair is not cause."

"Ah, yes, but it is amazing how a proof of physician's grave mistakes can suddenly surface, whether they are founded or not."

His patience now in tatters, Rafiq shot from the sofa and pointed at the door. "Get out."

Shamil's ensuing laugh sounded sinister. "You are ordering me out of my own establishment?"

"Yes, and if you do not leave, I will have you forcefully removed by my guards and have you escorted to the airport. They are very loyal to me, and I have no control over what they might do on the way. A man would have a difficult time surviving in the mountains without supplies, clothes and transportation."

He saw the first sign of fear in Shamil's eyes. "You would not dare give that order, as you would be the primary suspect."

No, he would not, yet he would allow Shamil to believe otherwise. "It is amazing how people mysteriously disappear. Since in all likelihood no one has been made privy to our meeting, and since it is well-known you are currently living in Yemen, you would not be missed for quite some time."

Shamil finally stood, strode to the door and opened it. But before he exited, he faced Rafiq again. "When you see Maysa, give my whore of a sister my fondest regards."

On the heels of his fury, and driven by absolute betrayal, King Rafiq Mehdi, who had always prided himself on control, strode across the room, drew back his fist—and centered it in the middle of Shamil Barad's face.

Nine

Maysa arrived in time to see Rafiq deliver the blow that sent her brother back against one stone column bracing the portico. She watched in horror when the guards restrained Rafiq as he went after Shamil, who used that window of opportunity to throw a punch. The impact to his jaw snapped Rafiq's head back and split the corner of his mouth. Two more sentries appeared from across the road, grabbed Shamil and wrenched his arms behind his back.

Shock kept Maysa momentarily planted in place, until she came around and found the wherewithal to retrieve her medical bag from the backseat. She rushed toward Rafiq, only to be restrained by the bodyguard who had kept Rafiq from mostly doing serious damage to Shamil.

"Unhand her!" Rafiq shouted and then swiped his

shirtsleeve across the trickle of blood seeping from the laceration.

"Did he break my nose, Maysa?" Shamil asked, stopping her progress.

She took a quick glance at the wound. "Yes, it looks broken. They'll take care of it at the emergency room."

"You will not treat it?"

"No, I will not."

"Sharmuta!"

"Perhaps I am a bitch, but at least I fight fairly."

"Take him to the hospital," Rafiq ordered the guards.

For some reason Shamil looked terrified. "I will drive myself."

"You will remain in custody until I decide what I will do in regard to your assault on the king."

"And you will make certain I arrive at the hospital safely?"

Maysa could not believe he was being such a sniveling child. "I will call ahead and inform them you're coming." That would be the only favor she would grant him.

As the security detail began tugging him toward one of the cars, Shamil turned a hateful glare on Rafiq. "Remember what we have discussed, Your Majesty."

Rafiq muttered an Arabic oath as he turned and strode back into the villa before Maysa could get to him. She followed him even knowing she could very well be walking into a hornet's nest, with the king serving as the head hornet.

After she closed the door behind her, Maysa came upon Rafiq restlessly circling the living area, his hands balled into fists as if he would like to hit something else. "Look, Rafiq," she began, "I know you're most likely angry with me—"

"I am not angry with you," he said without looking at her. "I am angry at myself for not maintaining control. For being such a fool and a failure."

"Who have you failed?" she asked, though she already knew the answer.

He finally looked at her, the weight of the kingdom in his eyes. "My wife, and now you."

She set her bag aside on the coffee table, hoping to eventually put it to good use when she treated Rafiq's cut. If he let her treat it. "You and Rima failed each other, Rafiq. You two should never have married in the first place. But you did marry her, she turned to another man, and it all ended in tragedy. No matter what happened that night, it's done and it cannot be undone."

He paused his pacing in the middle of the room. "How long have you known about her affair with Shamil?"

The query came as no surprise. "Not until he told me the day you arrived at my house. I had my suspicions, but I never confirmed them."

"Yet you chose not to tell me."

"Shamil threatened to ruin my medical practice. At the time, that mattered most to me." Before Rafiq had come to matter more. "You and I were barely on speaking terms. I had no idea we would reconnect the way we have."

"Yet when we did become close, you still did not reveal what you knew. You should have said something, Maysa."

"Then you are angry with me."

"Disappointed that you did not feel you could tell

me after what I told you earlier." He both looked and sounded resigned.

"I did plan to tell you tonight, if that's any consolation." And now she was charged with delivering the final betrayal blow. "There is something else you need to know."

"Nothing you could say would surprise me at this point in time."

"Perhaps you should sit down, just in case."

He remained planted in the same spot. "I would rather stand."

Of course he would. "It's about the baby Rima was carrying. Shamil was the father." She waited a moment for the news to sink in before she continued. "I only discovered that this morning, after you mentioned the timing of the pregnancy. Rima was close to entering her second trimester."

"How do you know this?"

Maysa decided she needed to sit and selected the straight-back rattan chair in the corner. "Rima came to me to confirm the pregnancy, although I wasn't certain why. I now believe she wanted to avoid using one of the palace's physicians for fear they would be suspicious since you had been traveling at the time she conceived."

He sighed. "I find little comfort in the knowledge the child was not mine. An innocent life was still taken, regardless of its parentage, and I find that incredibly sad."

The declaration demonstrated the depth of his honor. Some men would be relieved, and not at all upset. "Did Shamil mention the baby to you?"

"He did not, yet I find it hard to believe that Rima would conceal it from him."

Maysa had no problem believing it. "I hate to speak ill of the dead, but Rima was always about appearances. I honestly believe she would not have divorced you for Shamil. She would never put herself in the midst of a scandal. I do think she let him believe she would for the attention."

"The attention I did not give her?"

"It wouldn't have mattered if you'd showered her with it every moment of every day. For Rima, it would never be enough."

"I did not realize you thought so little of her."

Clearly he had been blind to the ongoing competition for his affections between her and Rima. "She craved that attention when we were schoolmates at the palace, and she would find it through whatever means." Including shamelessly flirting with the other two Mehdi brothers behind Rafiq's back. But he had heard enough secrets for one day.

When Maysa noticed Rafiq's lip had begun to swell, she stood and gestured toward the sofa. "I need to take a closer look at your cut."

He trudged toward the divan as if on his way to the gallows. After he settled onto the cushions, Maysa went to work. He winced when she applied antiseptic, yet he remained still when she applied the strips to close the wound.

"That should hold the edges together if you're careful. But if it opens, you may need stitches."

As she began to put away the supplies, Rafiq clasped her wrist. "What are we going to do about us?"

"Is there an us, Rafiq?"

He released her and forked his hands through his hair. "Shamil continues to threaten to expose our affair. We would have to be cautious if we continue to see each other."

If they continued to see each other. "Then I suppose it's probably best we end it now, as originally planned."

"You are willing to walk away after what we have shared?"

She summoned all her courage before she answered. "Yes, because you are not willing to defy tradition and have an open relationship with me."

"To do that would only subject you to constant contempt and ridicule."

"Are you certain you are not referring to yourself?"

"I am the king and will remain so, whatever anyone might believe about me. But I would face resistance from the council when attempting to make decisions for the country. The majority still adhere to the old ways."

"Then in part this is also about your reputation and your unwillingness to discard the old ways."

"I am only trying to protect you, Maysa."

A spear of anger mixed with resentment hurled through her. "I divorced a husband who was basically a terrorist. I left my homeland for a strange country with only the clothes on my back. I worked my way through medical school and returned to Bajul to face the worst possible scorn, and I have survived it all. What makes you believe I need your protection?"

"I care about you and your well-being."

"If you truly cared about me, Rafiq, you would never propose I be your *sharmuta,* as Shamil so aptly put it. That being said, you may consider your sabbatical officially ended, and our affair permanently over. Feel free to return to the palace knowing your secrets are safe with me. Now I have to return to the clinic and salvage what is left of the day." And what was left of her heart.

Fearing she might reconsider or cry, Maysa snatched the bag and headed for the door. She didn't have time to open it before Rafiq came up behind her and slid his arms around her waist. "I do not know how to let you go a second time."

"Then don't, but only on my terms."

He turned her to face him. "I cannot risk failing you the way I failed Rima. I cannot abide you hating me. If avoiding that possibility means letting you go, then I have no choice."

Little by little, her heart began to splinter, one fissure at a time. One word at a time. "Everyone has choices, Rafiq. You have to decide whether you want to risk making them, or if you wish to settle for safety. I will not play second chair in your royal orchestra. I will not stand by while you choose another queen and enter another loveless marriage for the sake of building a fortune and making Mehdi babies. Either we are truly together, or we are not. I need all, or nothing."

She held her breath while she waited to hear his choice, and silently prayed it would be the right one.

Her hopes soared when he held her closely. They plummeted when he said, "I cannot risk hurting you again."

Oh, but he already had. Twice. She pulled away to gain some distance, at least physically. The emotional ties would be much harder to sever. "Then I wish you well, Rafiq, in your endeavors. And please do not try to contact me for I will not accept your calls."

"Will you honor one last request before you leave?"

The pain in his eyes called to her, and she tried not to listen. "That would depend on the request."

"Will you kiss me goodbye?"

Her mind rejected the appeal, while her shattering heart told her to answer. And she would for the sake of what they had meant to each other. A lasting memory to live on until she was ready to move forward.

Maysa wrapped her hand around his neck and brought his lips to hers. They remained that way for a long moment until the threat of tears forced her away from him. "God speed, Rafiq."

"Ana bahebik, habibti."

How long had she waited to hear those words? And now they had come too late. "I love you, too, Rafiq. I have since the first time I saw you. But I find it tragic that we still live in a place where love is simply not enough."

She walked away with her head held high and her soul in tatters. This time, the goodbye hadn't broken her. Not completely.

In the two weeks since Maysa had told Rafiq goodbye, she'd immersed herself in work, thankful for the diversion. Yet the nights had been the most difficult, and uninterrupted sleep had been at a premium.

Fortunately, today she finally felt more like her old self and prepared to meet any challenges. She was not prepared for the patient seated on the exam room table. "What are you doing here, Madison?"

"Guess."

Maysa didn't dare. "I hope you have a cold or some other minor ailment."

Madison tightened the band securing her blond

ponytail. "I'm not sure what I have exactly. I've been a little queasy in the morning and tired. But then being a mother to triplets can be exhausting."

Apparently the overtired mother was having a mental lapse. "You mean twins."

"I'm counting the father of my babies, so that basically makes three children. Did you know the man has no clue how to fold towels?"

She smiled. "Of course not. Someone has always done it for him."

"That someone is me because I refuse to have the staff do something I am quite capable of doing."

As much as she wanted to visit with Zain's wife, she still had six more patients to see before day's end. "Back to your symptoms. Is it possible you could be pregnant?"

"I have no idea. My periods are still irregular even after my one functioning ovary spit out double deuces."

"Let me rephrase the question then. Have you had unprotected sexual intercourse?"

Madison looked more than a bit sheepish. "Yes. The day we went to the lake."

The day they had stopped by to reveal the rumor mill was in full spin. "I knew I should have given you condoms."

"Zain hates using condoms."

"So does Raf..." She wanted to yank her wayward tongue out of her mouth. "Many men take exception to them, but they're necessary if you wish to prevent disease and pregnancy."

"It's okay," Madison said. "I know you and Rafiq were sleeping together. I could tell the minute I saw the two of you together at your house."

"Actually, we weren't sleeping together at that time."

"But you did sleep together later, right?"

Maysa grasped for an excuse to change the subject. "Let's get you a pregnancy test, just in case." She turned to the counter, retrieved the box, then offered it to Madison. "You know the drill. The restroom is right across the hall."

"Gotta love peeing on a stick," she said as she hopped off the table and headed out the door.

While Madison was gone, Maysa debated whether she should ask about Rafiq. Probably unwise. She would hate to learn he had already begun the queen candidate search.

After Madison returned, Maysa placed the test on the counter and set the portable timer to await the results. "In ten minutes, we should have the answer."

Madison scooted back onto the table and sent her dangling legs into motion. "I'm having a moment of déjà vu from the last time you gave me a pregnancy test. We have to stop meeting like this."

Maysa laughed. "I agree, but it's better than if you had something serious, such as malaria."

"Very true."

A few moments of awkward silence ticked off before Maysa spoke again. "How are the children?"

"Fine. Getting fat as little pigs."

"And Zain is doing well? Other than his domestic issues."

"Very well and frisky as ever. He has been busy with the water project, but he's never too tired for… you know."

Yes, she definitely knew, and she couldn't quell the envy onset. She studied the anatomy poster on the wall to her left in an effort to avoid Madison's scrutiny. "Elena and Adan are doing well?"

"Yes, and it's okay if you ask about him, Maysa."

Could she possibly be more obvious? "All right. How is he?"

Madison scowled. "He's horrible. He has turned into the meanest king in all the Middle East. He orders everyone around nonstop and refuses to come to dinner. And that blasted pacing. Makes me want to glue his butt to the office chair."

She smiled in part over Madison's comment, and in part because she liked to think Rafiq was experiencing some regret over his decision. "The pacing is a long-time habit. He's nervous."

"He's lovesick. He misses you, Maysa. I don't really know what happened between you, and you certainly are under no obligation to tell me."

She needed to tell someone, and she felt she could trust Zain's wife with the information. "Archaic tradition happened. He can't be openly involved with a divorcée, and I refuse to be his mistress."

"I don't blame you." Madison suddenly shifted her weight from one hip to the other, a possible sign of discomfort. "I do know about Rima and your brother's ongoing affair, and that the baby wasn't Rafiq's."

"Rafiq told you that?" she asked, attempting to temper the shock in her voice.

Madison shook her head. "No. He told Zain, and Zain told me. We don't have any secrets between us. He's also concerned that if Shamil decides to leak the information, I'll have to do damage control."

"It could definitely be damaging, depending on how

the information is perceived. The country seemed to take a liking to Rima immediately."

"I personally never cared for her," Madison said. "She seemed a bit self-absorbed at times, and cold. But then maybe I'm being too harsh. I never really had the chance to know her that well."

Maysa had known her all too well. "She's always been aloof since our teenage years."

"Then you knew her before she and Rafiq became engaged? Or maybe I should say before they went under contract."

"Actually, Rafiq and I were seeing each other up to that point in time." And after, a fact she decided not to divulge. "We were very close."

Madison sent her a sympathetic look. "It must have been difficult knowing she was taking your man right out from under you, and you could do nothing about it."

"It was very difficult, and at times it seemed she went out of her way to flirt with Rafiq in my presence. But then we were teenage girls, and you know how petty they can be sometimes."

"Speaking of teenagers, did you know Rima slept with Adan when he was only seventeen?"

She could tell Madison regretted the statement the moment it left her mouth. And Maysa had a difficult time believing Adan would betray his own brother.

"Are you certain that really happened?"

"Positive. Adan told me the night of the wedding. He claims Rima had argued with her one true love and she turned to him for comfort. Adan being Adan, he jumped at the opportunity. When I mistakenly thought he meant she'd argued with Rafiq, he hinted someone else was involved. I assume that someone else was your brother."

That made perfect sense to Maysa. "Does Rafiq know?"

"Not hardly, and I hope Adan doesn't have a sudden crisis of conscience and blurt it out. That would probably send Rafiq right over the edge. Losing you has been bad enough. That's why I wish you could work it out and save us all some grief."

She saw no end to the impasse. "In order to work it out, one of us will have to give in, and it will not be me. I highly doubt Rafiq will, either."

"You never know, Maysa. Just look at what Zain did to be with me. He gave up the crown and moved back to America."

Rafiq would never do something so drastic when it involved duty. That much she knew.

When the timer dinged, Maysa walked to the counter and picked up the test to read it. "This is either good news, or not so good news. You'll have to tell me which one it might be."

The woman looked as though she might vault off the exam table. "I'll let you know as soon as you tell me what it says."

"You're not pregnant."

Madison's shoulders slumped. "In a way, I'm a little disappointed. In a bigger way, I'm glad. I'm not sure either Zain or I could handle having another baby after dealing with twins. At least not for another year or two."

Maysa tossed the test into the trash and smiled. "If that happens, you must be sure to confirm the pregnancy with me. We'll make it our own tradition."

"And maybe before then, you'll be the one in need of a pregnancy test."

Not likely. "Single mothers are not always viewed favorably, and I don't intend to look for a husband in the near future."

"You could always go the artificial insemination route." Madison snapped her fingers and pointed. "You could even do it yourself."

That appealed to Maysa about as much as having a tooth filled. "No, thank you. I'm also fairly sure sperm donors are few and far between in Bajul."

"I know of one man who would gladly donate his sperm the natural way. Of course, he'll first have to realize he's in danger of giving up the best thing that has ever happened to him, meaning you."

"Forgive me if I don't hold my breath until that happens. I'd require a ventilator."

Madison slid off the table, gave her a hug and paused before she left the room. "Don't give up on him yet, Maysa. He just might come around, marry you and tell all of Bajul to go to hell if they don't like it."

As far as Maysa was concerned, that would take a full-fledged miracle. And though she had witnessed a few miracles in her career—the birth of a child, a patient's unexpected recovery from a devastating illness—she wouldn't let allow herself to hope for one this time.

Ten

"Miracle of all miracles. You are actually sitting down."

At the sound of the grating British accent, Rafiq looked up from his notes to see Adan filing into the office, Zain and Madison trailing behind him. "I do not recall summoning any of you."

Zain claimed the chair across from the desk without seeking Rafiq's permission. "Since you did not summon us in response to our request for a family meeting, we have taken the initiative to seek you out."

Rafiq gripped the gold pen in both hands with enough force to break it in half. "The council meeting will be held tomorrow afternoon, and I need to prepare. Therefore, this meeting is officially over."

Adan assumed his usual perch on the edge of the desk, as if he had been raised by baboons. "We are not leaving until we have our say, Rafiq."

If he chose to argue the point, he would only prolong their departure. "Then have your say and be done with it. But make it quick or I will leave the whole lot of you here, retire to my bedroom and lock the door."

While Madison remained a few feet away, Zain and Adan exchanged a glance before Zain began to speak. "We are here on Maysa's behalf."

The sound of her name instantly filled Rafiq with further regret. The same regret that had haunted him every moment of every day since they had parted. "She has contacted you?"

"She has no idea we're discussing her," Adan said. "However, since you apparently have left her high and dry, we feel it is necessary to advocate for her. In other words, remove your head from that part of your anatomy in which no self-respecting head belongs, and beg her to come back to you."

If only that option existed. "Impossible. Any public connection she has with me will only serve to destroy her good standing in the community. She has already endured entirely too much hardship as it is." Some of which he had recently imposed on her life.

"If you're referring to her status as a divorcée," Zain began, "it's a common occurrence in America. People change spouses as often as they change underwear."

His brother had clearly forgotten he was in Bajul, not Los Angeles. "Need I remind you we are not governed by the same laws and customs here?"

"No, you need not," Zain said. "I personally experienced the results of those antiquated customs. Perhaps I should remind you that I chose to marry Madison, and we have suffered no serious ill effects from that decision."

"You are no longer king, Zain. You handed that honor to me. My private life is put under a microscope daily, and I will not subject Maysa to constant scrutiny."

"Instead, you are willing to subject all of us to your bad temper because you are so consumed with her, you can barely function," Zain said.

His ever-present anger began to escalate. "My duty has not been affected by my decision to cut all ties with her." The decision that she truthfully had made for him.

Adan scowled. "Duty be damned, Rafiq. Your duty cannot replace a woman's affections, or save you from your determination to punish the world for your own failures."

He did not need to be reminded how he had failed, or whom he had failed. "If you know what is good for you, Adan, you will go fly a plane and leave me be."

Madison raised her hand as if they were in a schoolroom, not the king's official office. "May I say something, Rafiq?"

He waved her forward. "Please. Everyone should have the opportunity to take a verbal shot at the king."

"That's not my intent," she said. "I simply wanted to let you know that when I've taken the twins for a stroll in the village, I've managed to talk with several of your subjects. They all seem to feel you are doing an excellent job."

"I am pleased to hear that." The first good news he had heard in quite some time, aside from Maysa's declaration of love. "All the more reason not to introduce a scandal."

Madison's gaze momentarily faltered. "I also took the liberty of digging into Boutros Kassab's history.

According to a few contacts I have in Europe, it seems he has a history of violence against women, specifically two of his three ex-wives and one mistress. Of course, he used his influence to get the charges dismissed."

"He is a known tyrant, so I am not surprised." He *was* surprised that Madison knew about Maysa's marriage to Boutros. Perhaps too much to be the product of a natural curiosity.

His suspicions were confirmed when she glanced at her husband before bringing her attention back to Rafiq. "Since Maysa suffered abuse at the hands of Kassab, we could leak that information. Then when you decide to publicly announce your relationship, people would know the reason behind Maysa's divorce."

He had been wrong to confide in Zain. "You told her about what Maysa endured when I emphatically asked that you not share that information?"

Zain seemed unmoved by Rafiq's ire. "Madison and I have no secrets. She is only attempting to aid in your happiness, and you will never be happy until you are reunited with Maysa."

When Zain stood and wrapped a protective arm around her shoulder, Madison said, "Thank you, sweetheart. And by the way, Maysa confirmed we're not pregnant."

Zain kissed her on the mouth, as if no one else mattered. The same way Rafiq had kissed Maysa only two short weeks ago.

"Then we shall have more time to practice in the next year or two," Zain said after they parted.

"Good lord," Adan said. "If you two do not stop this nonsense, I will send you both to your room and sell your children to the highest bidder."

Zain shot an acrid glance at Adan. "You are jealous because you have not kept company with a female in quite some time. Perhaps you should take care of that and leave the adults to solve Rafiq's problems."

As the brotherly bickering continued, Rafiq's temper arrived in the form of a solid slam on the desk. "Enough! I am capable of solving my own problems, and I am tired of the intrusion." He regarded Zain's wife. "Madison, I appreciate your assistance, but I will not be in need of the information. Revealing Kassab's tainted history will only force Maysa to relive a past she desires to forget and open old wounds that have finally begun to heal." Until he had inflicted the emotional wounds upon her.

"I understand your decision," Madison said. "And you can trust me to keep the information confidential."

Rafiq came to his feet and willed his anger to calm. "I am finished answering questions and entertaining suggestions, so if you will excuse me—"

"Not until you answer my questions, *cara mia*."

As always, his former governess had an uncanny knack of appearing before Rafiq could escape the inquest. "I will allow one more question from you, Elena. But only one."

She wedged between a surprised Madison and Zain. "You will answer as many questions as I ask. First, do you love Maysa?"

He tracked his gaze from one expectant face to the other. "With all due respect, that is a private matter I will not address."

"Bloody hell, Rafiq," Adan said. "Just admit it."

"I assure you the sky will not fall on your head if

you say the words," Zain added. "Otherwise, I would have suffered several concussions."

"Do you love her?" Elena repeated.

"Yes, I love her." With all his once-hardened heart. "Are you satisfied now?"

The woman looked extremely satisfied, and somewhat smug. "Do you love her enough to spit in the face of convention and claim her as your partner for all time?"

When he failed to answer, Elena marched forward and stood immediately before the desk. "Rafiq, you have two choices, the first being you can disregard public opinion and ask Maysa to marry you because I know *she* is strong enough to handle any repercussions. Are you?"

He did not view that as a viable option. "And my second choice?"

"You can end up like me. Alone."

"You have never seemed to have an issue with being alone before."

"I was never truly physically alone, Rafiq, but I was lonely. I spent a lifetime loving a man who refused to acknowledge our affair for fear of upsetting the royal applecart."

His mind was fraught with more confusion. "What man is this, Elena?"

"Our father, you fool," Adan said. "I have suspected as much for years."

Elena looked completely baffled. "How could you have known?"

"I arrived late from the academy one night and I saw you enter his suite," Adan stated matter-of-factly.

"I assumed everyone knew and just never mentioned it out of respect for your privacy."

"Then you were the one sleeping with the king?" Zain asked, his tone heralding the shock Rafiq now experienced.

Elena lifted her chin, her eyes slightly misted with tears. "Yes, I was sleeping with the king. Right up until the day before he died. And no, I was not responsible for his death. I *was* responsible for giving him many memorable moments during his final hours on earth."

Adan kissed her cheek. "Good show, old girl. And while we're confessing…" He turned to address Rafiq. "I wish to apologize for sleeping with your wife."

The shock returned with the force of a grenade. "You did what?"

Adan held up his hands, palms forward. "Before you come across the desk to slug me, I wish to add I was only seventeen at the time. Rima apparently had a tussle with Shamil and she looked to me for comfort. I did not plan it, and neither did she."

If he heard one more revelation, he would not be responsible for what he would do to his youngest sibling. "You also knew Rima and Shamil were lovers?"

He shrugged. "I assumed everyone knew—"

"You assume too much, Adan," Zain said.

Adan presented a wry smile. "Obviously."

Rafiq turned a glare and a question on Zain. "Do you wish to confess anything?"

Zain held up his hands in surrender. "I solemnly swear I did not bed your former wife."

"I am so glad to know that, honey," Madison said.

So was Rafiq, if he could actually believe Zain. He no longer knew what to believe.

"It is now time to put the past to rest." Elena braced her palms on the desk, leaned forward and directed her gaze at Rafiq. "*Cara,* you have shown signs of being a great leader, yet most likely not greater than your father. But you can be a better man than your father. You can have the life you were meant to lead with Maysa, or you can enter into another loveless marriage and be miserable until your time on earth is over."

Or he could spend the rest of his life alone. He had no need to produce an heir, now that Zain had fulfilled that requirement. His father had completed his reign as a widower, and no one had condemned him for the decision. Of course, no one had known about his relationship with Elena. Yet he had dishonored the cherished surrogate mother to Rafiq and his brothers by not standing up to the elders and making a commoner his queen.

"I will consider all that you have said," he told Elena, the only answer he could presently give.

Elena straightened and smoothed a hand over her graying hair. "That is all anyone can ask. And I know you will make the right decision for all concerned, as I have taught you to do. Never forget what makes a man a true king and a hero. Honor."

And he had clearly forgotten that honor over the past few weeks. "If it is all the same to you, I wish to be alone now."

"Let us leave your brother to his thoughts," Elena said as she started toward the door, gesturing for everyone to follow her.

And everyone did, except for Zain. "I do have to know one more thing, Rafiq."

He released a weary sigh. “I am in no mood to answer more questions about Maysa.”

“This doesn’t involve Maysa,” he said. “It does involve her brother. Why have you not yet dismissed him from the council?”

If he did, he risked Shamil revealing damning information to the press about his relationship with Maysa. Yet if he decided to make it known to the world that he was in love with the beautiful doctor, and he planned to make her the next queen, that would no longer be a concern. But the possible uproar over taking that course could be very concerning.

Since he had not quite reached that decision, Rafiq provided only a partial truth. “I had thought to ask him to step down first. If he does not, then I will demand his resignation.”

“I personally would opt to humiliate him tomorrow at the meeting by relieving him of his duties,” Zain said. “Perhaps he will then think twice before he tangles with another Mehdi and receives another broken nose.”

After Zain exited the room, Rafiq weighed his brother’s suggestion. He agreed that dismissing Shamil publicly would be effective, and worth considering. First, he had to determine whether he would attempt to reestablish a relationship with Maysa. A permanent, public relationship.

With that consideration rolling around in his mind, Rafiq would be forced to face another sleepless night—without Maysa. Would he be wise to ask her to make it his last?

You have shown signs of being a great leader, yet

most likely not greater than your father.... You can have the life you were meant to lead with Maysa....

Elena's words of wisdom suddenly struck a chord in Rafiq. He could be a better man. Maysa could assist him with that. In some ways, she already had. She was stronger than most men he had known, at times even him. Determined and intelligent. Worthy of respect. She had much to offer this country. She had much more to offer him. Much more than he probably deserved.

Rafiq could not bear the thought of spending another long day—and night—without Maysa Barad. Now that he had made the supreme decision to alter tradition, as well as his life, he had to formulate a plan. As the kernel of an idea filtered into his brain, a scheme that would cover two pressing issues at once, he smiled for the first time in weeks. He prayed that what he had planned would bring about Maysa's smile, too.

She wasn't particularly thrilled to be summoned to the palace by Rafiq's assistant, Mr. Deeb. Yet when Maysa had learned she was expected to speak on current health care issues before the royal council, her attitude immediately changed. She could not wait to enlighten each and every one of them.

And now here she was, waiting in the anteroom for her turn to finally have the chance to give the members a good dose of her reality. Unfortunately, the opportunity meant she would have to face Rafiq, as well as her brother, who amazingly still held his position on the governing board. Despite his verbal threats, and his physical assault on the king, Shamil had somehow come out of the situation smelling like a rose, while she still carried the thorns of Rafiq's rejection.

Maysa refused to worry over that now. She would walk into the room as the only woman among all men and let them know she was a force to be reckoned with. Her bravado began to diminish when Deeb appeared at the main door. "They are ready for you now, Dr. Barad."

And she was ready for them—for the most part.

After silently demanding her nerves be still, Maysa entered displaying a confidence she didn't exactly feel. To make matters worse, Rafiq happened to be the first person to invade her field of vision. And what a vision he was, dressed in his finest black silk suit, the official sash of the king draped around his neck, his face free of facial hair, his dark eyes without obvious emotion. She had no idea what he was feeling, only what she was feeling for him—undeniable longing.

"Gentlemen," he began in Arabic. "You all know Dr. Barad."

Maysa took inventory of their reactions and wasn't pleased with the results. No one spoke a greeting aside from Zain and Adan, although a few nodded in acknowledgment.

Rafiq pulled out the chair next to his and gestured her forward. After she settled in, she realized she was now face-to-frown with her brother. Lovely.

She turned her attention to the king as he outlined future plans for hospital expansion and patiently waited for her turn to present her thoughts on rural health care.

But before that turn arrived, Rafiq centered a bitter gaze on Shamil. "Sheikh Barad, as presiding Minister of Health, it is my opinion you have failed in successfully overseeing Bajul's faltering health care system."

Shamil's face turned so red, Maysa feared his head

might explode. "I take exception to your criticism, Your Excellency. I have served our people well."

"I disagree," Rafiq said, switching to English. "And I take exception to you sleeping with the queen, you traitorous son of a bitch."

Maysa had no way of knowing how many members understood the English curse, but she understood it very well. However, she had never heard Rafiq speak the words before, and she found it somewhat amusing, and appropriate for the situation.

Her brother stood so abruptly, he knocked his chair back in the process. "You are out of line, Rafiq."

Rafiq remained surprisingly calm. "And you are hereby facing charges of high treason if you do not vacate your position, and the premises, immediately."

Shamil sent a pointed look at Maysa before returning his ugly sneer to the king. "You are willing to make my sister your sacrificial lamb?"

A slightly mocking smile curled the corners of Rafiq's mouth. "No, but I am willing to appoint her as the new health minister, if she agrees."

Maysa looked around at all the confused men lining the table. But she didn't know if their confusion resulted from Rafiq offering a woman a position on the council for the first time in Bajul's history, or because Rafiq still spoke in English. "I would be honored, Your Majesty." Honored and thrilled and amazed.

"This is a travesty!" Shamil shouted. "A monumental mistake for this nation!"

"And men like you are a scourge on our nation," Rafiq said as he signaled a nearby guard, then returned to speaking in their native tongue. "Escort the sheikh to the airport and inform them that by my order, he is permanently barred from crossing Bajul's borders."

Shamil shook off the guard's grasp and pointed a shaky finger at Maysa. "You will regret this decision, and you will suffer the wrath of the people once they learn you are the king's secret whore. They will shun you."

"Not if she is the queen."

Shamil looked stunned, while Maysa turned wide eyes on Rafiq. "What did you say?"

"I am unofficially asking you to be my wife." And he did so where everyone could understand his proposal. "I will do the official honors after the meeting. You may give me your answer at that time."

As security escorted a cursing Shamil out of the room, Maysa sat in shocked silence. Yet several members of the council broke theirs by issuing protests over both Rafiq's decisions.

He commanded their attention by rapping the table with his palm. "Silence! I ask who among you has the right to judge Dr. Barad when she has done nothing but divorce a tormentor and care for the poorest of our people. Who among you has given more than your wealth to do the same?"

"She is a harlot who has taken the king as her lover," one man said. "She is a divorced woman who has no respect for the sanctity of marriage."

Rafiq glared at him. "And you do, Sheikh Saab? Do you not dishonor your wife nightly by bedding the innkeeper's wife?" He then turned to another protester. "And you, Sheikh Najem. Did you not divorce your first wife to marry a woman much younger than yourself?"

Najem looked as if he would like to disappear beneath the conference table. "It is different. I am a man."

"And that is where we differ," Rafiq said. "Both my brothers and myself believe we are overdue implementing changes in attitude when it comes to the backbone of this country, women such as Dr. Barad."

Zain and Adan verbally added their support before Rafiq spoke again. "Now that the business at hand is settled, including going forward with the water project, this meeting is officially adjourned."

Before Maysa could mentally digest the chaotic events, Rafiq took her by the hand, led her through the lengthy first-floor corridor, and up the stairs at a fast clip. He slowed a bit as they climbed to the third floor, but not enough for Maysa to catch her breath or gather her thoughts.

She suddenly realized they had arrived at the royal living quarters when she peered through the open bedroom door to her right. "What just happened in that meeting?"

"You agreed to become Bajul's newly appointed health minister to replace your brother, whom I have permanently exiled."

"And?"

He hinted at a smile. "I unofficially asked you to be my wife, and now I wish to make it official." Like a storybook hero, the king of Bajul went to one knee and clasped both her hands in his. "Maysa Barad, will you do me the honor of being my wife and my queen?"

She'd imagined this moment many times in her youth, and "youth" was the key. Now she was an adult, with adult concerns.

"Well?" Rafiq asked with a touch of impatience in his tone.

She wanted to say yes, but she wasn't quite ready to do that. "I'm still thinking."

He stood, his expression showing his disappointment. "I have asked too much of you, and I have waited until it is too late."

"I didn't say no, Rafiq. But before I say yes, I have to know what changed your mind."

"Not what, but whom," he said. "Elena forced me to see the error of my ways, immediately after she revealed she carried on a long-time affair with my father, who refused to make her his wife due to outdated mores."

Maysa was quickly reaching revelation overload. "How did they pull that off without anyone finding out?"

"Adan claims he knew, but Zain and I only heard rumors that our father had a mistress. We never suspected it would be the woman who raised us."

She, too, had heard the rumors, yet never in a million years would she have guessed Elena as the mystery woman. "It's sad to know that she was never able to show her love for your father out in the open."

"And that is what I am trying to avoid with us. I understand that I am asking you to endure continued bias, and I would not blame you if you refused me—"

"Let me stop you right there. As I've said before, I have survived much worse than a few insults. I survived the members' caustic remarks in the meeting only a few minutes ago. But if I agree to marry you, I will continue to be who I am, not who everyone feels

I should be. I will still be a doctor, and I will insist on treating the patients who need me."

Rafiq streak a hand over his jaw. "You realize that will require a security contingency at the clinic at all times."

That was something Maysa had yet to consider. "I accept that necessity, as long as the men do not frighten away my patients."

"They will also be required to accompany us when we travel to the outlying areas."

"We?"

His smile arrived, fully formed and completely gorgeous. "Yes, we. I believe I still have much to learn about our country's medical needs. Who better to guide me than you? However, I will make certain we have better accommodations, or at the very least, a comfortable cot for the tent where I will make love to you the next time."

"I will definitely agree to that, Your Majesty."

His features turned suddenly serious. "Then you will agree to marry me?"

She saw no harm in keeping him in suspense for a while longer. "I am leaning in that direction."

He slipped his arms around her waist and tugged her closer. "Maysa, if you refuse me, and I pray you do not, you must know I will never marry another. I refuse to settle for less than what we have together, an abiding love that has spanned years of separation. I will never feel for another woman the depth of what I feel for you. I simply cannot."

That alone convinced Maysa to deliver a resounding "Yes, I will marry you."

They sealed this unlikely betrothal, not with a contract, but with a kiss, as it should be. That kiss ended when a household staff member cleared her throat before she rushed by.

"Let us retire to my bedroom now," Rafiq said as soon as the woman disappeared around the corner.

Maysa glanced at the open door, specifically the bed, and questioned the wisdom in his plan. "I'm not sure I would be comfortable doing that, Rafiq."

"She never slept in my bed, Maysa," he said, as if he had channeled her concern. "I suppose I have been saving the bed for you, though it took me a while to realize I have been waiting for you all my life."

"And I am honored you reserved the permanent space beside you." As well as deeply touched.

"If you are also worried that I am only interested in making love to you," he added, "and I used a marriage proposal to achieve that goal, I assure you that is not the case. I have simply not been able to sleep without you in my arms."

Such a sweet thing to admit, but Maysa was still a bit suspicious. "It's a little past four o'clock, Rafiq. Isn't it too early to retire for the night?"

He presented an endearing grin, with a side of sexy devil tossed in for good measure. "Perhaps we could consider it a long nap?"

Now that her adrenaline level had plummeted, Maysa could probably nap standing up. She released Rafiq and stretched her arms above her heads. "I am very tired; so I suppose we could manage that."

Rafiq then swept Maysa into his arms, carried her into his bedroom as if she were already his bride and laid her on the bed for their "nap." After they undressed down to only skin, they did actually sleep for a while before they officially made love as an engaged couple. A soft, sensuous lovemaking session that almost brought Maysa to tears. Joyful tears.

And in the peaceful moments that followed, they were content to hold each other as if they had no other plans for the foreseeable future—until Maysa remembered they did have one monumental plan to make.

"When do you suggest we have the wedding, King Mehdi?"

He nuzzled her neck. "Tomorrow would be preferable, unless we can find someone to officiate tonight."

She elbowed Rafiq's side, causing him to release an exaggerated wince. "I am serious."

"And I am now injured, as well as serious about wanting to marry you quickly, before you change your mind. But I suppose we need sufficient time to make the arrangements."

"We only need a month at best," she said. "Just enough time to organize a small, intimate ceremony. Perhaps we should consider traveling south to the beach, or perhaps here at the lake. I have always thought it would be nice to marry without shoes."

Rafiq lifted his head from the pillow and frowned. "You do not wish to wear shoes or have an elaborate undertaking?"

"I wish anything but a large wedding. We have both been through the pomp and circumstance before. I see no need to repeat that now. And yes, I want to marry without my shoes and feel warm sand beneath my feet."

"I will leave the decision to discard footwear to you. But when a Mehdi king takes a new queen, he is expected to hold a large celebration in honor of the event, complete with a feast and thousands of people, most of whom he has never met, nor does he care to meet."

That was not Maysa's idea of a good time. "I will agree to the feast and the hordes of strangers, as long as we exchange our vows in private with only close friends and family in attendance."

He scowled. "I hope family does not include your brother."

"Bite your tongue, future husband. I would rather consume a plateful of salt than have Shamil at our wedding."

He kissed her gently. "I agree, my future queen. Your brother is not welcome in our world."

She smiled. "And for future reference, I prefer to be addressed as Dr. Queen. I believe I have earned the title."

Rafiq laughed then—a rich, deep laugh that provided masculine music to Maysa's ears. "As you wish, Dr. Queen," he said, followed by a lingering kiss. "And I believe I have thought of the perfect setting for our wedding ceremony."

"That cove by the lake?"

"No. The place where we began our journey together. Our past."

Epilogue

Exactly one month later, the reigning king and the physician queen exchanged vows, surrounded by olive trees and fifty or so of their closest friends and family. The bride had exchanged her preferred gauze dresses for a gown made of champagne-colored silk. The groom sported an open-collared, white tailored shirt with a beige jacket and slacks. Neither wore shoes, a sincere scandal in the making.

Maysa's attendants, Madison and Demetria, wore aqua dresses, while Zain and Adan reluctantly donned matching navy suits to meet their responsibility as groomsmen. None of the bridal party appreciated the no-shoe policy, a true uprising in the making.

Perhaps the ceremony wasn't quite as intimate as Maysa would have liked, but everything was going as planned…until two international news helicopters began buzzing overhead, forcing them to hurry their vows and the official kiss.

The disruption sent everyone to their awaiting cars for the brief trip to the palace. A trip too brief for the bride to agree to the groom's suggestion they begin the honeymoon on the journey. Just as well, Maysa decided. Had she agreed, the wedding guests would probably see guilt written all over her face.

Moments later, the newlyweds entered the massive banquet hall to a round of rousing applause. Maysa was extremely thankful for the show of approval and somewhat surprised. Fortunately, the press coverage had been favorable, and she hadn't been exposed to overt hostility, aside from the palace chef, who had not been pleased when she'd changed her mind about the menu twice.

Maysa could not recall being so blissfully happy, or so ready to begin her life with Rafiq. First, she had to assume her first duty as the queen—mingling with some of the most influential people in the world.

She spent well over an hour exchanging polite greetings with guests who'd waited a long while in the lengthy reception line to meet the monarchs. During a brief break in the line's flow, she surveyed the decorations made from bouquets of fragrant jasmine and the candles set out on the tables. And when one esteemed, unfamiliar guest held Rafiq captive with endless chatter, she turned her attention to the bounty of food spread out on the nearby tables. Enough food to feed half of Bajul, and she would swear more than half had come. By the time the last well-wisher left, she was ready to consume her fair share. Unfortunately, Rafiq had been detained again, this time by a woman at least twenty years his senior. That didn't stop her from fawning all over him, and Maysa didn't mind a bit. After this free-for-all food fest ended, the king would be taking her to Cyprus for two weeks filled with sea, sand and on-demand sex.

Thinking about the honeymoon led her to seek out her husband. When he caught her gaze and winked, she considered dragging him away now, a very un-queenly thing to do.

"Have you been enjoying your first hours as the queen?"

Maysa turned to Madison and frowned. "I am not enjoying having to wear these high heels. I'm definitely not enjoying the limited time with my new husband."

"They both take some getting used to," Madison said as she acknowledged a guest with a wave. "Both the heels on your feet, and the human kind who think it's their right to have the king's ear, even when that king is the groom."

Madison waved yet again, this time at a handsome, middle-aged gentleman. "I have no idea who that was," she said through a fake grin. "Some dignitary I invited I think. I believe he's from Albania, or maybe it's Australia. First rule of thumb, smile and pretend you know them, even if you don't."

"That's what I've been doing since we arrived, and I didn't understand what some of them said to me. It's a true disadvantage."

"I'll be glad to teach you some basic foreign greetings if you'd like," Madison said. "I know at least fifty."

"You and Zain will return to California before I master even five."

Madison brought her attention from the crowd and

gave it to Maysa. "Actually, we've decided to stay in Bajul indefinitely."

Maysa decided her sister-in-law deserved a hug for delivering such glad tidings. "I'm thrilled to know you're staying. I'm going to need all the support I can get. Rafiq will be pleased, too. But exactly why did you decide to relocate from Los Angeles and leave the beach behind?"

"We want the children to be raised here so they can learn about their heritage. And I want Cala to lead the future generation of Bajul's kick-ass women, just like her aunt Maysa, who defied all odds and received the ultimate prize."

"Rafiq?"

Madison frowned. "No. Premium tickets to the local sheepherder's ball."

Maysa grinned. "I was not aware of that perk."

"Of course I meant Rafiq, silly queen. He's always been considered quite a catch, just like Zain before he came to his senses and married me." Something, or someone, behind Maysa drew Madison's attention. "Speaking of our catches, here they come, plus the lone bachelor prince who mysteriously went missing after the wedding."

Maysa turned to see the approaching trio of gorgeous Mehdi brothers. Rafiq and Zain's resemblance to each other had always been remarkable, but even more so now that her husband decided not to regrow his goatee. Yet Adan, with his lighter-colored hair and skin tone, as well as his deep, deep dimples, did not favor his siblings aside from his tall stature and distinctive gait. Clearly he had inherited his looks from some unknown relative.

After Rafiq came to Maysa's side and kissed her soundly, Adan inserted himself between them. "Congratulations to the bride," he said, then leaned to kiss Maysa's cheek. "And my apologies for my tardiness in arriving here tonight."

Rafiq demonstrated his disapproval with a scowl and showed his possessive side by wrapping one arm around Maysa's waist and pulling her close to his side. "May I ask where you went after we left the grove?"

Adan adjusted his collar that seemed perfectly fine. "Since I am a gentleman, I will only say that I was preoccupied with a lovely little lady right here in the palace, and she is quite charming."

"Only you could manage to pick up a woman in less than an hour's time," Zain said.

Adan grinned. "Yes, I definitely picked her up."

Zain pointed at him. "Enjoy your freedom now, because mark my words, I predict you will soon meet that special someone and she'll drag you onto the marriage merry-go-round." When Madison glared at him, he added, "I meant she will introduce you to the state of marital bliss."

"You are wrong, brother," Adan said. "I intend to adhere to my plan of waiting until I am at least forty before I settle down. And as of this evening, I have decided to remain celibate for a while."

"That will most likely be the longest ten minutes of your life," Rafiq said, drawing laughter from everyone but Adan. "Now that the festivities seem to be dying down, have you notified the airport of our impending departure?"

"I have and the plane is ready and waiting." Adan began to back away as he spoke. "And I am prepared to deliver you to your destination safe and sound, after I say goodbye to the lady."

"Hurry," Rafiq called after his brother before Adan disappeared through the double doors.

Madison pushed up her sheer sleeve and checked her watch. "The celibacy thing didn't even last seven minutes."

The conversation continued until Adan suddenly returned with a beautiful baby girl wearing a pink satin dress, her thumb planted securely in her mouth. But not just any baby—Zain and Madison's baby girl, Cala.

He walked up to the group, a mischievous look splashed across his face. "Did I not say she was special?"

Zain kissed his daughter's cheek. "The most special lady in the world, and the niece of quite the deceiver."

Madison moved closer to examine Cala's dress. "Where did this come from?"

Adan's grin expanded. "I saw it in a boutique window the last time I visited Paris. I could not resist buying it for her. I bought Joseph a miniature tuxedo for the occasion. He's wearing it now, but unfortunately he passed out in Elena's lap and will be missing the party."

Who would have thought a reputed rogue like Adan would have such a soft spot for children? Not Maysa. She only wished Rafiq shared in his brother's enthusiasm. As far as she knew, he had never held his niece and nephew, and she wondered if he would ever recover from losing the child he'd believed to be his for months. Then as if by magic on this magical night, Cala reached for Rafiq.

Everyone went silent while Maysa held her breath as she awaited her husband's reaction. He hesitated a moment before he took the baby from Adan. Cala extracted her thumb, touched her uncle's face, then laid her head on his shoulder, as if she sensed he needed help with his healing. The scene was so very, very sweet, Maysa's already full heart filled with more joy.

"She apparently realizes who to go to when she needs her demands met," Adan said, shattering the silence. "I hate to disappoint you, Cala, but he will make you jump through hoops before he'll grant you your wish. But if you learn to curtsy—"

"She will not do any such thing," Madison chimed in. "Bow maybe, but never curtsy."

Rafiq tenderly kissed the now sleeping Cala's cheek before returning her to her father. "It is time for us to go now."

Maysa was more than excited to get on with the honeymoon and get out of her heels. "Good night, everyone, and thank you all so much for being there for us."

After doling out hugs and kisses, Maysa and Rafiq entered the armored limousine flanked by escorts on motorcycles. Adan took another car, leaving them alone at last.

Maysa rested her head on Rafiq's shoulder and sighed. "Today is perfect."

He lifted her chin and kissed her softly. "You are perfect."

He might not think so as soon as she asked the question she'd wanted to ask for some time. "Rafiq, do you want to have children?"

"At one time I was not certain I did, but now I am sure I do want children. Perhaps as many as five."

"You cannot be serious, Rafiq. We're both four years past thirty. We wouldn't have time to—"

He touched a fingertip to her lips to silence her. "I am not serious, but I would like to have two. I would also prefer to wait a year before we begin the process, but as Zain said, we may practice frequently until that time."

"I wholeheartedly agree with practicing often and waiting a year, but not any longer. We do need time together before we start a family."

"Fortunately, time is now on our side."

Thankfully, that was true. "There is something else we need to cover. Actually, a few rules."

"So we are back to rules again, are we?"

"A few minor rules. First, I believe it's all right to go to bed angry, as long as we make up in that bed before morning."

"You will receive no argument from me."

"Second, we both need autonomy and time away from each other now and then. We will appreciate each other more when we are together."

From the sour look on his face, evidently that rule did not set well with the king. "How much time?"

She tapped her chin and pretended to think. "I would say perhaps the occasional lunch hour, but never breakfast or dinner. We might want to shower separately—"

"I draw the line there."

She was not surprised by the command. "All right. I wasn't particularly fond of the idea anyway."

He gave her his smile and took her breath in exchange. "Anything else, my queen?"

"I prefer Dr. Queen, remember?"

He lifted her hand and laced their fingers together. "I prefer to call you the woman who saved me from a lonely life. The center of my existence. The love of my life."

The vows were less rushed and more poignant than those they'd exchanged earlier. Beautiful vows coming from an equally beautiful man. "And you, Rafiq Mehdi, have always been, and always will be, the king of my heart."

He touched her face with reverence, then said the words she would never tire of hearing. "*Ana bahebik.* Always."

She laid her hand on his palm, and entrusted him with the rest of her life. "*Ana bahebak.* Forever."

Dr. Maysa Barad-Mehdi had received several miracles at last—permanently reuniting with the man she had wanted most of her life, a career that continually fulfilled her and, most important, realizing that abiding love could be more than enough.

* * * * *